Denting the Bosch

Denting the Bosch

a novel of marriage, friendship, and expensive household appliances

❧

Teresa Link

THOMAS DUNNE BOOKS
St. Martin's Press
New York

THOMAS DUNNE BOOKS.
An imprint of St. Martin's Press.

DENTING THE BOSCH. Copyright © 2012 by Teresa Link. All rights reserved. Printed in the United States of America. For information, address St. Martin's Press, 175 Fifth Avenue, New York, NY 10010.

www.thomasdunnebooks.com
www.stmartins.com

LIBRARY OF CONGRESS CATALOGING-IN-PUBLICATION DATA

Link, Teresa.
    Denting the Bosch : a novel / Teresa Link. — 1st ed.
       p. cm.
    ISBN 978-0-312-64341-6 (hardcover)
    ISBN 978-1-250-01050-6 (e-book)
 1. Middle-aged persons—Fiction. 2. Empty nesters—Fiction. 3. Female friendship—Fiction.
4. Divorce—Fiction. 5. Domestic fiction. I. Title.
    PS3612.I554D46 2012
    813'.6—dc23

                                                              2012011014

First Edition: August 2012

10 9 8 7 6 5 4 3 2 1

In memory of my brother,
Christopher Link

Acknowledgments

FOR WIT, SUCCOR, AND GUIDED TOURS, my Canadian brother Greg Link; for discernment and insight, my editor, Margaret Smith; and for midwifery, my sesh buddies, Lisa Maria and the sagacious Mrs. Kornhauser.

What we call a home is merely any place that succeeds in making more consistently available to us the important truths which the wider world ignores, or which our distracted and irresolute selves have trouble holding on to.

—Alain de Botton, *The Architecture of Happiness*

Preface

THE BEST AND WORST OF TIMES, for most of us, are marked not by revolution but by mere discontent; oversalted margaritas, undercooked fish. We are glutted, sated, full to bursting, all the presents have been opened and now what?

Three couples; the best of friends. In the plump, juicy center of their lives. Midlife? Who can say? Do those who die young have their midlife crisis in childhood? Still, we are a species driven to measure and mark. The homes of the three couples all have scribbles on the doorways of their children's rooms, noting their height at each birthday. Well, two of the homes, anyway. Not the condo, which belongs to the relative newcomers. Two of their children were already grown when they moved in, the third well into his teens. They left the penciled numbers behind.

A cold front is moving in from Canada; the northeast buckles down. The aisles of Stop & Shop and Whole Foods are brimming with housewives stocking up for the predicted storm, ticking off ingredients for the soup recipe downloaded from Epicurean.com, filling their carts with extra this and thats, just in case. They know each other from dropoff and pickup, from book group, from the gym. They stop for a quick chat, exchange urgent promises to get together soon. The light is vivid, exaggerated, just before the clouds seal it up. Lines form at the gas stations, too; everyone filling their tanks, preparing. Those who have procrastinated their garden cleanups rush about emptying the last of the geraniums from the pots, stripping the lawn chairs of their cushions, lowering umbrellas and awnings. Husbands are called at work and reminded to pick up firewood on the way home from the train station. Snowplows are checked and readied, storm windows are lowered, the last of the autumn leaves are swept up and bagged. Pickup trucks full of illegal Guatemalans drive through the woody lanes and wrap the tender saplings they've planted in their clients' gardens with burlap. Mothers pray it won't be bad enough to close school. Children pray that school will be canceled for days and days. The oil companies send out extra trucks to top off everyone's tanks. Squirrels scrabble at the hardened soil, dig up what they can, and scamper up the trees. As daylight dims into an indigo sky streaked with violent slashes of pink, the frenzy ebbs, the streets and shops empty. Lights go on in the windows in the gathering dusk; the smell of wood smoke mixes with frigid air. Tires crunch on gravel and garage doors thunk shut as the husbands come home. Houses fill up with the scent of roasting chicken; windows steam up; in every home the weatherman points to big maps and explains how the storm is moving toward them. The screens flicker with images of the snow that is already falling in parts of New England. It could be a Big One, they're saying. Everyone is advised to prepare, to not go out if they don't have to, to stock the larder.

But not here. Not in Carlsbad, California. Adele has the TV on while she grates cheese and potatoes for the kugel she's preparing for dinner. The balcony sliders are wide open; the cherry geraniums bloom vigorously in their pots; the late-afternoon sun casts molten gold over the blue Pacific. Adele, watching the Weather Channel, does not gloat, as her husband would, at the news from back home. Adele, oblivious to the view from her condo, is remembering. She is remembering the smell of the coming storm, the camaraderie in the grocery aisles, the energizing anticipation. She is indulging in what Drew calls her Happy Hindsight. He says it with a face meant to imply that her homesickness is a form of lunacy. Rationally, she knows he is right. Their life out here is so much easier, so much more pleasant! It is incontestable. But what is she to do with this feeling, this boulder of sadness she lugs around with her, this longing she feels as she imagines, down to every detail, the way it is right now back home in Bedford, New York, as everyone gets ready for the storm.

Straw

⁓

You easy lovers and forgivers of
mankind, stand back!
—WENDELL BERRY

One

THERE WERE NO STORMS in Southern California. There were earth-quakes, mud slides, fires—but no storms. When it rained, they called it a storm. "San Diego prepares for another winter storm," the newscasters announced grimly, sending Adele into snorts of derisive laughter. The thing about a storm, a real storm, was that you could prepare. You could hunker down. You could feel cozy, waiting it out. It wasn't at all like the fires two years ago, turning the sky yellow and raining ash on the roofs. They'd got-ten a reverse 911 call to be ready to evacuate and Drew had loaded up the car with valuables; Adele had practically gone catatonic with horror. No, she'd take a blizzard, a hurricane, a nor'easter over fire any day.

It made her feel a little guilty, watching the sun wash over her kitchen, while back home, they were checking their sump pumps and hauling out their generators. She thought of Cordelia, her old best friend, and won-dered—as she so often did, even after all these years—what she was doing at that moment. Her two oldest sons and Cordy's two boys had grown up together, the two families inseparable, until 9/11 changed everything. In-stinctively, Adele's hand fluttered, a tic she had developed whenever such thoughts intruded. Brushing them away. Not now, not now.

She and Drew had just returned from three days at Sea Ranch, celebrating her friend Sylvia's fifty-fifth birthday. Sylvia's husband, Carl, had a cousin who owned a house there, and he'd loaned it to them for the occasion. There had been six of them. Three couples. Best friends. New best friends. California friends. The best friends from home sent e-mails, called sometimes, once every year or so came out for a visit.

Not Cordelia, though. She had curled into herself, shut everyone out, and who could blame her? The look on her face, when Adele had told her they were moving to San Diego. That look still haunted Adele. Adele, who had remained so unscathed. Who still had her whole family. Who apparently had chosen to abandon ship.

An architect by training but not profession (a sore point on blue days—Drew's career always came first, as well it should; her job had been the children), Adele had been excited about visiting Sea Ranch. Her favorite professor in college had studied with Charles Moore, the postmodern designer who, along with the landscape architect Lawrence Halprin, created the community in the mid-1960s. She had read, at the time, of the five-thousand-acre site on the windswept cliffs, the utopian ambitions of the design team. Sylvia's invitation had stirred dormant fervor in Adele. The nights before going she'd had dreams of dew-drenched hopefulness, woken to a fresh sense of promise. It had spun her back into her youth, those days when the idea of a shared community of like-minded people seemed to be the way the world was going. *Maybe this is it,* she'd thought, anticipating a thrill of recognition. *Maybe this will be where I'll build my house, and the whole California diaspora will make sense.* Drew had promised her, when they sold their house in Bedford, that after Noah left for college they'd buy land somewhere for her to build on. Anywhere she wanted, he'd said, except back east. He wouldn't go back east. Though she'd always imagined her someday house being east, somewhere—Vermont? Pennsylvania?—she agreed to his terms. She had reconciled herself to a state of homelessness, taken it on as an ancient inheritance, and hoped that a new promised land would be revealed to her. That promise had kept her going for years.

But Sea Ranch—initially intended to be weekend houses, small in scale, with American vernacular post-and-beam construction and an imperative to harmonize with the environment—had been a disappointment. Three decades and the new millennium had corrupted what Adele had expected to be an oasis of architectural purity. Halprin had required the owners to live close together, to build small, to cluster the houses at the tree line in order to keep the open sweep of the meadow and the bluffs for common use, to keep the ocean views open. Carl's cousin's house was one of the new ones, right on the bluff, huge and overdone, with views from every room of the cobalt sea and the rugged cliffs. There were three bedrooms, a media room, and a small gym. The kitchen had a six-burner Viking stove and double dishwashing drawers. While the others oohed and aahed over the house and the views, Adele nursed her disappointment with a stern reality check: What had she expected? How naive could she be? *Move on, Mrs. Gold*, she told herself. *You won't be building a house in California; that's the good news. And at least you're not in SandyfuckingEggo. This place is entirely different: enjoy yourself.*

She'd allowed herself to be lulled into a sort of infantile comfort, there, swaddling herself in a blanket on the couch in front of the fire. They'd taken long walks, prepared elaborate meals in the big open kitchen, gone antiquing in Gualala. Carl had bought Syl a beautiful old locket on a gold chain. The shop's proprietor, whom Maggie swore she recognized as a famous poet, threw in a little beaded bag for the necklace when he heard it was Sylvia's birthday. Adele had been cheered; she'd felt the heavy cloak of discontent lightening a bit. Driving back along the Pacific Coast Highway, she had delivered a history of the Ranch, and remarked how sad it was that it had ultimately failed.

"What do you mean, 'failed'?" Sylvia had protested. "How can you call this a failure?"

"Only in the sense," replied Adele, "that its original intention never came to fruition. Or rather, it flourished briefly, but now it's been compromised."

"Money," Drew had pronounced. "It all comes down to money."

Back in Carlsbad, the familiar disorientation had crept back into her. This morning she'd gone out for donuts, to bring to Sylvia's. A long line had formed, typical of a Sunday morning. The boy behind the counter had asked who was next, and the man behind Adele began to give his order.

"Excuse me," Adele had said, "I'm next." She hadn't been rude or confrontational, just assertive. She was a New Yorker. Lines were inviolable. The next thing she knew, the whole place was calling her a line Nazi! Snickering and exchanging glances of shared derision. She had been furious until she got in the car, when she'd burst into tears. She just didn't get it, out here! And then she'd gone to Sylvia's, where they were supposed to talk about building an apartment over the garage, which she was going to design, and instead there was Maggie on the couch, with Syl sobbing in her arms. Carl— pudgy, bumbling, pussy-whipped Carl—had announced, that morning before going off to play golf, that he wanted a divorce.

It didn't make sense. There had been no clue. No red flag among the credit card bills, no late nights at the office, no souring toward Syl. Up north they'd been observed necking on the couch after the others had gone to bed, weary of *Wild Hearts Can't Be Broken*, which still flickered on the TV screen when Adele got up for a glass of water and some Advil. She'd crawled back into bed with Drew and snuggled against him, thinking how lucky they were, how precious this inclusive friendship, how extraordinary that they had weathered such storms and all emerged, battered but whole, into the rapturous, sunny utopia of middle age. Of all the marriages she might have speculated would implode once the kids were gone, Syl and Carl's was the last. *Poor Sylvia,* she thought, as she broke the eggs into a bowl. She'd sobbed like a baby. Adele had been a little shocked at her utter lack of reserve, her childlike meltdown. The woman was without defenses; she was as trusting and eager to please as an earnest little girl.

Sylvia and Carl were not the sort of people Adele would have had occasion to meet, let alone befriend, back home. She thought of them as quintessential Southern Californians: transplanted midwesterners, house-proud, vaguely Christian, not widely read or traveled. In fact, she reflected, not without a twinge of shame at her snobbishness, they were, frankly, unsophisticated and charmingly provincial. But she had grown terribly fond of them, especially Syl. She was bighearted and guileless, dependable, unintentionally comedic. Seeing her dissolved on the sectional in Maggie's arms, Adele had had the urge to find Carl and reprimand him, demand an apology, force him to make up with his wife. Unexpected shocks and undone friends were not a new experience for Adele, but schooled as she was, she found it wrenching to witness Sylvia's distress. As always in the face of the unimaginable, she tried to piece together something cohesive, but she was stuck on the image of Carl wrapping his arms around Sylvia from behind and squeezing her breasts while she shrieked and slapped him, delighted. This had occurred just yesterday morning, while they'd been milling around in the kitchen at Sea Ranch making coffee and toasting bagels.

Sylvia had choked and gulped her story out in typical Sylvia fashion; winding around non sequiturs and irrelevancies, distracting herself with random digressions. Adele had had to struggle with the inappropriate laughter that kept bouncing up in her as she sat next to Syl, stroking her hand, trying not to look at Maggie lest they both lose it. Had she allowed herself a peek at Maggie, she would have seen no mirth, for Maggie's fury and sense of righteousness were galloping apace.

"Beth said we needed a sleigh bed," Syl had stammered, "or she and Franco would have to stay at a hotel. Adele, when was she here last? More than a year, right? I told Carl you were coming over this morning to talk about the garage and he said . . . he said . . ." And here her face crumpled like an overripe camellia and she wailed unself-consciously. "Oh, you guys . . . " she gasped in a moment, having accepted the tissues and caresses of her friends. "What would I do without you guys?"

Recalling the moment as she diced the onion, Adele allowed herself a moment of levity. What was it Mel Brooks had said? "Comedy is when you fall into a hole and break your leg. Tragedy is when I get a hangnail"? Something like that. Syl said Carl had told her he would always love her, but that he hadn't felt the same about her for a long time. That he loved her like a sister. That he had fallen in love with someone else. And that someone else, she had wailed, was his secretary. How humiliating was that?! His fat Russian whore of a secretary, is what she'd said, spluttering about how just last month Carl had asked her, Sylvia, to pick out a birthday present for her! And Syl had gone to Anthropologie and bought her a beautiful, expensive set of bedding! Bedding! And Carl had thanked her, and kissed her, and all the time he was thinking how he was going to screw the bitch on those beautiful sheets! (At this point Syl had pressed her face into the shiny leather couch cushion and contorted, flailing, as if she were trying to crawl inside it.) "We have to get you a lawyer," Maggie had pronounced, but Syl said no, Carl had already secured a lawyer (the infamous barracuda of divorce lawyers, unfunnily named Mort Sahl) and that he would take care of them both, it would be a no-contest divorce, and not to worry, Carl would always take care of Sylvia. (Already gotten a lawyer? Adele marveled. So the whole time at Sea Ranch he'd been faking it?)

"That is just not okay," Maggie had said. "You need your own lawyer." But no, Sylvia insisted, "Carl said there's no sense giving all our money to the lawyers, that I just have to trust him."

Adele had called Drew, who was a doctor, and left a message on his cell for him to procure a supply of Xanax; she would explain later. Maggie had gone online and started making a list of lawyers to call, pointedly ignoring Syl's protestations. Adele had manipulated the little ball of Day-Glo-orange Play-Doh that she carried around to keep her encroachingly arthritic right hand from hardening into a claw like her mother's had. She'd formed it into a little man with a potbelly and a droopy little penis and placed him on the coffee table. "Let's get pins," she'd suggested. "Syl, do you have a pin box? I made a little voodoo Carl."

It was interesting, Adele mused, blowing her nose and wiping away onion tears, how adamant Sylvia had been about trusting Carl, even as he betrayed her. She'd actually snapped at Maggie to stop talking about how she should protect herself. Said she wasn't going to "go there," that she was going to "support Carl's decision." *First the grief, then the rage,* Adele thought. *How we all scamper into predictable human behavior when the ground collapses under us.* And then, like a person hearing about someone else's cancer diagnosis, Adele watched her own thoughts leap onto the hamster's wheel: *Could it happen to me?*

But of course that was silly. Carl was silly. There was something buffoonish about him, despite his success in business. He always made a big deal about adoring Sylvia, in public. As they had no reason to doubt his sincerity, that had endeared him to Sylvia's friends. Why should it come as such a shock that he was duplicitous? Why should that have anything to do with Drew?

Around and around the wheel she went, her thoughts careening between fragmented memories of shock and betrayal, of pleasure and connection. Her marriage had always been easy. She and Drew were pals. More than pals: soul mates. Lovers, of course, though that had dwindled, naturally—but mostly pals. She couldn't remember a time when she'd thought of herself as separate from him. This kugel she was making, for example. At the grocery, earlier, she'd had the inspiration to make it for Drew; it was a favorite of his, and she hadn't made one for a while. No sooner had she put the groceries away in the kitchen than the phone rang and Drew asked about dinner. When she told him what she was making he was amazed, saying that was exactly what he'd been hungry for. That kind of thing happened often, between them. She'd assumed, naively, she realized, that all good marriages were like that. Apparently not, she mused, marveling at Carl's ability to be so doting, so positively uxorious, so Mr. Jolly Host of a lovey-dovey weekend, all the while preparing the wrecking ball. She wondered, as she poured the kugel into a loaf pan, if Drew had known about Carl's affair. Admonished herself for the fleeting suspicion: Drew would have told her. Of course he would have. They didn't have secrets between them. Drew would be as shocked as she was. She experienced a little frisson of excitement in anticipation of sharing the gossip, and was instantly ashamed. This was terrible news. Sickening news, really, and with that thought, something leaden stirred within her, some slouching beast she had thought was finally slumbering. "No more," she said, aloud. "No more. Leave us alone."

The snow had started in New York. A bundled-up newsgirl stood on Central Park West, talking into the mike about how here it was: the first of the season. Adele squinted at the screen—she was on Sixty-ninth Street, it looked like. When the image dissolved and was replaced by dancing sponges, Adele felt a tug of regret. She could have stood there all night and watched the snow fall on Central Park. Outside, the sun slipped into the Pacific Ocean and the sky turned rosy. She closed the sliders and turned on the lamps in the living area. Not really a room; the condo had what was called an open floor plan. She slid the pan into the oven, poured herself a glass of the Shiraz they had bought at the winery near Sea Ranch, settled onto the couch, and waited for her husband to come home. On the end table was a snow globe, a going-away present from a friend when she'd left New York. Inside the globe was a tiny compression of Manhattan: the Empire State Building, St. Patrick's Cathedral, the Brooklyn Bridge, the Statue of Liberty. Even a wee little yellow taxi. She wound it up, and its music box tinkled out "New York, New York." She shook the globe, and it swirled with glittering flakes as the music slowed, then spluttered into silence.

Two

MAGGIE HAD NEVER LIKED HER sister-in-law, but it seemed to her
that as she aged, the woman was growing increasingly strident. Her husband's devotion to his sister had always irritated Maggie, though she
couldn't have explained why and knew it was unfair of her. She dreaded
these monthly Sunday afternoon "luncheons," as Patsy referred to the spread
of cold cuts and jars of condiments, and made little effort to hide from
Paul the sense of imposition they oppressed her with. Patsy lived in Vista,
and it always depressed Maggie to have to drive east to Vista. The only
enjoyable part of the day for her was when, on the way home, they caught
their first glimpse of the sea as they drove west on 78.

Patsy and Paul had become embroiled in one of their affectionate dis-
agreements about the past—who had married whom and when so-and-so
had died—and Patsy's husband, Brian, was blathering on about the idealism of the sixties, interjecting what he considered apt commentary on the
siblings' reminiscences, when Maggie was jolted out of her ennui by mention of the bomb on West Tenth Street.

"That was Susan," Patsy was saying. "You remember, Paul. We were at
school together. She's the one who gave clothes to those naked girls who
ran out into the street."

"She was your friend?" Maggie said. "The one who took them in and gave one of them a very expensive coat, and then they vanished and never returned it?"

"What are you talking about?" Paul said irritably, glancing at his wife.

"The Weathermen," Patsy said.

"Actually," Maggie corrected her, "it was the SDS." She turned to Paul, brightening at the turn the discussion had taken. "A radical group from the SDS borrowed a town house belonging to the father of one of them, on West Tenth Street. They were building a bomb in the basement, which they intended to blow up at an enlisted men's dance."

"It was the Weathermen," Patsy said.

"No, really, it was the SDS."

Patsy's lips tightened. "I'm quite sure, Maggie, that it was the Weathermen."

"No, it was the SDS. Anyway, this was the group Bill Ayers was associated with. You know, the one they used to try to associate Obama with terrorists. 'Palling around with terrorists,' Sarah Palin said. Ayers had told his girlfriend, Diana Oughton, hours before the explosion, that he couldn't be monogamous because it violated his political beliefs, and there's a theory that she detonated the bomb on purpose because she was distraught, and also because she had been having second thoughts about blowing up innocent enlisted men—at a dance, no less—to make a political point. All these kids were blue bloods, to the manner born, daughters of the wealthy and accomplished. And when the bomb went off it killed Diana Oughton, and the other two ran into the street stark naked. I guess the bomb blew off their clothes, or maybe they were working naked, and Susan—this woman I guess you know—the story goes that she took them in and dressed them, rather expensively, and never saw them or her clothes again. Don't you remember? The whole building blew up. I think Dustin Hoffman lived there."

"It was the Weathermen," Patsy said.

"Darling, is there any more of that sponge cake?" Brian asked his wife.

Patsy's nasty little shih tzus jumped up on her lap and she began her disgusting routine with them, smacking her lips, rubbing noses. "In the fridge," she directed her husband. "Bring some for the babies."

Maggie was stung by the disinterest in her information. Not a spark of curiosity! And Patsy, so bent on being right. The Weathermen, the Weathermen. Like one of her stupid little dogs, growling and shaking a sock. And Paul. Even he had brushed her off, as if she were an annoying child reciting poetry at a grown-ups' lunch. He and Patsy had gone off again, on some tangent about this Susan person's various husbands. The Weathermen! As if Maggie wouldn't know! Maggie, who was arrested twice for lying down in the street at peace rallies! Who majored in political science and planned on law school before marrying Paul!

Later, though, doubt began to gnaw at her. Had it been the Weathermen? She was sure it was the SDS. There *was* a distinction—not that anyone cared, anymore. Other than Patsy, evidently, but she only cared in terms of being Right. She and Paul had gone on and on about this Susan, way beyond relevance to the conversation at hand, telling long, drawn-out stories about her various marriages and divorces and travels and homes, interrupted only by the obnoxious adorableness of the shih tzus as they slobbered on Patsy's face. Maggie had sat sullenly, her whole life called into question by the choices of these people whose values and interests were so frivolous and so far from her own. Had it been the Weathermen? It was like a seed stuck between her teeth; she couldn't stop returning to it, prodding. And if it had been the Weathermen, what did that say about her, a pushy didact who didn't even have her facts right? This was the trouble with her life, she decided. Something must have gone awry in her childhood to make her so pointed and snappish. Who cared about the Weathermen and the SDS or even Bill Ayers, now that Obama was safely in the White House? Who cared, and what prevented her from being the kind of person who could shrug, allow Patsy her little point of correction? It wasn't as if she was on *Jeopardy!*, for Christ's sake. And if it was the Weathermen, and she'd been so adamant about it being the SDS, what else had she been wrong about, ignorantly proclaiming her rightness? Was this something she'd always done? Was this the part of her personality that grated on

Paul? Because she knew, deep down, that there was something about her that set him off. Where was her *mind*? Who gave a rat's ass about whether it was the SDS or the Weathermen? Why couldn't she just *Let. It. Go?*

That's what Paul said to her in the car, on the way home. They'd driven in silence until they reached the 5 South, and then, just as Maggie was experiencing the loosening in her chest that meant she was close to home, he said, in that flat, cold voice that effectively slammed a garage door between them, "Sometimes, Maggie . . ."

"Sometimes what? What, sometimes, Paul?"

He hadn't answered, and they'd gone to bed without speaking. In the morning he had rolled over and they'd had urgent, sweaty sex before he left for work.

Maggie and Paul lived in Carlsbad, just east of the 5, in a sixties tract house on the edge of a development that had been built on a landfill. Sometimes she daydreamed about going back to school, getting that law degree, but things had fallen into a comfortably familiar routine, and she somehow lacked the energy to go beyond the occasional Internet search. The search itself—the prickle of excitement as she perused course descriptions and syllabuses—satisfied her, left her with a sense of having taken some vaguely edifying step. She worked part-time from home as a freelance online marketer, in the spare room that they had set up as a family office. It was a skill she had learned during a stint at a national fitness company. Before her son, Josh, was born, she'd liked the job because of the perks and camaraderie; after Josh, she'd negotiated home hours on a contractual basis. While she missed actually going to work, she liked the luxury of staying home with her baby, and found that she could generate enough income to keep her from feeling dependent on Paul, which alleviated a lot of tension. Paul was brilliant, with an engineering degree from Berkeley and a B.A. from Columbia, but he was, Maggie felt, curiously unambitious. He was happiest when he was puttering around fixing things, or engaged in projects like building the playhouse for Josh in the backyard. As she stood at the kitchen sink, washing up the breakfast dishes, she looked out at the playhouse—now Paul's workroom—and mused on how, last week at Sea Ranch, he had opted to stay at the house to fix a gutter that had separated from the roof, instead of going with them to Gualala for the afternoon. "Don't be an ass," Carl had said—it was his cousin's house. "He pays guys to do that stuff."

But Paul was glad to be excused from the excursion to Gualala, and when they returned he was in an excellent mood, having found several other things requiring his ministrations. It annoyed Maggie, but she wouldn't have admitted it. She would have preferred him to put his energy into getting a better job. Not for the money—Maggie was an uncompromising anti-capitalist—but for his own sense of self-worth. It was not something they could, or would, ever discuss, but there was something in Paul that seemed, to Maggie, defensive. Patsy was the only one in his family she knew, his parents having died before she met him. He'd been phlegmatic about his childhood, insisting, when she'd tried to go digging around in his psyche, that there was nothing there of interest. That she "invented drama where none existed." Whenever she had tried to engage him in a conversation about the future—about his dreams, his ambitions—he'd get irritable, tell her to stop trying to psychoanalyze him. But it troubled Maggie; it grated against her idealism to see him trudge off to work, day in, day out, leading a flatliner kind of life, a life she'd never expected to live. He'd been in middle management in the engineering department of SDG&E for years. Time and again opportunities arose for him to advance, but he never seemed to position himself correctly, or even to take any interest. "Is it because of me?" Maggie had asked him once, thinking he might have mistaken her staunch old hippiness for contempt of accomplishment. She couldn't remember how he had responded. Probably with one of those quizzical looks, as if he had just woken up and was startled to see who he was married to.

That trip to Sea Ranch had been all over the shop—as her mother used to say—for Maggie. Moments of joy followed by sickening thuds of misery. Which is how her days usually went, but in such compacted circumstances it was intensified. She loved the place. Northern California was home; she had grown up in Berkeley. A friend of her mother's had owned one of the original Sea Ranch houses—a shack, really—and as a child she had wandered the windswept bluffs and had relationships with each of the gnarled, stunted cypresses at the edge of the meadow. And the six of them, the three couples, always got along so well. But Carl and Drew had their routine about money, teasing each other and making a big deal about who was going to pick up the check, and Paul always just sat there and let them bicker. Then he'd say, "How much do we owe?" and count out the dollars carefully. It was embarrassing. "Can't you just pick up the check, sometimes?" Maggie had complained, to which he'd replied, "Not on my salary." She suspected that was why he'd wanted to fix things at the house; to sort of pay their share, even though no payment was expected. His nervousness about money had the effect of making money a component of their marriage, which was a continual source of anguish for Maggie. She hated money! Sometimes she looked around their weary little tract house and wondered who lived there, felt sorry for the inhabitants and the compromised lives it embodied. It was a mystery to her how she had landed there; she had always envisioned herself in a life less grounded, more fraught with significance. What vexed Maggie was that Paul was so smart, so educated, so qualified! If he'd wanted to, he could have been out there doing something meaningful, building houses in Rwanda or working for UNICEF or Bono. But no, he wanted a quiet, secure life; he wanted Josh to grow up with a hometown and his little handprint sunk in the driveway cement. Fine, but what was stopping him, then, from earning the precious money he seemed so conscious of not having? He could easily have commanded as much as Drew, the big-shot doctor, and more than Carl, who had glad-handed and kissed ass and who knew what else to get where he was. God knew the secret to his success wasn't smarts. Once, years ago, when she and Sylvia had first become friends, Carl had come on to her. They'd all drunk a little too much at dinner, and for some reason she was alone with him for a few moments, and he'd said something, or done something— she couldn't remember exactly what. It was disgusting. She'd never mentioned it to either Syl or Paul, but from then on she'd kept her wits about her with Carl. With good reason, it turned out. All week Maggie's heart had been racing with outrage at Carl's unthinkable sleaziness. How could the man *be* such a bastard? Last week, when Sylvia'd sat weeping in her arms, she'd wanted to say, *Hey! The jerk has done you a favor!* Carl was funny, and fun to hang out with, but she'd always felt he was a little slimy, a little eel-like. Not someone to trust. She'd never understood what Sylvia saw in him. But then, wasn't that the case with most couples? What did people think of her and Paul, she wondered. Did they speculate about what kept them together? "Sex," she said out loud.

At Sea Ranch, Paul had woken her in the middle of the night and led her to the kitchen, where he hoisted her onto the granite counter and made love to her with authority and scrutiny, while outside, in the vast darkness, seals barked in the waves. Afterward, he carried her back to bed, tucked her in, covered her face with tender kisses. At breakfast the next morning, while they were all standing around with their coffee, Paul had run the flat of his hand on the smooth stone and said, "Nice." This had led them into a discussion of various kitchen designs, during which Syl and Adele argued about whether granite had had its day and would soon be considered dated (Adele, yes; Syl, never) while Paul leveled a knowing gaze at Maggie. Even after all these years, even after having and raising a child, despite the banality of the everyday and the accrual of marital dissatisfactions, he still got to her, that way. Sometimes at the end of the day Maggie would be afflicted with a kind of panicky melancholy, a sense of accidental momentum having thrust her into someone else's life. She would flail around, mentally, trying to find an anchor, a bellwether to cling to. At dinner, she would telegraph her need to her husband, hover anxiously, hoping he would catch her and ground her, fasten her securely to their life. But Paul was a silent eater, not a conversationalist; he preferred to watch the news, to tinker around in his workshop or leaf through one of his *National Geographics*. Maggie had learned, over the years, to get out of his way, to rope in her neediness. Because there was always bedtime. And bedtime, no matter how distant he had been all evening, was the flower, the fountain, the garden of their marriage. Whatever slights she had nursed, whatever vexations he had grimly borne, the sanctum of their bedroom soothed away. In the dark, in the silence, she was never alone, never frightened. The warm cave of his body always accepted and enveloped her, and the demons of the daylight dispersed in their intimacy. This was how her marriage nurtured and stabilized her, whatever her other complaints. Driving home from Sylvia's last week, she had tried to imagine what it would be like if their roles were reversed, if Paul had been the one to let the axe fall. But she couldn't wrap her mind around such a thing. Maggie knew Paul would never be unfaithful. She sometimes wasn't sure if he liked her. But she knew he loved her, she knew he desired her, and she knew he'd never go to anyone else. Not as long as he had her.

Three

"WHETHER YOU'RE RIGHT, whether you're wrong. Man of my heart, I'll string along. . . ."

Sylvia sang quietly, rocking in the glider on her patio. It was now exactly one week since Carl had taken the knife and plunged it into her heart. It was a glorious day, blue and fragrant, with gentle breezes caressing her and mockingbirds filling her ears with distracting chatter. She sipped from her glass of chilled Chardonnay, idly contemplating the weeds that had sprung up between the pavers by the pool. Everything seemed the same. She had made breakfast for Carl that morning; they had taken their coffee onto the patio and talked about his trip to New York tomorrow. After he had left for the day (where had he gone? He hadn't said; she hadn't asked. He'd left his golf clubs behind), she had gone into Beth's room, where he'd been sleeping, and made the bed. She had hugged the pillow to her—it was soft and gushy, like Carl—and told herself that everything was going to be all right. The worst had happened. Life had resumed normalcy; Carl was still here; the sky hadn't fallen. It was something he had to go through; he'd get it out of his system and realize that nothing was worth losing his home and family for.

Let him screw his dirty whore. She could have him. It wouldn't be such a bad thing, Syl thought, to let him have a mistress. She could have him for the sex and Syl could keep him for everything else. Everything else was what she wanted, after all. Syl would show him, over time, how broadminded she could be. How irreplaceable she was. How precious it was to have her to come home to, no questions asked. He'd see how lucky he was, what a bad idea it was to take it as far as he meant to. He'd be begging her for forgiveness, just wait. And then, when it had all blown over, they'd start work on the garage apartment.

Sylvia allowed her mind to wander into decorating mode, which always soothed her. She pondered colors, imagined the new guest quarters as a cool, beachy retreat, all sea greens and pale blues, with gauzy curtains fluttering at the windows. Then redecorated it as a sophisticated, crisp aerie, in dove grays and browns, minimally furnished, something functional and no-nonsense at the windows, like those slatted blinds from the Smith and Noble catalog. But then Carl intruded into her fantasy, yelling, in that ugly way, "Why don't you just throw all my money into the fireplace?"

She shivered, hearing him again. Oh horrible, horrible moment that had been, worse than an earthquake, worse than the fires; an unimaginable sensation of the ground beneath her cracking open, everything tumbling down, down. She gulped the last of the Chardonnay. Swung out of her perch to go to the kitchen for a refill. She had to stop thinking about that. Because he had come home, hadn't he, after stalking out and staying away all day? He had come home, late in the night while she lay in bed, shivering, emptied of all her tears. She had heard him come in; it had been like the sound of her parents coming home when they'd left her with a babysitter, how she'd forced herself to stay awake until she heard them return, then fell into sleep even before they peeked in to check on her. She had heard him come upstairs and go into Beth's room, and then she hadn't known anything until the morning, when there he was just like always, almost, and she'd made his breakfast and asked him if he'd be home for dinner. And that's how it had been all week: no more yelling, Carl going to work and then coming home. Every night but Monday he did come home for dinner, and she took extra care to give him his favorites, and asked him how his day had gone, and they had watched the news together and then he'd said good night and gone to sleep in Beth's room. Which actually suited her fine, if truth be told.

After he'd stormed out last week she had called Maggie, who had rushed right over. Then Adele showed up, whom she'd expected anyway, and they had been wonderful. They had calmed her down. Friends were everything, she thought now, with a sob of sentiment. You give everything to your family—your body, the sweat of your back, your whole heart—and then they cut you open, and who do you have? Your friends. After they'd left, Syl, despite her assurances that she was okay, had panicked. The empty house had mocked her, she'd had a frantic impulse to run, hide, somehow escape her own body. So she had called her daughter. The closest and dearest being in her life; her raison d'être, her most profound comfort. She knew it would enrage Carl that she would spill the beans, that she would get to Beth first, that she would deprive him of whatever wool he meant to pull over their daughter's eyes when he actually got to see her in New York. Pleased with her one-upmanship, she called Beth, told her the incomprehensible news. Beth's response had been, "Duh, Mom!"

She'd expected to brush up her mothering skills, expected to console, reassure, even, yes, because it was incumbent upon her in such circumstances, to defend Carl. "Your father has a right to be happy," she'd been prepared to say, and in the practicing of it had felt her heart swell with the grandeur of expansive selflessness. But Beth's reaction—"Duh, Mom!"—had utterly deflated her. "You knew?" she had gasped into the mouthpiece, picturing her daughter in the Tribeca loft she shared with her boyfriend, which Syl had visited exactly once.

"Well, knew," Beth had replied, "no, not knew that he was, specifically, screwing Yelena. But knew that he was unhappy? That he had a roving eye? That the two of you were headed to the junk pile? Duh, Mom."

What is a woman left with? That was the question that tormented Sylvia as she paced alone in her house, wandering past her daughter's bedroom, devoid now of any sense of Beth, a room of shame now. The room where Sylvia had spent the better part of two decades offering up the love that usurped all others. Nursing Beth under the framed Beatrix Potter prints. Tending to Beth when she was ill, rocking Beth in her arms when her teenage heart was broken. Helping Beth paint the peony pink walls an unsettling purple when the time came for her to declare her independence from her mother's taste. The purple walls remained, but the last time Beth had visited—more than a year ago!—she had suggested redoing the room as a generic guest room, replacing the twin bed with its chenille bedspread and its nest of pillows and stuffed animals with a queen-size sleigh bed. "Otherwise," her daughter had said, with what Syl secretly thought was rather appalling superciliousness, "Franco and I will have to stay at a hotel when we come to visit."

That had been the impetus for the garage apartment. Which she had brought up last Sunday morning, fresh from the glow of their lovely birthday holiday in Sea Ranch. Again she winced, remembering how innocently she had mentioned it, anticipating a conversation with Carl about decorating choices. Instead, he had gotten ugly about money. Money! When what she was proposing was designed to make their daughter more welcome, to encourage her to come home more often! Oh, the look he gave her when she pointed that out! "I'm not building a hotel room to lure her home to shack up with her boyfriend," he'd spat, which had made her nag him about how they should go to New York, then, to visit them, which had made him say those unspeakable things he'd said. About being in love with someone else. And how that someone else was Yelena, his secretary ("She's not my secretary! She's my assistant!"), the very woman she had bought and wrapped a gift for, just weeks ago. Oh, the mortification of that! Syl had actually enjoyed doing that errand for Carl. She had given thought to what that bitch would like, she had been proud of her selection, had taken pleasure in Carl's approval of her choice. She had even called him at the office (oh God!) and asked how Yelena had liked the gift! Did they laugh about it, as she unfolded the expensive linens? Make lewd jokes about Sylvia providing them with feathers to nest their filthy bed? She should have bought her a gift certificate at Borders, she reflected. Something sure to be stuck in a drawer and forgotten.

She decided to make pancakes for herself. In the kitchen, she cracked eggs and poured milk into the mix, heated syrup, stirred frozen blueberries into the batter. She turned the radio on to her favorite oldies station, sang along as the scent of cooking wafted through the kitchen. Nothing like pancakes to make things right. She ate the whole stack, soggy with syrup and butter, savoring each bite. Heated up what was left of the breakfast coffee, poured another glass of Chardonnay. Patted her tummy with satisfaction. Could Yelena cook? she wondered. She doubted it. Syl had only met the woman twice, briefly, and afterward had told Carl how unattractive she'd found her. "There's something dubious about her, don't you think?" she'd said. "She looks like a cosmetician. What's her story, anyway?"

How had Carl responded? She tried to remember. Couldn't. She hadn't paid much attention, obviously, not being in the habit of suspecting her husband of cheating on her. And now Carl was leaving her for that woman, that shifty-eyed, bulgy woman, that Russian Mafia moll. For some reason, Sylvia's thoughts darted into her closet then. She'd been feeling a little tatty lately, a little dated. She'd been thinking of updating her wardrobe but hadn't gotten around to it. Had been postponing it until she'd dropped a few pounds. Now would be a good time, she decided. A little pick-me-up. A trip to the mall would be a lovely way to spend this solitary Sunday, the one-week anniversary of the Betrayal, while her husband was out doing God-knew-what. Ordinarily she wouldn't have contemplated a shopping trip without running it by Carl, even though she knew what he would say, what he always said: "Sure, sweetie. Enjoy yourself. Just don't bankrupt me." As she heard his voice in her mind saying those familiar, husband-like words, the sky suddenly darkened with a passing cloud. And in that moment a shudder went through her, a violent tremor of loneliness and rage.

Sylvia had never given a thought—not one single, solitary, momentary, passing thought—to what she might do under these circumstances. It had never occurred to her. Once upon a time she had worked, briefly, in the publishing industry. But her skills, when added up, were heavily weighted toward the domestic. She had devoted herself to her home and her family. Her energies had been spent first on Carl, then on Beth, then on the threesome, then back on Carl. She'd been good at it. She'd been a loving and efficient nurse, when needed. She'd created a home that everyone commented on; her taste was widely acclaimed in her social circle. She'd been an asset to Carl in the early days, when a pretty and charming wife counted for something in his climb to his present position as CFO of a chain of retail stores. She had never been the type to go wild with the credit card; she was an excellent cook; and Lord knows she had allowed her husband sex on demand, which was far more frequently than she would have preferred. She had loved Carl since their first meeting at class registration at the University of Michigan, when his myopic, slightly crossed, milky blue eyes had reminded her of her parents' old Siamese cat. Everything had proceeded smoothly, throughout thirty-two years of marriage. And now, it seemed, Carl had been abducted by aliens. Or, perhaps—and this was harder for Sylvia to contemplate—perhaps it had been coming, as Beth had pronounced, and she simply hadn't noticed.

She brought her fresh glass of wine back outside, surveyed her rose garden. Carl had labored, for her, digging and carrying, amusing her with comic antics, shuffling and bowing, acting like her slave. "We're never moving," he'd said. "Not after the sweat I just poured into that garden."

Never moving. Never, ever. Sylvia loved her house with a tenderness and indulgence such as she had lavished on her baby girl. She loved the way the light moved through the house, warming different rooms at different times of day. She loved how every nook and cranny held a memory. It was just a tract house, really, built in the seventies, east of the 5 but with a distant view of the ocean. Still, over the years they had improved and upgraded, made it perfect. Made it theirs. Hers. No, she vowed, thoughtfully wiping a lipstick smear off her glass, *we're never moving.*

Four

CARL HAD HIT A TRIPLE. He tipped his hat to the cheering crowd. Way to go! First, he'd set up a business trip to New York to coincide with Beth's birthday, which also effectively removed him from the war zone at home, where the bomb he'd dropped continued to smolder, concealed by Sylvia's passive-aggressive tactics of entrapment. And, rounding into third, by postponing the quarterly meeting with his guy at J.P. Morgan he scored an edge, toggled the switch a little on the punk's overconfidence. His old guy, Vic, had retired and been replaced by this upstart. Over the years Carl and Vic had developed an almost friendship. Vic used to fly out from New York, "smiling and dialing," he joked, and would sit in Carl's office and go over the corporate accounts. Then they'd golf at Torrey Pines and have lunch at the clubhouse, Vic picking up the tab. "I'll come east next time," Carl would say, and Vic would beg him not to, make believe these jaunts to San Diego were a kind of vacation for him. Once Carl had suggested it might be nice to visit Vic at his house in Connecticut, meet his wife and kids. Vic's response had confirmed Carl's suspicion. "Nah, come to the city," he'd said. "Connecticut's not for you. No point. Better yet, stay here in paradise and let me come to you. I'm begging you; it's like mainlining Prozac, coming out here." Carl knew, then, what Vic was anxious to hide: that even though he was Vic's client—or his company was—his income wasn't close to Vic's. Those Wall Street guys! Vic didn't want him to see his Connecticut spread, his driveway full of Beemers and Range Rovers, his landscaped acreage. Carl got it. He backed off. But this new kid, no way was he barging in on the old routine. No, Carl informed him, I'll come to you. Two things rankled him: the knowledge that this kid made more than he did, and the kid's condescending chumminess. "Carl's Baaad," he would growl into the phone, a stupid pun that had grown old before it reached Carl's ears the first time. Why did everyone in New York think that anyone who lived outside of New York was inherently inferior? But Carl had detected the undertone of nervousness when he'd put off the meeting, and he was pleased. *Shrewd,* he praised himself. *Shrewd one, Carl.* Three in one blow. He imagined himself at the skeet range: "Pull!," then *blamblamblam.* Yes!

Carl lived in a world of private reckonings. Every encounter was a contest; his days were full of scorecards. Someone tried to bully him on the 5, watch this: he'd slice in front of him just before his exit. Some plebe at work tried to one-up him, tried to steal his thunder or undercut his idea, watch out! More than one smug wunderkind had learned to cover his balls after pushing Carl too far—but he always accomplished it on the sly. He was not only aware of his persona as somewhat of a Mr. Magoo, he actually cultivated it. It gave him cover for his dealings. While everyone chuckled and exchanged collusive glances over his fumbling, he systematically went about his business. The fact that no one had caught on to him after all these years was a source of private glee. Did they think he'd achieved his success by accident? Were they under the impression that he was unaware of their "affectionate" derision? No, Carl was a shrewd customer. He'd been prescient in securing the infamous Mort Sahl before Sylvia could get him, seamless in his affair with the pulchritudinous Yelena, nothing short of brilliant in his handling of Sylvia. "Ducks in a row," he muttered to himself as he settled into the banquette at Union Square Cafe, ten minutes early for the birthday dinner with his daughter.

On the phone, Beth had said, "Is this a smooth-things-over-before-the-divorce dinner?"

That had come out of left field. He had specifically told Sylvia not to blab to Beth. Convinced her that it would be better to wait, to do it when they were all together. Then, having accomplished it in his own way and time, he'd explain to Sylvia that it had just come up, that he hadn't meant to tell her, that he'd been put on the spot and couldn't avoid the truth. He should have known. She'd probably been on the phone before his car was out of the driveway last week.

The tone of his daughter's voice threw him. He scrambled to reposition, annoyed at being caught off guard.

"Honey," he'd exclaimed, his voice resonant with hurt. Her voice had been hard. Cynical. His daughter was the only person he'd surrendered to, the only one he loved without calculation. The day she was born—in point of fact it wasn't day, but that nether hour between deepest night and dawn—Carl had experienced, for the first and only time in his life, utter captivation. He'd been patient with Sylvia, who had borne her pregnancy with the same plodding sense of duty and unimaginative goodwill that she bore everything. Throughout the long, stop-and-go labor, he had stayed by her side, applied cool washcloths to her forehead, murmured encouragement. After a particularly grueling contraction during which she had grunted and grimaced like a farm animal, he had gazed lovingly into her eyes while forming the whole and complete sentence in his head, *My God, I do not love this woman.*

It wasn't as if the admission shocked or even saddened him. Sylvia was pliable enough. If anything it reassured him, freed him to collect himself. But then Beth was placed in his arms, tiny, fragile Beth, who gazed up at him with his very own milky blue eyes, and his heart sailed right out of his body, never to settle back safely again.

And now here she was. Carl watched his daughter wend her way through the crowded bar area, scan the dining room. Spotting him, she nodded—a curt little smile—and maneuvered deftly through the aisles. As a child Beth had been chubby, but as a twenty-something (twenty-eight today, actually) she was lean and taut as an ice dancer, clad in stretchy black, her once-springy chestnut hair cropped close like a helmet. When had Beth turned so brittle? Carl wondered, with a flicker of dismay, as she pecked him on the cheek and settled primly into the chair across from him, ignoring the invitational pat he'd made on the leather banquette next to him.

"Cosmopolitan," she said to the waiter who materialized as she sat.

"Scotch," Carl said. "Rocks, twist."

He smiled at his baby girl. "You look beautiful," he said.

She blinked, gave her head a little shake. "I haven't been sleeping well," she said.

Carl chose to ignore that, as he chose to ignore any reminder that his daughter was cohabiting, sharing her bed nightly with some guy. When he'd called to invite her to dinner, she'd been offended that her boyfriend hadn't been included. "I so rarely get to see you," Carl had explained. "I'm sure he'll understand."

"How are things at the magazine?" he asked now, surprised to find himself feeling bashful in front of this self-assured young woman.

Beth sighed and aimed those unsettling eyes directly into his own. "Can we cut the shit, Dad? Can we cut to the chase?" she said, and then, oh daggers, glanced at her watch.

Carl swept his arm in a courtly gesture, inviting her to take the floor. In a moment of uncalculated ineptitude, however, his sleeve caught the edge of a bud vase holding a single rose and sent it crashing to the floor, where it shattered. A quick glance at Beth reassured him that this unplanned buffoonery had worked in his favor—her tough chick persona had been pushed aside by this display of Daddy Magoo, and she ducked her head to hide her bright giggle.

"Where the hell did that come from?" Carl wondered aloud, staring at the mess on the floor as if it had ambushed him, playing slyly into her weakened defenses. For now Beth cocked her head, freeing an overgelled lock of hair to fall out of place, and said, mournfully, "Oh, Daddy . . ."

It was all Carl needed. He reached across the table and grasped his daughter's hands. "Beth, honey . . ."

She bit her lip and looked away as the busboy knelt beside her to clean up the broken vase. Freeing one hand, Carl reached into his jacket pocket and withdrew the pale blue box, fresh from Tiffany's. He placed it between them. "Happy birthday, sweetheart."

No woman in Carl's experience could set eyes on that telltale blue box without getting over it, or at least dropping her defenses long enough to provide an opening. Beth was no exception. He thrilled to see her drop her hauteur and give a delighted gasp. For a moment her face was his little girl's again as she darted him a shy, breathless look. Inside the box was a diamond tennis bracelet. As she lifted it, it caught and reflected thousands of glimmers of light, the diamonds being full cut and not the chips put in the cheaper versions. "If it's not what you want . . . " he began, but she cut him off.

"It's actually exactly what I wanted. Exactly. How did you know that?"

"You're my girl," Carl said. "Brain meld." He performed a little routine with his fingers on his forehead, receiving psychic messages.

"Thank you, Daddy." Beth allowed him to fasten the clasp, held up her arm to admire the gift. "I really love it."

"I really love you," Carl replied, once more on his game.

She pushed the errant lock of hair behind her ear, ducking her head away from him.

"Beth? Talk to me."

But she averted her gaze, shook her head. "It's your life," she said, "none of my business."

"Of course it's your business. We're your family."

The drinks arrived, and he attempted to clink glasses with her, but she ignored him and took a healthy swig. "Tell you the truth," she said, "I always kind of expected this."

Carl flinched. "I don't know why you would say that. I didn't."

She gave a very unladylike snort. "Oh please. Like I don't know Mom drives you nuts."

"I loved your mother. I still do. Always will."

"Gag me, Dad."

"I'm surprised by your attitude, Beth. I'm sure you're hurt, but—"

"I'm not hurt! I could care less! I'm busy with my own life, in case you hadn't noticed."

Once upon a time, Carl had taught this girl how to play tennis. He'd been so proud of her when she got good enough to maintain a volley. For some reason he thought of that now, as he cast around for an appropriate response to her. He was saved by the waiter, a real flamer, who popped up with a tiny blackboard upon which the specials were scrawled. Eyeing the Tiffany's box, he simpered, "Ooh, somebody's happy!" Beth seemed to like that, but Carl bristled, wondering if the fag realized she was his daughter.

"I'll have a half order of the field greens salad," Beth said, without even glancing at the menu. "No dressing."

"And for your entrée?"

"That's it." She took another slug of her cocktail, casting a self-assured glance around the room. Her eyes rested on Carl and she gave him a fond, conciliatory smile. *My God*, thought Carl, *my daughter's a little sexpot.*

"Come on, honey, have a nice dinner," he said. He had a sudden fear that she'd become one of those nutcases who starved themselves. She was awfully thin.

"It's all I want," she said, and Carl detected a flush of embarrassment, so he ordered himself a rib eye and waited for the poofter to depart before leaning in and saying, "Beth, why aren't you eating?"

Beth shifted and did that little snappish thing with her head again, as if some tiny bug had alit on her cheek. "Well, Daddy, I'm sorry, but actually I'm having dinner with Franco, um, afterward. I mean, it is my birthday. I mean, Dad, I do live with Franco. He's my boyfriend. And you didn't want him to join us? I mean, it's kind of awkward. So I'm meeting him. After."

"I see," said Carl.

"Sorry, Dad."

"No, no, my fault. I didn't realize. I didn't mean to be rude. It's just, I see you so seldom. I wanted . . ."

"You wanted to have the divorce chat."

"I wanted to reassure you."

"Of what?"

"I wanted you to know . . . your mother and I . . ." Beth gazed at him expectantly. What was it he had wanted her to know, exactly? His ducks weren't lining up. It was himself he had wanted to reassure, he realized. Unloading Sylvia was liberating, but his adoring, adorable little girl—was she going to side with her mother? The possibility hadn't occurred to him that Beth might choose to freeze him out. It was unacceptable.

"I only have one question," Beth said.

His mouth full of overbuttered bread, Carl raised his eyebrows in inquiry. Beth leaned across the table and brushed a crumb from his chin. "What took you so long?" she said. "I've been waiting for this for I don't know how long. At least since high school."

"I really don't know what you're talking about. Your mother and I have had many happy years together."

"Whatever."

"Come on, Bethy. Cut the hard-assed routine. I love you, your mother loves you, we want to make sure you understand this has nothing to do with you. We want you to know we're still your parents, will always be your parents."

Beth let out a harsh bark of laughter. "What am I, five?" she said. "It's fine, Dad. Chill. It's your life. I'm just glad I'm out of it."

"Beth!" This was too much.

"I mean, you're the asshole here, am I right? You're the one doing your secretary. Mom's only guilty of being Mom, which I guess she can't help, so you better let her keep that house or she'll go berserk, you do know that."

"You . . . your mother . . ." Carl began.

"She'll be fine as long as she gets to keep the house and you give her enough money."

"What are you, her lawyer?" Carl worked his tongue around his back molar in an effort to dislodge a lump of sodden dough, then took a gulp of scotch. The cubes had melted and it was watery and flavorless. He cast his eyes around for the waiter. Beth nibbled at her plate of greens, smiling a supercilious little smile.

"So, the artifice crumbles," she said.

"I find your attitude offensive. You're not being fair. We gave you a good life, we had a happy home," Carl said.

"Yeah, if you want that kind of life. Big house, important job, Mom's perfect dinner parties. Not what I want."

"What *do* you want?" Carl snarled. He raised his empty glass and pointed at it pointedly. Mr. Take-It-Up-the-Butt gave him a thumbs-up and headed to the service bar.

"No need to get hostile, Daddy. My childhood was fine. I'm not going to be traumatized by your midlife crisis." She glanced at her watch again.

Carl fought an impulse to pin her down, keep her sitting across from him. *You are staying right where you are, young lady. Don't think for a minute you are leaving this table,* he wanted to say. The startling truth that she was beyond his dominion, that she could get up and walk away from him with impunity, made him tremble. "Listen," he said, "why don't you call Frank? Tell him to join us."

Beth shook her head in disbelief, leaned her cheek on her hand, gazed at him as if he were some street waif observed through the windows of a passing limo. "Franco, Dad. And I'm afraid that's not doable. He wouldn't come, and besides, we've made other plans."

"Oh come on, Beth. Don't you think you're laying it on a little thick?"

Beth shrugged. "I work for the biggest prima donna in the industry, Dad. I spend my days coming up with solutions to all kinds of interpersonal problems. One thing I've learned for sure is you can't make everyone happy. I'm really sorry, but I've got to go. How long are you in the city?"

"I leave tomorrow, after my meeting."

"Want to have lunch?"

"My meeting is lunch."

"Oh. Gee. Too bad you couldn't have stayed longer."

Carl considered changing his flight, but that would have made him appear weak, and as if his job weren't important. He smiled ruefully as Beth leaned across the table to give him another sterile peck on the cheek. "You're really going? You really have to rush off?"

"Really do. Can't be late for my own birthday party."

Carl nodded grimly. "Happy birthday, sweetheart."

"Thank you, Daddy. I love the bracelet. Call me, okay?" She looped her purse over her shoulder and turned her back on him. He watched her for a moment, then pulled his gaze away in an impulse of self-protectiveness. But at that moment she turned, and, rushing back to him, threw her arms around his neck and pressed her face against the side of his head. "I do love you, Daddy," she whispered. He squeezed his eyes shut and held her taut little body tightly against him. Then she broke free and rushed out, and he watched her until she was indistinguishable from the throng.

She had left the Tiffany's box on the table. He thought that was odd. Sylvia wouldn't have done that. Sylvia would have saved it, used it to store little trinkets. Those blue boxes were like trophies to women.

He ordered a third scotch and dessert, then coffee, then had a brandy at the bar. By the time he got back to his hotel he was really missing Yelena. What bitches his wife and daughter were! He longed to sink his head between the fragrant pillows of his lover's breasts. On the corner, in the shadows, a Somali was selling knockoff jewelry. "Rolexes, Cartier," he called softly to Carl. Carl had seen him, or one of his countrymen, earlier, working with a partner. One of them hawking, the other scanning for police. He'd seen them pack up and vanish at the hint of a bust. He stopped now and glanced at the wares, arranged on black velvet. They certainly looked authentic. He chose a pair of earrings and counted out the bills. When he looked back, the Somali and his stand were gone. He patted the little blue box his daughter had left behind, sagely salvaged by him. How well this had worked out, without his even planning it! He imagined the look on Yelena's face, the way she would lean in and plant a fat kiss on his mouth, how she'd purr with pleasure and gratitude. He wondered if she would even know the significance of the blue box. He'd have to figure out a way to prep her, drop some casual reference to Tiffany's while at work. Knowing her, she'd go straight to the computer and Google it, one more piece of Americana to master. He pictured her eyes widening at the array of jewels, at the prices. Then, when they were alone, he'd slide the blue box out of his pocket. Picked up a little something for you when I was in New York, he'd say. Bull's-eye.

Five

THE FIRST TIME Adele laid eyes on her future husband was at NYU freshman orientation. She was raised in a big prewar apartment on Riverside Drive, and the city was full of people she'd grown up with. That day she'd discovered several old acquaintances and they'd fallen in together, all flushed with the newness of college, joking and jostling each other, pretending to be overwhelmed by all the information they had to process. She heard one of her friends say "Sorry!" but didn't pay attention. Then the girl said, in a high-pitched stage whisper, "I *said* I was sorry. Geez. Excuse *me!*" At that point Adele focused and saw a compact, wiry boy in faded high-water cords standing alone in line. His lips were compressed, and he gazed over everyone's heads in a way that conveyed, to Adele, extreme self-consciousness. She tried to smile at him, but he ignored her, and her friend poked her and giggled, mouthed the word *creep.*

Adele didn't think he was a creep. She couldn't stop sneaking glances at him; there was something about him that she almost recognized. It took her weeks to get him to look back at her, but soon they were friends. He said he'd ignored her because he thought she was making fun of him. "Why are you so defensive?" she'd asked him. He told her, in dribs and drabs, over months of friendship, about his situation. Rattled off the names of the meds his mother wouldn't take. Showed her the bone that stuck out of his elbow after having been shattered on the playground.

Truth be told, Adele was the seductress. Drew was so reticent she wondered if he was gay. It never occurred to her that she intimidated him, that she personified all that he longed for, that he feared her affection was some kind of joke. The first time they made love—which Adele still remembered in detail—their nervousness quickly melted into a familiarity that seemed cellular in its depth. Afterward they were both teary, touching each other's faces in wonderment.

At some point the momentum had gathered and the years started tumbling by, one blurring into another. Those fuzzy, bubbled years of grad school, survival jobs, med school. The decision to marry. The arrival of babies. The days bleeding into years, choices made in the moment, for expediency, always thinking *Later, later when I can focus, I'll reevaluate.* Choices like working temp jobs because the money was better than interning at an architectural firm. Choices like not wanting her parents to help them. Choices like not raising the kids in the city. Never hearing the doors slamming behind her, because she wasn't listening. Why should she? She had a great marriage, great kids, and when her father died the money was well-used in obtaining the house in Bedford. Life was good.

It was Jake, her oldest, who had started it. When he announced that he wanted to go to UCSD, Adele thought it was a joke. "But you have acceptances from NYU and Columbia! Why would you want to go all the way out there?" she had wailed. Oh, how she'd wept, when he left.

She and Drew flew out several times to visit him, sometimes with Danny and Noah in tow, staying in the Best Western near campus. As his freshman year was drawing to a close, he informed them that he wanted to stay out there for the summer. He'd gotten a job, he said. He had friends with an apartment; he could room with them. It had hit her very hard. She hadn't realized, when he'd flown off, that he wouldn't be back. "Of course he'll be back," Drew had said, exasperated by her sadness. But she knew. By next summer it wouldn't even occur to him to come home. "Let's at least go see him," she'd said. "Get him settled in the apartment. Make sure he has an actual bed to sleep in." They went, just the two of them, making it a holiday; instead of the Best Western they stayed at the Four Seasons Aviara. Adele soon learned that it wasn't just the job that was keeping Jake out there. He had a girlfriend, whose parents lived in one of those ubiquitous developments in Carlsbad. Adele and Drew invited them all for cocktails at the hotel.

It happened that nature conspired to seduce Drew, hitherto an enthusiastic participant in Adele's derision of all things Californian. Toward evening, the June Gloom (which would later become so familiar to them) lifted and presented a glorious sunset over the Pacific. All day there had been a sluggish precipitation, and suddenly the sun broke through and a rainbow appeared over the sparkling sea. A young man of extraordinary courtesy and charm brought them their drinks and chatted amiably with them about his studies. Adele watched with amusement as her husband became besotted. Gleefully, she anticipated teasing him once they were home in New York. Jake's girlfriend was adorable, bright, and clearly head over heels for him. In fact they did become engaged, briefly, but they broke up before a date was set. This was a tremendous relief to Adele, not just because she was Jake's first serious girlfriend, but because the thought of sharing in-law status with the girl's parents was inconceivable. They were nice enough, but, to Adele, comically bland. "Were you able to detect any sign of intelligent life?" she said to Drew later in their hotel room. "I mean, seriously, Drew—did you hear what she said when the waiter brought the amuse-bouche? She said, 'Oh golly.' Did you hear that? How could I make it up? 'Oh golly.'"

He hadn't bitten. All he'd said was, "I thought they were nice."

The following day Drew went for a run, and when he returned to the hotel he informed Adele that he wanted to purchase a condo. I love it here, he said. I feel great. The air, the sea, the mountains. Adele remembered the moment as if it were five minutes ago. How she'd stared at her husband, a guy for whom Fort Tryon Park was the wilderness. The move out of the city to Bedford had traumatized him, for God's sake; it had taken him a good year to learn to appreciate the fresh air. She'd laughed. "You're kidding," she'd said. She thought he'd gone temporarily insane.

She remembered it all so well. How incredulous she'd been, how she'd thought he was joking, right up until the last moment. She'd refused to go with him when he took off in the rental car to go condo shopping. "We have the money," he'd kept saying. "We have the money."

~

On the Saturday morning a week after their trip to Sea Ranch, Drew returned from his run to find Adele on the balcony, poring over *Architectural Digest*. "Look at this crap," she said, showing him the feature article on the Hollywood manse of a movie star couple barely out of their teens.

Drew glanced at it, indifferent. "What are you up to today?"

"Look at this stupid cupola on the pool house. Unbelievable." Adele sighed a sigh of deep, resigned injury, and tossed the magazine down. "Let's do something," she said. "Let's take the Coaster to L.A. Visit some museums, get out of here."

Now Drew sighed, turning away from his wife to hide his flicker of annoyance. *Get out of here!* What was her problem? It was a spectacular day, even by San Diego standards, and the last thing he wanted to do was sit in a train to L.A. "I don't know why you won't learn how to play golf," he said.

"I told you. No sticks, no balls, no holes or goals."

"You'd enjoy it. And we wouldn't have to have these arguments."

"Who's arguing?"

"I can't understand why, when you have a day like this, you would want to go to L.A."

"You can't?" Adele tilted her head in exaggerated wonderment. "Okay, then how about La Jolla? Or Coronado? We can have lunch at the Del."

"Actually, sweetie, I committed myself to play some golf today."

"On a Saturday?" Adele heard the plaintive tone in her voice and fell silent, taming the impulse to protest. She'd been looking forward to a leisurely day with her husband, just the two of them. Sundays he usually played golf. Not Saturdays.

"I should have told you, I'm sorry," Drew was saying. "Sven Olssen has people in from out of town; he booked the course for the afternoon. Asked me to join them. I can't say no to Sven, you know that."

Adele did not know that. Sven was some big shot at Scripps, she knew that, but so was Drew. "What about tomorrow?" she asked.

"Tomorrow's my regular game." Why was she laying this guilt trip on him? He picked up the binoculars he kept on the balcony and gazed out to sea. Lots of surfers out there today. A lone sailboat, far out. He wanted a boat. He wanted to be out on that boat, right now.

Adele wordlessly gathered her things and went inside. So Drew had booked himself solid for the weekend. Lovely. This kind of thing never used to happen. Back home, weekends meant the city; museums, a show, a new restaurant to check out. He played golf occasionally, seasonally. Now it was becoming an obsession.

Drew followed her in and attempted to hug her. She didn't exactly push him away, but was stiff and unresponsive in his arms. "Don't be mad," he said. "I'm sorry. I didn't think. I'll make it up to you."

"How?" He nuzzled the back of her neck, tickling her with his stubble. He knew how sensitive she was there; he knew exactly how to dissolve her. "Stop!" she erupted, and of course he didn't, and of course she went help-less with laughter. "How?" she repeated, catching his cheeks in her hands, holding his face away from her.

"Dinner? Your pick."

"Just the two of us?"

"Unless you want to invite somebody to join us. It's up to you."

"I thought we'd invite Sylvia for dinner tonight."

He groaned. "How did I know you were going to say that?"

"We don't have to. I'll take her to lunch, now that I have the day free."

He glanced at her to gauge the quality of the dig, saw that she was play-ing it, which meant she'd forgiven him. Had a surge of affection for her. "See, this is why I love you," he said, kissing her nose.

Later, after he'd left, Adele allowed herself to fume a little. She hated that she'd whined, but for so many years it had been a given that Saturday afternoons were together times. He hadn't even bothered to tell her! "Can't say no to Sven," she muttered, dialing Syl's number. No answer. She didn't pick up her cell, either. She called Maggie, but Paul said she'd gone out and left her cell on the kitchen counter. Adele floundered, feeling stuck and abandoned. It was like being in some kind of benign prison, slowly dying of boredom. Adele didn't actually believe in boredom, but she'd already read the library book she'd taken out that week, and there was no pressing household chore to claim her time. Though she was generally self-sufficient, what had thrown her was the unexpectedness of the empty day, with nothing but her own company. *If I were home,* she thought. *If I were home . . .* and then her mind started buzzing with what she'd have done, whom she'd have seen, how she'd have filled the day, if she were home. She knew she had to avoid thinking along those lines, so she got in the car and drove down the 101 to the Pannikin in Leucadia. Got a latte and a muffin. Settled in at one of the outside tables with the *Times.* In the Weekend section she read about all the millions of things that were going on in Manhattan that she would miss. The train thundered by. At the table next to her, two women were deep in conversation about colon health. "And it's so easy here," one of them was saying. "Ninety percent of my diet is from my garden, all year long."

Adele gazed across the highway past the railroad tracks to Vulcan Avenue, where an old Volkswagen van covered in paint-dripped peace signs tootled by. Someone in the trailer park on Vulcan had erected a kind of obelisk, decorated with pieces of broken glass and mirrors, which sent jagged spears of reflected light all the way to where she sat. It was November, and back home it would be chilly and gray. The weather was lovely here, that was incontestable. Warm enough to sit outside in the sun, the breeze gently cooling. No bugs. Not like home, where she had to slather herself with Avon Skin So Soft to keep from being eaten alive. No, this was the Golden Ring. Everybody out here but her, apparently, knew they'd won the prize. *Aren't we all so very very lucky.* Drew certainly felt that way. She knew he thought there was something wrong with her, some perverse strain of resistance, else why wouldn't she drink the Kool-Aid? "How can you miss New York?" he'd exclaim, throwing his arms wide to the view.

The weather, the weather. As if weather were the only thing that mattered in life. "You misunderstand," she'd said to Drew. "I don't hate it here. It's very nice. It just isn't home, and it never will be." It made her sad that she couldn't love California the way he and the boys did. It was the biggest thing that had ever come between them. She had said to Maggie, once, that it was as if San Diego were a perfectly nice man who you found yourself married to—no complaints, except that you were still in love with your ex. Maggie understood. She was from Northern California, and before that, the UK. She and Paul had just sort of migrated here, she'd told Adele, and next thing you knew, Paul had his job and Josh was in school, and for better or worse it was home. Not Syl, though. Syl loved it here. She and Carl had come out after college; they were big flourishers of the Golden Ring.

The boys had been jubilant to learn that Dad bought a condo. They all became giddily bicoastal, flying off to Carlsbad every chance they got. Even Adele got caught up in the excitement, despite herself. She wouldn't admit it, though. Her curmudgeonliness about California became a family joke; they all vied with each other to find things that she would have to admit were cool. What she most enjoyed was being able to see Jake frequently. That was compensation for the bygone days of European vacations, the carefully researched trips to Sardinia and Prague. There wasn't even discussion anymore. Vacation equaled Carlsbad, end of conversation. Then Danny graduated and followed his brother to UCSD. Noah, who was just starting high school, began a campaign for them to move full-time to California. Danny and Jake egged him on. "Absolutely not," Adele replied. "Forget it. In your dreams. What don't you understand about *no*? No way, José. N.O. When hell freezes over. Over my dead body."

This was in August 2001.

After 9/11, Drew talked of almost nothing else. "We're getting out," he kept saying. Adele, preoccupied with Cordelia, hadn't paid much attention to him. And then came the offer from Scripps. How they'd argued over that! Never, never, Adele protested. It is unthinkable to pass this up, Drew insisted.

The Clean Colon Gals were sharing pictures on their iPhones and laughing raucously. There was a loud, clattery sound as a pack of preteens rode their skateboards down the sidewalk. Something knocked roughly into Adele, causing her to spill coffee on her thigh. It was a big dog, nosing around for crumbs. "She's friendly," said her apparent owner, a blond boy in dreadlocks. Adele glared at him. She had been thinking of the meeting at Noah's school, when they were drilled on lockdown procedures and advised to have family emergency plans. Such a beautiful, crisp autumn, her favorite time of the year. She'd left the packet of paranoid suggestions from the school on the dining room table, where Drew picked it up later and read aloud from it, emphasizing words like *terrorist* and *bomb* and *your children*. The boy with the dreads bore a slight resemblance to Henry, Cordelia's younger son. Something sweet and hopeful in his face, his cheeks ruddy and Rubenesque despite his attempt at grunge. Adele stared at him, her face tingling.

In the weeks and months after 9/11 rumors circulated daily: don't go to any mall over Halloween weekend, watch out for Grand Central. Then there was the plane crash in Long Island. One of Drew's interns was on it. Adele's protestations became weaker when Drew started talking about the Jews who wouldn't leave Germany, the people with their heads in the sand. He laid his deal on the table about the house she would get to build someday. Finally, unable to stand alone against the tide any longer, she agreed. Their house went straight into a bidding war. They were offered more than three times what they'd paid for it twenty years earlier. She'd sobbed throughout the closing.

How she had loved that house. It was such a goyim house, to be sure. Her mother's lips had gotten thinner and thinner as she wordlessly walked through it, the first time she came to visit. Adele had found her in the kitchen, scrubbing the old soapstone sink with bleach, wearing rubber gloves and a gauze mask. "For what you paid for this, you could have had a nice new house in Rye Brook," she'd said.

It was true. Falling in love with an old farmhouse was the last thing she'd expected of herself. Mid-century modern was her passion; Saarinen and Eames and Neutra. Her notebooks were full of sketches inspired by their ideas. The Bedford listings her Realtor had sent her were all boxy things, new construction or leftovers from the seventies that had been fudged over. Raised ranches with bomb shelters that had been turned into gyms, stuff like that, stuff she could have worked with, though with a toddler and an infant she had to admit to a certain longing for a simple turnkey, something clean and uncomplicated with a yard for the boys.

Adele drifted into a reverie as the din of 101, the rushing trains, and the earnest chatterers blended into an indistinguishable swell of white noise. She thought of the day she had first met her house, so many years ago. A lot of things had occurred that day, some of them minor annoyances, some of them eerily omen-like. She didn't like to believe in omens, but there certainly seemed to be a conspiracy of forces at work that day. First, getting out of the city had been hell. The babysitter who came to watch Jake was late, claiming a subway delay. Adele was still nursing Danny, so she brought him with her, and she barely made her train. There was a derailment on the Metro-North and they'd sat there for over an hour. She fully expected the Realtor to have given up on her, but there she was, with coffee and muffins. Danny had been fussing and squirming all morning, but as soon as they got out of the train in Bedford he became charming and sunny, batting his lashes at the Realtor so that she was more than happy to hold him while Adele wandered the properties. It was a glorious autumn day; the leaves were in full color, the air brisk with just a hint of wood smoke. When they drove up the drive to the house that would become hers, the Realtor had said, "I know you're not interested in antiques, but this one is so special I just wanted to show it to you."

Abruptly, Adele rose and dropped her newspaper in the bin. Her mind had embarked on the flight of the bumblebee again, buzzing around, driving her mad. This was precisely what she had wanted to avoid, why she had hoped to be distracted. She should drive over to Syl's; maybe she was out working in her garden. Maybe Maggie was there with her. It would be fun to spend the afternoon with them. They were good friends. Adele was grateful for them. She would miss them when she left.

For she would be leaving. Noah would be finishing his degree this year, finally, after taking a gap year to tag along with a skateboard team his friend was on. Danny was wrapping up his veterinarian training at UC Davis; Jake was interning at Scripps. Her three little pigs were off to make their way in the world, and it was time to hold Drew to their deal, to his promise. For years she had been drawing, clipping ideas from magazines, researching properties. He could keep his precious condo—she knew she'd never get him entirely out of California. But she also knew that if she didn't act soon, her dream would disintegrate. Another few years and she'd be in her sixties. Would she really want to take on such a project then?

The most startling omen, that day in Bedford, had occurred as she stepped out of the back door and saw the fringe of woods and the pond. She'd been admiring the fieldstone fireplace with the hidden silver cupboards, pelting the poor Realtor with questions she couldn't answer concerning the history of the house, what she knew about the builder. The Realtor had escaped her, taking Danny to rock him on the swing that hung from the front porch. Everything had grown quiet, then, as she stepped out the back door. The flaming leaves shimmered in the sun, soughed in the gentle breeze. The water glittered. It was utterly still, until something leapt from the surface of the pond, swiveled, flashed silver in the sun, then slid back, seamlessly, into the depths.

In all the years she lived there, she never saw such a thing again. The boys used to fish in the pond, but they never caught anything. Never even saw a fish. Her insistence on what she'd seen became a family joke. "Mom's fish."

She left the Pannikin and drove to Sylvia's, but there was no sign of her. She went home and took a nap and a bath. Decided on George's at the Cove in La Jolla for dinner. But Drew came home tired and convinced her to settle for the Coyote Bar and Grill. There was a band playing and it was too noisy to talk much. By the time Adele had finished picking at her dinner she was in a fully mushroomed cloud of gloom. Drew was so happy! He wolfed down a burger platter and a couple of beers, chatted with the waitress and the other "diners" who were sharing their fire pit, bopped along to the music. He kept beaming at her, reaching over and squeezing her knee, as if he actually imagined that she was enjoying herself as much as he was. In the car on the way home, he teased her. "Judge Curmudgeon," he chanted. "Mudgie won't budgie." It was a stupid thing they had started calling her, when she was Woody Allen–ing their California high. "Look at Mom, doing the Mudge Trudge!" The boys had laughed, imitating her insulted stalk.

She turned her face away from Drew and stared out the window as they drove. "Sorry you had a bad day," Drew said, in a tone that implied how impossible it was to please her.

"It's California's fault," Adele muttered, though she knew how childish she sounded. It never used to be this way. They'd always had fun together.

It *was* California's fault, she thought, because the little seed of tension that moving here had planted seemed to be growing into a nasty weed.

Back at the condo, while Drew was in the bathroom, she made a mug of chamomile tea, dumped her stack of research on the table. "What's that?" he said, on his way through the kitchen.

"Our future."

"That sounds ominous. What're you up to?" He opened a liter of water and sat at the table opposite her. Gave her an amused, indulgent smile, which she responded to with an impassive stare. "I would like to have a discussion with you," she said. "I am feeling overlooked. 'How can I get over this?' I asked myself, and the answer was, isn't it just about time to call in my husband's promise?"

Drew's indulgent smile grew rigid. " 'Promise'?" he echoed.

"Drew. It's going on six years since we sold Bedford. Noah's almost done with college. I'm not getting any younger, in case you haven't noticed. It's shit or get off the pot time."

When he didn't reply, she continued, riffling through her stack of clippings. "They're offering tax breaks in Portland to support the waterside redevelopment. Factory lofts; raw space. That might be interesting. It's a start. Let's go to Portland next weekend, look around." When there was no response, she raised her head to find her husband gazing at her, his expression inscrutable.

"What?" Adele said. "Oregon's always been on the list."

Drew passed his elegant surgeon's hands over his face, the long, capable fingers gently massaging his sinuses. There was something exasperated in the gesture, and Adele took umbrage.

"It's time, Drew," she said. "It's now or never. Don't you even want to discuss it?"

"Adele," he said, into the palm of his hand. "My darling Adele."

"What? Your darling Adele what, Andrew?"

Their eyes locked, and for a moment Adele felt her heart stop. Her ears yawned as if she were holding a shell against them.

"I . . ." He shook his head, that exasperated gesture. "Why can't you let it go? Why can't you enjoy this life we have?"

"What are you saying?"

Again, the head shake. She wanted to reach across the table and give him a smack, make him snap out of it, make him come back. Come back from where? Where had he gone? A chasm of loneliness yawned inside her. "Drew? What's the matter? What's going on?"

"Sweetheart, I just . . . I'm not into it. I know I said you could build a house someday, but you hate it here, and I love it here, and . . . I don't know."

"This is unbelievable. You can't really be saying this to me. You would take this away from me?"

"No, you deserve your house. You do."

"Thank you. Then, what?"

"I . . . just don't want to be in on it."

"What are you talking about, you don't want to be in on it? What are you saying?"

"I'm . . . having doubts."

"Doubts about what? The house? Me?"

Drew nodded, avoided her eyes. "Both. I think."

Adele sat motionless, gripping the edge of her chair. It was how she had always reacted to danger, as far back as her childhood. By holding perfectly still, not allowing so much as a rising breath to alert the enemy. Who was the enemy? Impossible that it could be Drew, her Drew. Something had gone wrong; it was a mistake. If she didn't move, didn't breathe, it might go away. Dissolve. She let her eyes glaze over. Let him go out of focus. They sat this way for a long time, it seemed. Or maybe it was only a moment or two.

He began to fidget with the things on the table. Took the saltshaker and jiggled it. "Agitate, agitate," he muttered, almost to himself. Then, directly to her, he said, "Never satisfied. Always bitching, always tweaking."

Adele weaved her head around as if it were ensnared in cobwebs. "What are you talking about?"

Drew arranged the objects in a V shape away from his water bottle. "This is us," he said. "Here's me, loving my life, and here's you, resisting. Refusing. Determined to hate it here. Closing your eyes to every possible . . . delight. Ridiculing every single thing."

Adele gaped at him wordlessly. "I mean," he continued, "things change. Life evolves. You think if you leave here and go somewhere else that suddenly you'll be happy?"

"I want to go home. But I can't go home. Because you said anywhere but back east. That was the agreement. This whole California thing was . . . was thrust upon me, Drew. I never liked it here. This was you, all you. Don't you point your finger at me for not being happy here."

"You haven't even tried."

"I have tried! I know how much you like it, and I've tried, but it just doesn't do it for me, Drew!"

"But what are we supposed to do, Del? I've never been so happy in my life."

"I know that. I agreed we won't sell the condo. Keep it forever. It has nothing to do with my house."

Drew gazed at her, got up and went to the sliders, where the lights of Carlsbad glittered a path to the sea. His heart surged like the inky waves out there in the night. His love for the place was visceral. He'd never expected to feel like this about life, about his life. It was so far from what he'd been born into, so far from what he'd been taught to expect. He turned back to his wife, who sat across the room looking at him. It was as if she were on a distant shore, and he was sailing farther and farther away from her. He hadn't realized, until she pushed it, how angry he'd been at her persistent griping. Now, he felt the anger gathering momentum, an eddy swirling up against the tide of bliss that was his life these days. The life she wanted to suck away from him. She was Adele, his Adele, his best friend— how could she have turned into this sour taste in his mouth, this old, old presence of oppression? From across the room she almost looked like his mother, which made his stomach grip. But that wasn't fair. She wasn't his mother, for Christ's sake. She was Adele, his Adele. "I don't want to fight with you," he said. "You absolutely should build your house. I'll do everything I can to help you."

"Help me?"

"Absolutely. For example, not that you need to, but it might be worth your while to look for a job with some architectural firm. Get back in the game. I could help you with that. Then you'll get the royal treatment when you start to build."

"Get a job?" Adele had completely lost her bearings. Groping for a way into communication, she said, "Drew, I'm fifty-six."

"So what? They'll be lucky to get you."

"I have no résumé. No portfolio. No experience."

"I'm not talking as an associate. I'm talking as a receptionist, something like that."

"Receptionist?" she echoed, wondering, suddenly, if she was having a stroke.

"Why not?"

"Why *not*? How did we go from 'Yes, we'll build a house' to 'Go get a job as a receptionist'?"

"Jesus, Adele, you're determined to turn everything I say into something negative."

"Drew, you said you're having doubts. About me. *I'm* turning this into something negative?"

From somewhere below, a parking alarm went off. It was a somewhat regular occurrence, as there was a garage and storage units below the condos. The strident noise ricocheted around the room. Adele and Drew looked away from each other. As suddenly as it started, the alarm shut off, and the room was thick with silence.

In those few moments, the actuality of what Drew was saying had cleared her confusion. Now, fury bubbled up inside her. "Your career always came first. I supported you. I raised your sons. I never complained, not for one second, about blowing off my own ambitions. How dare you stand there and accuse me of being negative? How dare you suddenly decide, big-shot California doctor, that your promises don't matter?"

Drew strode to the table and grabbed his water bottle, took a long swig. Wiped his mouth with the back of his hand. "Here we go," he said. "I've been dreading this."

"You've been dreading this?" Adele leapt to her feet. She circled the table, clenching and unclenching her hands. "You've been dreading this?" she repeated. *"Dreading this?"*

"People change," Drew said. "Haven't you felt it? It can't be just me. Haven't you felt us growing apart?"

"Have you met somebody?" Adele stared hard at him. "Is that what's going on?"

"Don't be stupid."

" 'Don't be stupid'? I'm sorry, am I stupid now, too, because I'm trying to understand how you can completely lose your mind? You're talking to me, Drew! Me! What the hell is going on?"

"You think I don't know who I'm talking to? You think I'm mistaken as to who you are? You think I'm not exhausted, trying to come up with ways to get you to stop bitching and kvetching my life away?"

"Your life away! *Your* life! Excuse me, what about *our* life? What about *my* life? What about the one thing I have ever asked of you? And by the way, please remember that it's my money we're talking about, not yours. What am I asking, except for you to support this dream, to honor your promise? Look at me, Drew! This is me, Adele! Who did everything you ever asked, including walking away from what I loved to follow you out here to your lunatic version of paradise!" As she said *paradise*, she grabbed her mug and hurled it across the room, where it smashed into the stainless steel dishwasher and shattered on the floor.

Drew leapt up and attended to the appliance as if it were a patient. "Jesus, Adele! You dented the Bosch!"

"Fuck the Bosch! I could care less about the Bosch! I just want to know *what is your problem?*"

"You! You're my problem!"

They were both panting now, gloves removed. Facing off across the room, they stared at each other like hostile strangers. Adele opened her mouth to speak but found herself mute. In her ears was a hollow roar.

"Do you have any idea how sick I am of this?" Drew spat out the words. "Sick, Adele. Living with you and your negativity is like being sick, like having an undiagnosed pathology lodged in my intestines. You're like a parasite, crouching and growing, gnawing at me. Nothing's ever enough for you; nothing's ever right. Everything you do, every step of our lives, you're looking around for the step we should have taken. You're never there; you're always judging, criticizing. You smash my spirits, Adele. You bring me down! I'm sick of it!"

Adele listened and watched as if from a great distance. His face had contorted, giving him the appearance of something feral and ratlike. His open mouth was hissing at her. She had no idea who he was. She felt like something washed up after a hurricane—like one of the horseshoe crab shells she and the boys used to gather on the beach back home; an empty, brittle husk. Scooped hollow, mute. Suddenly, inexplicably, she saw, in her mind's eye, the fish leap from the pond, twist, shimmer, vanish.

The air in the room was stale, still. After what seemed like a long silence, she spoke. "I was happy, back home. I was happy when I was young. I was always a happy kid. I was happy raising the boys. Happy with you. I don't think I've ever been unhappy, actually, until we came here. I can't believe what I'm hearing, actually, Drew. I never knew you felt like that."

Drew looked pale, drained. He moved toward her, reached out to touch her hair; she jerked her head away.

"I'm sorry," he said. "I didn't mean . . . I'm just . . ." He squeezed his eyes shut, shook his head. "I don't know. I don't know, Del."

Adele spoke, feeling her voice float out of the top of her head. "Are you leaving me, Drew? Are we done?"

Their eyes met. Adele felt the room tilt; instinctively reached out for something to hold on to. She expected to find his arm; she expected him to steady her. But she grasped air. His voice came as if through a tunnel.

"I don't know. I love you, Adele, but . . . but I think . . . I don't know."

Six

Syl and Adele were accustomed to going to yogacize class together on Tuesday mornings. Adele enjoyed the classes because there were a couple of ex–New Yorkers who were regulars, and they shared complaints and sarcasms directed at the instructor, Brie (or, as they called her, Gumby). Adele had barely moved all day Monday, and had to force herself to show up at Total Woman, where Sylvia had already set up two mats next to each other. It was no use—Adele lay there as if pinned, inertia pressing down on her like a gassy cloud. Are you on your cycle? Brie asked her, and she didn't even answer, letting the snickers of the other women suffice.

Their routine was to go to Starbucks after class and reward themselves for their exertions with lattes and muffins. Sometimes Maggie, who staunchly refused to attend the classes, would be waiting for them, deep into her soy chai and whatever nonfiction book she was reading. It was Syl's turn to treat, and she protested when Adele wanted just coffee. Straining her leotard and wearing her new expression of stunned distress, Syl whispered to Maggie, while Adele was dumping Splenda into her coffee, "Adele's in a really bad mood."

Maggie chuckled. Sylvia was such a mother hen, clucking and fussing over her brood. "Did you tell her that's not allowed?"

"Shh. Don't say anything." Syl licked the foam off her lid. "Carl called me from New York last night."

"What did he want?"

"I'm not sure. He'd just had dinner with Beth; it was her birthday. Twenty-eight! I swear I was nursing her five minutes ago. He called from his hotel room. It was almost like he was . . . checking in. Like everything was normal."

"Was he alone?"

Syl's face crumpled. "That was mean."

Adele plopped down next to them. "Here we are," she said, "the three weird sisters."

"Anything new?" asked Maggie.

"New?"

"New. Like, different. How're things?"

Adele looked sharply at Sylvia. "Why are you asking?"

Maggie laid her book down. "Adele, what's wrong?"

"What's wrong with *you*? Why are you both looking at me like I have a frog on my nose?"

"I knew it." Sylvia scooted her chair up close to Adele. "Adele, you are in the worst mood I have ever seen. What's wrong?"

Adele bent her head, stirred her coffee. "Nothing's wrong. Are bad moods against the law?"

Syl persisted. "Are you coming down with something? Are you on your cycle?" To Maggie's incredulous look, she said, "Tout le monde wants to know."

Maggie gave Sylvia a warning look, and they fell silent. Sylvia cut her muffin in threes and distributed their portions. Ate hers, daintily, while the others ignored theirs.

"What'd you do all weekend?" Adele asked Maggie.

"Worked at the Lagoon. We're trying to clear away all of the ice plant."

"Why?" Sylvia looked as if she'd been told that child labor was making a comeback. "I thought ice plant was good! Doesn't it keep fire away?"

"It's invasive. Chokes out all the food sources in the wetlands."

"Really?" Sylvia said this with such exaggerated interest that Maggie laughed, and Adele, after a moment, joined in. Syl giggled, then said, "Why was that funny?"

"What's that you're reading, Syl?" Maggie snatched a magazine out of Syl's bag. It was an ongoing routine between the two of them, to make fun of what the other was reading. Syl reached for Maggie's book. "*The World Is Flat*," she read. "*A Brief History of the Twenty-first Century*." She made a snoring sound; drooped her head. Maggie, squinting with exaggerated distaste at the cover of O, *The Oprah Magazine*, read "Getting Divorced? Watch Your Purse and Your Driving."

"Yeah, they say you should be extra careful because when you're going through a divorce you're so preoccupied," Syl said. "Also, they suggest taking an inventory of everything in your house."

Adele pulled her Play-Doh out of her pocket and began to knead it absentmindedly.

"Really," Maggie said. "And how about this: 'Increase the Depth of Your Orgasms.'"

Syl tried to grab the magazine away, and there ensued a friendly little scuffle among middle-aged women. Adele seemed not to even notice. She just sat, kneading and gazing into the distance. Syl and Maggie exchanged glances. Maggie said, "Adele."

"Adele," said Sylvia.

"Hmmm?"

"Why don't you tell us what's going on." Sylvia ignored Maggie's frown. "Where are you? What's the matter, sweetie?"

"I told you, nothing is wrong."

"You should talk about it. Maybe we can help."

"You can't help."

"Are you mad at me? Did I do something?"

"Sylvia," said Maggie, "it's not always about you."

"Are you mad at Maggie?"

"I'm not mad at anybody." Adele sighed. "Something's going on with Drew. I don't know."

"Oh my God." Sylvia clapped her hand over her mouth. "Oh my God, Del. What has he done?"

"He hasn't 'done' anything, Sylvia. He's just . . . confused, I guess."

"Confused?" Maggie shook her head. "Drew, confused? What about?"

And so, reluctantly, Adele chose bits and pieces of what had occurred and presented them to her friends, trying to make it seem as if it were something silly, some routine domestic irritation. As she heard the words coming out of her mouth, though, she felt them solidifying, as if the things he had said to her had been specters that were now assuming shape, shapes that loomed on the periphery of her consciousness in a scary, threatening way. She heard herself reassuring her friends, as if they were the ones who needed comforting. She even suggested Drew might be "going through something of his own" and would "snap out of it."

Maggie kept her hand pressed against her heart, trying to still the trembling. As shaken as she was by Carl's defection, Adele's announcement completely unmoored her. She sensed a kind of déjà vu of the future during the conversation, in which *she* was the woman making the announcement while the others comforted *her*. Rage at Drew and Carl churned within her. It seemed to her that Adele's reticence with details was a form of protectiveness toward Drew, which, while frustrating, she understood and respected, even as Sylvia pried for more details.

"Did he actually leave?" Maggie was envisioning Drew peeling out in his BMW, bunking down in some doctors' quarters somewhere.

"No, of course not. He just moved into the guest room, until he figures things out."

"Is there another woman?"

"He says not. I don't think so. No."

"Did you ask him?"

"Um-hmm. It seems a logical question, under the circumstances."

"And what did he say?" Sylvia seemed intent on clearing this point up.

"He said, 'Don't be stupid.' And then, when I asked him again this morning, he said, 'That's neither here nor there.'"

"What does that mean?" said Syl.

"Exactly," said Maggie.

"Stop. Drew's allowed to . . . to examine his life. I'm not really worried."

She's lying, Maggie thought. *She's worried sick*. She caught a glimpse of their reflections in the display case. Their three heads, a veritable Cerberus. It used to be their kids they'd be commiserating about. She wondered, not for the first time, if there wasn't some biological logic to their increasing irrelevancy in their husbands' lives. At least Paul . . . at least Paul, what? Would never leave her? When she'd dropped the bomb about Carl, she'd watched him carefully for signs he may have known. A shifting of the eyes, a twitch of his mouth, anything that would indicate he might be privy to details he had withheld. His response had been alarming. He'd shrugged. Shrugged! "Paul!" she'd cried. "These are our best friends! He's behaving as if—"

"As if he's tired of being unhappy?" he'd said, acidly.

That had been a scary moment. "Are you unhappy?" she'd asked, steeling herself.

He had sighed. Kissed her forehead. A dry, avuncular peck. "Life has its ups and downs," he'd said, and gone off to work.

"Carl closed the joint account," Syl was saying. "He said he'll give me an allowance. He said he's not going to let me starve."

"That's big of him," Adele said.

"I don't think he can do that," Maggie spluttered. "Goddammit, Syl, we need to get you a lawyer. Both you and Del. Maybe we can find someone who'll do two for the price of one. Damn, I wish I'd gone to law school. I'd love to skewer those two bastards."

"I don't need a lawyer! Calm down. Drew says he still supports 'my' dream. The money's earmarked. He says I deserve to be happy, because he got what he wanted, coming out here." She shrugged. "I guess I'll go build a house, somewhere, with or without him."

"Excuse me, what do you mean, 'the money's earmaked'? You guys— you don't get it. You can't let them pat you on the head and say, 'You've been a good girl, here's a lollipop'! It's your life! It's your money! They don't get to 'give' it or 'take' it."

"I hate talking about money," Syl said.

"I don't care about money," Adele said.

Maggie slapped the table with her newspaper. "Goddammit!" she said. "Goddammit goddammit goddammit! It's not the money. It's your self-worth! You're going to lie down? You're going to sit there and take your little pittance, say, 'Thank you, sir. Oh, thank you, kind sir'? I don't think so! I'm opening my own account and shifting half the joint account into it now, before he has the chance to try that with me!"

Syl and Adele stared at her. "You?" Adele said.

"I just mean, half of everything's mine! You don't grovel for handouts!"

Syl put her hand on Maggie's thin, brown, freckled forearm. "Mags? Did something happen?"

"Don't be ridiculous. Everything's fine with us," Maggie said curtly. "But listening to you two makes me realize I need to protect myself. Just in case."

"Maggie, you have so much anger," Syl murmured. "You need to get in touch with that. I worry about you."

While Maggie and Syl embarked on one of their affectionate bickers, Adele slid into a brief reverie of the recent trip to Sea Ranch. In her mind's eye she saw the six of them gathered around the table, raising their glasses first to Syl, and then to their friendship. Maggie had been her first friend in California. They'd met through their sons—Maggie's Josh had taken Noah under his wing, taught him to skateboard and surf. Adele had been attracted to Maggie's un-California-like aggression. She was forever scheduling meetings at school to address this or that injustice, to champion some underdog scheme, to chair some committee or other for the improvement of whatever. *Get a life*, Adele had first thought, but then, when some junior neo-Nazi types had scrawled "Jew" on Noah's car, Maggie went ballistic over the school's idea of quietly suspending the culprits and single-handedly organized a Holocaust Awareness Day. Elie Wiesel respectfully declined the invitation to speak, citing health and scheduling problems, but he sent an emissary from his organization, who spoke so eloquently and made such an impression that there was a surge of attendance at the temple's teen classes. "You're not even Jewish," Adele had said to Maggie, to which Maggie had replied, "We're all Jewish."

Paul had always been somewhat of a mystery to Adele. At first she thought he was just a nice, dull guy. He surfed with his son, toiled in middle management, never drank too much. "Pussy whipped," Drew said. But Adele had noticed that the opposite seemed to be true. Maggie seemed anxious around her husband. Her volubility and self-confidence dropped a few decibels, and she appeared always to be glancing to him for approval, as if she were gauging his response to her every word and action. Who knew what kept a marriage together, or tore it apart? Adele wondered.

A young mother with three little ones bumped past where they were sitting, next to the open door. They watched her idly, each of them feeling a tug of nostalgia for the days when their own children were still tiny and helpless, adorable and adoring. The woman began an arduous process of ordering something to eat and drink for each of her charges. "No, sweetie, you can have a sandwich but not a muffin. Do you want milk or juice? I'll have a double caramel latte. Tyler, stop that right now or you won't get anything." Adele was taken by the little girl, who wore a sagging, torn tutu. She nursed a secret sadness at not having had a girl. It wouldn't be long before she had grandchildren, though, and she hoped for an excuse to buy dresses and dolls; pink, girly things. She'd always imagined her grandchildren running in and out of the Bedford house, their frazzled mothers grateful for her calm intervention. What now? How was she to bear this state of exile? How did the life she'd so assiduously built unravel? She remembered being happy. She remembered the measured, predictable days, the surety. Now she felt, all the time, as if she had vertigo. Everything whirled. Everything spun; kept her unbalanced.

Maggie was banging on the table again. "Of course we don't have a 'right' to be happy! I never said that, I never said anything about a 'right'! But Sylvia, don't you think we have a responsibility to do everything we can to pursue happiness? Isn't that what this country is all about? Isn't that our biggest responsibility, as humans?"

"Our biggest responsibility is to our children," Sylvia replied. "If I do what you want me to do, everything will get so ugly. My job in all this is to keep things as emotionally stable as possible, to keep this as small a blip on the radar as I can."

"For who, for Beth?" Maggie was incredulous. "You think Beth is crying herself to sleep at night over this, Syl? In her New York loft? You want the lesson Beth will learn from this to be to lie down and take it, don't stand up for yourself, a woman's job is to be a rug? Please!"

"I'm not you, Maggie. I'm not full of rage."

"Why not? You should be, Syl! Okay, I'm not saying give yourself cancer. I'm just saying have a little pride! Take a stand!"

"What am I supposed to *do?*" Sylvia imitated Maggie's gesture, slapping her hand on the table. "Maggie, I don't want to go to war! I love him! I just want my life back!"

"Oh, Syl." Maggie scooted her chair closer to Syl, rubbed her back. "I'm sorry. I didn't mean to upset you."

Syl hiccoughed into her folded arms. "I am so miserable," she moaned.

The young mother herded her flock past them, casting a sympathetic glance at Sylvia. Her eyes met Adele's, briefly. Adele smiled sadly at her, and she smiled back. A tentative, puzzled smile. *We're the crones,* Adele thought. *The crones in our hut by the river, full of disappointment and sadness and disillusionment, and, supposedly, some kind of hard-won wisdom. Proffering our salves and poultices to our daughters, who don't know they're destined to occupy our skins, sooner than they could ever believe.*

Suddenly the little boy, Tyler, bolted from his mother and raced after a pigeon, straight into the path of a black Jeep Cherokee that was going too fast. The mother screamed. The Jeep slammed on its brakes just as it hit a speed bump, making a screeching squeal and sending it into a shuddering, scraping stall. The car behind it smashed into its rear. Someone else screamed. The little boy, frozen and terrified, looked up at his mother as she rushed to him, her infant in her arms, the toddler abandoned on the sidewalk. People gathered around the two drivers, who were yelling at each other in Spanish. The mother hauled off and smacked her son, an action recognizable to any mother anywhere as coming from a place of terror, after the unimaginable had almost just happened. "I told you to stay next to me!" she yelled, as his loud cries mingled with the shouting. "Hey!" another voice bellowed, and then there was a man with a beard and an "Old Guys Rule" T-shirt bounding up to the mother, getting right in her face. "What's wrong with you, lady? You just *hit* that child." He pulled out his cell phone. "What's your name," he demanded, poking his finger at her. "I'm reporting you."

Maggie was there in a shot, defending the woman. The little boy was wrapped around his mother's leg, wailing. The woman was also crying, and now there was a police car, and the crowd was starting to disperse. Adele and Sylvia watched the whole thing unfold in a kind of silent slow motion. Finally Maggie succeeded in dismissing the man, who wandered away shaking his head, as if the world were a confounding and violent place and he a beleaguered, defeated knight. Maggie walked the woman to her car, then returned. The shouting had stopped, the two drivers had exchanged their insurance information, the police, having seen them drive off in different directions, slowly drove away. The whole thing had taken maybe ten or fifteen minutes, at the most, and now it was completely calm again, as if nothing had happened.

"She shouldn't have hit him," Syl said. "I know how she felt, but still."

They gathered their things to leave, and Adele couldn't find her purse. They looked under the table, on the condiment counter, asked the barista if anyone had turned it in. "Maybe you left it at the gym," Sylvia offered, and called on her cell to ask them to check. "No, it's not there," she reported.

"It's probably in your car," Maggie said.

But it wasn't in her car. Her keys were in the pocket of her fleece vest, but the purse was nowhere to be found. They offered to go home with her, but Adele was getting increasingly anxious and wanted to be alone. Their solicitude grated on her. She regretted confiding in them, felt disloyal to Drew. Even felt that she had somehow validated his misgivings by discussing them with outsiders. She snapped at her friends, then apologized. "I'm sure it'll turn up," she said. "Please don't worry. I'll let you know when I find it."

Adele sat in her car and waited until Maggie and Sylvia had left. It was hot and stuffy. Finally she started the motor and lowered the windows. The parking lot stretched on and on, the size of the Sheep Meadow in Central Park. The midmorning light blazed outside her windshield. To the east, the mountains loomed like the dirt piles they were. Brown, brown everywhere. Scorching, dreary, blistered, sere, paved, and undulating in the glare. The flowerpots full of succulents, prickly and spiked. It was like a foreign planet. She did try, she did. She'd made friends and familiarized herself with all the museums, she'd gone to all the theaters and became a friend of the library, which was actually a rather nice library. She did try. But what could she do? How can you love something you don't love? The more she tried to share Drew's enthusiasm, the more she hated the place. The simplest things became fraught with thwarting. Of course things had gone wrong back home, but never with such regularity, never with the sense that some supernatural force was pushing her away, which is what it always felt like here. *Maybe it* is *me*, she thought. *Maybe there's some essential joylessness inside me that acts like some kind of scrim between me and this promised land.*

But she knew that wasn't true. She knew, because throughout her life she'd had glimmerings of the vast capacity within her. She'd known—just for moments, but it was enough—boundless joy, infinite love, shimmering wonderment. She was no kvetch, goddammit. She wiped her eyes with the edge of her vest, and glared with raw hatred at the silly palm trees sticking up into the cloudless sky.

Seven

AFTER SYL SAID GOOD-BYE to her friends, she went back into Starbucks and bought four more apricot blueberry muffins to get her through the day. By the time she got home, one of the muffins was gone. Brushing the crumbs off her yoga pants, she felt her thighs jiggle. *Oh dear. Better start walking in the morning again.* So much had fallen by the wayside these last few weeks.

She'd been doing a lot of housecleaning, lately. Not that her house needed it—she was a fanatic, according to Maggie. But housework was default mode for Syl. And she'd been on red alert, devising implements to suck dust out from under the dryer, clean the refrigerator coils, the venetian blinds, the blades of the ceiling fans. She was particularly pleased with a gizmo she'd ordered from a late-night TV ad, a sort of sponge with claws that snaked into all those crevices that she'd despaired of ever getting clean.

She made a pot of coffee and flicked on the radio to the oldies station. Replayed, yet again, the image of that woman smacking her son. She herself had never laid a hand on her child in anger. There was that photo of Princess Di, poor thing, spanking one of the princes—Harry, the younger one. He'd run out onto a polo field or something. It had circulated the world, that photo; she'd seen it in *People* magazine. Chuckles all around. Children deserve a good smack every now and then, seemed to be the prevailing attitude. No one had ever hit her, when she was little. Sometimes there had been punishments, but they were always some form of deprivation; no dessert or TV, that sort of thing. Never violence. Of course, it was clear for all to see that the woman at Starbucks was a good mother. She'd been thrown into her worst self, in that moment of panic. She'd lashed out because of her fear. She hadn't wanted to hurt her child. She'd wanted him to learn a lesson, to associate what he'd done with physical pain. Or maybe not; maybe she smacked her kids all the time at home. They seemed like happy enough kids, not that Syl had paid all that much attention to them, being preoccupied with Maggie's needling. Easy for her to egg Syl on; her husband wasn't leaving her, wasn't sleeping with his secretary. She tried to picture Paul saying the things to Maggie that Carl had said to her. Paul was a funny man. Not funny ha-ha, funny interesting. Very attractive, Syl had always thought. Still, something was simmering in there. Kept Maggie on edge, that was for sure. But no, Syl couldn't imagine Paul losing his mind, as Carl had evidently done. He was like a big watchdog, Paul, like one of those aloof but loyal breeds, quietly watching from the corner. Not like Carl, who was more of a big sloppy golden, drooling and shoving his head between your legs. And what was Drew, then? A whippet? A Doberman pinscher?

Syl had always thought of Drew and Adele as two peas in a pod. They were the kind of couple everyone likes to be around because they were so easy with each other, they laughed at each other's jokes, never jabbed or took shots at each other like some couples did. Adele's news had shocked Sylvia almost as much as Carl's announcement had. The whole business gave her a headache. It was as if the world had undergone some sinister metamorphosis overnight, while she was asleep. Adele was too private a person to let anyone see how devastated she was, but if anyone understood, it was her, Sylvia. "Maybe they're both having a midlife crisis," she had suggested to Adele, to which Adele had replied that if Drew thinks this is a crisis, he'd better fasten his seat belt. Syl hadn't been exactly sure what she meant by that.

Mama Cass broke into her thoughts, singing about California dreamin'. Syl turned up the volume, sung along. This was the song she and Carl had sung while they'd driven from Michigan to San Diego. By the time she got to the chorus, Syl's face was soaked with tears. She blew her nose into a paper towel. Took a clean mug from the dishwasher for her coffee. There were no dirty mugs in the sink, no eggshells or crumpled paper towels in the trash. With herself the only occupant of the house, it was remarkably simple to keep order. It soothed her. Of course, it had always been like this when Carl was away for business, after Beth had gone. It was a snatched pleasure, sweet in its finitude. For Carl would be back, and Carl was, let's face it, a bit of a slob. The flickering irritations of his messiness would soon reimpose themselves on her, and she would sigh as she knelt down to wipe up the drops of coffee and the crumbs and the bits of orange peel that Carl left in his wake. That was her life. A life she had never wanted to alter.

Now, as she stirred skim milk into her coffee, a smothering sadness draped over her, shooing away the momentary pleasure she'd taken in her orderly kitchen. What if this was the way it would always be now? What if every time she came home, everything was exactly as she had left it? Never finding the shiny granite counter awash in sandwich makings, her husband out by the pool with his lunch and the paper. The house always as clean and sterile and untouched as a magazine photo.

Sylvia had always known her life was charmed. Her childhood had been loving and uneventful, her college years filled with good times, friendship, and Carl. Their relationship had never been fraught with drama, like so many of her friends'. They started dating and never broke up. They both wanted the same things: a family, a house in California. All their dreams had come true. Had she not been grateful enough? Had she committed some sin she was unaware of, that this punishment had been brought down on her? This house had been their first. They'd lived in an apartment in La Jolla at first; then, when they had the money and the timing was right, they'd found this place. Just a little tract house, but it was at the top of a hill, at the end of a cul-de-sac, with views of the ocean to the west and the mountains to the east. Everyone who came over oohed and aahed. The neighborhood became desirable, which was why they'd never sold and

"moved up" when Carl began to do well. Instead, they remodeled, custom-
ized, added on, landscaped. Their plot was large for the neighborhood—
almost half an acre. They'd planted trees, put in a patio and a pool, gardens.
The kitchen and dining area both opened onto the patio, which was on
the west side of the house. The French doors stayed open most of the year,
to welcome the warming sun and the cooling ocean breezes. There was a
manageable patch of lawn—they'd kept it small to save on watering—and
Syl's rose garden, which was modest but robust. Carl had a little kitchen
garden installed for her, where she grew herbs, salad greens, and tomatoes.
It was altogether a perfect house, glistening and glowing with years of care
and maintenance.

"We should be able to triple our original price, at least," Carl had said
during that unspeakable conversation.

Syl stiffened at the recollection, remembering how she'd hurled a roll
of paper towels at him when he'd said that. They'd been in the kitchen and
her eyes had fallen on a silver bowl full of lemons that she'd have liked to
have thrown; but she prudently realized that she'd probably miss him and
damage something, so she'd reached for the paper towels instead. "You are
not selling my home," she'd said, fury in her heart. And then she'd crumpled, sobbing and pleading with him not to leave, and he'd been Carl; he'd
held her, comforted her, reassured her. "I'll see what I can do," he'd said.

It would be silly, of course, to live in such a big house all alone.

Why? Why would it be silly? It was her *home*. This was Southern California; people didn't sell and move when their kids left. Everyone else sells
and tries to move *here*. She and Carl had never discussed "downsizing"
when Beth left. Why should they? It wasn't a mansion. So what if there
were a few extra rooms? And thanks to Prop 13, their taxes were ridiculously low, unlike those of most of their neighbors, who had bought during
the market peak.

It made no sense to leave. Just because Carl had gone insane and
wanted to turn his back on their life! Why should Syl have to pay for Carl's
lunacy? It was outrageous. No. No, she would not leave her home. She loved
this house. Life without it was unthinkable. What, did he think he was
going to stick her away in a condo? Turn her, Sylvia, devoted and adoring

wife and mother, into one of those haunted San Diego divorcées with a designated parking space and a few potted plants on a four-by-six-foot balcony? While he what? Married his scheming Russian gold digger and moved to Rancho Santa Fe, where he'd hang out at the coffee shop with the other pathetic old men on their second and third families, whose wives were younger than their own daughters? "Over my dead body!" Syl yelped, aloud.

Fortified by this surge of outrage, Syl went upstairs to shower. At the top of the stairs she experienced her usual tingle of delight as she stood on the landing and gazed down the hall into the master bedroom. That had been a major project. They'd built it over the garage, turning the existing master bedroom into an office for Carl. It had been Adele's vision, and the two women had cemented their friendship during the course of its creation. For Sylvia, the room was like a favorite child. Every inch of her home was dear to her, but when she beheld this room, her heart swelled and melted. It had a raised ceiling with exposed beams, painted a pickled white. French doors opened onto a balcony looking out over the backyard and to the sea beyond. The fireplace had a surround that Adele had devised with someone she knew who was a mosaic artist. The tiles depicted, in whimsical design, all that Sylvia held dear. There were sea horses and mermaids and starfish; there was an imprint of Beth's little hand, and one of the paw of Duckworth, their old yellow Lab, the memory of whom still choked Sylvia up. Why hadn't they gotten another dog? They'd spoken of it, vaguely, but it had never happened. In front of the fireplace was a cozy seating area, where Carl had often brought a glass of wine to Sylvia at day's end. A small corridor led to the bath, and the two walk-in closets. The bath, done in Juparana granite, had a deep Jacuzzi tub, a bidet, a double-headed shower stall, his-and-hers sinks.

Sylvia put her coffee mug on the counter and pulled off her sweats, humming. It never took too much to cheer her up. She reached over to turn on the shower, and as she did so, confronted herself full on in the floor-to-ceiling mirror. Stark naked. "My God," she said aloud.

She observed herself clinically, with perverse fascination.

There was an aging fat woman in the mirror. How had that happened? Syl had always had to watch her weight. Carl liked that; he liked, he said, having something to grab onto. But this had gone a bit far. No wonder her clothes had been feeling tight! In fact, now that she thought of it, there was a whole section of her wardrobe that she'd stopped even attempting to occupy. Without thought, she'd opted for whatever was loose and stretchy, telling herself she wanted to be comfortable.

She'd never asked herself why she no longer wore her old outfits. She'd been in some sort of denial, she realized. She hadn't noticed, or perhaps had carefully avoided, what was happening. To her very own body.

To her very own marriage.

"What the hell?" she exclaimed, turning this way and that. She couldn't pull her eyes away. There were mounds of herself.

Thanks to Adele's wizardry, there were mirrors everywhere, so it was possible to contemplate multiple images of herself from every angle, without having to contort or strain her neck to see her behind. It was all there. All of it.

Syl had never considered herself vain. She'd never felt competitive about her looks. She knew her good fortune had extended itself into her appearance; she'd been effortlessly pretty, if not a beauty. Because of this security it had never bothered her that Carl looked at other women. Sometimes she even pointed someone out to him, and they had lazy debates about what made this or that woman beautiful or not. Looking at herself now, it wasn't hard to imagine what would be said about her, had she been a stranger in their sight.

She had just turned fifty-five. When the inevitable age jokes were made, she had laughed them off. Why should I be upset about getting older, she had said, when you consider the alternative? Most places in the world— places that weren't San Diego—celebrated this time of a woman's life, a time for gracefully entering into a kind of pre-cronehood, a pillowy middle age when a plushy butt and ample hips meant protection from early-onset osteoporosis. Sylvia had often shaken her head sadly at the sight of aging women who spent every waking hour fending off the inevitable, dressing like teenagers, faces puffy from Botox. Still, it was incumbent upon her as a wife to work at being reasonably attractive, and she had always been conscientious about that. Fat lot of good it had done her, apparently. What was to stop her from letting go? Who cared? How far could she go, if she just *let go?*

From the radio downstairs she heard snatches of Linda Ronstadt singing "Our Love Is Here to Stay." She loved that song. "It's very clear," she murmured along. The woman in the mirror raised her arms to the mike and what used to be her triceps jiggled and shuddered.

This must be a mistake. The mirrors might have warped, or something. It didn't make any sense; she wasn't a piggish eater. She exercised. Maybe she ought to get her thyroid checked; she had read somewhere recently that the thyroid often went on the fritz in middle age. No doubt a prescription could be written, and she'd be back to herself in no time.

"Who cares? The Rockies may crumble, Gibraltar may tumble, they're only made of clay . . ." Syl sang softly, forcing herself to look full on at what used to be her figure. "My bosoms have tumbled," she sang, "my butt flesh has crumbled, my waistline has gone away . . ."

How long had she looked like this? Had Carl noticed? She had thought Yelena was the fat one, the way she bulged out of those cheap dresses she wore to work. "Why doesn't someone tell her she needs to go up a size or two?" she'd said to Carl. Now she winced at the recollection. Had he jeered inwardly at her for that? Had he found Yelena svelte compared to her?

She sank down on the edge of the tub and continued gazing at herself in fascinated horror. She'd had an hourglass figure! Looking at the roll of fat around her waist, she realized she couldn't remember the last time she'd worn a belt. Briefly, she caught hold of a snatch of optimism—she'd fix this; she'd get that medicine they advertised on TV and even diet for a while; she'd get her body back—but then a heavy sadness descended on her, and she saw her face settle into an expression of resignation. It was the same look she remembered seeing on her grandmother's face, and on her mother's, too, now that she thought of it. That look of disappointment. A kind of draining of hopefulness. *So this is it, then,* is what the look said. *I didn't even hear the bell ring.*

Sylvia felt sorry for that woman she was staring at. She was embarrassed for her. Protectively, she wrapped her arms around herself, rocked lightly.

She wished Beth hadn't gone to New York. She wished she could call her right now and make a date to meet for dinner. She longed for the sight of her daughter's face. How wonderful it would be to laugh with her, to feel the heaviness lifting in the presence of her beautiful child! And yet, the truth was she felt oddly self-conscious with her daughter. At some point— when was it?—Beth had adopted a kind of disdain for her. Syl had never taken it too much to heart; it was just a teenage thing. But it had been a while since Beth was a teenager. And, Syl realized, it had been a while since they'd laughed together. Since they'd been close. She thought of the little girl in the ragged tutu, earlier, the way she had stood riveted on the sidewalk while the drama unfolded. Whatever happened to Beth's toe shoes? She had packed them away in her own little trunk, she remembered that clearly. Where was that trunk? Beth was so alarmingly unsentimental. She'd wanted to save all that stuff for Beth's own daughter, and Beth had laughed at her. Not laughed. Sneered, more like. Said she was taking it all to the hospice shop. God, Syl thought with a start, was all that stuff gone? All those beautiful little things she'd so carefully tended to?

She realized she was chilly, sitting there ruminating, naked. Got into the shower and let the hot water lull her. Afterward, dressed and cozy in her room, she lay on her bed and thought about things. Worried, briefly, about Adele's purse. Worried less briefly about Drew. Thought about Maggie's outburst, her need to control everybody. She loved Maggie, really, but she always felt that she was waiting to get some kind of grade from her. She wasn't as pushy with Adele. And certainly not with Paul. Why did she always pick on her, Sylvia? Was there something about her that made Maggie particularly protective? Or was it disdain, like Beth? Did she think Sylvia was a helpless fool? No, that wasn't fair; they were best friends. What was really bothering Maggie, she decided, was that she perceived an injustice that she was powerless to interfere with. And for some reason Syl didn't really understand, that thought comforted her. Again she saw that mother smack her son, watched Maggie spring to action, butting in, bossing everyone around. Well, she couldn't boss Sylvia around. She couldn't boss Carl around. This was *her* beautiful life, she thought, curling up on her bed, and, cold comfort though it was, it was *her* mess. Maggie would just have to mind her own beeswax. Somewhere outside a lawn mower started up, its familiar hum like a childhood lullaby, and as she drifted off she saw herself lying under a giant tent, with tiny people all around pounding stakes into the ropes that held her down, and she smiled to herself, amused at their misconception, thinking she needed to be restrained, when all she wanted was to sink into the soft, fresh-cut grass.

Eight

AFTER SHE HAD FINALLY CONVINCED Maggie and Sylvia that she was perfectly fine, and promised that she would call them both as soon as she got home to let them know if her purse was there, Adele sat in her car with the motor running for she didn't know how long. Thoughts were swirling about in her head without taking any specific shape. Finally, some sense of urgency on the periphery nudged her into the present. What was it? . . . Oh right, her bag. Where the hell was it? She tried to go over her actions of the morning, but there were blanks she couldn't fill in. She remembered putting on her exercise clothes—remembered being in class— but for the life of her she couldn't conjure a recollection of leaving her house. She kept her keys on a hook by the door, so it was possible she'd grabbed them and left her bag. Better go home and check. But when she got to the Coast Highway she turned left toward Encinitas instead of right toward Carlsbad. "Damn," she muttered, getting into the left lane to make a U-turn. But at the next intersection she kept straight, almost as if someone else were steering the car. She drove all the way through Encinitas, where people actually walked around on the sidewalks. It was one of the few local places that felt real in that regard, and Adele liked coming here for lunch. She had an idea that it might be nice to stop and have a bite at the St.

Tropez Bakery in the Lumberyard, and she wandered into the left-hand turn lane. But when she got close she changed her mind—she wasn't hungry and besides, what was she thinking, she had no money with her—so she pulled back into the non-turn lane without looking, and almost hit a car. She had to jerk the wheel to the left to avoid it, gasping with a rush of adrenaline. There was a blast of horns, then the next car sped past, not letting her in. She'd come to a full stop on the 101 now, and she was so flummoxed she sat there until a grizzled guy in a pickup slowed down and waved her in front of him.

Adele was a good driver. She just hadn't been paying attention. "Focus," she instructed herself. She was reaching the end of town and still didn't know where she was going, why she was heading south away from home. In front of her the gold-domed roof of the Self-Realization Fellowship glowed in the sun like the proverbial goose's egg. She slammed on her brakes and made a sudden right turn onto I Street, parked on the hill opposite the entrance to the garden, turned off the engine.

Her heart was still racing after she'd almost hit that car. It would have been entirely her fault. She might have hurt somebody. And she didn't have her license with her. It was in her wallet, which was in her bag, wherever that might be. She got out of the car and crossed the street into the SRF gardens, drawn to the peace and quiet they offered.

This was one of the places she had made fun of when they first arrived in Sandy Eggo. It was right next to Swami's surfing beach and across the street from Swami's Cafe, and the picture of the long-haired, orange-robed monk who had started the place epitomized everything New Agey and la-di-da that she found off-putting about North County. But then she and Drew heard that the gardens were a destination spot, and they spent an afternoon there together that even Adele had to admit was magical. The property had been a gift from a wealthy devotee, and was cultivated and maintained by the monks who lived there. Strategically placed benches along the bluffs encouraged contemplation and meditation; fat koi swam in a pond among blooming, fragrant flowers. The shady, manicured paths bordered by the blue, infinite sea did indeed feel like a kind of heaven. Adele had picked up the brochures and read about Paramahansa Yogananda, whose guru had sent him here from India in the 1920s to teach the West how to meditate. Intrigued, she had even gone to a couple of Sunday services at the temple. Drew wouldn't join her, though. She knew the thought of so much as setting foot inside a foreign temple threatened him. He clung to his Judaism as a sort of life jacket, which Adele found touching, though she didn't share his feelings. Her upbringing had been less threatened, more inclusive. His had been chaotic and unguided, his solitary excursions to temple giving him the safety and structure he didn't have at home.

Perhaps it had been a mistake to come here, reminding her as it did of that day with Drew. She needed to abolish this nostalgic sentiment; she needed to get angry. She had to stir up some of Maggie's outrage. She thought of Maggie's outburst this morning. Passion was certainly one of her friend's endearing qualities, but her rants usually fizzled amiably when the topic changed. This time she'd seemed possessed. Was it really loyalty and protectiveness, or had Paul too become infected with whatever seemed to be going around among the men?

She was bothered by her missing bag, and knew she should start canceling her credit cards if it wasn't at the condo, but as she climbed the stone steps she felt a kind of comfort envelop her. She didn't want to go back to the condo. She didn't want to turn off the road past the sign PELI-CAN SHORES and punch her code into the box so the gate would swing open. She didn't want to park and put her key in the lock and enter the bright, boxy place that was supposed to be home, where Drew lurked in every cushion and glass, where he had nurtured his detachment from her. No, this was where she wanted to be, right now. Up here on this sandy cliff, gazing out past the surfer-dotted sea to the cloudless horizon. She wanted to empty her mind, banish from it the leaping, cavorting thoughts and images that seemed to clatter against her skull. She sank onto a stone bench, and instantly fell into a memory of the big flat rock that lay on the ancient stone wall by the barn in Bedford. She'd loved that perch, used to sit there in the morning with her coffee, or in the evening with a glass of wine. It looked out over their meadow, which eased into the wetlands. They'd put a purple martin house out there, and waited years for the birds to show up and nest. Finally they came, and thrived, eating thousands of mosquitoes every summer. That purple martin house had been a triumph.

Adele had had big plans for the barn, someday. She'd meant it to be her workshop, where she would paint. She'd always meant to start painting again. But the boys had claimed it and used it for boy things, which changed as they went through their various phases. Even now, after all these years, she sometimes daydreamed about that barn, redesigned it in her mind. Oh, it was a burden that scarcely a day went by that she didn't long for home! For her old farmhouse, for the city, for the feeling of her feet upon the ground of the East Coast, where she felt like a native plant in native soil. She thought she'd hidden that from Drew, because she'd seen how he thrived out here. She loved him, and didn't wish to cast a pall on his happiness.

You smash my spirits, he'd said. Bitching and kvetching my life away.

The sun was hot on the top of her head. Her body felt weighted, sluggish. Right this moment, she thought, someone might be running up thousands on her credit cards, or stealing her identity. Well, they were welcome to it. Take it, please. Let someone else take over.

Drew used to say, "Why worry? The things that happen are the things you forgot to worry about." He'd say that to comfort her when she was fretting over one of the boys. Not that she'd been a big worrier, but the largeness of her life, the vulnerability of her charges, used to sometimes overwhelm her. Four of them—the boys plus Drew—to feed and dress and nurture and track. All those years of it. Never once in all those days, the many, countless days of domestic routine, of socializing, of rising from bed each morning and tacitly agreeing to go on, of shouldering that day's responsibilities, of releasing yesterday's fears and steeling herself for this day's vicissitudes—never in all that time had she thought to worry about her marriage. She and Drew shifted in thousands of subtle ways to accommodate each other, the bearing and raising of their children, the astonishing variety of ways in which love was manifested, the glad giving over of her self, newly, each morning, with never a doubt or wish that it be otherwise.

Your negativity, he'd said. Living with you is like being sick. Judging, criticizing.

Across the lawn from her a man sat on the grass, his eyes closed, his face turned to the sun. His legs were crossed and his hands rested on his thighs, palms up. He was the picture of serenity. She longed to be able to do that. To empty her mind. Her thoughts were wiry vines that wrapped around and squeezed the breath out of her. They were Mexican jumping beans, Ping-Pong balls. She tried to silence them, to not think. But here they were, leaping about. Maggie banging the table, warning them to claim their shares. Should she be worried about money? Was it possible that Drew could ever wish her ill? No. No, it wasn't. No, Drew couldn't do that to her. Could he? Should she worry? Should she shove this pain out of the way and make room for some kind of plan? For example, what was she going to do with the rest of her life? Without Drew! Did she still even want to build a house, without him? She gasped, turned away from that chasm.

A sudden memory intruded: Drew in college, before they'd become friends. She'd seen him in the library one day, bent over a textbook, scribbling notes. There were several study groups nearby, the members slumped against one another, passing papers around. In fact, Adele was on her way to join one of them. Drew was alone. She'd stared at him, hoping he'd feel her gaze and look up at her so she could smile and say hello. But if he did feel her gaze he ignored it, burrowing deeper into his book. Her friends had spotted her and were waving her over, but she had stood rooted, yearning to go to Drew, to touch his shoulder, to offer him something. She knew she had a crush, but it was something else about him, too, something that made her settle, when he was near. His proximity, even if he was unaware of her, reassured her.

The monks had put new ground cover down since the last time she'd been there. It was a mixture of mosses and sedums, in different shades of green, different textures. Gardening for Krishna. Most of the monks were nice midwestern boys whose spiritual journeys had led them to this path. This garden reflected the discipline and purpose of their lives. It was reverential, inspired. She felt the teeth in her gut unclench a bit as she gazed past the empty swimming pool out to sea. As always, the surfers in their shiny black wet suits swarmed like seabirds on the waves. She watched idly as one, then the next, glided down the swells, swooping left, then right, till the wave sighed itself back into the sea and they fell gracefully off their boards, only to paddle back out again. "A wave is of the ocean, but a wave is not the ocean." That's what the monk had talked about the day she'd gone to the service here. At the time she'd found that a pretty sentiment but hadn't given it much thought. It came back to her now. She tried to imagine herself out there on one of those surfboards, hopping a ride, sea foam all around her. Those shiny black surfer birds looked as much a part of the sea as the dolphins that could often be seen, leaping and ducking in their fluid pods. Yet each of those people out there would paddle in eventually, shed their sea suits, and become man, or woman, again. Go back to their lives.

And what am I? Adele thought. *I am of my marriage, but I am not my marriage. I am of my family, but I am not my family.*

Then what was she? With the foundation suddenly gone, what did she stand on? Who was she, of what relevance to anyone? And why did this terrible sense of emptiness seem to insist that she define her place in the world, justify herself?

Nothing had prepared her for this. Life had swooped her up; she had risen to its demands. She had built a house of brick, laid on a strong foundation. So she had believed. But apparently she'd been wrong. *I've been dreading this,* he'd said. So maybe her house hadn't been so solid after all.

Adele was not one to waste time licking wounds. She had to take action of some kind. She had been frontally attacked, and she needed to rally her forces and prepare a retreat, cut her losses and formulate an alternate course of action. This was in her bones. Her family history was typical of Jews of her generation: her grandparents had died in the camps, her parents had survived and built a new life in a new country. Their sorrow was Adele's legacy. Though they gave her a good life and loved her well, they were never able to protect her from the haunted looks in their eyes, from the ghosts that lurked behind the curtains and in the silverware and the coat closet. She should have heeded the warning. She'd been lulled into complacency by the promise of the new world; she was spoiled by the fruits that had come so easily.

A woman in a burka had spread herself out on the lawn and was feeding her two children something out of Tupperware. The children, a boy and a girl, kept their heads down and talked quietly with their mother. They seemed to have woven a web around themselves. They passed food among themselves in the intimate way of families. Then the father joined them, and they all four sat together on the grass and ate. It was made clear in several different places that food was not welcome here, but Adele thought there couldn't have been anything more natural than this little impromptu picnic. There was an ease and a familiarity between them that, despite the strangeness of the burka and the snatches of guttural language that floated over the breeze, struck a nostalgic chord in Adele. She wanted to lift up onto a current of air just as the gull there over the water was doing, float down next to them, join in their secret language and their casual, affectionate touching. She had been a little girl like that, once. Safe in the womb of her family, taking food from her mother's hand. And she had been a mother, blowing on hot things to cool them off before offering them to the tiny open mouths of her brood. The man spoke softly to his wife, and she gave him a doe-like, private look, conveying with her eyes and the tilt of her head a placid intimacy. A quiet, private smile, a smile with no imperative to convey anything. Adele had felt that look on her own face countless times, with her husband.

She sucked in her breath, squeezed her eyes shut, and turned her face to the sun. Tiny geometric shapes spun before her, as if she were peering through a kaleidoscope. A trick of the light. Motes in her eye. Pluck it out.

Nine

MAGGIE, STUNG BECAUSE ADELE had refused to let her follow her
home to make sure she got there safely, said a curt good-bye to Sylvia and
almost clipped a Prius on her way out of the parking lot. It had clearly
been her fault, but she honked and flipped the driver the bird anyway. She
was fuming. Ears flattened, tail flicking, rage gathering, and ready to pounce.
It was an old, crusty rage, easily stirred. She loathed its presence but knew
it to be bred in her bones. "Don't get your knickers in a twist," her mother
used to say. "Why are you so angry?" a therapist had asked her once, to
which she replied, like Thoreau, "Why *aren't* you?"

She was still trembling over the incident at Starbucks. That asshole
getting in that poor woman's face. Shouting at her about how he was going
to call child protective services and report her for hitting her kid.

"Can't you see how upset she is?" Maggie had said, incredulous at the guy's
meddling stupidity.

"She's upset? She's upset? What about the kid?" the guy had spluttered,
spraying Maggie's face with spittle.

The poor woman—she'd gone completely ashen, Maggie feared she was
going to faint. The little boy clinging to her, wailing. He'd gotten the message, all right. He wouldn't soon forget. Unless he was stupid, he wouldn't

be dashing in front of any moving cars again anytime soon. That young mother had been doing such a good job, so patient with her children, so loving. Maggie had watched her out of the corner of her eye while listening to Adele's reluctant story. Women doing the right thing, good mothers, good wives, and look what they had to endure. Outrage unspooled in her heart and choked her with frustration. Why isn't it enough, why isn't it ever enough? What does a person have to *do* to be released from accusation and betrayal?

She'd been sick with worry over Syl, and now there was Adele. It was too much to take in; it was undigestible. Hadn't they all just had that lovely weekend together in Sea Ranch? Hadn't everyone loved everyone else so very very much? Drew and Adele—they were joined at the hip. When she'd first met them she'd been a little jealous of them, of the genuine friendship they seemed to share. They finished each other's thoughts, they smiled at each other, they made each other laugh. They weren't like her and Paul; there was no discernible undercurrent. Sometimes they argued, but it was almost like a comedy routine; they'd roll their eyes and play to their audience, and they always ended up laughing.

It was the element of surprise that had shaken her so, she told herself: she'd lost her footing. Her own life suddenly felt unstable and threatened. Had she suspected unrest in her friends' marriages, the outrage and hurt would have been tempered with a sprinkle of vindication. This was chaotic; nothing made sense. Maggie was hugely uncomfortable when she couldn't make sense of things.

She'd vowed to start cleaning out the garage today, but she wanted to clear her head, so she drove to the Batiquitos Lagoon for a walk. She fervently wished she could have gone for a long run, the only cure she'd ever found for her rage, but her knees had given out years ago. Walking helped, but it took longer. Maggie hated wasting time. Like now, for example, some asshole in a pimped-up pickup truck was dawdling at thirty-five in the passing lane, and another asshole right next to him was doing the same, so no one could pass them. And there were bumper stickers on his stupid truck. Maggie hated bumper stickers. Who cares about your opinions? Just drive! This one said I'LL KEEP MY PICKUP AND GUNS, YOU CAN KEEP "THE CHANGE."

"Asshole!" Maggie yelled, leaning on her horn. What was the *matter* with these people? Do you realize, she'd said to Paul, how many assholes are *still* driving around with Bush/Cheney stickers? Can we not pass an ordinance?

They had had unbelievable sex again last night. Hoping the tension there'd been between them lately had dissipated, she'd gotten up and made him French toast for breakfast. But he'd seemed irritated by her presence in the kitchen, told her to go back to bed, said, Thanks anyway, but I just want coffee and toast.

"Anything wrong, Paul?" she'd said. She was sure she hadn't imagined the exasperated look on his face at the question. "Did we not have a gorgeous time last night?" he'd replied, patiently. Patiently! Then he'd kissed her on the forehead and gone off to work.

Like a child, like a chastised child, she thought now. You had your ice cream and cake; now go to bed like a good girl. And now she had that fear trickle. It'd been there all day, that unscratchable itch that wouldn't subside until Paul came home, and they had dinner and went to bed again.

She had married Paul because he loved her. There had been a long list of his attributes, but the one that really mattered to her was the surety of his commitment and desire for her. He was nice. He was dependable. The opposite of her college boyfriend, Mitch, who had broken her heart repeatedly, and whom she kept forgiving. Not just because she was in love with him, she'd learned after years of therapy, but because she'd wanted to hitch her wagon to his star. And oh, he had been a star, at Berkeley. She'd had no doubt, nor did anyone else, that he was going places. Brilliant. Passionate. Fearless.

Mitch. Whatever happened to him? She'd Googled him; nothing ever came up. How could he not be somewhere, if not in the Gore ranks, then surely on the Obama team? He must have died; that would be the only explanation. But there were no obituaries online either, nothing in his hometown newspaper. No one knew where he was. Someone suggested he might be in India. Deep in the Himalayas, practicing out-of-body techniques.

Mitchell. God, how she'd loved him.

But then Paul, so nice, so polite, so devoted. Her therapist had wondered if there was a rebound thing going on. "From rags to riches," she had said. Maggie had spent years in that woman's office, on a tree-lined street in Piedmont. What a joke. What a charlatan that woman had been. The cliché queen, she'd called her. Sitting there like a tired Yoda, spewing clichés.

Maggie remembered working herself up, once, as she dredged up the feelings of displacement she'd experienced when her mother and she had moved from England to Berkeley after her father died. She'd been seven. According to her mother, she'd apparently stopped talking for a while. She didn't remember. She did remember the long nights of terror, tucked into a new bed in a strange place, feeling the earth whirling beneath her. "Fish out of water," the therapist had pronounced.

And another time, when Maggie had been railing against Mitchell's parents for suggesting she was anti-Semitic, for Christ's sake, just because she had mentioned, at one of their Seders, that Son of God or not, you couldn't dismiss the beauty of Christ's teachings. Then, after the insult, they'd actually laughed and called her a goyim, and the therapist, listening to Maggie splutter with outrage, had nodded that all-knowing nod of hers and uttered, "Pot calling the kettle black."

Paul had never been much of a conversationalist. It had always been a source of loneliness for Maggie, for whom talking was like breathing.

She parked her old Saab and grabbed the binoculars she kept in her glove compartment, in case she was lucky enough to catch some bird action. Her mother, English to the bone, had been an avid bird-watcher. It was the one activity they had enjoyed together. They'd drive out to Point Reyes and stay overnight in a cluttered guesthouse owned by some academic acquaintance, and Maggie would be enchanted by the tenderness in her mother's voice as she'd hand over the binoculars, whispering instructions about what to notice in the bird she'd spotted. Maggie had never loved the birds as deeply as her mother did, but she did love the memory of her mother's love of them, and she was often drawn to the lagoon when she felt stressed or overwhelmed. The snowy egrets never failed to appear in their usual post, poised elegantly at water's edge, gazing down their noses at the double-crested cormorants with their hooked bills and their grasping fishing techniques. California towhees perched on the bare branches and trilled their inquisitive Quee, quee? Because, because, her mother used to sing back at them. But now Maggie was hoping for a glimpse of the Kentish plovers that had recently been sighted nesting in the lagoon, thanks to the dredging. Their return would signify a kind of hopefulness that she felt in need of.

Poor Sylvia, she mused, trudging up the narrow path. There was something so childlike about her, so marshmallowy. She worshipped the ground that asshole Carl walked on. She cut recipes out of magazines that she thought would please him; when she talked about him her voice got mushy. "Carl said this, Carl did that, Carl always says . . ."

Personally, Maggie had always thought Carl was kind of dopey. But he was amusing, and he seemed to worship Sylvia back. It pierced Maggie—it almost made her knees buckle—to think of Sylvia's defenseless little heart being broken. She wanted to hunt Carl down and beat him to a pulp. Wipe off that dimply little grin of his with a fistful of nails. The violence of her anger took her breath away. She sat on the bench that looked out toward the highway and watched a flock of pelicans, silhouetted against the sky.

And now Adele. Hadn't she practically martyred herself for Drew? Hadn't she caved to his every whim, been his perfect companion for the entirety of their marriage? Had he gone insane? Maggie had, for years, harbored a little secret crush on Drew. There was something about his wiry, hairy forearms, with the pulsing tendon, that stirred her.

Paul was of Irish descent, pale, freckled, smooth-chested. Not her type at all. In the beginning she hadn't been attracted to him; she'd let him court her to soothe her ego after Mitchell's final betrayal. But when they went to bed together it was a different story entirely. She'd never realized how selfish and fumbling her previous lovers had been. Even Mitch, whose touch turned her into a puddle, was raw and clumsy compared to Paul. Paul, so reticent and formal in the daylight, was another creature entirely in the dark. And it hadn't taken Maggie long to become addicted to that person. As for the daytime Paul, well, that had never been easy. He was fine as long as they kept things light, but for Maggie that felt like being in shackles.

Having Josh and raising him had kept her busy, kept things at bay. But now Josh was off on his own, so what next? Was this empty-nest syndrome?

Was she "borrowing worry," as Paul said? Did she imagine that her husband only loved her when she kept her mouth shut, did she read his expressions wrong, was she neurotic and paranoid, could she not just relax and stop looking for trouble?

Maybe she should go back into therapy. Or get a real job. Possibly she could parlay her online marketing into something. Maybe it was time now to reclaim a sense of mission. Besides, they could use the money. Paul had finally risen to management despite himself, but still, things were tight, especially by California standards. Money! Maggie spat into the dirt. Once, while doing the laundry, she had turned a collar of Paul's that had frayed. She'd been rather proud of that, of dredging up that old skill learned from her British mother. But Paul had bristled, told her not to do that again, insisted that they could afford new clothes and to stop "playing at poverty." Remembering, Maggie felt her face grow hot. Somehow money was tangled up with a vague sense of shame in her life. How had that happened? Was it some infectious baggage of her own, or did Paul introduce it? Maggie had never cared for or aspired to the high life. That ridiculous remodel Sylvia and Carl had done had strained the friendship, frankly, coming as it had during Katrina, when Maggie had tried to raise rescue money and Syl had, she felt, been stingier than she would have if she hadn't been busy picking out granite. Any job she might get wouldn't be for the money, that was for sure. Pocket money, would be all. Still, anything would help. Her inheritance from her mother had bought their house, and between their two incomes they got by. Josh had a partial scholarship at Berkeley, where her mother had taught, which helped. They got by.

Got by! She spat, again, and trained her binoculars on what looked like movement in a nest in the marsh. Got by! What an ambition! What a summarization of a life! "We got by."

"Still waters run deep," she had said to Dr. Blatt, in defense of Paul. "Sometimes," the therapist had replied.

Ten

For Drew, California was "the Great Event."

On those evenings with friends, when everyone was sated with good food and wine and someone would posit: "What would you say was the happiest moment of your life?" and everyone would answer, predictably: "The day I married ———," or "The day our first child was born," Drew, feeling his wife's eyes on him, would assume a thoughtful concentration.

"Hard to say," he'd venture. "There've been so many. The birth of my boys, of course. My wedding." (Which he barely remembered, it seemed so long ago.) "The day Adele discovered that the purple martins had nested."

That was pure sycophancy, calculated to make Adele's eyes sparkle with tears of nostalgia. Knowing that, on the drive home, she would squeeze his hand and say what a lovely evening it had been, instead of going on one of her rants, which were, in fact, thinly disguised attacks of homesickness. He knew that, but it didn't make him sympathetic. He was confounded by her refusal to let the past go, by her insistence on finding fault with everything West Coast.

That purple martin event had indeed been a joyful moment, accompanied by whoops of triumph, high fives, the snapping of pictures, and pleasant hours with the binoculars and the Audubon guide, the boys eager and excited, Adele triumphant.

But truly, the happiest day of Drew's life was the day he'd bought his very own slice of paradise, as he called it. It was a love that dared not speak its name, given how carefully he'd had to prep Adele. You'd have thought she was scouting for Woody Allen, the way she kept up a running monologue of all that struck her as ludicrous, inadequate, bizarre, about California. The nudges, the rolling of the eyes, the suppressed hilarity that she'd release as soon as they were alone in their hotel room!

They'd come out to visit Jake, that time. For Drew, whose previous trips to California had been brief and uneventful, the mysterious conversion that had occurred was nothing less than a divine revelation.

They'd had drinks at the Four Seasons Aviara, where they were staying. Invited the girlfriend and her parents. Nice people, he'd thought, feeling protective toward them in the face of what he knew were Adele's snap judgments. The wife was pretty, in that blond California way that seems to last well into a woman's sixties. The girl, though—what a body she'd had! Jake, who'd always been the quiet one, studious and socially indifferent, had sat on the sofa in the lounge, his hand draped in casual possession on the girl's thigh. His son, Drew had noticed, seemed to fill out the space around him in a way he never had back home. He was tan and robust; he joked and chatted. All day there had been a sluggish precipitation, what Drew later learned was known as June Gloom. Suddenly the sun had broken through, and a rainbow had appeared over the sparkling sea. Tuning out the conversation, he sipped his gin and tonic and settled into the comfortable lounge chair, gazing at the ridiculously beautiful scene. A sense of well-being seeped into his bones. A relaxation such as he was not accustomed to experiencing.

The glow of that first love hadn't left him. The day when he signed the papers on the condo was the happiest of his life. Happy in a different way from all the usual happinesses, the birth of his sons and such. Those were joyful events, but they were Life as he'd foreseen it. This was different. This was a visitation of sorts, proof that God loved him. Who knew such bliss was available to him, Drew Gold? When the job offer from Scripps materialized, he saw it as further proof that some unseen, benign hand had taken up his cause. He'd published a paper in *Archives of Surgery* about laparoscopic gastric binding, which he'd been working on at Columbia Presbyterian. Out of the blue Scripps had called, wondering if he'd come out to discuss "possibilities." They didn't even know he already had a foot in San Diego. He'd had to force himself, during the interview, to act as if relocating was a huge consideration. He didn't even tell Adele at first; she thought he was going off to play golf. And he did golf, after the interview, at the world-famous Torrey Pines course, in the spectacular setting on the La Jolla cliffs. Where he couldn't concentrate on anything but the offer they'd just made him. Unthinkable to pass it up.

When the boys were growing up, they'd vacationed in Florida, the Bahamas, or the Caribbean. Drew had loved the moment when, having left some variety of meteorological misery at JFK or La Guardia, he'd step out of the airport into the soft, warm air, palm trees sticking up like lollipops, like gold stars on an A-plus paper, like a smiling reward handed over by a beaming God.

It was like that every morning in California. Soft and bright and easy, the days long and gentle. The new job was fantastic, too. Drew had left all his personal baggage back at Columbia Presbyterian; here he was simply Dr. Gold, revered for his skill and accomplishments. It was as if they couldn't believe their good fortune in having him at Scripps, instead of the sense, like at CP, that the halls were filled with resentful colleagues, bitter ex-classmates who hadn't done as well as he.

It was as if someone had turned on the lights. He woke, every morning, to astonishment that it hadn't been a dream, that in fact his life had turned into this glittering, balmy palliation. He drank his coffee on the balcony, watching the marine layer dissipate to reveal the seemingly infinite Pacific. His pale, New Yorker's skin turned perpetually golden. The days were a cornucopia of pleasures: body surfing, tennis, golf.

And girls.

He'd been faithful to Adele, never giving much thought to it. He'd been far too busy, back home, to be distracted, and their sex life was fine. Who had time for fooling around when there was always something demanding attention: a fresh snowfall you had to dig your car out of, some minor crisis with the boys, leaves to rake, a new leak in the roof after a heavy rain, a derailment on Metro-North. Always something. And the days, in retrospect, were short, cramped. There was never enough time. Every night, when he crawled cold and exhausted into bed, his mind was awash with to-do lists for the next day, frustration at what he hadn't gotten to that day, dread of what the weather might do to mess up the days to come.

He'd been a good husband. Adele had been a gift to him, he knew; she'd appeared in his life like an angel, holding out her hand to him to lead him from the nightmare of his childhood into his just reward. He'd always known, deep in his heart, that he was meant for more than the circumstances into which he'd been born. Or rather, not known it, but suspected it, so that when things presented themselves to him he responded with a mixture of wonderment and gracious acceptance. The image he used to carry around with him was of ducking from God when something good happened. Don't let him see; he'll take it away. Even though the other half of his heart was going, Aha! I knew it!

Adele had been the first of such gifts. The astonishment of all that had faded, of course, through the years. At the time, though, he had distrusted the possibilities she offered him. Then, finally, dove into them.

One of the things he liked about San Diego was that the shattered bone in his elbow didn't ache like it did back east, in the cold. The elbow was one of the reasons he'd decided to be a doctor. When he came home from school with it, his shirt ripped, the pain shooting through his whole body, his mother had refused to take him to the hospital. She was afraid of hospitals. She was afraid of everything. She'd filled the tub in the kitchen and made him get into it and sit there, shivering, while she stirred whatever of her meds were lying around into a pot of Campbell's chicken noodle soup. He'd had to make believe he swallowed the soup and that the pain had gone, to get her to stop. He'd ended up, as always, taking care of *her*, though he was only nine and nearly passing out with pain.

He was a skinny little Jewish kid in Hell's Kitchen, living in a fifth-floor walk-up railroad flat with his beautiful, crazy mother. The kids he went to school with—the McManuses, the Reillys and Hogans—were sons of the thugs who ran the neighborhood. No teacher took his side; no priest stepped in to protect him. The only thing he had was his brains, and his suspicion that he was meant for something better.

But he never expected anything like this. He wouldn't have dared.

Drew saw it almost as rungs in a ladder. First Adele, then the various accomplishments of his profession. The boys, the life. He'd had childish fantasies of returning to the old neighborhood someday, flaunting his success to his old schoolmate bullies, who would no doubt be spending their dreary afternoons in the bars, just as their fathers had. But that fantasy faded along with the vivid memories of those horrible years, replaced by the immediacy of the life he'd built. And Adele, dear Adele—she'd been a good wife. He hadn't even been aware that he was only living half a life, that there was all this joy in store for him.

The girls . . . they were everywhere. Barely dressed, their breasts warm and risen like fresh popovers, their slim hips clad in low-riding jeans that hardly covered their pubic hair. When they reached up or bent over, the red silk of their thongs formed a little vee where, at the base of their sacrums, delicate tattoos like lipstick marks drew his gaze. "I can see why you like it here," he remarked once, to Jake, after some such girl had served them their burgers. Jake had blushed and drawled, "Seriously."

The first time it had been an accident. Drew had been having dinner at Jack's in La Jolla with a few of the research guys from work, and there'd been a commotion at the bar. A New Yorker to the bone, he'd ignored it until someone shouted for help, with what Drew recognized as a sincere note of panic. It was nothing, really. Some kid at the bar had choked on, as it turned out, a shrimp's tail. Drew performed a routine Heimlich, the thing dislodged, and that was that. Later, as he walked back to his car, someone said, "Doctor?"

The spectacular sunset had concluded, the sky was an iridescent dark periwinkle, and out of the shadows a girl emerged. He recognized her as having been at the bar. In fact, the choker had been her date; he'd seen her look of distaste when, freed of danger, the poor kid tried to laugh it off. She was wearing some kind of stretchy tubular thing that couldn't actually be called a dress, just a sort of perfunctory acquiescence to legality. Her breasts rose and sighed like waking kittens; her long legs moved like undulating reeds as she floated up to him on stiletto heels. Her long, blond hair glinted and threw off sparks of light.

They did it up against his car. It was fast, rough, thrilling, and when he shuddered into her, the excitement was almost painful. When it was over she slipped away, back into the shadows she'd emerged from, and he simply got into his car and drove home. As he sped along the 5, fleeting, random thoughts and images swirled in his head. Every now and then he said, out loud, "Wow!" and "I don't believe it!" The excitement and magnificence of the encounter was something out of a dream that Drew hadn't even dared to have. The sweet, girly smell of her hair, the slight stickiness on his lips from her fruity gloss, her taut, smooth skin, her youth, my God, her youth!

She could have been his daughter. What the hell was she doing, stalking around like a cat in heat, throwing herself at a stranger, in a parking lot! For that matter, what the hell was *he* doing? He was no better than an animal. Well, he *was* an animal, after all, and what male animal shuns sex on a plate, with a cherry on top?

It was wrong. It was so, so wrong. How could he do this? He was horrified at himself. This wasn't him, Drew Gold! Drew Gold was a family man, a loving husband, a devoted father, a mensch! Jesus, what if Adele found out about this? But that was too scary a thought to contemplate. Hurting Adele? No, he wasn't capable of that. Don't go there. The boys, too, what shame to bring on them. And then a devilish little thought nudged in, suggesting that they'd be proud of their old man. *Way to go, Dad! Score the babe!*

Who was thinking these thoughts? Who was taking him over? The old, childhood image of ducking from God returned. That was it. He'd finally noticed, finally realized little Drew Gold had tricked him, gotten out, achieved happiness in this vale of tears. That girl was a succubus, sent to drain the life from him. What next? Would this bleed into his job? What if some scandal erupted, what if he lost his job over this?

He was sweating profusely. Saddlebagging, his sons called it. His shirt soaking wet, from the armpits down to his waist. "Get a grip," he muttered. "Pull yourself together."

Back home, he gazed down at a lumpy, sleeping Adele, snoring softly on her side of the bed. Relief swept through him. Everything was normal.

But in the shower, scrubbing away the evidence of his sin, he realized that nothing would be normal ever again. He was different now. He hadn't asked for it, but it had happened. He got into bed gingerly, dreading the thought of waking Adele. She didn't stir. He lay on his back and stared up at the ceiling, and as he drifted off an image floated into his head: himself in a red Lamborghini convertible, passing his wife in her Volvo station wagon, giving her a little wave, then gunning it onto the exit ramp.

In the morning nothing was different. Nothing, and everything. Life went on. Did he go looking for it? No, not really. Not at first, anyway. But something fundamental in him had shifted, and now he emitted a kind of radar. Like he'd emerged from a cocoon and suddenly existed on a different plane, where he communicated with a species hitherto unknown to him.

The second time it happened he'd been more savvy. While it thrilled and surprised him, he took it more in stride. He knew he'd still get up in the morning next to his wife, still go to work. He didn't succumb to panic, but supplanted it with gratitude. Maybe God wasn't going to squash him. Maybe this was a special gift, a kind of reward. He'd worked hard, he'd been good. He'd had a lousy childhood and had worked his ass off throughout his adulthood; maybe this was a little bonus. All part of the California cornucopia.

It was stunning, how easy it was. Though he was not usually one to remember such things, something Maggie had said years earlier occurred and reoccurred to him, floating up in his consciousness when he entered the noisy, crowded bars. They'd come over for drinks, she and Paul. Adele liked her, and he'd been happy to see his wife bustling around the condo preparing for guests. There'd been the obligatory oohing over the view, the scrutinizing of the framed family pictures. Then Maggie had said, "Be careful. Keep your eye on Noah."

Both his and Adele's hackles had risen, for different reasons. Adele's ears pricked up, anticipating yet another reason to be wary of their new home. His thought was, *Great. This interfering busybody's going to fill Adele with some wholly unconsidered paranoia.* But what she'd said surprised him.

"The girls. They're predatory. Starting so young. When Josh was in sixth grade they shoved him up against a wall and demanded that he choose one of them as his girlfriend."

Relieved, Adele had laughed heartily. "Noah can handle himself," she'd said.

But Maggie wasn't letting go. "No, really. It's a cultural phenomenon. I blame Madonna. And Helen Gurley Brown. Those two should be jail mates for what they fed preadolescent girls. I'm telling you, they're having orgies in grammar school!"

Here, Paul had interjected, "Okay, you made your point. I'm sure it's the same back east."

"Is it?" Maggie had risen and begun pacing, like a caged puma. "Seriously, I'd be curious to know. I thought it was mostly out here, where they hardly wear any clothes. Is it the same back east?"

"Danny's had girlfriends since grammar school," Adele volunteered. Drew saw her discomfort. Glared at the pacing woman, willed her to shut up.

"I'm not talking about girlfriends! I'm talking sex, hooking up, little girls crawling around on their hands and knees in movie theaters performing anonymous oral sex!"

The combination of Maggie's aggression in making her point, the unpalatable information, and most of all the look on Adele's face made Drew frantic for diversion. He and Paul glanced nervously at each other, and without a thought Drew blurted out, "Really? Where were they when I was in high school?" At which Paul laughed and gave him a high five, and Maggie and Adele made a big deal of being disgusted with them. But basically he had defused the moment and the evening progressed pleasantly enough, without further incident.

It had come up, though. The boys had confided certain things. Noah had told him that the girls carried little airplane bottles of hard liquor around in their purses, because it got them to their goal faster. Their goal being to get wasted enough to have sex. Drew had talked to all three boys about being careful—scared the piss out of them, he hoped, with graphic descriptions of the various strains of STDs that were out there. Not to

mention the cry of rape once she sobered up. Other than that, and a few
rueful reflections on how life would've been if he'd grown up here, he didn't
really think about it. Until the tray was passed to him. Laden with delec-
tables. All on the house, it seemed. All for Doctor Drew. It was a shocking
reversal of what he'd considered the natural order. He'd been so scared of
girls, so grateful when Adele had taken the upper hand. There were three
kinds of women, he'd always believed: the ones you couldn't approach in
your wildest dreams, the ones you might be able to court if you did it right,
and prostitutes. How did it happen that the zeitgeist had shifted so dra-
matically? He wondered if it was biological. Perhaps a response to the
male/female ratio, or an overreaction to the gay proliferation. Combined
with Maggie's theory of cultural influence in the form of black lace bus-
tiers in junior size 4.

The girls were everywhere. Some of them barely into their twenties,
some of them well past the first blush of youth, but still delicious. Nurses,
med students, waitresses, secretaries. Plump, juicy apricots dangling on the
branch. He had them in closets, on desks, in his car, in dark corners of
parking garages. He had gotten adept at deflecting their postcoital rou-
tines; the coy entering of their numbers into his phone, the dropping of
their bad-girl personas as they suggested "next time"s. Sometimes they'd
hint about not having the money to pay next semester's tuition or their
rent or car loan. Once, a girl he'd just made love to on a twin bed in the
room she rented leapt into the air pumping her fist, shouting "Yes! Yes! I
won!" How had he felt when she explained that sleeping with a rich older
man was part of a "scavenger hunt," a game she and her friends had cooked
up to make sure they "experienced everything in life"? Shocked, at first,
and then embarrassed, but he'd chuckled about it on the way home.

Scavenger hunt or not, he was experiencing a level of sexual exhilaration he'd never dreamt of. He knew he was okay, looks-wise, but he certainly never suspected that women might find him irresistible. And yet
here they were, dropping, literally, into his hands. He examined himself,
naked, in his full-length mirror. The only difference from his old self that
he could see was his tan, and maybe a touch of insouciance he hadn't noticed before. But actually, now that he sized himself up, there *was* a differ-

ence. The guy looking back at him was a success. He looked like a player. He looked like someone with money. He was aging well. He used to be skinny and city-boy white. Now he was wiry and tan. His hair was thick, salt and pepper. His teeth looked very white against his bronze skin. He imagined how he looked to that foxy hostess, handing the keys to his BMW to the valet. He could see how he'd come across as some kind of prize.

It was extraordinary, what was happening to him. He was some sort of medical anomaly. He felt almost as if the aging process had reversed, as if the sap in a dormant tree had started running again. Life was good. It was excellent, in fact. The money from the sale of the house in Bedford was with his guy in New York, bringing in a solid 3 to 10 percent, safe from the rumbling in the markets. He simply smiled when people spoke of doom. His guy was a wizard; very picky about who he took in. Drew'd been introduced by a grateful patient who said she had connections, and despite his skepticism, the returns had been consistent. The condo, of course, was free and clear. There wasn't a cloud on his horizon. He was even newly fond of Adele, in a sentimental way. She wasn't aging as well as he was, but then women never do. Even though her constant bitching about California bugged him, he still loved her. His desire for her had certainly cooled—but she didn't seem to mind that. Women go off sex at her age; it wasn't her fault. Just as well, then, right? And he still liked to snuggle with her in bed at night, wrap himself around her and breathe in her soft, fragrant, familiar scent.

But now Noah was about to graduate from college, finally, and Adele had begun singing the old "I want to build a house" song. She was talking about the Pacific Northwest. The Pacific Northwest, where it rained all the time! Was she out of her mind? Drew didn't like the whole topic. He'd have said anything to get her to agree to leave New York. He couldn't believe how she'd clung to that house, how stubborn she'd been about relocating out here. That whole thing about her building a house someday— he'd honestly never thought she'd pursue it. He was sure she'd succumb to the life out here, and at the time of his promise he knew nothing about the San Diego real estate market. Now he knew all about it, and his idea was to wait for the market to hit bottom, then buy something on Del Mar

Terrace, where he'd be close to Torrey Pines and its two eighteen-hole championship golf courses.

She wants to build a house so bad, she can build it on Del Mar Terrace. But no, that's not good enough for her. The Pacific Northwest! Ha! No fucking way was he leaving here.

She had forced that confrontation. She never could leave well enough alone. He'd been caught off guard; he was tired after the long day. It was typical of the way they'd grown apart; he'd spent the day glorying in the delights of where they were lucky enough to live; she'd spent the day stewing and fueling her discontent. He didn't want to leave her. Everything was fine the way it was, but she had to push push push. He'd moved into the guest room, and frankly, that was fine, too. She'd calm down, after a while. He did love her. She was the mother of his boys, for God's sake. Let her build her house somewhere, get it out of her system. Divorce didn't have to enter into the picture. Just a big financial nightmare, that's all it would be.

This morning he was off to Torrey Pines. There'd been a symposium on robotics all week, and some of his colleagues from New York had come out for it. They were staying at the Inn, and Drew had cleared his day to have lunch with them and play a round or two of golf.

The 5 was okay till Manchester, when it came to a sluggish backup he knew would last through Del Mar, so he exited and headed to the Coast Highway. It was early. Drew was fanatically punctual, and he wended his way enjoyably through the hilly streets of Cardiff: Glasgow, Liverpool, Oxford. In Westchester the streets bore the names of English villages, or trees, or some native Indian tribe. Up in Leucadia they were all Greek gods and mythological figures: Hermes, Glaucus, Jupiter, Vulcan. In Carlsbad they were named after the presidents: Jefferson, Grant, Roosevelt. Cardiff had this British thing, and then the composer district, where Liszt intersected with Paganini. It was one of the things Drew loved about the area. He found it oddly endearing, the attempt to impose a linguistic order on the hastily created neighborhoods. He imagined the early settlers as stunned with love as he'd been, tossing their hats into the blue sky as they threw up their beach shacks and planted their avocado trees, ascribing these importunate names to their narrow, crooked streets. "No civic planning," Adele liked to crow. "Why did they put the train tracks right on the coast? What were they thinking, selling off the bluffs?"

Drew twitched, hearing her voice. *Don't think about her. Let her stew.* He was driving into a perfect blue day to play golf at one of the best courses in one of the most beautiful places on earth. And there it was; the sea, visible as he rounded the hill by the San Elijo Lagoon. Spectacular. He was in his new BMW, top down, salty air blowing through his still-abundant hair; he was twenty again. He turned up the radio and sang along, eased on the gas pedal and took the curve like a pro, then felt, rather than heard, a deep *thunk*.

He braked and switched off the radio. Looked behind him to see if there was something in the road he hadn't seen: a branch, a sneaker. Nothing. He pulled over, got out of the car with the intention of checking his muffler, and saw, lying inert, a little dog. He glanced around at the houses. No one. He went to the creature. It was one of those fluffy ones, clean, with a collar and a tag. Someone's pet. Who had been so stupid as to let the dumb little thing roam around? It was still alive. Its round, black-button eyes stared up at him. Again, Drew looked around; again, not a soul was stirring. Gently, he scooped the dog up into his arms. It was fat. Its breathing was labored, its hind leg clearly broken. Shit. The tag had a phone number on it, and a name. Patrick.

"Patrick," Drew said, and the creature blinked. "Patrick, you stupid little fuck." The dog blinked at him, made a pathetic little whining sound. Drew stroked his head. His internal organs didn't seem to be affected. If he got him to a vet and got the leg taken care of, there shouldn't be a problem. Problem was, he didn't know where the nearest vet was. He couldn't go driving around looking. People were expecting him. Where was the damn owner? Laying the dog carefully on the side of the road, he got his cell and called the number on the tag. Got voice mail. "Your dog . . ." Drew said, and stopped. "Your dog was running free; it darted . . ." and then there was a beep and he was disconnected. Assholes! He looked at his watch. It wasn't early anymore. He'd just decided to deposit the dog on a doorstep and ring the bell, giving a hasty explanation and claiming a medical emergency—human—that he had to attend to, when a pickup truck appeared. He waved it down.

"S'up, dude?" The driver looked like a preteen. Bare-chested, tattooed. The truck was full of surfboards. Next to him was a girl in braids and a bikini, clutching a Starbucks cup, gazing at Drew with the aggressive friendliness of her ilk.

Drew explained, briefly. He told lie upon lie. He was only doing about forty, it darted out, he swerved to avoid it, called the owners twice, tried to rouse the neighbors, was on his way to Scripps for an emergency call, could they please . . .

Back on the 101, Drew fought a growing rage. Why did people have pets if they couldn't be responsible for them? What was the matter with the moronic beast that it ran right under his wheels? How dare those surfer brats ask him for money? "What if they want us to pay?" the jerk had said. It has an owner, Drew objected, nevertheless pressing a fifty into the boy's palm.

By the time he got to Torrey Pines the sun had weakened, he'd missed tee time, and he was fighting a migraine. And though he was pretty sure he'd imagined it, it looked as if those kids had written down his license plate number.

Eleven

MAGGIE DECIDED "the girls" should go on a trip. Something cleansing, regenerative. Somewhere out of California, away from the hurtful husbands. She began researching with a vengeance.

"What's this?" Paul asked. He was sitting at the computer, looking at a page Maggie had neglected to close. (On purpose? she wondered, later—though at the time, being "caught" had flustered her into taking the offensive.)

"I was in the middle of researching something. Can't you ask, before barging in?"

"Ask? I need permission to go on the computer? You're not even using it."

"It's just rude, Paul. If you were on the computer I'd ask, before butting in."

"You're not on the computer. You're sitting in the middle of the floor, surrounded by old magazines that should have been thrown out years ago."

"I'm in the office, which implies that the computer is in use. And all these magazines contain articles that I've saved on purpose."

"No doubt. For your research. Why are you researching raft trips on the Snake River, or am I out of line to ask?"

Maggie sat back on her heels and narrowed her eyes at Paul, who towered over her. "I am researching raft trips on several different rivers. Is there a law against that?" And then, seeing that she'd reached him, she added, "I'm thinking Adele and Sylvia need to get away. I want to plan a holiday for the three of us." She said "holiday," reverting to her mother's Britishisms, knowing that Paul found these insertions into her otherwise native American English charming. And was instantly vexed with herself for trying to charm him. Two seconds ago she'd been ready to wage battle, and now she was circling back, offering conciliatory crumbs. Why did she feel like a child with him? She didn't need his permission to go on holiday with her friends! When was the last time he had suggested a vacation? Never! He was content to putter around every weekend, tinkering with gutters and drainpipes. They'd never have gone to Sea Ranch had they not been invited. His idea of a wild time was driving to his sister's for Sunday lunch.

"I was going to tell you, but I'm only just now looking into it. I'm sure you agree, what with everything that's going on, that everybody needs a break."

"Everybody?"

"They're my friends, Paul."

"And mine."

"Right. So what's the problem?"

"I didn't say there was a problem, Maggie. All I did was ask you what this rafting page was."

"If it's the money, don't worry. I'm not asking you for anything, I've got my own savings. And I'm looking for something cheap."

Paul smiled at her. It was a kind smile. Perhaps a little rueful, but affectionate.

"What?" she said.

He shook his head. "Maggie, Maggie."

"Maggie, Maggie what?"

But of course he didn't answer. He sighed and turned back to the computer, closed her page, and began typing. In a moment, peeking from where she sat among her stacks of old *Travel and Leisure* issues, she saw the screen fill with numbers and symbols. "What's that?"

"Just checking the markets."

"I didn't know you did that."

"I don't do it every day. But I like to know where we are. Especially now." He was tapping the keyboard, pulling down columns of squiggles and graphs. He drew his breath in sharply.

"What? What's the matter, Paul?"

But he closed the screen, swiveled back to face her. His face was impassive, unreadable. He seemed to be appraising her, in a detached, clinically curious way. "I know you don't like to concern yourself with the vulgarities of the marketplace," he said, "but you are aware, I assume, that the markets are taking a huge hit."

Maggie tasted that metallic tang that meant she was going to be forced to discuss money. Early in their marriage she had surrendered their finances to her husband, gratefully. He took over, in his phlegmatic, efficient way, and she went about her business cheerfully relieved of checkbook balancing or tax return preparing. She signed where he told her to sign, handed her own paychecks over to him to deposit in her account, spent money as she needed to without asking or telling. Both thrifty by nature, they never argued; he had never demanded an accounting. They had an agreement that the money she made from her own work was hers, and that his salary would pay for their household expenses. This was fair, because it was her inheritance that had purchased their house. Now, staring at her husband's grim face, she realized that she had no idea where they stood financially, and she knew that this ignorance was a grave error on her part. Paul could have gambled away all their money. She imagined some lawyer sliding a ledger across his desk at her, telling her she had nothing, it was all gone, too bad about your husband. It sparked that infantile place in her that she hated; she fought the impulse to curl up on Paul's lap and cajole him into reassuring her. The nerve that was touched when Adele and Sylvia disclosed their money issues with Drew and Carl was now peeled back, throbbing in the glare of Paul's fish-eye gaze. "Does that affect us?" she said, trying to keep the tremor out of her voice.

"It affects everybody."

"I didn't know you played the market."

"I don't 'play' the market, but my pension's wrapped up in it, and our IRA, and we do own some stocks I've bought over the years."

"I guess I should know that."

"It's not privileged information. All you had to do was ask."

Maggie's hackles rose at that, that passive-aggressive reprimand, that patriarchal air, again, making her feel like a child. "So it's all the same to you if I log on whenever I feel like it, check out our finances?"

"Be my guest."

"Don't I need to know your password, or something?"

"My password's the same everywhere. The security system, the garage door opener. You honestly don't know my password?"

"How would I? I never use the security system, do you? I didn't even know we had a garage door password. I just use the thingy. I can't believe I'm only just now finding this out."

"Me either. I've told you before. You just didn't listen."

"Oh, that's a good one. *I* didn't listen to *you?*"

Paul shook his head and rubbed his eyes.

He was a tall man, broad-shouldered by genetic gift, enhanced by the sports he'd excelled at in his youth. His prickly little wife, pacing around chewing on her pinky finger, hissing and flicking her tail, was crowding his already cluttered mind. Theirs had never been an easy marriage. She was skittish and overimaginative, a nervous, exotic feline who needed to be soothed. When soothed, she melted and purred; he adored her then. But at the first loud noise she'd dart away, back arched again. The soothing never lasted, never sunk deeply enough into her; off she'd dart to glower and stalk. He knew he'd been given the cue to soothe, but he was tired. He resented being required to put aside his legitimate concerns to tend to her. He'd been under a lot of strain at work. Every day more pink slips were issued. Their meager portfolio, which he'd assiduously developed over the years, had shrunk alarmingly. A few years ago, when mortgage rates had dropped so low, he'd refinanced the house and invested the money, which was now evaporating. They lived modestly, but they still lived in San Diego, where everything cost more. No, he was too tired to get into it with her now. With an aggrieved sigh, he rose heavily and started out of the room. At the door, he turned and said, "2680 Piklbe. P-i-k-l-b-e." He shut the door behind him.

Maggie stood, hot with shame. 2680 Picklebee. How could she not have known that? Picklebee was a private joke between them, from their Berkeley time, and 2680 had been her phone number when they'd met. Goddammit, but Paul could make her feel like shit! She'd been in such a good mood just a little while ago, full of ideas for consoling her friends, excited about planning this trip. She kicked the stack of magazines, watched them slide across the rug. It was probably a stupid idea. Rafting was her idea of a good time, not Syl's or Adele's. Defeated, she stared down at her feet, her eyes unfocused, seeing swirls of dollar signs and numbers. As she blinked away tears, her eyes fell on a picture where one of the magazines had fallen open. "Beautiful British Columbia," the words over the picture said. Maggie felt a funny stirring, almost a sense of recognition, which was odd because she'd never been to beautiful British Columbia. She sank back down and within minutes was deep into the article, all else forgotten.

Sticks

It is ignorant money I declare myself free from.

—WENDELL BERRY

Twelve

On the plane, Sylvia read to them from the brochure she had downloaded. She was on an upswing, giddy and flushed with excitement about the adventure. Adele, who had the window seat, sat staring at the clouds, occasionally interjecting sarcastic commentary. Maggie was experiencing a relieved satisfaction, as if she had single-handedly arrived at some panacea and her friends were the beneficiaries. When she'd broached the idea, Syl had literally clapped her hands, while Adele had said, "And the point would be?"

"To get away. Clear our heads. Experience the beauty of British Columbia."

"I just experienced the beauty of Sea Ranch. This morning I experienced the beauty of my balcony. Tonight I will experience the beauty of my own bed."

"Come on, Adele. It's a new experience. Natural hot springs, virgin forests."

"And it's cheap," Syl chimed in. "A hundred fifty bucks a night—with a view. Are these current rates?"

Now, Syl pored over the pages of information. "Haynesworth Hot Springs," she read, "in the heart of the Kootenay wilderness, nestles into the side of a mountain and overlooks Kootenay Lake and the Purcell Mountains. Deep in the British Columbia interior, the area has enfolded many an exile."

"'Enfolded'?" Adele said. "What does that mean, 'the area has enfolded many an exile'? How do you 'enfold' an exile? Who writes that crap?"

"Listen to this," Syl continued. "Shut up, Del, listen: 'Thousands of Doukhobors settled there in the late nineteenth century, fleeing persecution in their native Russia. Also many Americans in the sixties, fleeing the draft. It is a place of pristine beauty, untouched by modern sprawl.'"

"Oh, thank God," said Adele. "I always wondered what happened to those Doukhobors."

Maggie had made all the arrangements, which entailed flying to Vancouver, switching planes to Castlegar, then picking up a rental car to drive to Haynesworth. All went according to plan, and Adele cheered up a bit as they drove through the forest. Fatigue hit them about an hour before they arrived at their destination, and the conversation dwindled, each woman lapsing into her own silence. Maggie drove, with Syl next to her and Adele in the backseat. Maggie kept glancing in the rearview mirror, checking on Adele's mood. She was thinking, as they crawled up the long driveway to the lodge, that she had really put herself out there with this. Adele had been uncharacteristically passive, indifferent to the planning, shrugging agreement, her objections muttered without conviction. Maggie was counting on the verdant un–California-ness of this place to console her friend.

"Tell me again how the hell you found this place?" Adele grumbled as they wheeled their luggage down an olive-green corridor to their rooms.

"I love it," puffed Sylvia. "It's gorgeous."

"Just give it a chance, Del, okay?" Maggie turned down a corridor, away from them. They had both booked rooms with views, but she'd opted for a cheaper room on the other side of the hotel. "Meet in half an hour at the caves?"

"Absolutely," Syl sang. "Be there or be square!"

Maggie's room had a mineral-y smell. A hard little bed, flat pillow, tired comforter. It looked out over the back entrance to the kitchen. When she cracked the window open, a smell of cooked cabbage wafted up. Dauntless,

Maggie did a little dance. She was free, alone, away! Vacations were good, she decided; she needed to do this more often. She arranged her toiletries in the cramped bathroom, hung up her clothes, changed into her bathing suit. In the mirror she saw Paul come up behind her, run his hands along her hips. Go away, she said, and he did, evaporating into the stained wallpaper. She closed her eyes and drifted back through the voyage she'd just taken, traveling far from home. Opened them to her empty room, smiled at herself. Something in her stirred and shifted open like the tiny door of a minuscule cage; a little creature flew out, heady with freedom, and swooped over the tops of the towering pines. The air was cool and piney; it seemed to curl like smoke around her. The heavy silence throbbed like the inside of a seashell; there was a stillness that made her sway on her feet. That little nudge of recognition she'd felt when she found the article about this place persisted. There was something familiar about being here, an insistent sense of déjà vu. As if she'd dreamt it and woke to find herself inside the dream. It wasn't that she recognized anything or had any clear memories of the place; it was a feeling. A sense of being helpless, in a pleasant, infantile way. An awareness of the presence of grown-ups tending to grown-up things. It was an indolent sensation, threatening to lull her onto the bed, into sleep, and she shook it off, determined to herd Adele and Sylvia into rehabilitation. She had assigned herself the role of the healing goddess Achelois, attributing the troubled dreams she'd been having to her penchant for over-empathizing. That's what she'd tried to explain to Paul. "But if you say I can't go, I won't go," she'd said to him.

"Why would I say that?" was his response.

She pulled sweats on over her bathing suit and headed out to the springs. Sylvia was waiting in the lobby.

"Adele's in a vile mood," she said. "She said she'd meet us later; she wants to take a nap."

Maggie looked at Sylvia, seeing her with eyes freshened by the new surroundings. Syl's hair, of which she was so vain and careful to keep up, had a skunk line of gray at the part. She was wearing pink sweats that sagged at the crotch and knees. Maggie simultaneously wanted to slap her and hug her.

They followed the signs to the locker room, where they were to store their clothes. It was old and dank, dimly lit, and smelled strongly of sulfur. "Didn't they keep talking about how there's no smell here?" Syl said in a loud stage whisper. "The stuff I read explicitly said the springs are so fresh there's no smell."

"Maybe it's whatever they use to clean," Maggie suggested. "Does it bother you?"

"Not really." But Syl looked doubtful.

There were several women sharing the locker room with them, old, heavy women in bathing suits that looked as if they were from the 1900s. They clucked at each other in what Maggie supposed was Russian.

"There's supposed to be a place nearby where we can get massages," she said to Syl, who was bravely struggling out of her sweats, wearing an expression of determined gaiety.

"Fantastico!" Syl said. "I'll see you outside. Gotta tinkle."

The air was colder than Maggie had expected, and she felt foolish in her bathing suit. She stood at the mouth of the cave, annoyed despite herself that Sylvia was dawdling, Adele sulking, and all those women were padding around, lending the place a sinister air. She wondered helplessly what she thought she'd been doing, dragging her friends to this place. The water was the color of mercury, and mist rose up from it. The cave looked like the entrails of some mythical beast. A dirty golden color, its walls were pocked and lumpy, and a faint yellow light glowed from within. It was the weirdest thing Maggie had ever seen. It was as weird as the fact that she was standing there observing it. The mist floated on the breeze and coated her skin. Off in the distance were snowcapped mountains, velvety against the periwinkle-colored sky. From within the caves came an ominous, bubbly sound, and what sounded like guttural chants. *Adele will never speak to me again*, she thought, dipping her toe into the water. It was hot. She yanked her foot out; the chill air nipped it. She stuck it back in. Warm. She stepped in a little further. The water swirled gently about her calves. The skin on her arms rose in goose bumps in the chill air. She swiveled around to check for Sylvia—how long did it take to pee?! Then, with an impatient shrug, Maggie plunged in.

Thirteen

ADELE TOOK THREE ADVILS, wrung a washcloth out with cold water, and, pressing it to her forehead, stretched out on the bed. The bad mood had been coming on since they changed planes in Vancouver for the brief flight to Castlegar. Syl kept reading out loud from all the stuff she'd downloaded, and Maggie had that smug cat look, as if she was going to be such a hero for finding this wonderland where they were supposed to forget all their troubles.

It wasn't fair to give in to this bitchiness. Adele was ashamed of herself. But the moment the plane lifted off that morning at Lindbergh she'd panicked. What was she doing, leaving? Drew had come in while she was packing, sat on the bed, looked bewildered. "You are coming back, aren't you?" he'd said.

As if he cared. As if it was any of his business. But Adele had said, "Of course."

Had he been trying to say something? Was she admitting defeat and relinquishment by removing herself? It was not a good time to abandon ship. That's what she should have said, those exact words, to fend Maggie off. Why hadn't she thought of that? She hadn't been able to think of anything, in the face of Maggie's insistence and enthusiasm. And now look where she was.

The washcloth was flimsy and threadbare. It had grown hot against her forehead. She tossed it onto the nightstand and pulled a pillow over her head. Her body jangled with the movement of the plane, as if she were still aloft. Drew's voice rattled in her pounding head. Why hadn't she thought to bring some Xanax? Maybe Sylvia had some. She'd like to take a whole bottle right now.

Two days ago, Drew had gone for a run, and she went out to buy groceries. One of her tires had gone flat overnight. With hardly a thought, she'd gone back inside and grabbed the keys to his precious BMW. She'd call AAA when she got back, she decided.

Driving Drew's car set off a string of sense memories and seemingly unconnected associations. Her mind, these days, was a whirling dervish. Sometimes she found herself having gone from point A to point B, physically, with no recollection of the time in between. There she'd be in the kitchen, for example, when the last thing she remembered was being in the shower. She roamed, mentally, through the years, entertaining images of moments she hadn't recalled noting at the time; long-ago conversations she remembered word for word. She was back in the Manhattan of her youth, as she drove along, with her friend Debbie in Central Park, when she heard the siren.

At first she thought it was part of her memory. Then its insistence jerked her back into the present. Apparently she hadn't noticed the flashing lights. He'd had to put the siren on and yell at her through that megaphone thing to PULL OVER, PULL OVER!

His hand was on his holster when he approached the driver's window. "You totally blew off that stop sign," he said. So young. Her glance fell to his gun, and she'd gazed at him, sadly, seeing the little boy who wanted to be a cop when he grew up. She had to search for the registration. "It's my husband's car," she explained.

And then the box, under the armrest. She'd stared at it, uncomprehending. "Something wrong?" the boy asked, and she looked up at his smooth, suntanned face, shook her head dumbly.

"What's the point of this?" Drew stormed, later. "Why do this? It's done."

The box of condoms sat on the coffee table between them. Flavored, ultrasensitive, textured condoms.

"I just want to know how long," she said. "And with whom. I have a right to know."

"No one special," was his reply.

No one *special*? Then . . .

"How many? How many, Drew?"

Pressing the pillow into her face as the conversation replayed itself, she moaned. The humiliation. The misery. As if she'd been erased. Even if she set aside her own sense of betrayal, what was she to make of Drew? She'd always felt they were two parts of the same person. Now she wondered who the hell he was. Was it possible he had some kind of brain tumor or something, to cause him to lose his mind? He was a doctor, for Christ's sake. Had he not given a thought to the sheer physical danger of his promiscuity?

And now, stuck in this rickety dump in the literal middle of nowhere! This was supposed to do her good? Be some kind of a consolation?

Adele was widely traveled; she considered herself a sturdy pilgrim; she had healthy digestion and could sleep anywhere. So the panic at takeoff this morning had unnerved her, made her sense an ill wind. And the flight had been bumpy, and she had honestly wanted to snatch the stupid sheaf of papers out of Syl's hands and fling them out the window. She had spent most of the flight staring out the window, kneading her Play-Doh. Keeping her purse clutched in her lap. She still became unnerved when she recalled the day she thought she'd lost her bag, only to find it sitting on her bed when she got home. She'd developed a habit of keeping it slung around her neck and shoulder, as she used to in New York to deter snatchers.

She wouldn't sleep. She wasn't a napper. Plus, the Advil was beginning to gnaw at her stomach. She was hungry. She would go in search of food. She wasn't going near those reeking caves. Let the others wallow and paddle; she was going to find food, and see if she could get a massage or a facial, or a hot rock something or other. There were bound to be plenty of places she could do that, around here. That and organic farms, that's what exiled hippies have done with their lives. Those enfolded, exiled hippies.

At the front desk she collected a stack of brochures. "If you want a

super massage, this is the place to go, eh?" a chunky blond girl said, drawing a big star on a homemade flyer. On the front page was a drawing of
what was meant to depict a grotto, with ferns dripping over a forest pool,
in the depths of which the artist hoped you'd discern a mermaid, gazing
up with bejeweled, Keane-like eyes. "The Pardes" was written across the top,
in gothic script.

Adele laughed. "The Pardes? What is this, some kind of kabbalistic cult?"

The girl looked hurt. "It's a spa, eh? A really good one."

"It's just," Adele said, "it's a funny name. Pardes—that means garden,
in Hebrew. Like the garden of Eden."

"Well, that makes sense!" The girl seemed delighted with this insight.
"A little slice of paradise, eh?"

"That would be nice," said Adele. "That's just what I'm looking for."

Fourteen

SYLVIA LOCKED HERSELF in the toilet stall and wept. She shuddered with heaving, stifled sobs, blew her nose repeatedly, chirped, "Be there in a sec!" in response to what she thought was Maggie summoning her.

But no one was summoning her. She had imagined it, just as she used to imagine Beth's plaintive, "Mommy?" only to be told, when she rushed to her child, "What? I didn't call you."

No, Maggie had no doubt gone ahead without her, and Adele was passed out in her room, and she, Sylvia, was alone, utterly alone in this damp, chilly, public toilet, thousands of miles from home.

Maggie had been so persuasive. And Carl had been so abominable lately! First he was moving out, then he wasn't moving out, then he wanted her to go, then he cried and said he'd never make her leave, then he said they had to sell, then he said they couldn't sell because the bottom had dropped out of the market. When Syl had mentioned the trip Maggie was planning, he went off on a tangent about bleeding money, and said hateful things about Adele, blaming her for talking them into the new addition, when the original idea had been his! And when Syl told him, after having been coached by Maggie, that she wanted him to split their assets so she could move on, he had exploded like she'd never seen. She actually worried that he was going to have a heart attack. She had calmed him down and soothed him with a Bloody Mary, just the way he liked it, with V8 instead of tomato juice, and he had gulped it down and then told her the money was gone; they were poor.

"Don't be ridiculous," she had said. "How can we be poor?"

Sylvia's life, while not without its sorrows, had been appropriately benign. She harbored no illusions regarding the depth and capability of her spirit, and knew that the Lord had provided for her according to her needs. Not for her the Sturm und Drang of Maggie's political passions, or the marketplace ambitions of her impenetrable daughter. Her parents had brought her up in comfort, if not luxury, and she had known from the beginning that Carl would do well in the world, that she would never be reduced to the kind of debilitating worry she witnessed all too often in others. So when Carl said they were poor, it was the cruelest blow. He must have known that. What she found unfathomable was why he wanted to hurt her. Falling out of love with her, dallying with Yelena, that was betrayal and pain such as she'd never dreamt Carl could inflict. But to hide the money, to lie, to strand her, to take everything away, or at least try to—her home!—that was unbearable. Of course she was aware of the recession; she wasn't stupid ("Do you think I'm stupid?" she had wailed at him), but that had nothing to do with them. They didn't take foolish risks, and they had a modest mortgage.

Now Syl remembered how Carl had shuffled things around for the addition—he'd refinanced, he said. Don't worry, it's all done with mirrors. Of course she hadn't worried. There had always been enough money, there would always be enough money, and that was that. They weren't greedy people. They weren't spendthrifts. The recession, she had heard one of those economists on the news say, was a necessary correction. It had nothing whatsoever to do with them.

Sylvia had been gratified to observe Carl's discomfiture at her going off on this jaunt. Carl wanted her home, despite his own thrashing around. He wanted her to preserve the status quo; he needed to know that he could always come home and find clean clothes and food in the fridge. She understood that. He hadn't said that, exactly—that would have been giving away too much—but she knew how he felt. What else did she know in the world, but her husband? "I'll be home in a week," she had told him, and he had pouted like a little boy whose parents were going off without him. That had been a triumphant moment. She considered warning him to keep his whore out of her house, but decided against it. He'd have flown into a rage, and Syl was too exhausted from all the fighting to endure another. It was better to be nice, let him see what he was giving up. Make him feel guilty for the way he was treating her. She did have an awful moment, walking out of her room with her suitcase. Glancing back at her bed, she imagined Carl and the whore bouncing around, that woman in her bed, on her sheets, using her bathroom, and it had cut deep; it had taken her breath away. She prayed that Carl would have the decency to keep her out of Syl's room. Out of Syl's house. Syl had set up little booby traps everywhere, just to tip her off when she came home, proof that someone had invaded. She'd set the soap a certain way in the dish, folded the towels carefully, slipped her nightgown under her pillow just so. Please God let them be undisturbed, she prayed, sticking her fingers in her ears to block out the sound of the fat women padding around on their succubus feet outside the stall, blabbering Russian to each other.

Maggie hadn't thought. She couldn't have known, could she, that this place would be full of Russian women? She wouldn't have brought Syl here if she'd known, would she? How could she not have known? Had she done any research? Everything about the place talked about the Doukhobors. When Syl had heard the door of her room click shut behind her, hoisted her bag onto the luggage stand and gone to gaze out the window at the snowy peaks, she'd felt nauseated. She had sunk down on the bed, remembering a time she'd gotten separated from her mother on a shopping trip; how frightened she'd been, as if the very ground she'd stood on had given way.

She had never vacationed without her husband, not in twenty-five years. Maggie had made it sound so jolly, so carefree! Syl had had an idea of the three of them in a pastel convertible, their hair flying in the wind as they waved at handsome guys in Alfa Romeos while Connie Francis sang "Where the Boys Are" in the background.

Of course it was pretty here, in a *Sound of Music* kind of way. Syl had pulled herself together and gone back to the window, looked from the mountains to the pool below, and that's when the gut punch hit her. The pool area was swarming with Yelenas. Jabbering and cackling, their hennaed hair brittle in the harsh sunlight. It was like a nightmare, like a cruel joke. "You need to get away, clear your mind, take some time where you don't even think about Carl," Maggie had said. And now her nose was being rubbed in the very dirt she'd come here to escape! She'd run to the bathroom and washed her face, changed into her sweats to meet Maggie. "My dear," her grandmother used to say, "you must make the best of it. Rise above it! Put on a happy face, and soon your heart will follow!"

One whole week. Actually, five days, with two for traveling. The first day was half over, at least. Five more days, and then she could go home!

She waited for the locker room to empty, then emerged from the stall. She wasn't in the mood for the stupid caves. She went in search of a cup of tea.

Fifteen

THE WATER ACCEPTED MAGGIE'S BODY, opened and closed around her; she swooned into its embrace. She'd expected it to feel like sinking into a hot bath, but it was different. It felt, actually, like nothing else she'd experienced, but familiar and welcoming at the same time. Oddly, the smell she'd anticipated from the dank locker room had vanished. An earthy, pleasantly mineral-y scent emanated from the golden walls of the cave. These walls had appeared, in the catalog, as encrusted and fossilized, but now, as she floated deeper inside, they revealed themselves as cushiony pulsations; they exuded a mesmerizing comfort. After the rattling chill of the cold air on her naked flesh, the warmth and silkiness of the water, combined with the dimly lit, beckoning deepness, touched something in Maggie that felt like fear, but without a sense of danger. A host of sensations were clashing; tears sprang to her eyes. Looking back toward the opening, she briefly panicked and considered getting the hell out of there, but the pull was too strong, the delicious, engulfing warmth too persuasive. The very depth of the soothing both seduced and horrified her. A sound emerged from her throat and reverberated; it, too, frightened her, as if it were made by someone, or something, else.

The bit of sky she could still see had turned gray. Great; now they'd have bad weather on top of everything else. She was nervous about her friendship with Syl and Adele, who had had to be cajoled into this trip with all the salesmanship Maggie could muster. *Why?* she wondered now. *Why did I insist? Why did I feel it was my job to console them?* Normal people would have brought casseroles, listened to the heartbreak, simply been there. Maggie wondered, with desperation, what was wrong with her that she couldn't simply be there. Why she felt compelled, all the time, to fix things, tweak things, right wrongs. How absurd to have dragged her friends away from sunny Southern California to this gray, frigid, damp place, where they probably couldn't even get a decent glass of wine.

And then she remembered.

The memory swooped on her so suddenly that she gasped aloud: yes, she *had* been here before. She and her mother had flown from Oakland to rendezvous with her uncle; she was seven. They hadn't been in America long. In fact, she realized, they must have just arrived, since she was seven when they left England.

There were ridges along the cave walls where one could rest, lean one's elbows on the edge and float. Maggie pressed her belly against the rock, folded her arms, and laid her head on them. Squeezed her eyes shut as the memories darted in and out of her consciousness.

She'd been afraid to go in the caves. She'd cried, resisted, made her mother angry. "It's for your own bloody sake," her mother had said. She was supposed to be consoled; that's what her mother and uncle had conspired. She had heard them, talking stupidly as adults do, under the conviction that children either aren't listening or don't understand. They were talking about her not talking. She'd gone silent. Yes, that's right, she hadn't remembered, but her mother alluded to it once: "That was your mute period."

And now, to the steady, humid drip in the steamy cave, she remembered something else, something that had never before risen to the surface. Her father. The sensation of his arms encircling her, lifting her up over his head, the heady swirl of the air so high up, the scent of pomade from his hair. And she remembered the way, when she was brought in to his bedside, she had plucked at the skin on the top of his hand, how loose it was; she had pulled it into a little tent and marveled at how a person can shrink, even her big strong dad, and leave their skin like a balloon that the air's seeped out of.

"Lady, you okay?"

Maggie yanked her head up to see two of the Russian women, each of them in a white bathing cap. They were looking at her grudgingly, she imagined, put out that they'd had to feign concern.

"I'm fine. Thank you." She heard the brittle ring of her mother's accent in her voice. Smiled at them.

"Sometimes you get dizzy, first time," one of them muttered as they paddled away.

Maggie felt as if she'd slid out of her Self. Watching the women vanish into the gloom, she experienced herself as some primordial creature, slithering through the rocks. None of it mattered; not her friends' grief, nor her startling recollections, least of all her anxiety over how she might have tilted her friendships. It all seemed like a dream, or a story she'd read. The real thing was, she was alive. She observed the sense of life, hidden under her bones, felt an inexplicable joy as she stretched her arm into the tender water, tentatively bent her legs and pushed off from the wall. She bobbed like a cork, slid like a tadpole. She was pure liquid, formless and mutable. The sound of her breath rolled across the water, echoed off the walls. A Being, it told the darkened crevices, a Being is emerging.

The caves were horseshoe shaped, and from the deepest belly, the pulsing center, you then rounded a corner and saw, in the distance, the dim light of the world. From the dark, wet silence, Maggie slowly, almost regretfully, made her way toward the light. Now was the time to decide whether to grow wings or legs, how to enter the world, how to best maneuver through it? As she approached, she became aware of people, congregated in the pooled end of the springs. The two Russian women, another woman with long, gray hair in a single braid down her back, and a bald, bearded man. Surprised at the shock of invasion she felt, she joined them, finding an empty spot where she could prop herself against the ridge. Out in the open now, steam rose up from the water and coalesced in the cold. The air was frigid. Suddenly the sun broke through the gathering clouds, just for a moment, just a moment of blinding, golden light, the mountains stark against the blue sky, the pine-sweet air like the breath of heaven, and, lifting her face, Maggie saw what must have been an eagle—too big for a hawk, yes, definitely a bald eagle—and she lifted her arms up to it. Yes, I choose wings! But it was too late. Her legs moved instinctually, treading the water. The clouds again usurped the sun, the warmth tugged her down, and she tucked her arms back into herself and sank neck deep, rested the back of her head on the edge. The sky looked like a simulation she'd seen in some museum; dark clouds scudded violently amid patches of blue, then the sun broke free, then vanished, then broke free again.

You were supposed to emerge from the springs and immediately enter the ice plunge, then hightail it to the locker room to shower and bundle up. But Maggie didn't want to contemplate the ice plunge; she wanted to stay just exactly like this, with the peekabooing sun and the heart-swellingly sweet air butterfly-kissing her face. She felt that she had never been so purely happy in her life. Closing her eyes, she lifted her face to the heavens, felt the smile that spread across it. When she opened them, everyone had left the pool but the bald man. She watched idly as the woman with the braid shot up out of the ice plunge, stretched her arms above her head, and then brought her hands down in a prayer-like pose to her heart, bowing her head, before hustling off to the lockers. The Russians were gone. The only ones left were the bald man and her. She wanted him to go, too, so she could have it all to herself. She hadn't really looked at him but did now, hoping to convey her desire for him to move along.

As she turned her eyes to his face, she saw that he was staring at her intently. He had been for some time, it appeared, by the steady levelness of his gaze. His eyes were glittering, as if he were enjoying some secret amusement. When she met his gaze he didn't avert them, and Maggie sensed a psychedelic elasticity of the world, yawnings and lazy shudderings, light and dark and light, and he was grinning now, a huge, beaming smile, and she was shaking her head, unbelieving. And he nodded—Yes, it's me. Is it really you?—and opened his arms, and she swam into them.

Sixteen

CARL PRIED HIMSELF off the soft, sticky flesh of the zaftig Yelena. Her skin was like the gently sucking feet of tree frogs; each "pock" of disengagement brought a new slurp of connection. The woman was a yawning chasm of sensual greed. When he kissed her plushy lips she drew back and opened her mouth to encircle his own; when he plunged into her the very walls of her vagina seemed to leap in the glee of capture.

Carl was besotted. He had taken to humming all the time; when he shaved he sucked in his stomach. He was kind to his wife. Though he lectured her not to be greedy, secretly he planned to be rather generous. It wasn't her fault she'd been ousted by a woman she couldn't hope to compete with. On some level he chose not to dwell on, Yelena felt like a sort of homecoming. It was funny, he reflected as he stood peeing into her pink toilet: for almost three years she had simply been his secretary, an affable, efficient presence who smelled faintly of buttermilk and tended to bulge at the seams. There had been other women, of course. After Beth was born Sylvia had lost all interest, though she was amenable enough. Amenable didn't turn him on. The encounters were purely physical, usually occurring on his business trips, sometimes involving currency exchange. Always discreet.

But then one day as he was leaving the office, there was Yelena in the parking lot, crying. He could hardly have ignored her. It was her car, she said; she had lost her keys. Of course he had offered to drive her home to get the spare set. Who could blame him for that?

At first he thought it was an incident, and worried that it would affect their professional relationship. But Yelena was superb, flawless. Never a side-long glance or a flicker of assumption. So great was his relief, so impressed was he by the absence of any coyness in her manner, that they began to meet regularly. Sylvia seemed not to notice the sudden increase in meetings and dinners he couldn't get out of. She seemed relieved not to have to put out for him when he fell into bed, exhausted. *Works for everybody,* he thought. *Way to go, Carl.*

The feelings had sneaked up on him. Yelena had a cousin, she said, who managed money, and if Carl wanted to give him a little bit—not much; say, a couple hundred thousand—he could make "a nice chunka change," she said, on a short-term investment. Carl had sent the check indulgently, not expecting much, and in ten months he'd received a substantially larger check back. Drew offered to try to get him into a fund he had with some wizard back east, but the guy wasn't interested in his money, so instead he took Yelena's advice and reinvested with her cousin. She began to make suggestions about his business. This client was yanking his chain; that client was capable of bringing in more business and should be treated extra nice. "Careful what you say in front of that one, and let me handle this." "Darling, he will take it better from me." Carl began to rely on her advice. About her own past she was reticent, and for that Carl was grateful. There was an ex and a son or daughter back in Russia, but unlike most women she didn't bore him with regretful stories. And she never asked him about Sylvia.

One late afternoon, saturated and hovering on sleep, he whispered into her engulfing breasts, "It's only you, Yelena. I haven't touched my wife since we've been together."

Yelena slapped the side of his head, rudely snapping him out of his voluptuous half sleep. "Bad man!" she scolded him. "Your wife, she needs love too!"

And that was the moment Carl handed his heart over to his wise mistress. Only his daughter had stirred him as deeply. Syl and he had been college sweethearts; fumbling urgency and the fierce attachment spurred on by their mutual insecurity threw them into marriage. When he was growing up on the farm in Indiana, Carl's dreams of the future were organized and predictable: a good wife, healthy children, abundant larders. He didn't have unrealistic expectations of a wife. Of course she would be pretty, and like sex, and would be devoted to him and have no ambitions other than being a wife and mother and helpmate. Syl had excelled in all those expectations. Every year when Carl did his employee reviews he let his mind wander to his wife, and with the satisfaction of a good manager he gave her a consistently good rating. That she had never conceived again after Beth was a sorrow that they glossed over, so swimmingly did their life together progress. Dear Syl. Carl loved her, as he loved all the females in his life, his mother and aunts and sisters and even the dumb, gentle cows who blew softly into his hands with their velvet noses when he stroked them.

His bladder emptied, he sat now on the edge of the bed and ran his palm along Yelena's curved flank. "Guess what," he said. "I have a surprise for you."

Yelena heaved herself onto her back and blinked her blue, mascaraed eyes at him. Raising a red-tipped finger, she touched his nose and traced the outline of his forehead and jaw.

"Okay, I'll guess," she said. "You are giving me a raise."

"That's not fair," Carl said. displeased. "You know you're maxed out on your job description."

"Exactly. You have to give me a new job."

"Yelena!" But before Carl's annoyance could take hold, she chuckled in her throaty way and reached down to stroke his penis. "You are so easy to tease," she cooed.

He stirred nostalgically under her touch, then gave up. From behind his back he produced the telltale blue Tiffany's box.

"I brought you something from New York," he said.

Yelena's eyes widened. Taking the box, she murmured, "But my darling . . ."

"Open it," he urged.

Inside the box were gold earrings. Teardrop shaped. The Somali had said they were exact replicas.

"Oh!" she said. "They are beautiful!"

Sloppy with love, Carl caressed her butter-plate-sized nipple. "Like them?" he whispered, knowing his putt had dropped into the cup with a neat, resounding *plunk.* Fleetingly, he regretted that he wasn't given to boasting to the boys. He could teach them a thing or two, no question.

"But why are they in a bracelet box?" She had picked up the rectangular bed of white packing and peeked underneath, as if expecting to find more.

"Don't ask me." Carl was offended. "That's the box they put them in, how should I know?"

Yelena was examining the earrings with a critical appraisal unusual for a woman who's just been presented with a blue-box gift. "Where did you get these?" she asked.

"From Tiffany's!" Carl laughed. "Surely you've heard of Tiffany's, on Fifth Avenue?"

One of Yelena's brows shot up as she threw him a quick, shrewd glance.

"Imagine, darling, even a Russian peasant immigrant knows of your famous Tiffany's, of course."

"But that's not my only surprise," Carl said, quite unhappy now with the way she was handling the earrings, half expecting her to whip out a jeweler's glass and turn on a fluorescent light.

"What else?" she murmured, distracted.

"I told Sylvia about us. I told her I'm leaving her."

Yelena did not respond. She appeared not even to have heard him, so engrossed was she in her examination of the stupid earrings. "Did you really get these at Tiffany's?" she finally said.

"Of course I got them at fucking Tiffany's!" Carl exploded. "Jesus, Yelena, did you hear what I said? I left Sylvia. I'm getting a divorce."

"Why would you do such a thing?" Yelena removed her attention from the earrings and turned it to him, gazing with quizzical scrutiny at his face.

"What do you mean, why? Because of you." In his flustered state, Yelena's face seemed to recede, all the familiar curves and planes taking on a waxy quality, so that Carl suddenly became self-conscious of his nakedness. "Because of us," he added, startled to hear a hint of wheedling in his voice.

"What do you want from me, Mr. Ott?"

She was teasing him. That was all. Putting on the little-girl routine. Grinning, Carl said, "Well, Miss Petrovich, what I had in mind might make you blush, might make me blush. In fact . . . in fact, Yelena, my heart, I thought that we . . ." He held his hand out to her, in a gesture he hoped would articulate what his mouth wouldn't. His heart was pounding in a way that made him feel nineteen. His desire for her stirred him.

But she did not take his hand. She dropped the damn earrings back into their box and deposited it unceremoniously—indeed, almost contemptuously—on the bedside table. Then she pulled the sheet over herself and hoisted herself into a seated position. "This is something we have not discussed," she said.

"We're discussing it now."

"It is after the fact. We are discussing something that has already occurred. So it is not a discussion, it is an announcement."

"I didn't expect this, Yelena. I thought you'd be happy." Sternness was called for, Carl realized. When the meeting takes an unexpected turn, gather in your cards, reappraise, adopt an air of displeasure. Get the other person off guard and then reclaim the lead. Obviously he had neglected some aspect of the female psyche, offended her in some obscure way, caused her to balk. No problem; he'd talk her down. She'd be on her knees in moments. Leaning back, he nonchalantly examined a hangnail on his pinky.

Yelena cracked her knuckles. It was an annoying habit of hers that irritated him. He glanced at her sharply. She smiled an odd, Cheshire cat smile at him. "You make a lot of assumptions, my darling," she said.

Carl chuckled, held his hands up in mock surrender. "Time out, sweetie," he said. "Maybe my timing's bad. Maybe I'm jumping the gun. No problem. We'll shelve the discussion for now."

"I would like you to give me a managership," Yelena said. "I would like to manage a department."

Carl instinctively cupped his genitals. He glanced toward his pants, which were draped over a chair across the room. "We can talk about that in the right place, at the right time," he said.

Yelena laughed. "You are a funny man, Mr. Ott, my darling. You are eager to make me your partner, but reluctant to make me a manager. Is that an American thing, or is it just you?"

Carl had made it to the chair and was dressing with as much urgency as he had undressed with a few hours earlier.

"Anyway," Yelena continued, "you have been robbed, I am afraid. You must get your money back from Tiffany's."

"You disappoint me, Yelena," Carl said, fully dressed at the door.

"No, my sweet darling," she replied. "I will never disappoint you. Your disappointment is not to do with me."

"Gotta run," Carl said, tilting his head at her with an apologetic air. "Sorry, honey—we can talk things over later." He shut the door on her in what he meant to be a conciliatory fashion, but the look on her face, his last glimpse of her, had him muddled. What the hell had just happened? He was put off his game. He'd expected a luscious puddle of gratitude, and instead she'd pulled some kind of moll routine. A managership! Ha! That would look good, after he'd made a point of grumbling about her pea brain to head off the smirks and leers he had begun to discern among his colleagues. Besides, he realized with a queasy feeling, he needed her. She had taken on more than she was responsible for, to the point where she'd have to brief him on his own accounts if she left. A definite debit in his column. *Have to get out of the dugout*, he told himself.

He pulled out of her parking lot, seeing her again propped up in bed, her red hair fanned out against the pillows, her face twisted in that inscrutably cold expression. What had gone wrong? What was with women? You'd think he'd have it down by now; you'd think he was immune to their ploys. He'd let her take the upper hand, goddammit, but at least he'd escaped before the situation got out of control. Let her stew in her ingratitude; let her reflect on how she'd blown it. He'd step back, he decided; wouldn't even call her. Keep things professional at work. She'd come begging. He hoped. A chasm of emptiness suddenly opened in him, so acute he patted his pockets for a Tums. But it subsided, leaving him with a dull ache. The world outside the windshield looked veiled and grim. He cupped his balls, turned sharply onto the 5. He'd expected to have dinner with Yelena— what now? He was hungry. There would be nothing at home, Sylvia having abandoned ship for Canada. Goddammit, goddammit, goddammit. "Regroup," he muttered. "Line your ducks back up." A steak sounded good. A steak and a scotch or two, and a pile of fries with lots of salt and ketchup. That was the ticket. He'd go to that place he liked in the village; they'd be happy to see him. Cheered, he exited the freeway.

Seventeen

At dinner, Maggie gazed across the room at the fireplace, where real logs burned in a real fire. Sylvia consumed the contents of the bread basket and finished her first glass of wine before they gave their dinner order. Adele, who hours before Maggie had been sure was going to check out and go home, was positively bubbly.

"It feels so good to be cold!" she enthused, heaping pierogies on her plate. "Syl, you need to try these. I had a long chat with the most interesting woman, a Doukhobor; she told me the water here is so pure the pierogies are actually better than in the Ukraine." She spooned a fat glob onto Sylvia's plate. "Did you ever hear of the Doukhobors? I never did. Fascinating. They came here in droves from Russia in the 1800s, fleeing religious persecution. Tolstoy was a big supporter. God, this wine is bad. Maybe we should have some vodka! You okay, Syl? You ate all that bread; you should have left room for these. We should get the recipe. I definitely want to learn how to make shashliks and pelmenis and vareniki."

Sylvia reached into her large, pink leather bag and did something that stunned them all. She lit a cigarette.

"You can't do that," Adele said.

"Says who?" Syl inhaled deeply and blew the smoke out of the side of her mouth, twisting her lips.

Maggie stared at Syl as if she'd just pulled a pigeon out of her sleeve. "Since when do you smoke? Put it out, Syl. I'm sure you're not allowed to do that in here."

Syl glared at Maggie. "You said there were spa treatments."

"I did not. I said it's a mineral spa."

"Spa, schma," said Adele. "Come on, Syl, jump in. You'll be back in Carlsbad in a few days, and then you can go and spend the whole day at La Costa. I'll go with you."

"I hate it here." Sylvia took a deep drag of her cigarette, puffing her cheeks out and immediately expelling the smoke. Maggie coughed, waved her hands in front of her face. Adele glanced nervously at Maggie, then leaned into Syl.

"Can't you make an effort? She did this for us."

Sylvia gave an insolent shrug. Petulant, Adele thought, as Syl reached for her newly filled wineglass. Funny what you learn about people when you travel with them.

Directly on the heels of this thought came amusement at her own good mood. She'd been ready to kill Maggie for dragging them to this musty old place. Then she'd taken a long walk, following a piney trail that wound through the woods and ended at a pristine lake. Just as she'd emerged from the woods the sun came out, splashing onto a big, flat rock that jutted out over the water. She'd sat on the rock while the sun came in and out of the boisterous clouds, and wept. The weeping did not feel like grief so much as relief. The whole California mishigas seemed like something that had happened to somebody else. Here, it felt like she was home again, only better: this was an earlier Bedford, less developed, cleaner and full of promise. After her cry she felt reassured, as if some primitive oracle had indicated that life could be normal again. She took this as a kind of promise that Drew would regain his sanity, that her shattered life would be glued back together. The cracks would always be there, but that was life, wasn't it. She could live with cracks. While she sat on the rock, fish leapt up from the lake, sometimes catching glints of sun on their shiny scales. The first time, she gasped, and cursed herself for not bringing a camera. Then, as they kept leaping and shimmering, she was filled with mirth. She could tell people and they wouldn't believe her, and so what? A loon called from somewhere, its eerie warble traveling across the water, bouncing back. A dragonfly skidded across the glassy surface, so close to where she sat that she could see the delicate veining on its iridescent wings.

Back at the hotel, she had drunk tea by the fire in the lobby and chatted with the nice Doukhobor woman, who lived nearby and came once a week for the baths.

"Personally," Sylvia said, "I'd like to go to some bar and get picked up."

Adele and Maggie cast each other alarmed glances. Though Maggie, Adele thought, was also acting strangely. What was the matter with her? She'd come late to dinner, glazed, explaining that she'd fallen asleep. She kept staring over their heads. She looked like she was high on something. Adele wondered, with a stab of suspicion, if she'd brought pot with her. Did Maggie smoke pot regularly? She suddenly felt she hardly knew her friends at all.

The waiter approached, an elderly, potbellied man with an air of deprecation and the few strands of hair he had left plastered to his pate in swirls. "So sorry, I must ask you to put out your cigarette, or else go outside."

"Outside?" Syl blew smoke at him. "It's freezing outside!"

"So sorry, madame. These are the rules."

Syl mashed the cigarette out in one of the pierogies. Her pink sweatshirt had some kind of a stain on it, and her hair was unbrushed, with that disturbing gray streak at the part. Adele patted her friend's arm.

"We'll find you spa treatments, sweetie. I got a brochure at the desk for a place near here called the Pardes. Isn't that a riot? It's Hebrew for garden. Not just garden, but *the* Garden—there must be a coven of Jews up here! Anyway, they have all kinds of treatments: hot rocks, mineral salt massage, reflexology—"

"Craniosacral therapy," Maggie added dreamily.

"Craniosacral therapy," he had explained. He'd scooted up so he was sitting with his back against the headboard, cradled her head in his lap and begun massaging her temples. "It's better than years of therapy." Maggie, for the second time that day, had floated out of her body.

"Oh, did you see the brochure?" Adele was saying. "I thought you were in the caves all day, swimming around like Gollum."

"Looking for your 'precious ring,'" Syl added, imitating the creepy Gollum voice.

"Not all day," Maggie said. "I told you, I took a nap."

"So, did you see the brochure, then? We should go tomorrow. Get Syl her mud wrap. I could use an exfoliation."

"I don't want a fucking mud wrap." Syl emptied her wineglass, licked the rim. "I want to get fucked." Suddenly her face became animated, her eyes widened, and she let loose a torrent of hysterical, snorting laughter. Apparently it struck her as the funniest thing in the world, this notion of hers. Mopping her face with her dinner napkin, she clutched Adele's arm, tried to pull her into the joke. "Can you believe that, girls? I am dying to just go out and get myself a big fat zipless fuck!"

She said "fuck" so loudly that Adele swiveled her head around the dining room, and indeed, there were some annoyed glances directed at them. "Sweetie," she said. "Sylvia. Let's go back to your room."

"Am I embarrassing you?" Sylvia turned to the dining room at large, and said, loudly, "My husband is leaving me for his whore of a Russian secretary."

Adele stood, pulled the suddenly pliant Sylvia up, propelled her out of the room. Maggie watched as Adele released Syl's arm and then put her own around Syl's shoulders, a gesture that from Maggie's vantage point almost broke her heart with its sweetness. She felt deep love for her two friends. Also for everyone else in the shabby dining room, the handful of souls whose lives had rubbed against hers for the moment. She knew she should follow Adele and Syl, but she was stilled by the tenderness that flooded her. She was afraid that if she moved, it would dissipate. It was a feeling she had experienced before, but not for a very long time, and only once or twice, and only for seconds at a time. She wanted to stand up and open her arms, let the love she felt pour out of her heart and soothe the troubled lives she sensed in all the faces in the room with her. The urge was so strong that she squeezed her eyes shut and bowed her head to contain it.

"It's all right," a voice said. She looked up and the waiter was there, a kind, concerned look on his face. "It happens. Your friend, she drank too much."

Maggie looked into his beautiful, old face, which seemed to be a bunch of features tacked onto the central buoy, a prominent, veined nose with cavernous nostrils in the depths of which tangles of undergrowth sprouted. "Thank you," she said. "Are you married?"

"Yes, miss. Forty-three years."

"Were you ever unfaithful to your wife?"

He drew back, guarded. "No, miss, never."

"Me either." Maggie sighed. She signed for the check, and as he walked away she murmured, "Until today."

"Stay," he had said to her. "Don't go back. Stay with me." They were entwined in her lumpy bed in her closet of a room that looked out over the kitchen entrance. The scent of cooking cabbage wafted up. The wallpaper, a grandmotherly affair with fat roses and viney trellises, had brownish-yellow stains from something dribbling down through the crown molding. They were naked. His penis lay limp on her thigh, his hand rested on her breast. Their skin was sticky and exuded the mineral tang of the springs.

At first, Maggie had been unable to comprehend what was happening. "How can it be?" she kept asking. "What are the chances of this happening? You dropped off the face of the earth. I Googled you, I wrote you; no one knew where you were. We thought you were dead. How can this be?"

But Mitch did not share her awe. "I knew," he said. "I knew it would happen someday. I'm just surprised at how long it took."

They traced each other's faces with their fingertips. They made love gently, a little clumsily; neither of them came. He was different. His wild warrior mass of springy curls was all gone, his flesh was loose on the bone, and she detected a little gurgle at the back of his throat in the midst of his exertions. But it was him; it was Mitch. The same Mitch she'd mourned all these years, the Mitch she held in her secret heart and turned to in her loneliness when Paul rolled off her and went to sleep.

They smiled into each other's eyes when they gave up. "Not what I used to be," he said. She thought of the two of them in Golden Gate Park, doing it up against a wall in the dark. They'd just posted his brilliant manifesto on every available space, stealthily, so as not to get arrested before the rally. The next day he would stand in front of hundreds of people and speak about the avarice of the military machine to resounding cheers, while she stood behind him, awed.

"Who is?" she said now.

He talked. He told her how he'd come there to avoid the draft, never left. "What's to leave?" he asked rhetorically, making an expansive gesture. The woman with the gray braid whom Maggie had seen making the prayer gesture earlier was his partner, though not in the traditional sense, he averred.

Nothing was in the traditional sense with Mitch. How could it be? They had three children, all of whom lived and worked at the Pardes. Three or four other families were involved. They owned it communally, and blah blah. Maggie sank into the soft flesh of his body and listened to the rumbling sound of his beautiful voice beneath his furry chest. "He was always a windbag," she thought, fondly.

"I thought for sure I'd see your name connected to Obama," she said. "Every time something interesting happened politically I scoured the papers, sure I would see your name mentioned. I kept thinking, If he's still alive, he's got to be behind this, or that. Or the other thing. You remember Audrey? She said she heard somewhere you'd gone to India. Did you?"

"India? No. I told you, I came here. Why should I go to India? Everybody went to India, all those meshugenas who needed to find out who they were, needed some old guru with mice in his beard to tell them. I knew who I was. I just wanted to get out of America. Now everybody does, right? You wouldn't believe how many people show up wanting to know how to get on our health plan, how to get landed immigrant status. I knew back then, Mags. I knew how rotten America was getting. I wanted to get out and beat the rush."

"I thought you wanted to change things."

"I did. But after a while I realized that it wasn't going to change, the seeds of decadence are in the DNA. Here's what the USA stands for: build a hero—make him poor, with lots of odds against him, let him make it to the podium, so everyone can worship him and for two seconds feel like isn't it great that in our country this can happen, where else can this happen? And then everyone starts to feel like shit about themselves because if it could happen to this schmuck how come they didn't make it happen for them? Because they're failures, that's why, or else because the poor schmuck had some kind of an edge, yeah, that's it, the guy can't be for real, and then they find a soft spot and go for it, and next thing you know they've pulled the guy off the podium and crushed him in the dirt. That's America."

Maggie was silent. She was surprised at the defensiveness she felt, at her urge to defend her adopted country. Plus, she wasn't interested in this line of conversation. She wanted to keep it about them, about their past, about this miracle of reunion, about this bubble of possibility she was suspended in.

"Anyway. Pardon my bitterness. I've been here so long, I see America for what it is, that's all. So, who's this person you're married to? If I'm gonna have to take him on, I'd better know something about him."

"You know him. It's Paul. Paul Hanlon."

"Paul Hanlon? I know him?"

"Well, you knew him. He's the guy I started dating after you dumped me."

"Are you kidding me? Tall guy, reddish hair, Mr. Young Republican?"

"He wasn't a Republican then, and he isn't one now. He's just clean-cut."

"You actually married him?"

Maggie didn't answer, because a tidal wave had risen within her and she had to concentrate to keep from bursting out of her skin. Paul's name, coming out of Mitch's mouth—Mitch and she, lying naked together, discussing Paul . . . Suddenly she saw her son Josh's face, so much like his father's. Josh, coming out of the surf with his board, so strong and young, his smooth chest glistening. "Oh my God," she groaned, turning her face into the pillow. "I can't believe this. I've never done this. What am I doing?"

"Uh-oh. Remorse. Have you seriously been faithful to the guy? How many years?"

"Twenty-six."

"Holy shit, Mags. Holy shit."

"Stop it. Shut up. Leave me alone."

Mitch snaked his finger into the hollow by her left femur—my God, he still remembered the place he knew would make her helpless. She twitched away. "Don't."

He had her. He kept poking until she was convulsed in giggles. "See," he said, straddling her, tickling her armpits now, her whole body a land mine of sensitivity, "I remember. Nothing's changed. Does your husband know how to do this?"

"No!" Maggie shrieked, thrashing. "Uncle, uncle! No," she said again, when they were quiet, face-to-face on the pillow. "No, he's not the tickling type. He has other skills. I feel like shit."

But looking into Mitch's eyes, what she'd really felt was a kind of homecoming. As if she'd been on a long trip, met some interesting people, and was now back where she belonged.

Then they had showered together, in the inadequate, fiberglass tub, and they had made love again with the water spitting out of the rusted head, and this time Mitch, his clumsiness gone, moaned and shuddered into her, and Maggie, with a spasm of the most intense love she had ever felt, left her body for the third time that day.

Eighteen

"Geez Louise, lady, have you ever, in your entire life, tried to relax these shoulders?"

"Ow!" Sylvia, lying on her back, looked up at the bald bearded man whose face was upside down and whose hands were wrapped around her neck. "Ouch! You're hurting me!"

"I am barely applying pressure. I'm not even sweating."

A fresh stab of pain shot from where his thumb kneaded her jugular down her leg to crescendo in a toe-clenching spasm. "This is not nice! It hurts!"

"Here's the good news: this can be fixed. Now that you're aware of it you can address it. If you choose to."

Sylvia seethed silently. Smug old hippie! Insufferable know-it-all! He'd greeted her with both palms turned up, extended, as if he were Jesus Christ himself. "I am Mitch," he had pronounced, and she'd almost giggled except that she was a little nervous. This place was nothing like the spas she was accustomed to. With nice clean lockers and girls in starched uniforms, sterile rooms where deferential young women kneaded her gently. This person was not putting her at ease. She tried to think of ways she could hurt him back. Steal something from his table full of bottles, or mess up the bathroom. Adele and Maggie had talked her into the deep-tissue massage. They were not her friends anymore. She had no friends, no one in the whole world. Even Beth was being a bitch. A torrent of ill will gusted through her, blowing the faces of her former beloveds into a fiery cauldron. Fuck them all! Never, ever, would she leave home again. Five days, five more days, and she would be in her own room, with the TV on to KPBS, the dear, familiar face of Katie Orr telling her what was going on in her town, the only place she cared about. Reassuring her that the next day would be sunny and in the eighties, like the day before and the day after that and the day after that. Five more days and she would be safely back in the predictable world, flossing her teeth in the overstuffed wing chair, her bed turned down, her fluffy duvet, her Tempur-Pedic mattress . . . "OW! Shit!"

"Sorry. Poor you. Sylvia, right? Poor Sylvia. This is good, though, what we're doing. You really, really need this."

"I want to go home."

"You want me to stop? We're only fifteen minutes in."

"I just want to go home. This isn't helping; it's making everything worse."

"Okay, I'll stop, but it's the wrong choice, Sylvia. I'm done with your neck for now. If you can just relax and breathe and go with me, this next part should feel really good."

"I don't care! Keep going, stop, I couldn't care less. I just want to get out of this place. I want to go home."

"Ah, home. Where is home, Sylvia?"

"California." The word rolled off her lips with a little moan of longing.

"Ah. The Golden State. Know it well."

"Do you? You've spent time there?"

"Grew up there."

"Really?" A glimmer of comfort appeared on the horizon. "Whereabouts?"

"A little town called Fairfax."

"Fairfax? In Marin?"

"Yup." Mitch breathed in deeply through his nose, then let it out noisily through his mouth. "Do that."

Syl obeyed. "Ooh. That feels good. Whatever you're doing there, that's good. That doesn't hurt."

Mitch worked in silence for a bit, the only sound gentle grunts of empathy as he explored her skull. Happy that he had ceased inflicting pain, Sylvia breathed deeply as he had shown her. She felt a subtle tug from somewhere deep inside her, and then a rush of lightness. The room seemed to brighten, even though her eyes were closed.

"It's okay," the man said, dabbing at her wet cheeks. "It happens. It's release. Go with it."

"My husband just left me."

"Oh. I'm sorry."

"He's in love with his secretary."

"Unimaginative."

"I thought we were so happy. We got back from Sea Ranch and he just says, out of the clear blue sky, 'I'm leaving you'!"

"Why?"

"Why?"

"Umm. Why did your husband leave you for his secretary?"

"How should I know?"

"You didn't ask him?"

The question offended Sylvia deeply. She regretted having allowed this man to fiddle with her. God knew what he was doing to her head, what black art he practiced to force intimacies from strangers, what use he made of them. Ask him? Of course she'd asked him! She had pleaded why why why why why; she had wept it into her pillow, she had blurted it into the still air of her car, she had left messages on his cell phone. Why, Carl? Tell me why! *Ask him*, this horrible, cruel man says. As if that would solve everything! Why didn't you pick up the dry cleaning since you were right there at the mall, Carl? Oh, because I forgot, sorry. So are you going to drive back and do it now? Of course not, *I'm* going to do it. Why are you leaving me, Carl? Oh, because Yelena gives me blow jobs. I give you blow jobs, Carl! I've been giving you blow jobs for years, even though I hate it and it makes me sick. When did I ever say no when you wanted a blow job? Oh, I forgot. You're right. Never mind; I won't leave you.

"I never said no," she said. "I'm a good wife."

His hands were so strong. Her skull was cradled in them, so strong, but so gentle. "Your story's not important," he murmured. Her eyes flew open.

"It's just a story. You think it's unique; you think no one understands. It's just the same old thing, the same old human thing. As stories go, by the way, this one's as common as it gets."

His fingertips were under her brow, pressing and lifting. It hurt, and then it didn't. She felt herself float. Her eyelids were so heavy. There was a scent in the room she hadn't noticed before, something green, like wet leaves and cut grass, her father mowing the lawn, the brilliant sunshine, her new shorts, yellow daisies on a blue background, the sprinkler making loopy rainbows and the magnolia tree dropping its pink teacup flowers . . .

"Look at you, Sylvia." His voice came out of a fluffy white cloud. She was lying on her back on the grass, gazing up at the cloud, at the blue sky, daydreaming. The sun was warm, and she rocked in and out of awareness. His voice was deep, velvety. Like a cello, like chocolate. It vibrated on her skin. "You're a beautiful woman," the voice intoned. "You're in the prime of your life. Forget your schmuck of a husband, think about your neck. Your poor neck. Promise me, when you go back home to California, that you'll find somebody—somebody who knows what they're doing—to work on this neck." And then Syl was yanked out of her reverie as he dug into a knot behind her shoulder, and she said, Stop, that's enough now, no more.

Maggie and Adele were still in their treatments when Syl was ushered into the sanctuary and given a glass of cucumber water. She sank into a beanbag chair next to a wood fire in an old cast-iron stove. There was a musty smell in the room, for which Syl imagined the carpet was largely responsible. It was threadbare and stained; a rusty orange color. The beanbag, too, issued an unpleasant odor, like unwashed hair. Syl pressed the glass of cucumber water against her forehead and conjured images of the La Costa Spa, with its pristine lobby and orderly, immaculate locker room. The fluffy white robes they gave you, smelling faintly, reassuringly, of bleach. The robe she wore now was a tatty, flannel thing, like something you'd fish out of a bin at Goodwill. At least there were no Russian women here. The girl who'd checked them in was about Beth's age, with princess hair—a

tumble of flaxen curls—and a shy smile that would have been adorable but
for the woeful lack of orthodontia. Adele had gone off for a facial; Maggie
was doing something with hot rocks, if she'd heard correctly, though she
hadn't paid any attention to Maggie. She'd found it hard to even look at
her when they met for breakfast. Syl knew she wasn't behaving well, but
she couldn't help it. It was almost as if Maggie'd brought her here to taunt
her. She'd always suspected that Maggie disapproved of her beautiful home,
thought her shallow and materialistic. When Syl had written her a check
for some cause or other Maggie hadn't even said thank you, but acted disappointed. "Of course I want to help as much as the next person," she'd
said to Carl, "but with Maggie it's never enough. They choose to live the
way they do, but why should she hold it against us if we choose to invest in
our home? We could give everything away and there would still be hungry
people!"

Still, the cucumber water was delicious. There was something about
the water here, she remembered hearing somewhere. And her head felt
good. Light. She'd awoken that morning from a fitful sleep with a raging
headache, which she'd smothered with three extra-strength Tylenols and
three cups of coffee. Now the headache was a memory. Okay, fine, whatever that man had done to her head was nice. No sense being spiteful; she
had to admit it.

The princess-haired girl slipped into the room and knelt before her.
"Let's keep your feet warm," she said. She stuffed Syl's feet into big fat warm
slippers, massaged her shins with surprisingly strong hands. Her nails were
bitten to the quick, Syl observed, thinking of Beth's manicured hands.
"What's your name?" Syl asked her.

"Rachel."

"Rachel. That's a lovely name! I have a daughter about your age. She
lives in New York City."

"Lucky."

Did she imagine it, or did the girl have a bit of an attitude? She must be
imagining it. What a place for a girl to grow up! Syl wished, with a rush of
affection, that she could take her to lunch, treat her to a mani-pedi, a service this place didn't offer. Do a little shopping. "Don't you like living

here?" she asked. She'd take the rental car, tell the others she'd discovered a decent mall; she and Rachel would share confidences.

"It's okay."

"Well, if you ever decide you want to visit New York, you should look up Beth. You'd like each other."

"How do you know that?" There was no misinterpreting the girl's hostility.

"Just a guess. I'll leave you her number, just in case."

"No, thanks. I don't plan on any trips to New York City, and why would I call someone I don't even know?"

Syl pursed her lips and shook the rude girl off her shin. "That's enough," she said. "I've had quite enough."

The girl looked surprised and a little hurt, which gave Sylvia pleasure. You reap what you sow! she thought. People think they can be rude and mean and thoughtless and you'll just keep smiling and offering your other cheek to slap. Forget it! *I've had it*, she thought. *No more sweet Sylvia. From now on I'm giving what I get, you can all put that in your pipes and smoke it.*

⬿

Sylvia said she wanted to go back to her room for a nap, and Maggie opted to stay at the Pardes for more "treatments," so Adele decided to retrace her steps back to the flat rock. It was raining steadily, rain such as she hadn't experienced since leaving Bedford, and Adele loved the rain. The people at the hotel desk found her a poncho and an umbrella. They didn't seem at all surprised that she wanted to go out, which gave Adele a deep sense of reassurance. In California, everyone panicked at the hint of a spritz, and it wasn't much fun walking in the rain there, for some reason. It felt less like a pagan rite than a ruined vacation. Stepping on the wet leaves into the forest trail, Adele felt a joyful tug of homecoming. The moist, earthy smell, the rhythmic drum on the shuddering treetops, the muffled coziness under her umbrella; it all felt achingly comfortable and familiar. It was as if she'd stepped through some Narnian door and was ten again, untethered and hopeful, playing in the woods outside her grandparents' house in Westchester while her future sat, wrapped in shiny paper, under the silver

Christmas tree her grandmother always insisted on putting up so the children wouldn't feel too Jewish.

"You're going for a walk?" Sylvia had said. "Are you insane?"

Adele felt disloyal to her friend, as if her inexplicable good mood was some kind of betrayal. But she was also irritated with Syl, who was displaying a hitherto unsuspected side of herself. Was it really necessary to be so bratty about her disappointment? Sure you needed to cut her a break because of Carl, but Adele was in the same boat, and she was making an effort! It was a matter of staying open, she decided, threading her way around a gnarled root system. She'd learned that, in her first years of California. "You're railing like Lear on the heath," Drew had said, and she'd said, "No, more like Moses in the fucking desert!" Just being here, in a dripping forest, reminded her of how she loathed the dry brown hills of Southern California. But she'd adjusted! Whether he realized it or not, she'd made an effort.

A loon warbled, directly overhead. She wondered if it was the same one she'd heard yesterday. "It's me!" she called out.

She'd never once, in all their years of friendship, felt irritated with Sylvia. Maggie, on the other hand, could drive you out of your skin. Like Danny, she thought. Funny I never made that connection before. He used to push Adele right up against her breaking point, then, with a toddler's sixth sense, charm her back to besottedness. Maggie did that. There'd been times . . . but then she'd shift, and you'd want to hug her.

It was interesting, Adele mused, traveling with women friends. Without the husbands, who acted as buffers. With the men around, there was a convenient repository for annoyance and complaints, but in their absence the girls were naked to each other, more vulnerable. She'd been short with Syl, driving back from the Pardes. "She's staying for more treatments?" Syl had said, with exaggerated incredulity. "Maggie the cheapskate? She won't go to La Costa for so much as a pedicure but she'll give these hillbillies money for their bogus so-called bodywork?"

The fact that Adele had had the exact same response to Maggie's announcement only fueled her vexation. "Leave her alone, for God's sake," she had snapped at Sylvia. "You're acting like such a baby!" Syl had sulked the rest of the ride, saying nothing more until they parted in the lobby, when she'd blurted, "I've never had a worse time in my life!"

Adele wondered what Drew would make of it all. Traveling with him was fun. Once, in a taverna in Barcelona, he'd jotted down on a bar napkin snatches of overheard conversation. "No, the blimp is in the Azores. The little man is hankering for his island." When a cabdriver shouted unintelligibly at them, Drew had turned to her with a grave expression, and, as if translating, said, "No, the blimp is in the Azores. The little man is hankering for his island."

That joke had lasted for years. Whenever one of them hadn't understood the other, they'd say it. "Adele," Drew would call from another room, "gobble gobble gobble." And she'd answer, "No, the blimp is in the Azores."

God, she missed him.

And now here was her flat rock, where yesterday she'd been so soothed. It was too slippery to venture onto today. She leaned against a giant hemlock and watched the lake, no glassy mirror like yesterday but a sheet of hammered pewter. Her face felt funny. It tingled from the mountain root facial she'd had at the Pardes, administered by an austere, tall woman with a single gray braid. It was unlike any facial she'd had before, and she'd had many. The woman scrubbed and scraped and prodded and squeezed. "Ow," Adele had said a few times, to no response. She'd tried to engage the woman in conversation, curious about the Hebrew implications of the place, but the woman, who had introduced herself as Grace, responded monosyllabically.

Yesterday had been so lovely, out on that rock. She'd hoped to recapture the sense of reassurance she'd felt. But it was cold now that she had stopped walking, and her face itched. When she scratched her forehead there were bumps all over it. She ran her fingers across her nose, cheeks, chin; more eruptions. Burning and itching. "Goddammit," she muttered. "What did Brunhilde do to me?" And then a wicked surge of anger shot through her, aimed at Maggie. Smug Maggie, who was wallowing in some filthy mud bath right now, while she and Sylvia had their noses rubbed in life without their husbands.

The wind picked up and the rain tilted sideways; her face burned and a chill rose in her from the bottom of her soaked Reeboks. She wanted to turn around and see the lights on in her house in Bedford, smell the wood smoke from the fire Drew had lit in the living room. She wanted to call long-dead Sadie the Lab and see her running to her, ears flapping, mouth stretched in a gummy grin. She wanted to rub the wiggling dog dry with the old towel in the mudroom; she wanted to kick off her boots and check the roast in the oven, call the boys down for dinner.

What had happened to her life?

And now there was a rumble of thunder and it got very dark. The rain poured down in sheets; a wind picked up and funneled straight at her with startling fury, yanked her umbrella right out of her hand and shot it out to the middle of the lake, where it landed upside down, pitching and bobbing like a storm-tossed ship in an angry sea. "Shit!" Adele yelled at the top of her lungs. Her voice fell on sodden air, not even an echo. She pulled the flimsy hood of her borrowed poncho over her head and stumbled down the muddy path back toward the hotel.

Nineteen

"ARE YOU GOING to make me pay for this?" Maggie spoke, dreamily, to the ceiling. Mitch, balancing on a huge rubber ball, sat at her feet, pressing reflexology points. "Big-time."

"Can't you take it out in trade?"

"Not today. This is my business."

Maggie, who'd been speaking idly, was miffed. "I was only kidding," she said. But the realization that she'd have to pay him for what he did to her body rankled. She fumed. Then, without forethought, she blurted, "Why did you dump me?"

Mitch pulled her little toe, made it pop. "It was a test," he said. "You didn't pass it."

"Ouch!" She jerked her foot out of his grasp. "Say that again?"

"Come on, Mag. We were what, eighteen?"

"You said yesterday that I was the love of your life."

"You are the love of my life."

"You said you haven't forgotten me."

"I never forgot you."

"Were you always such an asshole? Did I just not notice?"

"See, this is what you always did." Mitch continued to sink his fingers into the tender coves of her foot. "What have you gone off on? Because I have to charge you for treatment? This is my business!"

"What did you mean I failed the test?"

"I was kidding."

"No you weren't. Why are you okay with—what did you say, Grace?— and having three children with her? Did *she* pass the test?"

Mitch squiggled his eyebrows at her. "You're ruining the effect of the treatment."

That expression on his face, those squiggled eyebrows, did her in. She had forgotten that look, and now here it was, the dear, beloved face looking at her as if she were still eighteen, as if he were saying, Cut class. You know more than that teacher anyway. Cut class; come with me. Oh, Mitch! How had they come apart? "You ruined my life!" she wailed.

"Oy."

"I can't believe you never came back. Did you tell Gray Braid about me?"

"You mean Grace? Yuh. I did."

"Did you tell her we were in bed together all afternoon yesterday?"

"I left that part out."

"Did you tell her you asked me to walk away from my husband and stay with you here? Did you leave that part out?"

"Passion of the moment, Mags."

"What? You're telling me you didn't even mean what you said yesterday?"

"I say what I mean, and I mean what I say. I'd love you to stay, if you think this life is for you. Personally, I don't think you'd be happy. Selfishly, it'd be great to have you around."

Maggie grabbed her purse from the chair where she'd left it, along with her clothes, and fumbled for her wallet. She pulled out all the bills and flung them at Mitch. "Here, then, liar, here's your payment!" She flipped her credit cards at him, even her library card. "This should cover today, and yesterday!" She emptied her change purse and hurled the coins at him. "And here's a tip, and here's for services rendered in the past. Here's for the camping trip to Big Sur, where you said you wanted to spend your life with me!"

Mitch picked a quarter out of his lap. "The exchange rate's not so good these days," he said.

"You broke my heart, Mitch! You killed me! I loved you so much. I would have done anything for you. Tell me, just tell me why. Tell me what happened. All I do is wonder what happened, why we're not together." Maggie had kicked free of Mitch's hands, was sitting up with her legs tucked under her. Everything hung on this moment, what he would do, what he would say. The sheet pooled in her lap; her breasts were exposed, her cheeks wet with unchecked tears. At her feet, Mitch bowed his shiny head and bounced gently on his ball. He'd always bounced, or shaken his foot, or drummed his fingers. "Mitch," she said, tasting his name on her lips.

"You ever see any of those movies about the French Resistance in World War Two?"

And this was something else about Mitch that she remembered. How shameless she could be with him. How anything could lead to an interesting conversation. How he never got silent on her, or walked out of a room when she was upset, or dismissed her feelings. Mitch was going to tell her something now, they were going to talk, and everything was going to be all right.

"You know," he continued, "how they were so pumped up, how they'd get tortured and hung up by meat hooks to bleed to death and watch their ancestral homes get torched to the ground, and it didn't matter because they knew they were right, they knew they had to fight for what was right, and their puny lives meant nothing compared to that?"

Maggie slid out of the heated sock on the foot he hadn't been working on. She was having a mother of a heat flash.

"Those guys," he continued, "those guys, they lived on the edge. That's what I wanted to do. That's what I did, right? But you can't stay on the edge. Look at Ayers. He wanted me to go on for my Ph.D., he wanted to mentor me. I would've been some constipated professor now, some deflated schmuck buried in academia."

"And you think this is better?"

Mitch looked at her. "I don't know. I guess I'll never know. It is what it is."

"So what does this have to do with me failing a test?"

"Ah, I just said that. I don't know what I meant. I didn't mean anything. Has your life been that bad, Maggie?"

Maggie considered. "No. No, it's been good."

"There you go. You have a son. A good strong boy."

Maggie nodded, her heart in her throat at the summoning of Josh. The joy of her life. He'd been a serious, determined little toddler, pulling himself up and falling down and pulling himself back up, never crying for her to help him, crowing triumphantly when he maneuvered himself all the way around the coffee table for the first time without falling. "So yesterday was what?" she said.

He ran his fingers along her shin, squeezed her big toe. "Yesterday was wonderful."

"And that's it?"

"What would you like it to be? You want to leave your husband, come live here? You're welcome."

"But you and me."

"You want to leave your husband, come live here? You're welcome," he repeated. "We'll see what happens." He gathered the scattered money and cards, dumped them in a pile in her lap.

"Are you happy, Mitch? With Grace? Do you love her? Do you ever wish it were me?"

"We're just two people, Mags. We're just another story."

"But the story's over, is what you're saying."

"No, I'm not saying that. I love you. Always did; always will. Such a gift, you swimming into my arms." He kissed the sole of her foot and went to the door. Before leaving, he said, "You can settle up at the front desk."

⁓

Sylvia was having the loveliest dream. She was floating on one of those pool lounges from Hammacher Schlemmer, the kind with a drink holder and an awning if the sun got too hot. She was floating in the bluest, warmest, biggest pool ever, but somehow she was still in her own backyard, though her real pool filled only a corner of the dream pool. Rose petals fell out of the sunny sky like a gentle rain, bursting into flower as they landed in the pool. She sipped from a crystal wineglass that snuggled in her palm like her own breast; in fact, it was her own breast. Its contours reflected shimmering rainbows onto the water as she sipped a honeyed nectar that slid down her throat and spread tingly warmth across her belly. Angels fluttered around her head, massaging her with their wings. Carl was somewhere— not the real Carl, but a sense of Carl the Husband, puttering around with the barbecue or something, and Beth, little Beth, the sweet, adorable Beth of six or so was pirouetting on a cloud that floated before her, her giggles like birdsong. She had honeyed princess hair, and as she danced she tossed handfuls of glitter at Sylvia, but it wasn't glitter, it was letters, weird letters; they sailed like Frisbees over Sylvia's head.

She'd gone to sleep on top of the bed and a chill had set in, causing her to roll over and reach for her blanket, which wasn't there. The dream began to fade; she floated to the edge of consciousness and reached out to clutch it, to hold on—she needed to understand those letters—but it crumbled away, and she opened her eyes to the walls of the hotel room. A framed picture of snow-covered mountains hung on the wall next to the window, through which she could see glimpses of snow-covered mountains. She tucked her hands between her thighs and squeezed her eyes shut, seeking the meaning behind those foreign letters. Someone banged on the door.

"Sylvia? You in there?"

Beth's giggles, like the tinkling of wind chimes. How she'd loved to laugh at her daddy! Carl would play into it, make her helpless with mirth, then share a look with Syl. Our girl.

She opened the door to Maggie, who stormed in. "Where's Adele?"

"I have no idea."

"She was supposed to pick me up. She completely stranded me. I had to ask them for a ride back."

Sylvia experienced a tingle of pleasurable spite, seeing the dreamy mien Maggie'd been wearing wiped away. Seeing Maggie back to her perpetually pissed-off self.

"I know you're not enjoying yourself," Maggie said. "I know you're both mad at me, you hate it here. I'm sorry, okay? I thought it would be better.

I was trying." Maggie paced, agitated. "But to strand me? In the pouring rain?"

"Honey, calm down. She must have forgot."

"Oh right, she forgot. I called her room. I called your room. Thanks for answering."

"I never heard the phone ring."

"Right. Where is she?"

"How should I know?"

"What, have you been in your room the whole time?"

Sylvia shrugged. "It's not like there's a lot to do."

Maggie sank on the bed, dropped her head into her hands. "I've never fucked up so bad in my life," she moaned.

"Oh, Mags." Sylvia sat next to her, put her arm around Maggie's thin shoulders. "Don't worry. I am having a bad time, but it's okay. I do hate it here, but it's not really your fault. We'll be home soon."

Maggie leaned into Syl. "How was your deep-tissue massage?"

"Nice. Actually, no, this horrible bald man hurt me. And said mean things, too."

Maggie gave a bitter snort. "I'll pay you back."

"Oh, don't be silly. It was interesting, it was fine, it wasn't your fault. It was kind of expensive, though, considering."

"Have you gone into the caves at all?"

Syl shook her head vehemently.

"You don't even want to try it?"

Syl kept shaking her head.

"Maybe that's where Adele is. It's probably nice in there, in the rain. Maybe I'll join her."

"She wouldn't go in there. Maybe she went to town. Is there a town?"

"Not really. Besides, the car's here. I saw it in the parking lot when Rachel dropped me off."

At the mention of Rachel, Syl's lips tightened. "That rude little girl? She drove you back?"

"Her father's the owner. It was the least they could do. I can't believe Adele did that."

"Maybe she's in the lounge with her new best friend, that Doukhobor."

"All right." Maggie rose. "I'll find her." At the door, she said, "Syl? Can't you just make an effort? We can have a good time if we try."

"I was actually thinking," Syl said, "of trying to change my flight reservations."

Maggie looked at Sylvia, slumped on the bed in the same dirty pink sweatshirt she'd been wearing since their arrival. Syl had gotten fat. She was fat, disheveled, and not terribly clean. Maggie felt the familiar hook tug at her, the impulse to fix, to reorganize, to shepherd her friend's life back on course. But she lifted the hook out, and said, "Whatever, Syl."

Sylvia called to her as she was rounding the hallway. "I almost forgot," she said. "Adele said she was going for a walk, but that was ages ago. Maybe she's in the shower, or asleep."

Maggie was cheered, despite her annoyance, at the thought of Adele taking initiative; making the most of things. Good for her. Sometimes Adele could be very picky and crabby; her good humor at dinner last night had come as a welcome surprise. It was almost enough to make Maggie forgive her for stranding her, forcing her to endure the humiliation of begging a ride back from Mitch's daughter. A rather sullen girl, she'd thought, but who could blame her. Still, to be sitting next to her in the pickup truck, this child of Mitch's, who called her ma'am! Surely the Furies had arranged it as punishment. *Suck it up*, she told herself grimly. *You can take it.*

Twenty

❦

OVER THIRTY SEARCHERS from local volunteer SAR groups had descended on the hotel and grounds. Maggie stood on the lawn and watched them, simultaneously reassured by their efficiency and alarmed by the grimness with which they assembled. "If we don't find her in the next hour or so, we'll have to wait until morning," one of them said to her, so softly she had to lean in to hear him. She guessed him to be fortyish, a large man in an old jacket that smelled of wood smoke and grease. He avoided eye contact and combed his beard with stubby fingers. Maggie wasn't sure she'd heard him right. "Wait till morning? Is that what you said?"

He nodded, watching over her shoulder as one of the group shouted instructions to the others. He was the leader, she assumed, the one who held everything in his hands, the one who would end this nightmare. She reached for the edge of his jacket, where the inner flannel had piled and curled, and clutched it in her fist. "You can't leave her out there all night."

Someone in the group shouted something to him, and he waved, and the group began to disperse. He cupped his hands around his mouth and bellowed, "Back here at twenty-one hundred!" To Maggie, he said, "We're doing an operation called a sound sweep. Hopefully your friend's conscious and will answer when she hears her name called."

Maggie stared at him. The rain had soaked her hair and was running in rivulets down her neck. "Conscious?" she echoed.

"She's been out there five, six hours. If she's just lost we'll bring her in. If she's hurt or unconscious, there's not much we can do, in the woods, in the dark and the rain. If we don't find her we'll resume at daybreak."

Maggie watched the yellow slickers disappear into the trees. One of them, an old woman with a shortage of teeth, had acted positively gleeful. "Knew we'd be gettin' out before this storm blew over, eh," she'd cackled.

Who were they? Just people, people familiar with this terrain, teachers and farmers and housewives who volunteered to go through the training and be prepared to jump up from their supper tables when the call came. SO THAT OTHERS MAY LIVE was painted on the side of the van that brought them. "You people are from California?" the leader had said, and Maggie saw the barely disguised smirk of contempt pass between him and the others. *Let them judge us*, she thought. *Let them hate us, who cares. Just let them find Adele. Bring her back.* She'd wanted to join the search crew, but they'd quickly squelched her. "Don't need to be lookin' for two of you," one of them had said. Maggie forced herself to acquiesce.

In the hotel lobby, Sylvia was sitting by the fire, wrapped in a blanket, a tray of tea on the table next to her. "They're being so nice," she said to Maggie.

Some people just don't do well out of their own environment, Maggie reflected. A chill shuddered her, and she realized she was soaked, her polar fleece as heavy as a dead pelt, a pool of water settling where she stood. Her mouth was dry; her head throbbed. She turned from Sylvia, obeying some prompt of common sense: must get dry, must get warm.

"Where are you going?" Sylvia called.

"To get dry."

"Don't leave. Sit by the fire, have some nice hot tea."

Maggie went and stood close to the fire. The heat made her soaked jeans sizzle. She stared at Sylvia, who was dunking a cookie into her tea.

"I don't know what she was thinking," Sylvia said. She giggled. "She's going to be so embarrassed." When Maggie didn't respond, she said, "Imagine having to be rescued!"

"You're not worried?" For a moment Maggie clutched at the possibility that the whole thing was an adventure, a great story to be told around the fire pit at the Coyote Bar and Grill.

"Course I'm worried. She'll be lucky if she doesn't get pneumonia."

A burst of tinny music erupted from Syl's lap. She pulled her cell phone out from under the blanket. "Carl's calling me back," she said, casting Maggie the look of a girl about to be asked to the prom. "Hi!" she gushed into the phone.

As Maggie walked away she heard Syl say, "What a disaster!" before lowering her voice to a conspiratorial murmur, no doubt to regale him with Maggie's failures. Why would Sylvia have called him? she wondered. Talk about turning to a cold nipple for comfort. And then she realized she hadn't called Paul, even though she'd told him she'd let him know when they arrived. She hadn't even turned on her cell phone since they left San Diego. There'd been no message at the desk, though, so obviously he wasn't exactly frantic with worry. He was probably happy to have the house to himself, happy to have her out of his hair. Paul seemed a million miles away. A lifetime away. Poor Paul—what would he do if he knew what she'd been up to? Not that it mattered. Nothing seemed to matter, much, in her present state of mind. *It's odd*, she thought. *You'd think I'd be turning to my husband for comfort and reassurance during all this. But he's the last person I want right now.* Back in her room, she peeled off her wet clothes and showered quickly. The water was mesmerizing, but she refused to allow herself to enjoy it. As wet and cold as she'd been, Adele was wetter and colder. Maybe right now they were bundling her up, giving her sips of the hot broth they had in thermoses. Maybe by the time Maggie was dressed and back in the lobby Adele would be sitting by the fire next to Syl, laughing with the SAR folks.

But she wasn't. It was nearing nine when the yellow slickers reemerged from the woods, when Maggie, standing in wait at the window, rushed out, tears of relief already in her eyes. But the faces they turned to her were grim. They'd resume in the morning, they said. Get some sleep, they said. Pray, one of them said. The rain had subsided for a bit, then picked up again. Staring into the tangled, dripping woods, Maggie tried to pray. She had never found it easy, praying. In the Anglican church of her youth there were calls and responses, which she didn't mind as it was a group effort, but one-on-ones with God had always made her self-conscious. And she had a niggling suspicion that she was being punished for her adultery. She knew it was a childish fear—she told herself that God wouldn't punish Adele for Maggie's sin—but "the Lord works in mysterious ways," wasn't that the party line? Ours is not to reason why. "Lord," she whispered now, but the words that came to her mind were "love a duck." Lord, love a duck. That's the kind of thing that always happened when she tried to pray. As if anyone were really listening! But she was desperate now—in a foxhole, so to speak—so she began to bargain with God. Whatever you want, whatever you want, she pleaded, but then her son's face rose before her and she gasped, Not Josh! Anything but Josh! Take me, take Paul, take Obama, even . . . that was bad, she knew. No, I take that back, not Obama. Not Josh. Me. You can have me. I'm the bad one; I'm the one you should punish. Just let Adele be safe. Just keep her safe. Maggie crafted a vivid fantasy of Adele, tucked in some fairy bower, wrapped in gossamer cloaks while benevolent sprites fed her cups of warm nectar and prepared a soft bed and sang her to sleep. A brutal image of Adele intruded and broke the reverie: Adele, facedown on the forest floor, not conscious.

She snapped the thoughts out of her head and pulled her sweater tighter around her. The fire was only embers now, the hotel quiet, dinner served and cleared up, the kitchen closed, the help gone home. Maggie had been urged to sit and eat, but she couldn't swallow a mouthful. Syl held court, scraping her plate clean, lowering her eyes and squeezing the hands of people who approached with kind words, offers of prayers, stories of miraculous survivals in circumstances far worse than these!

She's enjoying this, Maggie thought. She's perked up for the first time since we've been here. She stood abruptly and excused herself, went back to her vigil at the window. She'd devised a little mental game in which she stared hard at the opening in the woods where the hiking trail began, then squeezed her eyes shut and visualized Adele stepping out, willed it to be so, then opened her eyes again to the empty darkness.

And so it went, hour after hour. At one point the fire swooshed into flame again, and she turned to see the old waiter, whose name, she had learned, was Leo, and who apparently wore several hats at the hotel, including resident manager. He was adding another log to the grate, and he'd placed a tray on the table next to the worn easy chair. "You should eat," he said. "I've brought you some soup."

Maggie buried her face in her elbow and couldn't respond, her throat choked with emotion. She preferred the taciturn judgment of the SAR volunteers, their unspoken blame. Didn't Leo know it was all her fault? How could he be kind? He should bring his ministrations to Sylvia, not her. She didn't want them. She wanted the courage to stride into the night and retrieve Adele.

Leo stood next to her. "You should eat," he repeated. "Try maybe to sleep a little."

Maggie shook her head, willing him to leave.

"Just say a prayer." When Maggie didn't respond, he touched her lightly on the shoulder before shuffling away.

At daybreak the SAR volunteers returned, accompanied by an ambulance, some RCMP, and a crew from the local television station. Maggie was asleep on the chair next to the dampened fire, covered by a knitted afghan that someone—most likely Leo—had draped over her sometime during the night. The rain had lightened into a misty drizzle, and Maggie had missed the sight of the bright yellow figures enveloped in the fog, disappearing into the forest. She had missed the ambulance driver chatting with the news crew, passing around a box of donuts, steam from their cardboard coffee cups rising to mingle with the fog. She had missed Sylvia, who came down showered, made up, and dressed in fresh clothes, arranged with the desk to order a taxi to take her to the airport, and stood watching Maggie sleep before deciding to write a note, which she left folded next to the cold, untouched bowl of soup.

But she was awake and back at her post, clutching a mug of coffee, at exactly 10:37, when one of the slickers burst out of the woods and ran, waving his arms, to the ambulance.

❧

The hospital was not really a hospital, more like a clinic. It was a one-storied cinder-block structure, next to a gas station. Maggie had been allowed to ride in the ambulance with Adele, but when she'd tried to hold her friend's hand she'd been reprimanded. "Not the extremities," someone barked at her. They'd whipped off Adele's clothes and wrapped her in a heated blanket, keeping her arms and legs uncovered. When Maggie reached for the corner of the blanket to tuck around Adele's leg she got yelled at again: "No! Keep her extremities cool!" A woman with a thermos of hot cider put a straw in Adele's mouth and told her to sip. The liquid bubbled down her chin. The woman was kind; she dried Adele's chin with a square of gauze and said to Maggie, "If the extremities warm up too quickly it pushes the blood back toward the heart, lungs, and brain, which could cause a cardiac episode."

Maggie could do nothing but try to stay out of everyone's way, and when they unloaded the gurney and rushed down the corridor, when the double doors swooshed shut behind them, she was left alone. In the sad little waiting room she sat on an orange plastic chair whose ridged seat was built to accommodate bigger bottoms than hers, and began the work of straightening out the jumble in her mind.

It was all snatches of images superimposed over each other, tumbled around like in a kaleidoscope. Maggie attempted to halt the momentum, freeze the moments that mattered so that she could keep them intact for the future. The first sight of Adele, her face swollen and streaked with red welts but her eyes open. Yes, Maggie had looked right into Adele's open eyes and at that moment experienced a gratitude akin to religious conversion—her prayers had been answered; there was a just God, after all—but she'd have to peruse the implications of that another time. Then there was the news camera swooping down on them, the girl holding a microphone asking Maggie if she was glad to see her friend alive. What had she done in response to that, she couldn't remember; it was a blank spot. The images fractured and then gelled on the hotel receding behind them as they sped away. When they'd driven up to the hotel for the first time—what, just yesterday? No, the day before yesterday—Syl had said, "Oh, so cute! Like a little house in a fairy tale!" As the ambulance doors shut behind her and she watched the hotel grow smaller through the little window, she was struck by how changed it was through familiarity, how odd the little tug of leave-taking was.

A woman with a clipboard appeared now and asked for information about Adele. Maggie answered her questions as well as she could, but she had no idea what Adele's medical history was or if she was allergic to any medications. It occurred to her that she should call Drew, that she should have called Drew yesterday, for God's sake, but what would she have said? Your soon-to-be-ex-wife has gone missing? She'd left her purse at the hotel, so the woman invited her to use the hospital phone. She got the answering machine. Adele's voice, clueless as to what lay in wait for her. Maggie pictured the condo, flooded with sunlight, the sweeping view of the sea. *Of course Drew's out playing golf,* she thought. She didn't know his cell number. Paul would know how to reach him. She began to dial his number at work, but stopped halfway through and put the phone back in its cradle. She couldn't bear to hear Paul's voice right now. She'd have to find Adele's cell and get Drew's number that way.

She had bent near Adele's ear and murmured inanities to her. Adele was conscious, yes, but her eyes were glassy and she didn't seem to recognize Maggie. Her face looked as if something had been chewing on it all night, and her nails had dirt caked beneath them. Maggie had learned from the SAR team that Adele had found a shelter of sorts, a shallow cave where she'd huddled. So she hadn't gotten completely soaked, which, they said, probably saved her life. They'd also found a wrapper from a granola bar she'd apparently had with her, which was a good sign, they said. At least she'd eaten something.

Maggie knew nothing about hypothermia. She knew someone whose brother had gotten lost on a ski trip and was found barely alive; he'd never been quite right afterward. Her heart ricocheted as she imagined Adele, bundled on her balcony in Carlsbad, staring vacantly out to sea.

It was almost noon and she'd eaten nothing since lunch yesterday. She was mortified at the hunger that overtook her. There was a vending machine that offered hot chocolate and bags of chips, the thought of which made her salivate. But she had no money with her. No money, no cell phone, no coat or ID. And she was wearing the clothes she'd slept in. In her pocket was the crumpled note from Sylvia, explaining that Carl had insisted she come home immediately. On first reading Maggie had barely absorbed the information, so focused was she on Adele. Now she reread it. So, a reconciliation of sorts was in the offing. Carl said jump; she jumped. Or maybe she was lying; maybe she would have made up anything to justify her abandonment. Carl was as good an excuse as any. She tried to imagine the four of them—she, Paul, Syl, and Carl—getting together for dinner, chatting and laughing, this episode just another story. Impossible. Impossible to forgive Sylvia for this betrayal. What kind of person leaves a friend in such circumstances? She knew Sylvia had been in serious denial, but still. To leap like a trained seal at the snap of Carl's fingers. But who was she to judge? Couples do it all the time, have affairs and then make up. Little ripples and bumps in the course of a marriage. She knew Paul had been faithful to her. What if he hadn't? What if he was with someone right now, taking advantage of her absence? How would she feel? She concentrated. Nothing. That was something else she'd have to examine at a later date, when this was over.

The sun had emerged, and Maggie stepped outside to stand in its warmth. It was a spectacular day. The sky a cerulean blue, with marshmallow clouds scudding playfully. The mountains glistened with fresh snow. The air smelled of grass and sweet pine, cool water. Maggie stood in the sun, breathing, ashamed of the pleasure it gave her. Ashamed of the fresh memories of Mitch's hands on her. She thought of that sidelong glance Paul always threw at her, as if he couldn't believe what he was saddled with. And then he'd soothe her as if her feelings weren't valid. Always walking on ice, with him, always skirting around the edges. Except in bed, when everything was swallowed up in darkness, everything except their bodies. The only thing in their marriage that worked, and she'd sullied it irrevocably.

"Adulteress," she said out loud. She should have a big red "A" sewn on her sweater. She should be arrested, she should be nailed to a wall, she should be picked apart by crows. If she didn't love her husband she should have the courage to leave him. She pressed her hand to her heart, then pressed that hand with the other. *It's okay,* she soothed herself. *No one really cares about a little extramarital sex these days.* Apparently Drew and Carl had no compunctions, even though neither Adele nor Sylvia had given them anything to complain about. Besides, did it really count as adultery when Mitch had had her before Paul anyway? And if God had wanted her punished, well, he did a good job of it yesterday. Utter humiliation. Never again, she promised, though she wasn't sure who she was promising. One of the mothers from Josh's school had run off with someone, leaving her children. She remembered the father, showing up at back-to-school night alone, looking lost and vacant. "You do it to your whole family," someone had said, the mothers trying to pull in the wagons, be a village for the abandoned children. Maggie would never, ever, ever have done what she did if Josh were still little, still home. She'd been a good mother. She'd been devoted to her family! Josh sometimes gave her that glance, too, learned by osmosis from his father. How they bullied her, sometimes! She tried to revive the memory of her father that she'd captured in the cave, but it didn't work. She'd probably made it up. Like she'd made up Mitch. Wasting her life dreaming of a boy who didn't exist, who'd existed for seconds in the scheme of things, colliding briefly with a girl who didn't exist anymore, either. Paul used to accuse her of carrying a torch. He never went too far with it because he could see it didn't serve him; it was the wrong road to go down. She felt her cheeks grow hot as Paul and Mitch appeared together in her thoughts.

If Adele was seriously damaged, Maggie would have to kill herself. What else could she do? Well, she could dedicate the rest of her life to caring for her, for however long Adele lived. That would be better. It was the only future she could imagine.

And then the door pushed open behind her and an all-too-familiar voice said, "Here you are!"

Maggie loathed herself for the gratitude she felt when Mitch pulled her into his arms.

"I called the hotel and they told me what happened," he said. "Are you all right?"

With her face pressed into his shoulder Maggie saw herself spiraling away into nothingness. He'd open his arms and she'd be gone. Dust to dust.

He took her to a coffee shop and bought her breakfast. He gave her his jacket to wear, gently chiding her for running out in only a cotton turtleneck. He told her that in the thirty-two–plus years he'd lived there, he'd seen SAR successes countless times.

"She was so out of it," Maggie said. "I'm worried she might be damaged."

"You don't get brain damage from hypothermia," he said. "You die from it, but if you don't die, then you're okay. The main thing is she didn't get frostbite; it wasn't cold enough. If it was next month she could've lost her fingers and toes."

"What about her face? It was covered with welts."

Mitch darted his eyes. "I don't know. Could've been an allergic reaction to something."

"To what? She ate a granola bar."

Mitch shrugged. "Could've been anything."

"Yeah, could've been the facial she got yesterday."

"Possible."

Maggie set her coffee cup down with a thud. "Is that what it was? Could that have been what disoriented her?"

"No, that's ridiculous. A little rash, maybe, is possible. Not probable. Everything we use is one hundred percent organic and pure, locally harvested, no additives, no animal by-products. No, she got lost in the woods, that's all. Happens all the time, like I said. She's going to be fine."

She's going to be fine. Maggie clung to the words. The sun splashed across the Formica table in their booth. She was warm now, and her stomach was full. The coffee shop had filled up with people who knew each other's names, called out good mornings to each other. A grandmotherly waitress came over and refilled their cups. In the bright sunlight, Mitch's face looked weathered. The face of a middle-aged man. It made her sad, to see the animated, youthful face of her fantasy Mitch fade away, replaced for all time by this person with bags under his eyes and a double chin under his beard. "You're not a doctor," she said.

"Nope." As if aware of her unflattering scrutiny, he sighed and gazed out the window. "Like I said, though. I've seen it before. Sometimes they don't get found until spring or summer. Someone trips over them, or someone's dog goes bonkers in the woods. Sometimes they never show up. Eaten, probably. Bones dragged off or buried. People don't get it. People are so fucking stupid. Oh, I'll go for a walk, they say, like it's Central Park or something. This is wilderness. We have cougars and bears up here. They eat people. We have weather. It's not fucking California."

"No, it certainly isn't." Mitch had pushed his plate away and was working a toothpick around his teeth. It was a disconcerting sight. Maggie was well aware of Mitch's prep school upbringing, the childhood dance lessons and wardrobe full of khakis and blue blazers. He'd been early in the process of shedding that part of himself when she met him, but the sheen of good breeding still clung to him. It had been endearing and just a tad comical, how he made a point of eschewing manners, was scrupulous about resisting his impulse to open doors and pull out chairs. It was all part of reinventing himself, becoming a man of the people. It had taken years, Maggie guessed, for him to acquire such natural coarseness as he now exhibited. This Mitch, prodding away with the toothpick, was an entirely different person from that boy who had shimmered and glowed in her heart all these years. He was just an old friend, Maggie thought. A friend of my youth. She had a floating sensation, as she emptied a packet of Equal into her coffee. It was as if she were hovering, suspended, over the little story of her life. Look, there's the house she lives in, and there's the family, and there's the circle of people she's surrounded by, and then the eye backs away and the circle widens; the tiny pinprick of her world surrounded now by the delineations of mountains and rivers and gorges and seas, wider and wider, opening into the mouth of infinity.

Mitch was talking. "From the day I set foot here," he was saying, "I was home. Everyone was coming up here to get out of the draft. There was this place I heard about—some people from California started it way back in the fifties, during the McCarthy era. They were Quakers, and they wouldn't sign any oath swearing they weren't communists. Quakers don't sign oaths, but they were fired from their jobs because they wouldn't sign, so they said fuck you and came up here. And they were just the most beautiful people. They welcomed everyone; they didn't care, they didn't judge. I stayed with them for a while, but it wasn't my thing, you know, Quakerism. I'm a Jew. And there were some other Jews, and we got together and starting reading the Torah, and then we started our own place up."

"The Pardes. Adele said it's Hebrew for garden."

"Yeah. It's been good. A good life."

"A good life," Maggie echoed. "Why'd you call me at the hotel?"

Mitch nodded, as if expecting the question. "You were so pissed off at me yesterday. I was afraid you'd go back to California and I'd never see you again, and I didn't want us to have that be the last thing we had together. That pissed-off conversation."

"Like the last time," Maggie said. Something like thirty-five years ago, she realized. The fury, the screaming, the tears. She remembered rushing at him, beating his chest with her fists, him holding her off, laughing. Yes, she remembered, he'd laughed at her rage, probably embarrassed by it, she realized now, but at the time it had felt like the worst betrayal of all, the dismissal of her pain. And that had been the last time they'd seen each other. Until two days ago.

"I'm not sure if I love my husband," Maggie said.

Mitch ran his palm over his scalp, a gesture, Maggie thought, left over from when he'd tug at his curls. "Unhappiness sucks," he said.

"I don't know what to do."

"Like I said. If you want to come here, you're welcome. There's always a place for you here. We'll figure something out."

Maggie laughed, surprising herself with the harsh, brittle sound. It was the laugh her mother used to expel, a puff of bemused resignation. "Why would I come here?" she said. "What would be the point of that?"

Mitch shrugged. "I just said."

And then, simultaneously, they reached across the table and grasped each other's hands. Another moment seared into her, scorching the edges of the old moments that had grown so frayed in her years of folding and unfolding them.

This was not the way it was supposed to go. In the fantasies, they met—and, to be truthful, even in the dreamiest of fantasies she hadn't come up with anything like what had actually happened—they met, and the years closed up and sealed them together, never to be sundered again. She would tell him the thing she'd told him in her mind for the last three decades. "I want to tell you something," she'd say, or "Guess what?" Or, "There's something you should know."

The fact of their reunion was the fulcrum of her fantasy. It would be a consummation; she would solemnly hand him this fact, this thing about them that she had carried alone all these years. "I was pregnant," she'd say. "I got an abortion." Sometimes they'd cry together, and he'd acquire a tragic gleam in his eye that would never go away. And of course they'd swear never to be parted again. "How can I make it up to you?" he'd say.

Sometimes she'd really stick it to him in the fantasy, she'd tell him how it was Paul who had taken her to the clinic, Paul who sat and waited, Paul who drove her home. Not to her flat, which she shared with several other girls, but to his room at the top of a stately old Queen Anne, a private, clean space where he put her to bed and brought her soup and tea. He had been so nice to her, Paul. They'd been friends, not particularly close, but it had been he who had put his arm around her and whispered, "What's wrong? I can tell there's something going on. Can I help?" Yes, she would serve that one up to Mitch. "Look who took me on, Mitch. Look who stepped up to the plate."

In some of the fantasies Mitch would face Paul, begging his pardon, thanking him for all of his trouble with Maggie before announcing that he was taking her off his hands forever. That fantasy extinguished now with a crackle of remorse, like an ember she ground into the dirt with her heel.

Here she was, sitting in a coffee shop in Canada, holding hands with Mitch. Not a dream, but a dingy reality. She wanted to inflict something on him. Even as he stroked her fingers she felt something dislodge inside her, sweep through her like a big lint roller, accumulating all the moss and dirt and spikey pebbles and broken glass in the alleys of her disappointing life. And now it left her body in a rush, it hurled toward clueless Mitch as he looked up from their joined hands with a soulful gaze. Just like that, she could annihilate him. Smatter him to smithereens.

"Thank you for coming," she said. "And for breakfast."

He nodded. "It's been amazing to see you, Mag."

"Mmm. You too. I'm glad to know you're . . . alive. And doing well."

He laughed, and she noticed, for the first time, a gap where he'd lost a tooth. "Yeah," he said, "doing well. *Ani veAtah neshane et haOlam.* You and I will change the world."

"I don't think so. I think it happened without us."

He shrugged. "As long as it happened."

"Take care of yourself, Mitch."

"We'll keep in touch," he said.

She extricated her hand. "Sure. I'll give you my e-mail address."

"We don't do computers. But you know where to find me."

"Yes, I do. The next time someone wonders what became of you, I will give a full report."

There was nothing more to say. He heaved himself out of the booth. Her knees creaked when she got up. When he dropped her off back at the hospital, they gave each other dry pecks on the cheeks. And when his truck disappeared around the corner, she felt nothing more than a vague sense of relief, like the way she'd felt when they'd finally closed the lid of her mother's coffin at the funeral home, after hours of smiling and shaking people's hands and saying yes, she certainly was a remarkable woman.

Twenty-one

AT THE FIRST ANNOUNCEMENT that her flight was delayed, Sylvia didn't mind at all. She browsed in the duty-free, bought some perfume for herself and Beth, cigars for Carl. Tonight he would open one of his good bottles of wine, the ones he told her not to drink when it was just her girlfriends, and she would present him with the cigars, and he would present her with something. What would it be? she wondered. Jewelry, of course; hopefully a ring with something inscribed in it—"A new beginning." Carl could be sentimental. She could see him choosing carefully, imagine his pleasure as he anticipated her response. He'd been so sweet on the phone last night, she'd gone to sleep hugging her pillow, all bathed and packed, her fresh clothes laid out for the trip home.

The second time the flight was delayed she grumbled with the others. She'd already eaten and shopped and had her grande caffè mocha and bought a pack of gum for the flight. She'd already browsed through all the magazines and done the Sudoku in the paper she'd bought. Two more hours to kill in this provincial airport. But oh well. *Look on the bright side,* she resolved. *At least I'm out of here. At least I'm on my way home.*

She sat with the others in the lounge and tried to read the paper. A ten-year-old boy had shot his stepfather with a hunting rifle. A church bazaar had been postponed due to the weather. The American stock exchange had dropped lower than it had since 9/11. Carl would be growling about that, she could just hear him. On the phone he'd said they were safe, not to worry about all the money panic. But then he'd said, "There will be no divorce; I can't afford it."

That had hurt Syl's feelings, and she'd responded with silence, but then he realized what he'd said and reassured her, "I didn't mean it like that." Syl had wanted to say, "What did you mean?" But she didn't want to risk annoying him when he was being so conciliatory. She'd asked him about Yelena, and he said she was gone. "Gone?"

"Yeah, gone. I fired her."

"Fired her?" She'd been momentarily confused. Fired her, as his mistress? "What do you mean, fired her?"

"She's no longer working for me. I've ended things. Leave it at that."

Her joy at those words was instantly tempered with concern. "How do you know she won't sue you or something? What about sexual harassment, Carl. How do you know she won't claim that?"

"I fired her as my assistant, not from the company. She actually got a promotion."

"Oh, that's different. So when you say she's gone, you just mean gone from your personal life. And from your specific office."

"She's gone, Syl. Can we not mention her again?"

Happily. Sylvia would happily never mention Yelena's name again. When she got back to Carlsbad the Thanksgiving decorations would be up all over State Street. Maybe Beth would come home, without that boyfriend of hers—they'd all be together again, in their own beautiful house, and then there would be Christmas, and then Carl's birthday. The wonderful order of life would resume and Yelena would be like a warty old crocodile slithering away in the murky depths, a big slimy predatory crocodile whose greedy jaws they'd narrowly escaped.

Certain images had floated before Syl since the day she'd found out about Yelena, lewd images that made her wince. In her secret heart she wished that Carl had never told her; let him have his filthy fling, for all she cared, better Yelena than her. Carl was a sweetheart and she loved him, of course, but the sex thing had long been an albatross around her neck. She had kept waiting for him to outgrow it, as she had, and settle down to the benign domestic rituals that were the meat of life. Often he had ruined what had been a lovely day by his snuffling and clutching when she was trying to go to sleep. In the months before his announcement, when he was evidently sated by Yelena's whorish ministrations, Syl had never been more content. She hoped he had learned something from this. She hoped that if he was ever tempted to stray again he would at least show enough respect for their beautiful life to keep his nasty secrets to himself.

She folded the paper and put it on the seat next to her for someone else. Then snatched it back to see if there was something funny in it that she could share with Carl, like the articles he brought back from the London papers when he went there on business. They enjoyed that, laughing over the antics of the non-them. Canadians didn't seem to be funny, though, not like the Brits. No, there was nothing funny. The ladies auxiliary was looking for volunteers to wrap donated Christmas gifts for the needy. Syl had done that once, at her church. She'd brought Maggie, pleased that for once, she, Syl, was the initiator of activism. It had been awful. They'd each been assigned a place on an assembly line at a long table in a drafty hall. Her job had been the Scotch tape. Hours she'd sat there, sticking tape on jolly gift wrap, pushing the packages to the ribbon person next to her. All around her the other women were laughing and chatting. She'd sat there staring at the tape dispenser, concentrating with all her might on not crying. The thought of the poor families, opening their charity packages of gloves and scarves and cheap toys, it made her tremble. She'd been upset for days afterward. She envied Maggie and the others who had no problem waltzing in there and doling out their little slices of good works. She hated the fact that she couldn't seem to separate herself, that she couldn't just do her bit and go home.

Sylvia had what she considered a very good relationship with God. She gave thanks regularly. She said her prayers. She went to church on Easter and Christmas, and sometimes on Thanksgiving if it was a year she wasn't cooking. She bagged her own groceries, and practiced random acts of kindness. She'd never been a bad girl. Once when she was a teenager she'd stolen a lipstick from a cosmetics display at CVS, but she'd felt bad afterward and given the lipstick to a friend. God had no reason to be displeased with her. She avoided the sin of self-righteousness, unlike some people she knew, and was a good wife and mother. God rewards the just, because here was her husband, returning to her, saying come home, saying the divorce is off. She had walked through the valley of the shadow of death and been led back to green pastures, because she was a good woman, a good person, and surely goodness and mercy would follow her all the days of her life. Yes, the Lord had tested her, and she had not been found wanting. And he was bringing her home, even if it was taking longer than it was supposed to. What was a few hours of delay in the face of this blessedness? She smiled at a whining child and bestowed a sympathetic glance on his mother. Sunlight streamed through the floor-to-ceiling windows; it would be a lovely flight home.

Home. Soon, she could start planning the garage apartment. How wonderful it would be to get everything back to normal again, to put all this behind them. In just a few days she and Del would be back in their yogacize class, laughing about this dreadful adventure. Teasing Maggie for dragging them to this Dogpatch place.

The thought of Maggie sobered her. Maggie would read her note, and judge her. She would despise Syl for caving to Carl, she would condemn her for abandoning them. Syl had looked at her this morning, curled up asleep in that chair, and thought that really Maggie was very smug. Acting like Joan of Arc, like Adele's disappearance was her personal tragedy.

Sylvia had her own theory about Adele. She wasn't worried about her at all, just miffed that she'd been excluded. There was no question in her mind that Adele had simply gone elsewhere. She hadn't gone for a walk; what a ridiculous idea. She wasn't an idiot. She'd meant to; that's why she'd borrowed the rain gear. But what kind of dope would stay out in the pouring, cold rain? No, she'd had a shitty facial, she was in a bad mood, and she'd needed some space. If she and Syl hadn't had that snappish moment when Adele had felt compelled to defend Maggie, she might have included Syl in her jaunt. Sylvia was absolutely sure that what Adele had done, in the same spirit of resourcefulness with which she'd found that horrible

Pardes place, was find a different hotel. Maggie had sneered at the sugges-
tion, had pointed out that Adele's stuff was still in her room. But Syl could
see it all clearly: Adele calling other hotels, finding one that would come
and get her. She wouldn't have taken the car; she wouldn't have stranded
them. She'd been picked up and gone somewhere for lunch, maybe even for
some legitimate spa treatments; she may even have found a place to shop.
And she'd stayed for dinner, and then she couldn't arrange a ride back, so
she'd taken a room and would return in the morning, all refreshed, intend-
ing to round them up and move them all to the better place. That would
be such an Adele thing to do. Why they had ever trusted Maggie to pick a
vacation was a mystery that could only be solved by taking into consideration the state she and Adele were in. Never again. From now on it was
Sea Ranch and Maui; that was it. If Maggie and Paul couldn't afford to go,
it wasn't her problem; they'd go without them. Maggie was probably telling
Adele right now about Syl's defection, in her outraged way, and Adele was
probably just as pissed at Syl for not waiting for her as Syl was at Adele for
not including her in the jaunt. Everyone would be pissed at everyone, but
it would be all right, once they were home. She and Adele would rag Maggie over it; she smiled at the thought: everyone laughing, glasses clinking,
steam coming out of Maggie's ears.

   The third announcement, that the flight had been canceled, left Sylvia
stunned. How could they just cancel a flight? It wasn't even bad weather
today! They said something about fog, marine layers and such—what did
they expect her to do? Convinced there was a mistake, she joined the others
clamoring at the gate, where they were handing out bus vouchers. No one
seemed put out; they stood there obediently and accepted their fates. The
woman with the whining child said to Syl, "It happens, this time of year."

   It was preposterous. She accepted her voucher and said, "What am I
supposed to do? When's the next flight?" She was told that she was guaran-
teed a seat on the regularly scheduled flight the following morning.

   Syl rummaged through her purse for her phone. Carl would be furious.
He would be chomping at the bit to see her. He would go online and find
the right people to yell at, and arrange for her to be taken care of. Someone
would approach her, say, "Mrs. Ott?," and lead her to a town car and de-

liver her to a nice clean hotel, maybe a Grand Hyatt, and she would spend a long but comfortable day and go home in the morning. No tragedy. Just an inconvenience, a little glitch; she could handle that. But where was her damn phone? Nowhere. She emptied the contents of her purse, combed through everything; no phone. Her heart was racing. Everyone had shuffled away, presumably to the buses. "I can't find my phone!" she said to the girl at the counter. "I have to call my husband! I have to call my hotel and see if they have my phone!"

It was Leo who answered the call. No, they hadn't found her phone, but he would send someone to her room to look for it. "And miss," he said. "Your friend was found."

"I beg your pardon?" Syl was standing at the counter on the airport phone, while two uniformed girls tapped away at their computer screens.

"Your friend. I believe she was conscious. The ambulance has taken her to the hospital."

For the second time in three days, Syl locked herself in a stall in the ladies' room and wept, pressing her face into her palms. Shame pushed horror out of the way and then fear crept in and then relief admonished them all. "She's all right, she's conscious," Leo had said. "She's being tended to." But how could she, Sylvia, have been so wrong, so thick, so horrifically selfish? Her bowels contracted and she sank onto the toilet and gasped aloud at the cramp that doubled her over. "It's all right," she called out. "I'm fine." How humiliating to have someone find her that way, flailing about in a toilet stall. She grabbed hold of the paper dispenser to keep from falling. The floor was whirling beneath her, her heart was in her ears, her brain was going to explode, her entire body was in violent revolt.

No one knocked to see if she was all right. The bathroom was eerily empty. Everyone gone off with their bus vouchers, she supposed. In time the cramp released. She leaned her forehead onto her hands and rocked back and forth until the pounding subsided. She breathed deeply until a mild settling occurred and she was able to sit up, blow her nose. It was so quiet. Quiet and deserted. She could stay here forever and no one would find her. She was like a mouse stuck in a glue trap. They'd find her folded up into herself, someday, and that would be a good excuse, the only excuse, really, for why she wasn't where she was supposed to be right now: at the hospital with Adele, wherever the hell the hospital was. Wherever it was, she'd have to find it, have to get there somehow. Have to tell Adele how sorry she was that she'd been wrong, have to make sure Adele was okay, have to get her home. Home, home. Have to get back home, to real life; have to get out of this Canadian bathroom. She managed to stand and leave the stall, to stagger to the sink, where she observed her swollen face in the mirror. She'd finally been inspired to apply makeup, but now it dribbled like animal tracks down her cheeks. She was a sight. So much for making an effort. *To hell with it*, she thought. *Face it, Sylvia, that's you in the mirror. Lord knows how it happened, but there it is.* Good thing she kept her toiletry kit in her carry-on. She'd clean herself up, use the airport phone again to call Carl. Explain the situation, let him know she wasn't jumping at his command, not when her friend needed her. Maybe they'd be able to get on a later flight tomorrow. Maybe she'd still be home by tomorrow night. Cheered by that thought, she dampened a paper towel and blotted the streaks of mascara, then reached for her tube of tinted moisturizer. There, tucked into the little mesh pocket, was her phone.

The bus had just shut its doors and was pushing away from the curb. Syl yelped and banged on the door, causing the driver to slam on the brakes and the bus to shudder and groan. He opened the doors for her but made no move to help her with her bag, even when she heaved it up the steps one at a time. A sea of faces stared at her impassively. "Can you take me to the hospital?" she panted.

"The hospital? That's on the other side of the mountain, eh."

"But that's where I have to go. My friend is there."

"The clinic," the driver said. "Your friend that Yank, eh, got lost up near the hot springs? They'd have taken her to the clinic."

Sylvia glared at a surly teenage boy who was obviously not going to offer her his seat, and fell into a metal pole as the bus lurched back into gear. She grabbed it and nearly wrenched her shoulder out of its socket as the driver cut the wheel and the bus spun onto the road. "You'll be the last stop," he said. "Got your voucher, eh?"

She sank onto a seat near the back that had a broken spring that stuck into her thigh. On the other side of the streaked windows the mountain-tops glittered with fresh snow, but Syl paid them no mind. She cradled her cell phone, on which she had hit number two on speed dial, and the word *Home* gazed up at her from the little screen, with an icon of a tiny house, her house, and her number with the 760 area code, and she didn't lift her eyes from the screen but focused all her might on it, as if it were a talisman that would protect her from all this vast foreign otherness. And then she hit five, and watched Adele's name and number appear, and her eyes prick-led and the trembling began again.

∾

Maggie was in the waiting room reading an article in an old *Maclean's* about the use of native plants in medicine and cosmetics. A botanist from UBC was researching the use of poisonous natives by holistic practitioners who claimed they had healing properties when used judiciously. *Acacia greggii, Linaria dalmatica,* and *Amaranthus blitoides*—also known as wait-a-minute bush, Dalmatian toadflax, and prostrate pigweed—were among the species culled for the treatment of certain skin ailments. Also *Decaisnea fargesii,* or dead man's fingers, which, though not poisonous, could cause severe allergic reactions, and jointed goatgrass, or *Aegilops cylindrica,* which had actually caused a child's skin to disintegrate (there was a disgusting pic-ture to illustrate it). It was an old issue, so she didn't consider it too criminal to rip the article out and fold it into her pocket. She was staring at the tiles on the floor, trying to obliterate the mental image of Adele's skin disintegrating, when there was a painful squealing of brakes from outside. She lifted her gaze to the window and saw an old bus shudder to a stop, the accordion doors creak open, and who but Sylvia emerge, lugging her suitcase.

"Don't say anything," Syl said, huffing into the waiting room. Maggie simply looked at her, expressionless. "Nothing you could say to me would be as bad as what I've already said to myself, so just don't say anything." Syl plopped onto a chair across from Maggie and tried to catch her breath. "Any news?"

Maggie shook her head, but just at that moment a nurse appeared and said they could go in and see their friend now.

Adele was sitting up in bed, an IV connected to her arm. Her face looked almost normal; most of the swelling and redness were gone. Maggie and Syl bent over her, reached for her hands.

"Paper," Adele said.

"What, sweetie?" Sylvia smoothed a lock of Adele's hair back from her forehead.

"Bring me paper. A sketch pad. And pencils. Ticonderoga number two. We'll talk after. Not now."

Maggie and Sylvia looked at each other, confused. *She's damaged*, Maggie thought, panicked. *It's all over.*

"Do you have any idea where we can get her that stuff?" Syl said. "Is there such a thing as a Staples around here?"

"There's a general store around the corner," Maggie said, remembering seeing it from the window of Mitch's truck. She looked into Adele's eyes. "Okay, I'll be right back. Are you all right?" Adele's eyes looked into hers. They didn't seem vacant. She nodded. "I'm fine," Adele said.

Twenty-two

DREW WAS PULLED OUT of a fitful sleep by the ringing phone. It was dark: 4:37, the clock said. It was Harry, his buddy from New York, and the words he spoke made Drew go rigid. "The guy's a crook. It's all been a Ponzi scheme. Everything's gone, every fucking penny. Please forgive me. I didn't know. I swear I didn't know. I gave him everything we had."

"What guy? What are you talking about?" Drew sat up and swung his gaze around the dim room, disoriented. "Slow down, Harry. Give me a second. What guy?"

The story unfolded on CNN. His guy who could do no wrong, his guy who got solid returns when everyone else was hemorrhaging, his guy who wouldn't even let you in without an introduction, was a crook. Drew watched the perp walk, the clamoring press, the stunned pundits. He sat in the middle of his California king bed and absently clenched and unclenched the six-hundred-thread-count Egyptian cotton sheets. Outside his window he felt the shaftway looming, as if he were in his childhood bedroom in the railroad flat in Hell's Kitchen. He wanted to get up and open the blinds to reveal the sea but couldn't make himself move. His mind shuttled and gauged. As a doctor he was well trained in detachment and calculation. A mental spreadsheet assessed the losses, diagnosed the chances. He still had his job, the condo, and his pension, which he'd transferred to Scripps. He still had a few CDs and some gold bullion he'd stockpiled during Y2K. What was gone was Bedford, and over ten years of savings and investments. What was gone was his dream of Del Mar Terrace. What was gone was anything he could spare for Adele. But how could it be gone? Where did it go? Some childlike sense of disbelief within him kept insisting that it was just lost, not gone, that it would be found and reclaimed. Over and over, on channel after channel, he watched the impassive face of the man he had trusted with his future as the newscasters told and retold the incomprehensible story. He had met the guy only once, briefly. He had seemed like a nice enough guy. Apparently he had spared no one.

The night before, Drew had had sex in a ladies' room at a restaurant in Pacific Beach. He'd gone there alone and was eating at the bar. He saw the girl, who was with a group. She smiled at him, and he gave her his Look. He'd learned by now that they responded to this Look, which was a variation on his well-honed bedside manner. A narrowing of his eyes, an interested concentration. They loved to imagine that they were of interest to him. Once Drew realized that the Look got results, he practiced it in the mirror. Laughed at himself, was fleetingly embarrassed. But it had become natural now to respond to a girl's gaze with the Look; he didn't even think about it. The girl had come up behind him at the bar, ostensibly to order a drink. She'd rubbed her breasts against his back as she leaned into the bar. He'd given her a long, brazen version of the Look, and she'd taken his hand, whispered, "Come with me," and led him away. She locked the door behind them and after a deep-throated kiss slid her panties down and bent over the sink. Evidently she found the visual exciting and assumed he would, too, as she didn't take her eyes off the mirror in front of them. "Fuck me, Daddy," she purred, in the voice of a child. In fact, she was barely more than a child, Drew realized, horrified when he saw the skimpy golden hairs of her pubis, artfully shaped by a bikini wax. He found it difficult to stay aroused as women with full bladders began pounding on the locked door. He actually faked an orgasm to get it over with and then, emerging into a sea of female irritation, said, "Sorry, ladies—I'm afraid she got a bad oyster. She'll be out in a minute." He was sure they smirked at him, and also sure that one of them worked at the hospital. At any rate, at least one of them was familiar. He'd walked straight out of the place to his car, and was already heading north on the 5 when he realized he'd left without paying his tab.

He sat now with his coffee as the sky began to lighten. The feeling rising in his gut was sickeningly familiar, from long ago. The dybbuk was back. It had been years since he'd experienced that ball of dread, that sensation of something chewing, gnawing, feeding on him. He remembered, as if it were yesterday, the first time he had money left over after paying all the bills. How he'd hoarded it in a secret savings account, how he'd look at the figures as they grew and feel such wonderment. He kept thinking it would disappear, but it didn't. After a while he became callous toward it; he spoke of it casually, discussed it with Adele, with the guy who did their taxes. He took it for granted. And then everyone was talking about big returns and tax shelters and playing with mirrors and buying something in the Hamptons because you couldn't go wrong with real estate, and when the guys would go out for a beer after playing racquetball everyone had advice, everyone had a tip, a guy you had to invest with, a scheme you'd be a putz not to take advantage of. Drew put money into a herd of cattle in Argentina. A racehorse. It was ridiculous, the money that appeared in his account. His accountant got real creative with ways to avoid shelling out to the Fed. And then this guy, this guy Harry said was like God. And he was, that was no lie. That's why Drew gave him all the Bedford money. Adele wanted him to put it someplace safe; she'd had a shit fit about it. "That's my house!" she kept saying. Drew had laughed at her. "Relax!" he'd said. "Trust me. It'd be stupid to let it just sit there, when it can work for us."

It was a lot of money. He wanted more.

And now it was gone. All gone. The sky brightened into about fifteen different shades of blue, and the clouds were like the underbelly of an abalone shell. It pierced Drew's heart, he loved it so. It occurred to him that this must be how it felt when you were told you had an inoperable tumor.

Suddenly, now that life was being taken away, you could burst with love for it. You'd do anything to keep it. You'd make any bargain. Anything, anything. Just don't take my life away. But this was silly; it wasn't life he'd lost, just money.

Just money! His lifeblood! Literally, the fruit of his labor, of his heartbeats, his youth. What was it all for, if not for this? This reward, which now, apparently, was being snatched away. He knew he was giving in to the weakest part of himself, stoking these thoughts. He knew he had to get a grip, do some serious thinking, figure out what steps to take. He had to go into defense mode. Everything had to be reassessed. Here he was all over again, dodging and ducking—what a schmuck, thinking he'd gotten away with it. Ha! That's what God was saying, Ha! Didn't think I noticed, eh, Drew Gold? Ha!

He'd gone over the numbers with his lawyer just a few weeks ago; it was a pretty picture. Adele would be appeased—she'd get to go build her damn dream house wherever. The boys would be fine; college was all paid for and there was enough to give all three a nice little nest egg to get started. And, most important, there was the cream, the beautiful, thick, buttery cream with which he would buy a house on the Terrace, and then his happiness would be complete. The condo could be rented; he'd hold on to it as long as he could. It was all good.

Now everything would have to be rethought, but not right now. His brain felt sluggish. A flock of pelicans flapped by, he gazed at them and got dizzy. His coffee had gone cold.

When the phone rang he spilled the coffee jumping up. He lunged for the phone. Maybe it was all a mistake. Maybe it was his guy's office, calling to assure him it wasn't as bad as the media was making out; he was still safe.

It was Danny, his second son. "Hey, Dad. Guess where I am?"

Drew scrambled to find something jocular and in control to say. Instead he was silent.

"Dad? Hey, I'm at the Pannikin right down the road. Can you come? There's someone I want you to meet."

"What's up, Dan?"

"My dad wants to know what's up"—this in a soft, tender voice, an aside. Then there were female giggles. "What's up, Dad, is—no, I'm going to tell him! What's up is, I just got engaged."

The words bounced off Drew's numb ears. "Ha!" he said mechanically. "Why aren't you in class?"

"We don't have classes till Thursday. We drove down last night so I could ask her father, officially. You know, for her hand. He said yes. They live in Cardiff. Come on, Dad, just get in the car and drive over, have some breakfast with us. I wish Mom was here; she's going to be pissed to be the last to know. Dad? You'll come, right? Her name is Kirstin. I told you about her, remember? Kirstin, from Cardiff. You'll love her."

The next thing Drew realized he was driving down the 101 to Leucadia. He'd had one of those weird lapses; he couldn't really remember anything between talking on the phone and being in the car. Stress, he diagnosed. Got to get a grip. He squinted at himself in the rearview. He hadn't shaved; he was wearing a baseball cap. He'd look like everyone else at the Pannikin. He was by turns amused and annoyed at the so-called "engagement." Danny had been a heartthrob ever since he was a toddler. He hadn't been without a girlfriend since the sixth grade. This girl must be something, to get a promise like that out of him. Still, it was out of the question. He had another year of graduate school to get through. Drew entertained a brief fantasy in which Adele was next to him in the Beemer, sharing a laugh with him over Danny's latest romantic indiscretion. He could just hear her. "Kirstin? Her name is Kirstin? Isn't that Jake's girlfriend's name? Don't any of the girls out here have names that don't begin with *K*?" But the thought of Adele quickly turned into something physical; an odd numbness made his skin tingle. It felt wrong that she wasn't with him now. But what a relief, too, not to have to face her just yet.

Danny had secured a table on the lawn. He jumped up and waved as Drew approached. They bumped chests, thumped each other on the back. "The line was super long, so I got you a coffee," Danny said. "Black, and a banana muffin. Okay?"

The girl was remarkably unremarkable. Blond, pretty, athletic. She was in a stretchy top, revealing lovely breasts, but no lovelier than all the other young breasts all around. She was wearing flannel pajama pants and flip-flops. Drew stared at her toes, which were stubby and adorned with silver rings. There was a tattoo of something snaking around her ankle. "Dad?" his son said. "You okay?"

"Why wouldn't I be?" Drew snapped, then chortled and opened his arms to hug the girl. "So, this is the lucky girl." The girl stepped toward him to return his hug, beaming a fetching, dimpled smile, a smile of such familiarity that for a moment Drew thought she worked at Scripps. But he was confused, because didn't she go to school with Danny? "Don't I know you?" he said, and he was sure she blushed. He was sure she darted a nervous look at Danny. He was sure, with a sledgehammer to the gut, that she'd been his, briefly, somewhere.

And then he wasn't sure, or else the girl had poise like a pro, because she giggled and flashed his son a look that said, See, he likes me!

Drew's throat was dry and he didn't feel right. He had surgery scheduled for that afternoon; he'd have to take a nap and some Advil. Couldn't afford to get sick. No, he was wrong about the girl. She did look familiar, but so what; they all looked pretty much the same. It had given him a scare, that was all. Or was it? Wasn't she giving him a look now that seemed like a plea? Or a warning? She had those lips, those plush, glistening lips they all had. . . .

And then she squealed and Drew almost spit up the coffee he'd just gulped, but Danny only smiled as the girl flung herself into the face of a fluffy white dog whose owners stopped to proudly indulge the admiration. "Ohmygod he is *so cute!*" Kristin or Kirstin or whoever she was gushed, cradling the dog's face as if it were a rescued child. Snuggling back up against Danny, she sighed. "Oh, I miss my baby so much!"

"She lost her dog not long ago," Danny explained. "Hit-and-run! Can you believe that?"

Drew found himself unable to speak. He attempted to murmur some generic condolence, but his heart was racing and his lips wouldn't move.

"I have his picture," the girl said, scrolling through her phone. "Oh, Danny, that dog reminded me of my baby! Look!" She thrust her phone at Drew, who had decided that some form of Biblical revenge was being enacted on him. Dumbly he took the phone, prepared to see the black button eyes of little Patrick. Prepared to bow his head and submit to the wrath of God, yet at the same time scrambling for words to get him through the moment, to avoid implicating himself, to shut the damn girl up.

The picture on the tiny screen was of some spaniel-blend mutt, black and brown and droopy-eared. Drew barked out a laugh. "This doesn't look anything like that one!" he said.

"Dad." Danny looked embarrassed.

Kirstin took her phone back and gazed at her dead dog. "Bastard," she muttered.

And then Drew's own phone rang. His son was used to the constant attachments on his father; first beepers, then cell phones—a doctor is always on call—and now that everyone else was, too, there was no need to apologize or explain. Still, out of long habit, Drew forced his legs to work and stepped away to take the call. It was Maggie.

A horde of spandexed bicyclists rode by the Pannikin on 101, their shiny leggings glinting in the sun. A train roared by; Drew simply held the phone and waited. Two dogs on leashes got into a tussle, their owners shrieking their silly names at them as if they cared. A plane went by. A few feet away sat his son, with a girl Drew had or hadn't tried to screw. And here was Maggie, telling him that Adele was in the hospital.

"She didn't want me to call," Maggie was saying. "And frankly I didn't want to, but we thought we should let you know. She's fine."

"Does she want to talk to me?" Drew asked.

"Do you want to talk to him?" Maggie said. Then, "Not really. She's fine. We just wanted to let you know."

"I'd like to speak to her doctor."

"She said you'd say that. She said no, everything's under control. She doesn't want you to talk to him."

"Tell her . . ." Drew stood, holding the little phone, while the sky swirled around.

"What?" Maggie said. There was a murmuring, there was a conversation occurring in the hospital room in Canada where his wife lay, but Drew, standing on the grass in Leucadia, couldn't discern the words. His vision had blurred.

"She said to tell you she'll be back Saturday," Maggie said.

"Tell her . . . send her my love," Drew said.

"Sure, Drew." And then the phone went dead, and Drew stood on the grass that was shifting sneakily under his feet. He wondered if it was a mild earthquake. He felt he was going to vomit. He turned back to Danny and Kirstin, both of whom were sitting with their eyes closed, faces turned up toward the sun. He took a step back to them, or at least he thought he did. But instead a searing pain shot up his left arm, and he knew what that was, all right. How could he not have realized what was happening? He opened his mouth to say "Call 911!," but his mouth was pressed against the ground, it was full of grass and dirt, and all that came out was a low grunt, and then he was being turned over and people were shouting, and as his son's face loomed up in front of him he stared, mute, while the blue sky whirled and whipped him into its black heart.

Twenty-three

WHEN SHE HEARD HER NAME called she thought it was her mother, who had been dead for years. *What does she want?* she'd thought, burrowing deeper into her pillow. Then she heard a different voice. Adele, Adele. Why didn't they leave her alone? She was just starting to get warm after being so, so cold, she was finally starting to relax and was ready to sleep, and now they wanted her to get up. *Go away,* she thought. *Leave me alone.* She was worried about the math exam—she wasn't prepared—and she couldn't find her clothes. And then someone called her again, and it was Drew's mother; they'd fallen asleep after doing it in his room. They were going to get caught and she was going to lose the shapes. It was crucial that she not lose the shapes. They'd been drifting at her in a turquoise light, a pulsating, diffused light, teasing her with tricks of angles and dis- tance. But then she'd caught them; puffy and light, they were, frothy meringues that set where she placed them and fit together joyfully, each one issuing a symphonic sigh as it nestled into its place. Adele! Adele Gold! Adele! Present! she called, though she was naked and unprepared. Still, some hope flickered: she was good at math; she would cover herself.

Adele lay now in a small bed in a bright room, remembering bits of things, trying to push thoughts out of her head and retrieve the shapes.

She understood that she had been in danger, that she had been saved, that her life had somehow re-formed, but all she wanted was for the shapes not to go away. And then Maggie and Sylvia were there, and she managed to say what she needed to, but each word she spoke made the shapes more elusive, and then suddenly she had what she needed and she began to sketch. There was buzzing and nipping all around her, people hovering. She shook her head in response to all queries and focused only on the paper, eyes half closed as the shapes loomed and receded, her hand moving quickly, obediently. She heard Maggie tell someone to let her be, and then there was quiet, warmth, light, and as the shapes assembled on the paper she was suffused with a sense of well-being, a childlike trust that all would be well.

Then she was done, and the shapes were captured, and she was hungry. Maggie fed her some chicken noodle soup. Sylvia rubbed her feet. Both of them kept looking at her anxiously, chattering inanities. Adele was completely happy. "You can talk now, but not both at once," she joked.

"No, you," said Maggie. "Tell us everything."

"Let me just say right off that I am a horrible friend," Sylvia said. "I didn't believe it. I'm so sorry. I thought you'd bailed."

"Sylvia," Maggie said. "This is not about you, right this moment. Can we hold off on the unburdening? Let Adele talk."

"I'm so happy to be alive," Adele said. Sylvia sobbed and blew her nose. "I know it sounds corny, but I don't care. Right now I just feel so grateful."

"Adele, I am so, so sorry," Maggie said.

"It's not about you," Sylvia hissed.

"So, you want to know?" Adele scooted up a little, prompting the other two to leap up and plump pillows, rearrange blankets. They sat on either side of her, each holding a hand. On her lap was the sketchbook, at which they both cast furtive looks.

"I was scared. When I realized I was lost, I couldn't believe it. It seemed so stupid. And my umbrella was gone, and the rain was pouring down, and it got dark really fast and I just had no idea where I was, which way to go. The path disappeared. I walked to where I thought it was, but then I got all tangled up in the underbrush and when I tried to go back I didn't know which way I'd come. I was furious. I was yelling at the top of my lungs, every curse word I've ever heard. I tried to calm down, but I was cold and hungry and it felt like I was the last person left on earth.

"Then I found this little cave. It was the kind of place I'd have screamed at my kids not to go near. It felt like a palace to me. Just to sit down on dry ground, not have the rain beating down on me. I was so happy, for maybe two minutes, and then I realized I might actually die. If I didn't freeze to death something would eat me. And then I had a meltdown. Thinking about my life, Drew, the boys, everything I've done and everything I haven't. I cried so hard for so long I got a headache. Then I started to fall asleep, and just as I was going deep down I knew that if I let myself go, if I fell asleep, I would never wake up. And you know what? I didn't care. So, I'll die this way, I thought. Big deal. Let them find what's left of my body and ship it back to Drew; let him beat his breast for the rest of his days, for what he did to me."

Adele had been speaking slowly, looking from Maggie to Sylvia, who were leaning in, taking in every word. Now, all of a sudden, she burst out laughing. "It's all so silly!" she said. "So pointless! Really, the things we do to ourselves. I raised my boys to be good men; I used to think someday their wives would thank me. They'll do what they'll do. They'll live how they'll live. At least they wouldn't have lost their mother till they were out of the nest. Then, I was watching my funeral—everyone was back in the Bedford house, sitting shivah, and I wandered through the rooms of my house, that house I loved so much, and I kept finding rooms I hadn't known were there. Passageways leading to whole wings of secret places, wonderful places, big sunny rooms filled with beautiful things, windows looking out on vistas I'd never seen before. And I was full of this joyful sense of hope! Like this was a happiness meant for me. All along it had been stored in a box under a bed in one of those rooms I hadn't known existed. So then I figured, This must be death; this feeling. I must be going now. And then a really weird thing happened. I don't know if I can explain it; it was physical. Like I was dropped out of a plane. You know that feeling you get when you're dreaming you're falling? Only it wasn't quite like that, more like . . . I don't know, like a power surge went through me. It literally made me jump, it made me hit my head against the back of the stone I was leaning on. And then all of a sudden there I was again, just sitting in this hole in a rock in the pitch black and the pouring rain and the freezing cold. I was wide awake, and I knew that if I could stay that way eventually someone would come looking for me. I found a granola bar in my pocket—God it was delicious—and then I just focused on not falling asleep. I went through all the presidents and conjugated every French verb and tried to remember the names of every plant I planted in my garden in Bedford. Russian sage, sandcherry, witches'-broom, buddleia, nepeta, rugosa. I kept falling in and out. It got harder and harder to pull myself out, I was so tired. And so cold. And then, I don't know . . . at some point I guess I must have given up and fallen asleep, and I was having this dream, not like a normal dream but more like . . . I don't know, does this sound too weird for you? It was like I was being given something. These shapes."

Adele disengaged her hands and touched the sketchbook with her fingertips. "It was my house. It's already built. I watched it all come together: the foundation, the frame, the masonry . . . all the beautiful pieces coming together. It's all here." Adele opened the sketchbook to reveal a series of drawings, black lines with numbers and arrows, brusque indications of elevation, squiggles of stairways and balconies. It seemed to be shaped like a star, with what looked like a donut around the middle. "See," Adele said. "This is the great room, the common area. It will be two stories, with a kitchen and a living area on the ground floor and a studio upstairs—for yoga, or meditation, or whatever. Just an open room, like a tower, with circular glass windows all around. Filled with light, and views in every direction of the woods and the lake. These"—she indicated the rounded points of the star—"these are the individual spaces. Each one will be completely self-contained, with two bedrooms, a small living area, a kitchen, and a bath. And this"—indicating the donut—"this is a circle of water. There will be little bridges connecting each unit to the great room."

Adele looked at them, her face serene. "I'm going home," she said. "I'm going home, and I'm going to buy a piece of land—I know just where—and I'm going to build my house. It's already built, as I said. I just have to make it real. It's going to be a sanctuary. For me, and for my friends. We'll grow old there together, taking care of each other. Snow will fall and melt, cardinals will come and perch on the holly branches. The ground will freeze and thaw and bluebells and crocuses and lilies of the valley will appear. You think I'm crazy, don't you? I can see, you're looking at me like oh boy, Adele got her brain freeze-dried."

"No," Maggie said. "Actually, Del . . . I'm amazed. I'm even a little jealous."

"I don't want you to go back east!" Sylvia said.

"You can come. You can both come."

Sylvia dipped her head. Maggie shot her an exasperated glance and gave Adele a look fraught with meaning. Adele made a birdlike, inquisitive movement. "What?" she said. "What happened?"

"The divorce is off," Syl said. "He's sorry."

Adele nodded. "Good. He'll do it again, you know. As long as you can live with that, then good."

"Adele, you probably don't want to hear this, but we should call Drew," Maggie said. "He should know, don't you think?"

"Umm. You mean about the house?"

"No, sweetie, about your brush with death and the fact that you're in hospital!"

"*The* hospital," Syl said. "It's not England. Why do you make believe you're so la la English? 'Bloody hospital'!"

"Sylvia, you really need to fuck off, you know that? Just fuck fuck fuck all the way off."

"All the bloody way off," Syl said.

"I didn't die, though," Adele said. "I actually really didn't die. Why worry him?"

Maggie snorted. "I can't believe you're worried about worrying him."

"You know how he is. If I get a cold he thinks somehow he's failed."

"Adele, you do remember, don't you, what's happening? What he did?"

Adele smiled weakly. "I haven't gone barmy, Mags. Of course I remember."

Maggie thought she looked positively beatific, her head nestled in the snow-white pillows, her smile Mona Lisa–like. She suspected that despite Adele's protestations, something had addled her a little. *Please God let it not be permanent,* she thought.

"Do you forgive him?" Sylvia asked.

"Oh, he can rot in hell," Adele said. "But I do love him. He can come home and live in my sanctuary too, if he wants to. But I doubt he'll ever leave his beloved California."

"I don't think Beth will come back either," Syl said. "She loves New York."

"What's his cell number?" Maggie said. "I got the machine at the home number."

Adele told her. "Okay, I'm calling him," Maggie said. "Drew? Oh good, I'm glad you picked up. It's Maggie."

Bricks

❧

My love must be discriminate or fail to
bear its weight.

—Wendell Berry

Twenty-four

"Well, you didn't call me, either."

Maggie sat hunched in the passenger seat, gazing into the side mirror at the traffic on the 5, behind them. They had pulled into a parking space at Torrey Pines. Paul had turned off the engine and stared straight ahead at the beach.

"I called you several times. Your phone was off."

"I didn't get any messages."

"I didn't leave any. I thought you'd check and see that I'd called."

"You could have called the hotel if you really wanted to reach me."

"Come on, Maggie."

"I'm just saying."

They continued not looking at each other. The air was thick between them. Maggie had her feet up on the dash; he hated when she did that. She was waiting for him to tell her to take them down, but he didn't. Finally, he said, "So did you get everything out of your trip that you wanted to?"

"What's that supposed to mean?"

"It was a simple question."

"It was a bust, okay? Does that make you happy?"

More dead space floated between them, and then he said, "An expensive bust."

"I paid for it with my own money!" She snapped out the words, overenunciating.

"'My *own* money,'" he mimicked.

They had driven here to go for a walk, but then Paul had been unable to resist needling her about not calling. He had been a trouper the night before, picking them up at the airport, delivering Syl and Adele to their respective homes. He'd been great with Adele; solicitous and thoughtful. He filled her in on his earlier visit with Drew, offered to pick her up and take her to the hospital in the morning. She'd declined, saying she'd go later in the day, after she'd had a good night's sleep in her own bed. Paul questioned that, back in the car. Neither Sylvia nor Maggie responded. Each of them had simply gazed silently out the windows of the car, watching the familiar sights of the Coast Highway, lost in their separate musings.

After dropping Syl off, Paul reached for Maggie and pulled her into a kiss. She'd kissed him back without enthusiasm, drawn away and patted his thigh. "I'm exhausted," she'd said. He'd responded by drawing her hand onto his hard-on and murmuring, "I can't wait to be in bed with you."

Maggie had stayed in the bathroom as long as she could. She hadn't expected this inner collision. Of course she'd been nervous about seeing Paul. She'd been grateful for his kindness. That was Paul; he always came through. Syl and Adele had hugged him with more warmth than Maggie could muster, she'd noticed. "My husband," she'd repeated to herself in the car, while he chatted with her friends. "He is my husband." When she'd finally slipped into bed he was all over her with an urgency that she simply couldn't respond to. When he finished she was relieved. When he tried to arouse her again she pretended to be asleep.

And now here they were, sitting in a car at Torrey Pines. The reentry had not gone smoothly. The molecules hadn't scrambled properly, or something. The brown hills in the side-view mirror looked distant and foreign; the cars whizzing by on the 101 jarred her. She thought of the silence in the Kootenays, how you could hear the tiny rustlings of forest creatures just by standing still. The night before they'd left she'd gone outside and stood, alone, staring up at the moonless heavens, and a shooting star had sped across the sky. At first she'd thought it was a plane, or a UFO. It was so fast. If she'd blinked, or blown her nose, or looked over her shoulder at the lights in the dining room, she'd have missed it.

After she'd turned from Paul last night, she'd thought of Mitch. Not like she had all those other nights, when he was her secret, her hiding place. She'd thought of him with grief. Lying there in the dark with her husband beside her, she'd felt utterly, desolately alone. Mitch would never again offer his vaporous succor; that had been spoiled. She'd fallen into a bone-weary sleep and woken from dreams of slithery moisture, distant pin-pricks of light, flashes of yellow in a tangled wood. Paul had brought her a cup of coffee, suggested a walk. He had been uncharacteristically chatty, perhaps in response to her uncharacteristic reticence. While scrambling eggs he told her that Josh had decided not to come home for Thanksgiving. He'd been invited to Baja with friends and hoped they'd understand. It would be their first Thanksgiving without him. For years Maggie had orga-nized an excursion to a women's shelter in Calexico on Thanksgiving, drag-ging Josh and Paul along to help ladle out gravy and mashed potatoes. She didn't want to go without Josh. And yet she couldn't begrudge him wanting to go surfing with his friends. He was grown up. He was pretty well gone. She had better get used to it being just the two of them; her and Paul. Paul, her husband, who was staring out the window, sucking on his back molar, saying, nastily, "My *own* money."

"Well, it is," she said. "I work for it. I can spend it how I like."

"I realize you've been off in the woods," he said, "but are you at all aware of what's going on in the world? Have you bothered to read a paper or watch the news?"

"I heard about the Ponzi thing, if that's what you mean. Poor Adele."

"Poor Adele?"

"Yeah, she said he had her money. Her house money."

"Really? I didn't know that." Paul looked full on at her; for a moment they were united in gossip.

"She said that's probably why Drew had a heart attack. She said they'd had terrible fights about it. She never wanted him to play with that money. That's her house money."

"Geez," Paul said. Then, pulling his guard back up, added, "Well, it's not just him. The whole economy has tanked. Everyone's affected."

"Not us, though, right?" Maggie squirmed, cracked the window open. Money, again. How she hated it; hated discussing it, hated thinking about it. And she hated the fact that Paul was so preoccupied with it, lately, going online to check out this or that stock or uptick or downturn. She had never understood why, with all his interest in the market and his degrees from Columbia and Berkeley, he had stayed in middle management. Not that it bothered her, having less money than her friends. She took a certain pride in that, and though Paul's lack of ambition puzzled her, she respected him for it, too. It was certainly preferable to being a workaholic, one of those guys who worshipped at the altar of greed. She liked working; their house was just fine; and she wouldn't have wanted all the stuff Sylvia seemed to need to make her happy. Why had Paul all of a sudden gotten so materialistic? She just wanted to walk, wanted the roar of the sea to drown out any chance of conversation.

"It boggles the mind, really, how naive you are," Paul was saying. "Of course it affects us! It affects the whole world! It's global. You've heard of the global economy, Maggie? The global economy is melting down."

"Well, excuse me, but I don't get it. How can money just disappear? What's a Ponzi scheme, anyway? Not that I care. And you know what, Paul? I don't care about the global economy, either. Let everybody go bankrupt. I say good. I say tear down all the malls and put the farms back, stop producing crap to supposedly make our lives better, crap that just ends up in toxic landfills, and start growing food so we don't have to buy it from China!"

"Ever the old hippie."

"Damn right, and pardon me for not giving a shit about all those people who have to auction off their artwork or whatever because their precious money disappeared. If they weren't so greedy in the first place it wouldn't have happened."

"Like Adele and Drew?"

"Drew *was* being greedy! Adele told him to just put it in the bank, but no, he had to double it, triple it, quadruple it. Drew is an asshole, and now Adele can't build her house. That's all she ever wanted, all she ever asked. What the hell, Paul? A little house, a sanctuary, where people could live in peace and grow their own food and take care of each other, that's not enough?"

"I don't disagree."

"And why are you still in that stupid job when they haven't given you a raise in two years? What do you care about the design of oil caps or whatever the hell it is you're designing?"

"I'm lucky to have the job, Maggie! That's what I mean. Your head is in the sand. You don't get it. The country is falling apart. Banks are closing, the mortgage industry has collapsed in on itself, we're in trillions of dollars of debt, we're at war with a country that did nothing to us, the bottom has fallen out of the market! Forty percent, Maggie! That's how far we're down. Forty percent! Do you have any idea how much money that is?"

Maggie was impressed. She'd never heard Paul so impassioned. Despite herself, she cheered up.

"The country's okay, Paul. Don't worry. Obama's in. It's the best thing that's ever happened. He'll fix it. First he has to clean up the mess Bush left; that's what this is all about."

"God, you're naive!" Paul sunk his head onto the steering wheel.

"You need to quit that job. Now's the perfect time. You need to go somewhere where they appreciate you. You're overqualified for that job."

Paul slammed the back of his hand onto the dashboard, so hard that Maggie levitated off her seat for a second. "No, I'm not," he spat.

"You are too!" The hairs had risen on Maggie's arms. She tensed, alert as a cat. "Degrees from Columbia and Berkeley? Designing oil thingys? I've never understood it."

Paul made a sound that was almost like a sob. Maggie waited for him to sneeze or something. "You okay, Paul?"

"I have to tell you something."

Here it was.

Maggie looked at her husband, curled over the steering wheel, his freckled hands clenched, the knuckles white. A cloud of extraordinary calm had settled over her. She felt light, strong. The feeling baffled her, but there it was. Whatever would happen would happen. The center was collapsing and look, the sun was streaming in long fingers through the opalescent clouds, the waves were swelling and breaking and ebbing, swelling and breaking and ebbing. She had been waiting for this moment, she realized, for years.

"Please," said Paul, in a muffled voice, "don't hate me."

"I won't hate you." A *door*, Maggie thought, girding her loins.

"I haven't been entirely honest with you."

"It's all right, Paul. Just say it."

"You keep talking about my degrees. How overqualified I am."

"You are."

"I'm not."

"Okay, you're not. Why not?" Maggie gave the dashboard a little kick, impatient for the big revelation.

"What year did I graduate from Columbia?"

"I don't know. Sixty-eight?"

"Right. Sixty-eight. What happened in sixty-eight?"

"I don't know."

"Sure you do. If anybody knows, you do."

"The Chicago convention?"

"What else?"

"I don't know, Paul. Goddammit, stop with the guessing games and just say what you have to say!"

"Sixty-eight was the year the students took over the administration offices at Columbia. Mark Rudd, remember?"

Maggie nodded. "Right. They were protesting the gym. It turned into a big racial thing."

"They occupied the offices for four days. Some of the records were tampered with, went missing, or were destroyed. There was no way to check on any of it. No backup discs, no computers. It was April; the school year was almost over. They decided to give everybody passing grades for that semester. It was chaos. Anyone could claim they'd graduated, that they'd earned a degree."

Maggie, who had been expecting something entirely different, simply stared at him. "I don't understand," she said.

"I had taken a few courses, that was all. I wasn't even a full-time student."

"But then how did you get into Berkeley?"

"'Get into' Berkeley? I didn't 'get into' Berkeley. I showed up and told them I had a degree from Columbia and wanted to enroll in graduate school. I told them my transcripts had been ransacked during the student occupation. They said I could matriculate classes until they were able to get information from my professors at Columbia."

"You're telling me you didn't graduate?"

"I have a high school diploma and some college credits, that's all."

"But why would you lie?"

"I don't know."

"But wait, why didn't you just go ahead and finish the degree at Berkeley?"

Paul looked at her. She stared back, stunned. "Me," she said.

After the abortion, they'd been inseparable. She'd stayed in his bed, in his attic room, and he'd nursed her and catered to her and eventually made love to her. She remembered now that she'd wondered about his classes. He'd make breakfast and go out for a while and then come back with lunch, and she'd say, "Don't you have classes?" And he'd say it was an independent study or he was done for that semester, and she'd never questioned him.

"Was I that needy?" she asked him now.

"It seemed best not to leave you alone for too long," he said.

"I was a wreck."

"You were . . . fragile."

"So you bagged your classes. But you told me you were done! Why lie? I wouldn't have cared!"

"I wanted to be good enough for you," he said.

"Funny. No one cares about college that much anymore. If you're good at something or can come up with some new Internet idea you're a millionaire. Who cares whether you have a degree or not."

"I'm not that good at anything. I'm no genius, and I'm no millionaire."

"So . . . at work . . . they think you have all these degrees."

"I don't know what they think. Hopefully they think, Oh, there's Paul, he knows what he's doing. He's good at his job, let's keep him."

"You must be good at it, after all these years."

"I am. I just hope I don't become obsolete. See, what I'm trying to tell you, Mag, is we're vulnerable. I need you to understand that. I've been saving for years, and I'm careful with my trades, and we don't live beyond our means. But forty percent is gone, anyway. And that's just our personal savings. That doesn't take into account my pension, which has also been gutted."

Maggie heard fear in his voice. She heard the word *vulnerable*. He was looking at her now, his face raw and pleading. "I thought you were going to tell me something else. That there was another woman, or . . . I don't know, something else," she said.

"There is no other woman. There's never been any other woman for me. Just you."

"So basically what you're telling me, Paul, is that the ground level of our marriage is a lie. I'm not saying our marriage is based on a lie, because really it is such a stupid lie, and it has nothing to do with anything really except for its own truth, which is that you have let us live with this lie for our entire life together."

"And you, on the other hand, have been a paradigm of honesty."

"I've never lied to you!" Maggie, attempting to digest Paul's confession as well as acclimate herself to the unexpected position of moral superiority, was hastily shoving her own guilt off the stage. *Till now,* she could have said, but she was preoccupied with the role of offendee, and mentally scrambled to calculate if his dishonesty could cancel out hers. In any event, she couldn't deny the hopefulness she felt, the sudden mitigation of guilt. But Paul snorted.

"Really," he said, drenching the word in sarcasm.

"What's that supposed to mean?"

"You've been nothing but up front and innocent, open book. Uh-huh."

"Well, I mean fundamentally. I mean, I certainly haven't told you every single little thing. God, who would want that? I mean, would you really want me to be completely honest with you about every single time I've wanted to kill you, for example? I don't think so."

"You've wanted to kill me?"

"I mean, not literally. You know what I mean. My point is, Paul, you've had this big fat lie between us. You can't accuse me of the same thing."

"Sorry," said Paul, "I'm not buying it."

"What, so now you're accusing me of lying to you?"

Paul rubbed his face vigorously, as though he'd suddenly broken out in a rash. "Maggie," he said, "we both know what I'm talking about."

"Oh, do we?" Maggie put her hand to her chest to keep her heart still. It was a gesture Paul knew well, and he knew what it meant. She had no idea how well he knew her, how well he could read her. She was guilty as hell about something; he knew it the minute he saw her at the airport. He guessed it had something to do with her keeping her phone off, not calling. She was trying to distance herself, to keep him out. It was the thing he most dreaded, the thing he had always had to be most vigilant about, with her. He had imagined the three of them, over the last week, reveling in man-bashing. Adele and Sylvia picking apart Carl and Drew like carrion with fresh kill, and Maggie—squirmy, never-quite-satisfied Maggie—only too susceptible to the invitation. He imagined her joining in, at first hesitantly, a little flicker of loyalty tugging at her, then leaping into the ring and feasting on his faults. He had suspected that would be the agenda for the week; he had steeled himself against a certain coldness in her reentry. But her distance had been too great to traverse, even in bed, where he usually leapt over her chasms with ease. And then this morning, when he'd told her about Josh not coming home for Thanksgiving, she'd fallen apart, and here he had thought it would be nice for them to be alone together, just the two of them. "I thought it would be nice to have you all to myself," he'd said, and she had gaped at him as if he'd suggested something obscene. That had stung. And looming over it all was the gut-stomping statement from his brokerage firm. He was careful, so careful, he played it so safe, and still there were those numbers on the page that he couldn't comprehend, 40 percent less than what used to be there. The last thing he needed was a reminder about how fucking smart and accomplished and overqualified he was with those bogus degrees, those stupid fucking seals of approval that he thought meant so much to her. And now she tells him it was stupid; the truth wouldn't have mattered. Now she bristles at his dishonesty.

"I always knew you didn't feel the same way about me that I did about you," he said. Might as well spill it all. What difference did it make, if you could work so hard, try so hard, and still have it all come to nothing? He was tired. Someone was flying a kite on the beach; it swooped up and ducked down, tails fluttering behind it. He wanted to reach up and grasp it, let it fly him away. This was an unfamiliar feeling for him, this sense of loosening. He let it take him, let it spiral like the kite. "I thought I could change that," he continued. "If I was a good enough husband, a good enough lover, a good enough father. If I was a person with all these degrees. If I even out the playing field, I thought, she'll come around. Hasn't happened, though."

"What do you mean, it hasn't happened?"

"Come on, Maggie. Please."

"Please what? What exactly are you saying? I'm still reeling from this news, Paul. I'm thinking about all the times I bragged about your academic accomplishments, I'm thinking about . . . about Josh, for God's sake! How are you going to handle *that*?"

"I'm going to tell him the truth. I've already thought about it."

Maggie sank her face in her hands. "Oh, dear God. Do you really think you need to do that?"

"Yes, I do. I'm sick of this act. You're the one who always made a big deal about it. I just kept hoping it would go away."

"So you really thought I wouldn't have married you if you weren't the overachiever you pretended to be? That doesn't say much for me, Paul."

"No, I think you still would have married me. That wasn't it."

Maggie reached across him and turned the key to start the engine; pressed the window button down to get some air. "What was 'it,' then?" She sighed.

"You're going to make me say his name?"

And now the hair on the back of her neck stood up, blood rushed to her face. Her ears pounded.

"Mitch," he said. "Okay? Mitch. Big Berkeley radical hot shot. Helluva guy; I can sure understand why you've kept the home fires burning for him all these years." He spoke so bitterly that Maggie instinctively clapped her hands to her ears.

"Don't," she said. "Please, Paul. Don't do this."

He reached for her and roughly pulled her hands away from her head. "No, I'm sick of it. Let's get it out in the open, once and for all."

Now it was Maggie's turn to rub her face, as it contorted like a bawling child's. Never had she and Paul talked this way before. Never had she seen him so unguarded. What did he know? Was he just guessing? How could he possibly know—not even Sylvia and Adele were aware of what had happened. They didn't even know of the connection. Had Paul been *spying* on her, somehow? They'd never discussed Mitch, not since their first nights together. Then, of course, she had cried in his arms, poured her heart out to him. She'd never dreamt he was her future husband. And then they'd never mentioned Mitch again; his name had never been uttered between them. She'd been grateful for Paul's sensitivity. For his reticence. It was one of the many qualities that made him so opposite from Mitch.

A couple stepped in front of their car, maneuvering their way down to the beach. They both glanced in the window, casually, at Maggie and Paul. So obvious what was going on, Maggie thought. A breakup. She saw the couple exchange a look and grasp each other's hands. We'll never do that, they seemed to be promising. So all these years, *all* these years, Paul had felt Mitch between them. Her secret wasn't a secret at all. And now the infidelity of the heart had become infidelity of the flesh, and it was she who had dealt the blow, she who had thrown the poison into the reservoir.

Unbelievable that he had let her brag, all these years, about his education! How she had brought it out like a medal, like a blue ribbon, to flaunt in company. When people would start talking about business, when this or that guy would go off about his latest venture or how they were going to spend his bonus and she'd been ashamed, ashamed of her prickling sense of inadequacy about her husband's mid-level job, how she'd opened her mouth and crowed! Caw, caw, she'd crowed, Columbia and Berkeley! Not only is my husband better educated than you, but he's morally superior, because he's not driven by greed, he's not frothing at the mouth like you for bigger, better, more!

Crowed like a scavenging raven, she had, snatching at little glittering things to hoard in her nest. Hypocrite! And how she judged, how she sat in lofty judgment over everyone whose shortcomings she appointed herself the tallier of. Hypocrite! The worst epitaph of her generation. She had hurled it at her mother countless times. Her mother had quoted Rochefoucauld: "Hypocrisy is the homage that vice pays to virtue." Maggie had never actually understood what that meant. An excuse, a justification. There's a place for it in the civilized world, her mother had seemed to imply. But not in *Maggie's* life, not in the way *she* had chosen to live. She had been so grateful to Paul. When he had spoken of love, she had been careless with the word. What did she know? Was *love* the searing agony she'd had inflicted on her by Mitch's betrayal? Or the unprecedented safety and security she felt with Paul? "I love you," she had told him, and she meant it, but she also knew it wasn't the way she felt about Mitch. That was something else, something best kept under a rock, something she could peek at through the years, when life got bland. She hadn't thought of it as hypocrisy. She hadn't thought of her pride in Paul's degrees as hypocrisy. Apparently she hadn't thought at all. She pushed her heart back under the skin, blew her nose with the clean white handkerchief Paul pressed into her hand.

"The way I felt about him was different from the way I felt about you," she said.

"I know."

"It was all tangled up in that time. Youth. All that. The excitement."

"I know that."

"But I love you." She wiped her eyes with her sleeve. It didn't help. He reached over and dabbed at her cheeks, which made her sob. "I'm sorry, Paul. I'm so sorry if you felt like I didn't love you. I did love you. I do love you."

"I don't know if you'll ever be satisfied with me."

"Stop saying that! Okay, you're right—I did care. I did use those degrees to . . . to justify you, Paul."

"I know."

"You're right. The lie did matter. I don't know how it would have been different if . . . if I'd known the truth. But I can see that you . . . why you did it."

"I wanted to deserve you."

"What about me? What about me deserving you?"

Paul took her face in his hands and kissed her cheeks where the tears were running. "I just loved you. I just knew I wanted you. I would have said anything."

"You are a much better man than I deserve." Maggie looked at him, his large body folded into the driver's seat, his pale skin, the roughness of his fingers. He hadn't shaved, and the effect wasn't so much ruggedly handsome as hastily disheveled. He hadn't shaved because he'd been busy making her breakfast and loading the dishwasher while she showered. He looked uncomfortable in his skin. It was so unfair. And all her fault. She wondered if it would be possible to tally up the number of little, daily sacrifices he had made over the years to keep up his image in front of her.

She wondered how many years it would take to make it up to him.

"Does that mean you forgive me?" he said.

"Forgive you?" Maggie laughed bitterly. "Sure. All is forgiven. Do you forgive me?"

"There's nothing to forgive."

"We haven't been honest with each other."

He nodded. Looked away from her, at a kite that was flapping in the air. "Do you want to walk?" he said.

Maggie looked at him sharply, misinterpreting. Then she saw that he meant here, on the beach, with him. Just the two of them, a middle-aged couple, hiking Torrey Pines on a Sunday afternoon.

She bowed her head, staring at her lap. This man next to her, her husband, had humbled her. He had never been anything but earnest and steadfast in his commitment and love to her. He had been a loving, responsible father to their son. Her mother, she reflected, had been widowed by the time she was the age Maggie was now. She'd honed her eccentricities and lived and breathed academia, in all its cutthroat scrabbling. Maggie had assumed a similar kind of life would be her lot. Not in academia, clearly, but some form of single-minded, self-sacrificing service. She had never expected to be loved. At what point had she scribbled, in invisible ink, these guidelines for herself? What rock-solid conviction had lodged itself in her heart, accepting the role of the lost, unwanted, misunderstood spirit? How transparent was the cloak of tragedy she had assumed, that moth-eaten old costume of mourning for the Great Love who had dumped her. All those times she'd bragged about Paul, about his degrees and his brilliance, she'd been apologizing for him. For her choice.

A sudden vision of Gray Braid intruded, stepping out of some yurt with Mitch's babies slung in papooses from her hips. This was what she had been mourning? What a waste of days! The shame and regret was almost physically painful.

And now he wanted to go for a walk on the beach with her. Then, because it was Sunday, maybe they'd go out for an early dinner somewhere, La Jolla, perhaps, and watch the sunset. It was an idea of such beauty, such simplicity and clarity, such elegance and heart-swelling generosity that she sat still with it for a moment, savoring the way it washed over her. Letting it cool the burning shame. Such gratitude, she felt. The feeling itself was a prayer.

She reached for his hand. Felt his skin against hers, the familiarity of the shapes of his fingers. "Yes," she said. "Yes, my love. Let's walk."

Twenty-five

❧

ADELE COULDN'T TAKE HER EYES off her boys. All together; a rarity these days. Three young men! How had it happened? The diaper days were still so vivid, it was like some kind of fast-forward to see them towering over her.

They were in the hospital cafeteria, having lunch. A jocular relief had settled among them; the boys were full of teasing innuendos and playful physicality. Danny took off Noah's baseball cap and whacked him in the head with it. Jake, sporting a fresh tattoo on his wrist, kept stabbing Danny's hand with a plastic fork.

Adele watched Danny with particular scrutiny. Of the three, he was the closest to his father. Jake had been her first, and they shared a special devotion. Noah, the baby, had been born into a raucous, preexisting society, and, like a family pet, loved everyone cheerfully and indiscriminately. But Danny had been Drew's boy from the first. In the long, early years of Drew's internship, when whole days would go by without the boys catching a glimpse of their father, Danny trained himself to wake to the sound of the car wheels on the gravel drive, and would bound out of bed to greet his exhausted father, even though he knew all he'd get would be a quick hug and an admonishment to go back to bed.

On the flight back to San Diego, Adele's thoughts had lingered the longest on her middle son. Apparently he had handled the whole thing with aplomb. It had been Danny who had called her, he who had ridden in the ambulance with Drew, he who had dealt with the paperwork, the formalities, the phone calls. "I'm glad I was the one," he had told her. "If I'd been the one getting the call I'd have freaked. At least I got to be with him."

Who'd have thought? Danny was the middle child: charming, social, indifferent to ambition. Where Jake had been full of nervous intensity and Noah effortlessly capable, Danny had repeatedly messed up, charming his way out of any number of social and academic crises. And yet here he was, this big man, explaining the regimen the doctors had outlined for his father, warning Adele about the necessity for strictness against Drew's inevitable revolt.

"You know he's going to say he's fine, he's going to throw all these technical terms around, he's going to be all, like, 'Excuse me, who's the doctor around here?' And you're just going to have to stay tough, Mom. You're gonna have to clamp down."

The boys, of course, knew nothing about what had transpired between their parents. Or of what she had just been through. And she doubted if they'd made any connection between the Ponzi scheme in the news and their own inheritance. They'd wanted to pick her up at the airport last night and bring her straight to the hospital, and when she'd demurred, pleading exhaustion and maybe a cold coming on, Danny's voice had gone cold. Paul, too, had acted like she was some kind of bad wife, not rushing to Drew's bedside. Everybody thinks they know everything, she'd thought, and she thought it again now, as she chewed indifferently on her soggy tuna sandwich and nodded obediently at her son.

They had just left Drew in his room, after visiting with him for about an hour. Having just crawled out of a hospital bed herself, it was surrealistic to find herself sitting there, whole and out of danger, surrounded by the family she'd feared she'd never see again. Drew was lying in the hospital bed hooked up to a multitude of beeping, dripping, humming machines. Her first sight of him brought a rush of relief and reassurance. In the jumbled hours between leaving Canada and being here, there had been such an onslaught of things to process that she had gone numb. But now there was some semblance of normality again: they were all together; no one had died. Then, as if released from having to contemplate the worst, she simply observed her mind with a kind of detached interest as it flashed back and forth between the wide, gleaming corridors of Scripps and the earnest little clinic in the Kootenays. With the hum of the boys' voices lulling her, she admired the big window in his private room, sunlight streaming through it, green, sweeping lawns below, comparing it with the windowless little nook she had occupied. Yet it had felt like paradise to her; that soft, clean bed. Drew did not appear to be in paradise, though as a big-shot doctor he was clearly getting special treatment. He looked diminished. His head, on the white pillows, looked like a little brown nut. There was an effeminacy to his hospital gown. He looked like a little man stripped of his powerful cloak. Adele had never seen her husband in a hospital bed before. She'd never thought of him as a smallish man. Pale, too, as if his tan were being drained. He looked awful. She realized that it would not be completely crazy to wonder if he had AIDS. "How many women?" she had demanded, after finding the damning box of condoms. "I don't know," he had said. "I don't know." He had lost count.

Earlier that morning, Adele had been having her coffee in the empty condo, having woken from a deep, dreamless sleep and taken a long shower in her own cheerful bathroom. It had rained overnight and was still overcast. Three times the phone rang, three times she let the machine pick up. The first time it was Jake, assuming she was either still asleep or in the shower, asking her to call him so they could make plans to rendezvous at the hospital. The next two calls were from Maggie and Syl, respectively, "just checking in," in cheerful voices meant to camouflage their fear that she had brain hemorrhaged in the night, or thrown herself from the balcony in despair over her imploded life. The doctor who had attended her in Canada had treated the whole thing as if it were a routine sprained ankle or something, chuckling as he signed her release papers about not getting lost on her way back to the airport. Once she'd been given an IV and had a nice warm sleep she was good as new. Perhaps she had stirred up alarm by sharing her drawings of the house with Maggie and Sylvia. She

should have kept the lovely visions to herself. How could she have expected anyone to understand? Then someday they'd stand there looking
at the real house, and maybe then she'd tell them where it had come from.
She was touched by their solicitude, but loath to talk to anyone. The solitude and quiet of the empty rooms had filled her like medicinal ether; the
jumble of shocks she had endured over the last week began to untangle. It
had been a cluster fuck, for sure, but now each event separated itself and
stood alone, ready to be acknowledged for what it was rather than as just
another wave of woe. At the airport in Canada, Maggie and Syl had hovered, getting her Starbucks, finding her a seat in the waiting area, treating
her like some kind of invalid. TV screens and newspapers all shrieked with
news of the Ponzi scheme, but she hadn't been paying much attention, until
suddenly she heard his name. The old Adele would have hurled something.

The old Adele would have rent her clothes in the marketplace, bewail-
ing her fate. As it was, she had frozen. Riveted on the nearest screen, she
watched the man, whom she had never seen, being herded through crowds
of clamoring reporters. The implications of what she was witnessing were
sudden and incontestable: one minute she was sitting there dreaming of her
house, the next minute she watched it disappear. She had fought bitterly
with Drew, she had begged him to reconsider, she had called him names.
Just put it in the bank! she had begged. Keep my house money safe! But
somewhere along the line Drew had caught the fever. He had to get more,
more, more, and she was just a housewife and didn't understand what he, a
big important doctor, knew: money begets money if you're one of the smart
ones. And now here was the smartest one of all being defiled in the marketplace; a thief, a swindler. And among his irretrievable loot was her house
money.

Some flicker of self-preservation helped her push the horror aside and
focus her thoughts on the immediate. On her husband in the hospital. On
her meshugena son, suddenly thrust into adulthood. Once home, she'd
fallen into bed, into that merciful sleep. Now, in the serene, private morning, she was surprised to find that the rage she'd expected to rear up hadn't.
She was surprised to realize that it was lovely, being home. Not real Home,
not Bedford, but here, in this place that had inadvertently, behind her

back, become home. Adele sipped her coffee and couldn't believe how good it tasted. It was the same brand they always used, brewed the same way, but it was as if she were discovering fire, or auditioning for a commercial. She knew she was behaving as if she were on *Candid Camera*, closing her eyes and shuddering with pleasure, inhaling deeply, drawing the liquid in as if it had been handed to her by Zeus. She was amused at herself, but she couldn't help it. It was just the most delicious, satisfying thing imaginable. She wrapped her hands around her plain white Pottery Barn mug and was astonished by the genius of its design. It held hot liquid! It warmed her hands! It curved beautifully, sensually, and its rim was smooth on her lips. In the shower, she had lathered her hair, massaging her scalp and swooning at the sensation of the hot water, the texture and scent of the soap, the fat, white, fragrant towel she dried herself with. As she smoothed lotion onto her legs she marveled at her skin. How extraordinary skin was, holding in all those muscles and bones and blood!

After breakfast, she'd done an uncharacteristic thing: gone to the beach. Adele was not a beach person. Adele was a city person, a Westchester County person. She didn't swim in the ocean, and she didn't like sand. Once, at a beach picnic Maggie had roped them all into, Drew had brought a DustBuster to keep her blanket sand-free, which everyone had found hilarious.

But now Adele got the urge to go to the beach, even though she didn't like beaches and even though it wasn't even a very nice day, and she followed her urge because she was in a State. That's what she told herself: I'm in some kind of a State. She figured it was a state of relief, which couldn't be much of a surprise, as she had just eluded death. She knew she was experiencing some kind of heightened sense of awareness, because of the Disney-esque way her surroundings were behaving. She half expected the coffee mug to sprout legs and start dancing, the bottles and jars on the glass shelf above the bathroom sink to burst into song.

So she went to the beach, and it was chilly and not all that pleasant, but as she was standing on the bluff overlook at the top of the stairs at South Ponto, gazing through the mist at the slick black-suited surfers bobbing in the waves, at the vague outline of the Oceanside pier to the north, at the

Batiquitos Lagoon to the east, past the little toy cars on the 5 to the mountains beyond, long fingers of sunlight reached through the gloom and cast an incandescent glow over the landscape. Adele remembered, then, how she'd wanted to be a painter when she was a girl. How she'd always doodled and crayoned, how she'd linger in the toy store over the paint sets, falling in love with the turquoises and vermilions. Her fourth-grade teacher, Mrs. Hiller—how funny that she should pop into her head, after all these years!—had been the first to tell her that she had talent. She remembered how special she'd felt after that, how she cradled this gift she'd been given. And suddenly, she recalled with vivid clarity a long-forgotten day— sometime around her twelfth birthday—when her mother had taken her to the Metropolitan Museum to see a Canaletto exhibit. They had walked together from painting to painting, and Adele had looked into the pictures at the golden light. She'd stared at the tiny people assembled on the bridges and the flats, at the green of the water and the blue of the sky. It had taken her breath away, she recalled; she had fallen in love. Her mother had bought her a watercolor set and she'd spent a whole summer trying to paint the light as she'd seen it in those paintings. She'd used up the set and then taken up riding and then met her first boyfriend and what with one thing and another hadn't thought much about painting again. During her senior year of high school, a famous architect had visited her school on career day and encouraged her when she showed him some sketches she'd thrown together. After that it all seemed to fall into place. She'd wandered the city with new eyes, loving the light, the shapes, the angles.

She was mulling this when the sun finally burned off the clouds and a rainbow appeared. It was immense, arching from east to west, its pearly greens and lavenders shimmering against the translucent blue sky. Adele, in her State, gasped aloud. She stood, riveted, while the rainbow faded, seemed to evaporate, and then reappeared. And then again faded, vanished, reappeared. The clouds were threads of mist gathering to veil the colors in gray; the rainbow a glimmering insistence, melting the clouds with its brilliance. Transfixed, Adele stood gaping as a spandexed "boot camp" from Frog's Gym arrived and began running up and down the stairs. "Cool rainbow!" someone called, and Adele was jostled out of her reverie. But as she walked back, she wondered if she might be about to have her own heart attack. She felt something expanding inside her ribs, a swelling sense of euphoria. Was this how Drew had felt, right before he toppled? She'd been secretly disappointed by the absence, in her own case, of any of those near-death experiences you hear about. There'd been no quick reel of her whole life spooling out, no white light, no music or sense of homecoming. Just those lovely shapes, that blissful vision of her house. Had that been a near-death experience? What she was feeling now felt more like one. She had to stop walking, so intensely did she feel something going on inside her.

Adele had always referred to herself as a cultural Jew. She had been raised with the Ethical Culture Society as a moral yardstick. Drew had been determined to bar mitzvah the boys, so they'd joined a shul and observed the High Holidays, but Adele had always taken pride in her intellectual approach to religion. It was necessary to maintain order, she understood: put fear of the wrath of God in the hearts of men and they'll be motivated to stay in line. But for the intelligentsia, for those who had the intellect to handle it, the God stuff was metaphorical. The moral compass was within. The rules were just and correct, but when you were done you were done. So why had she felt cheated, rather than vindicated, when she could report no white light enshrouding her as she'd begun to slip away?

And now she was having this acid trip over a rainbow, as if it were the first she'd ever seen, which of course it wasn't. But it was the first she'd seen since she'd almost died. And now it came to her, here it was: at Noah's bar mitzvah, the rabbi had engaged the congregation in an exploration of the meaning of the covenant. Adele had been distracted, dizzy with pride at Noah's exemplary reading of the Hebrew, preoccupied with her mental checklist of the party to follow. She remembered wishing they would shut up already about the covenant. "Does it have to be so Talmudic?" she had whispered to Drew, who kept raising his hand to chime in with his insights. "It's all about promise," he kept saying. They had all chuckled about the pot of gold, the leprechauns, the vernacular symbolism the rainbow had assumed. "It is the arc of the covenant," the rabbi had repeated. The "ahk of the covuhnant." It was a promise.

Adele's skin prickled as she looked over to where the rainbow had been. What if it's still there? What if it's always there, she wondered, but we only get to see glimpses of it? People used to think the moon disappeared, but it's always there. It's just on the other side of the world, until we come back to it.

Adele glanced suspiciously at the split-rail fence, wondering if it would attempt to animate itself as her cup and bottles had. And damned if she didn't see, looking at its weathered surface, the living trees from whence these posts had come. Trees like those in the forest where she'd wandered, dropping pine needles to cushion the path, spreading their leaves to catch the rain.

This is ridiculous, she thought. Is this going to last forever? Maybe something did go awry in my brain. She'd seen the looks Maggie and Syl had exchanged. She knew she'd had hypothermia—the doctor had explained it all to her, though she didn't remember much of what he'd said. She'd have to do some research. Oddly, her skin looked great. Apparently it had looked like a huge diaper rash when they'd found her, but now it was smooth and sort of glowed.

And this feeling, this breathlessness, this swelling—its name suddenly floated up: joy. Joy. Tears sprang to her eyes; she was buoyant with gratitude. She had lifted her face to the now bright sun, felt its warmth radiate through her. "I'm alive," she had breathed. "I'm alive. Thank you."

⇜

And now she was sitting in the cafeteria with her beloveds. Outside, the palm trees stood still in the breezeless San Diego afternoon, no trace of the rainbow in the cloudless sky. Noah was rubbing her back. Jake, on her other side, was stroking her fingers, a gesture between them since babyhood. "What do you think, Mom?" Danny was saying.

"Think? About what?"

"We're saying you and Dad should go somewhere when he gets better. Take a nice long vacation, a cruise or something. You should start planning. It would be good for him. You too. Go somewhere you've never been."

"Or somewhere you have," added Jake. "You loved Italy. Maybe you should go back there."

She had held Drew's hand. The boys had arranged chairs around his bed, and she had sat there and held his hand. The first thing he'd said to her was "Are you all right?" His eyes had roamed between them all, the boys and her, with glistening eagerness. She wondered if he was in a State, too, or if that hadn't happened yet. Or if it would, to him. She wondered if he could see how different she was. Or if it interested him. The boys did all the talking, taking up so much space and air with their robust maleness. There was talk of someone named Kirstin, to whom Danny had apparently just gotten himself engaged (one more piece of indigestible information conveyed over the phone), and Kristin, Jake's girlfriend. Adele entertained a lazy curiosity about a girl who got a promise like that out of Danny. She didn't take it seriously, of course. She couldn't even think about it right now. Occasionally, Drew's eyes had rested on hers as the boys bantered, and she had met his imploring gaze with a mildly reassuring smile. Curiouser and curiouser, she'd thought.

"What do you say, Mom?" Danny repeated.

They were all looking at her, their faces full of love and concern. A miracle, they were.

She would have liked to tell them about what she had just lived through, share her sense of wonderment with them, but their father's heart attack, she decided, was enough worry for them right now. Another time, perhaps. Now, she simply drank their dear, worried faces in, and smiled with as much reassurance as she could muster. "We'll see," was all she said.

Twenty-six

SYLVIA HAD TRIED, unsuccessfully, to get Maggie to go Christmas shopping with her. Spurned, she'd driven alone to the mall, where the bad mood she'd kept simmering on the back burner had spilled over into an urge to spit at people. She'd always loved Christmas, and hoped that the familiar songs and window displays would cheer her up. Now she wanted to find the mall manager and demand that they put Karen Carpenter to rest, for God's sake. Throngs of rude people made it difficult to even get her bearings, and a line of parents stood waiting to thrust their children onto the lap of a Santa-for-hire. As she elbowed her way through, a shrieking child was being yanked onto the dais by his mother. She glanced at Santa, and for a moment thought she detected an eerie resemblance to that character in the so-called spa who had said those mean things to her while handling her body. The recollection put a sour taste in her mouth. It was overcast, and her throat was scratchy. She went to the food court and waited in a long line to order a double cheeseburger, fries, and a chocolate milk shake, then wandered with her tray, seeking a place to sit and eat.

She ate too fast. After the first few bites, the food was tasteless. She sucked down the milk shake, taking perverse pleasure in its lack of nutritional value, its high caloric content. Carl had said she needed to lose weight. He hadn't actually said "that's why . . . ," but the implication was, How can you expect me to be attracted to a fat woman? As if Y—— (she wouldn't allow her name to be spoken, even in her thoughts) was some sylph! And look who's talking, she fumed, swirling her fries in a puddle of ketchup, shoveling them into her mouth—like Carl's some hottie! He had a paunch on him you could stuff a kangaroo in, and his privates looked like an old turkey.

She finished her lunch and bought an ice cream cone. That morning she had performed oral sex on Carl, and forced herself to swallow, even though it made her gag. He'd kept saying yeh, yeh, and she assured herself that his moans were risings of love for her, though she couldn't entirely dismiss the suspicion that he'd been on the verge of speaking the name of she who shall remain unspoken of.

Syl caught a glimpse of herself in a mirror: a rather bulgy woman slurping at a double-scoop Chunky Monkey. Tough shit, she thought, glaring at herself. Like it or lump it. Love it or leave it.

She wanted to go to Coach to buy a purse for Beth. She'd wanted Maggie along, because she had a plan: she was going to enlist her help in picking out something for Beth, and that way see what Maggie liked. Then she was going to come back and buy it for her. The plan had filled her with delight when first conceived. She'd imagined Maggie's surprise, her joy, her gratitude. Maggie would carry that bag for years; it would be the gift that kept on giving, and Syl's gratification would be renewed every time she saw Maggie with it.

But Maggie wasn't going to get her bag, after all, because Carl had been such a prick. Syl winced as the word rose to her mind, then she repeated it softly, giving it breath, tasting it on her lips: "Prick." Forever after, she'd taste Chunky Monkey whenever she heard or said that word.

"We have to pull in our belts!" Carl had yelled. At first Sylvia thought he'd meant they both had to go on diets. But he was talking about money.

"We didn't have any money in that Ponzi scheme, did we?" she'd asked. Carl had snorted; he had made an ugly face at her. "He didn't want my money," he'd sneered. "Drew asked, but he blew me off. Wrong demographic, no doubt."

Syl had been sickened by the conversation. Her grandmother had taught her that money was a vulgar topic and mustn't be spoken of by ladies. She had been relieved that Carl didn't discuss their finances with her. This conversation was an abomination, considering everything. After what he'd done! And she had just, only an hour earlier, given him a blow job!

And now here he was using words like *limit* and *allowance* and *outlets*!

"I am *not* cutting back on Christmas," she had hissed.

What he had done then made a fresh wave of nausea rise up in her scratchy throat as she relived it.

He had leapt up from the table, violently, so that she thought he was about to hit her! And he'd run out of the room, knocking over his chair, and he'd come back with papers, which he'd slammed down on the table in front of her. They were bank statements; columns of numbers, pie charts. "Oh please," she had said, turning away, and then he had grabbed a fistful of her hair and shoved her face down into the papers, when just an hour earlier he had reached down between his legs and stroked that same hair!

"Prick," she said again now, savoring the word. All the shops had SALE signs in their windows, and Christmas hadn't even come yet. The world was falling apart. For the millionth time, Syl called up the scene at that little shop in Gualala where the five of them had browsed, aglow with good fellowship, where Carl had held the antique locket against her neck and said, "Like it? It's yours." October, that had been. Just a couple of months ago!

How could everything have changed so much? How could money just disappear? How could a man love his wife one minute, and the next toss her out like Chinese leftovers? Carl had ranted about the addition again this morning, and when she'd tried to remind him that it had been his idea, he'd gone off on a tangent about Adele's "ridiculously expensive" design, Sylvia throwing around "his money." He kept reminding her about the second mortgage they'd taken to afford the construction. He said she should prepare herself to say good-bye to the house as soon as the market went up again. The sweet reconciliation that Syl had flown home to from Canada had lasted less than a week. Now it was prick time. "Prick time," she muttered aloud.

No Coach bag for Maggie. It had been an impulse, not uncommon for

Syl, to make a generous, loving gesture. Maggie'd been carrying the same old canvas Gap bag for years. It had ink stains on it and a little frayed hole in one of the outer pockets. Syl had envisioned presenting Maggie with a buttery soft, new leather bag of her choice; she had so looked forward to the look on her friend's face, the softening, the feeble protests she'd make. This Christmas, Syl had decided, would be a time of healing, of mending rifts and recommitting love. In that spirit she had called Beth and had a lovely, long conversation with her. She'd been unable to convince her to come home for the holidays, and she'd been disappointed in Beth's response to the news of her parents' reconciliation. "Huh," she'd said.

Syl had floundered. "You must be relieved," she'd offered. At that, Beth had been a little snooty, saying something along the lines of "If that's what you want to settle for." Syl couldn't recall the exact words, nor did she care to.

But Beth had talked freely about herself, her job, her boyfriend. They'd been like girlfriends, chatting away.

So she ticked that smoothing off her list and turned to Maggie, whom she'd hardly spoken to since they'd returned from Canada. Maggie was not a person whose bad side you wanted to get on, and Syl was afraid that she'd never be forgiven for her admittedly bad behavior on that trip from hell. She and Maggie frequently butted heads—it was almost a joke between them—but this time she sensed the rift might be harder to bridge. Her last two messages had gone unanswered. They'd seen each other only once since their return, when they'd taken Adele to lunch and then all gone to see Drew in the hospital.

Sylvia tried to avoid thinking about Adele. There were too many uncomfortable feelings colliding; it was too much. And really, Syl had to concentrate on getting her own house in order. Surely Adele understood that. It would all be all right, eventually, and they'd all forgive each other everything. More than anything, Syl yearned to turn back the clock, to have things be the way they were. Adele had been weird since her brush with death, and Syl couldn't dispel her suspicion that in fact something had gone wrong with her brain. The way she'd gone on and on about that house with the donut pool, and then the creepy, Yoda-like calm with which she'd told them, on the plane, that her money was gone. She'd been so quiet, sitting in the window seat, staring out at clouds. Nothing Syl or Maggie said elicited anything beyond that acquiescent little murmur. "Ummhmm," she'd said. "Uh-huh." With that little nod, that disturbing little smile. So Syl, snuggling next to her, had said, "Tell me more about your house," and Adele had said, "Oh, there won't be any house. Did you see that man on TV? He had all my money. They said it's all gone now."

Sylvia really wanted to discuss this with Maggie. She wanted to know if she was overreacting to Adele's weirdness. She wanted to compare notes, be reassured. But Maggie was avoiding her.

She would have bought that Coach bag anyway, despite Carl's warning, if Maggie had agreed to come today. But Maggie blew her off. "You know I hate all that Christmas shit," she'd said in response to Syl's invitation.

Syl went to Nordstrom's, just for the heck of it. Carl had given her a pair of Tiffany earrings, the night she'd come home from Canada. He'd handed her the little blue box, told her how sorry he was to have hurt her. She'd hoped for a ring, and when she saw the box she thought it was a watch. But the earrings were lovely. Maybe not exactly her style, but she would wear them anyway, as a signal to Carl that their pact was renewed. The first time she'd worn the earrings her lobes swelled a little, which was odd because that only happened when she didn't wear gold. Also, they felt light for eighteen carat. It saddened her to think that Tiffany's was slipping in quality. Of course she'd said nothing to Carl, but after the horrible way he'd acted this morning she felt she deserved something in the way of restitution, so she went to the jewelry counter at Nordstrom's to buy herself a little something. "Prick," she breathed as she looked at the glittering things in their velvet display cases.

There was quite a crush at the counter, and only two salesgirls. They were both flustered, and there was a sense of verging panic in the air. A flock of teenage girls had descended and were picking and cooing, sending the salesgirls in and out of the display cases with overlapping requests, so that the counter was littered with pieces that should have been put away. It looked like a shoe sale, Syl mused, all the trying on and discarding. She kept to the edge of the flock, wishing to be unobtrusive and being in no hurry to choose.

Sylvia loved jewelry. Already she was experiencing the buzzing comfort of a new acquisition, warming to the prospect of selection. She would take her time, compare, get in the zone. When she was in the zone her intuition would kick in; she would know exactly which piece was meant to come home with her. In anticipation of the moment when she handed her credit card over, butterflies kicked up in her stomach. *Shut up, you prick*, she imagined saying to Carl when he shook the bill in her face. Besides, Maggie wasn't getting her Coach bag, so it was a wash.

Hysteria had set in among the girls. They were probably just mall rats, killing time until their rides home showed up. They were draping themselves and each other in baubles and beads. They were all talking at once, shrieking in that high-pitched dog whistle way, jostling each other for mirror space. Sylvia tried to catch the eye of one of the salesgirls to give her some sympathy, but the girl was darting like a cornered mouse. Please, she said, several times, attempting to retrieve individual pieces from the accumulating pile. The other girl had abandoned her for a solitary older man at the other end of the counter, who was fingering a pearl choker with sinister concentration. Sylvia's eyes fell on a David Yurman bracelet, which would be beautiful with her grandmother's ring. She had recently had the ring resized and had taken to wearing it again, on top of her wedding ring. It was a bigger diamond than the one in her own engagement ring, and the antique setting and cut were more elegant. That bracelet would look fabulous with it. It lay, undisturbed, under the glass. Once more she tried to catch the salesgirl's eye, giving her an inquisitive look, pointing to the bracelet. This time the girl responded—gratefully, it seemed—turning away from the squawking flock to slip the bracelet out of its display and fasten it on Sylvia's wrist. "Beautiful," the girl said, and Sylvia agreed, pleased with the satisfying heft of the gold. She lifted her hand to admire it, and as she did her eye was caught by a quick movement next to her. It was so quick and deft she wondered if she had imagined it, and stared, blinking. The girl's eyes met hers briefly, dangerously. They were hostile eyes, warning. In just a fraction of a second Sylvia had witnessed a crime, and been warned to keep her mouth shut. She stood, rigid with shame. Afterward, when she went over it in her mind, she would wonder why she hadn't said something, quietly, to the salesclerk. But at this moment she drowned in collusion, standing stock-still and silent as the girls skittered away like sandpipers.

The price tag on the Yurman piece completely cowed her. No, it was impossible. It would have carried the act of rebellion to full-out revolution; she didn't have the stomach for it. "I'm so sorry," she said to the salesclerk, who really couldn't have cared less, so relieved was she that the girls had left.

There was a man in a tux playing Christmas songs on a grand piano near the escalator. There were models dressed in gowns, twirling and smiling with cruelly painted lips. Sylvia thought she might go have a manicure, or a cup of tea, or a quickie massage at the Healthy Back store. She hadn't bought one present, and she wasn't in the mood anymore. She had suddenly had it with all the noise and the crowds, and she felt a little queasy, and her throat hurt. How she had loved Christmas when she was younger! It never failed to delight her, year after year, the familiar things that Adele referred to as kitsch. She'd driven to the mall hoping to be cheered, to be reassured, but instead she felt angry. Why shouldn't she buy that bracelet? Over and over her mind went back to the quick movement, the flash of gold as it vanished into the pocket. Her heart sped up as she imagined doing such a thing. She remembered the lipstick she'd filched, so many years ago, the thrill of getting away with it. She wondered if the other girls had taken things, too, or if it had just been the one she saw.

She drifted back to the jewelry counter, idly perused the less expensive things that hung on racks. Department stores went to great lengths to catch shoplifters, she had heard. Hidden cameras, detectives, two-way mirrors. Especially during the holiday season, she supposed, and especially during a recession. On the radio, driving over, they'd warned people to keep their doors locked, even if they weren't accustomed to doing so, as the police expected a lot of robberies. Last year someone Maggie knew had had her house broken into on Christmas Eve. They'd taken every last present from under the tree. And this year things were worse; it wasn't just the poor people who were desperate. Sylvia slipped a necklace from the rack over her head and checked herself out in the mirror. It was pretty—amber beads, with a heart pendant of silver dangling from its center. Fake amber, of course. Just glass. And cheap silver; Mexican. Still, it was pretty. Reasonable, too.

Wouldn't even make a blip on the credit card statement. There was no sign of the clerks, however.

In the mirror, Syl checked the milling people behind her. No one appeared to be paying the least attention to her. She removed a second necklace and draped it over the first. While checking her reflection, she managed to tuck the silver heart inside her blouse. Then she removed the second necklace, studied its price tag, examined its clasp, then replaced it on the rack. She would amble over to the Misses department and look for a rust-colored V-neck, she decided. Just for the heck of it. Then she'd come back and return the necklace. If anyone asked, she'd explain that she was trying it out. There'd been no one there to assist her, she'd point out. She was shopping for her daughter, who was an executive in New York City, she'd say, and had wanted one of the young salesgirls to model the sweater and necklace together. But they seemed a little understaffed, she'd complain. Not angrily, just mildly critical. "I am attempting to shop," would be her attitude, "and, frankly, you are not doing much to attract my business."

By the time she had chosen some sweaters to try on, her heart was thundering. She cast surreptitious glances to where she thought cameras might be hidden. In the privacy of the dressing room, after examining all angles and assuring herself no one was watching, she was able to admire the necklace. It really was pretty. Nothing she'd have chosen for herself; she was strictly a gold wearer. But she liked the way the heart nestled in her cleavage, and the beads were smooth against her skin, and gave off a warm glow. She chose a cotton scoop neck, the color of maple syrup. Dressing, she concealed the necklace under her blouse. She paid for the sweater, exchanging pleasantries with the older woman at the register. She roamed through shoes. Then ladies intimates, where she bought a nightgown for Beth. She went to the men's department and bought some socks for Carl. He preferred black cashmere, so she bought brown wool. Her shopping bags bounced cheerily against her thigh. "Oh my, I forgot I still had it on!" she'd say if someone placed a heavy hand on her arm. "See, this sweater I purchased . . . my daughter . . . how embarrassing. . . ."

But no one stopped her. She waltzed right out of Nordstrom's and into the Hallmark store, where she hovered in the rear aisle, pretending to peruse sympathy cards. So easy! And how nice to be among the living, again. She smiled at strangers. Relaxed by the fountains and had another Ben and Jerry's, savoring each creamy bite, the cold soothing her throat. She was glad Maggie hadn't come. It was fun, doing this alone. She would do it more often, she resolved. Not the shoplifting; that had been an aberration—a game, really. She certainly wasn't going to make a habit out of that. But it was good to shake things up a bit. Maybe she'd give Maggie the necklace for Christmas. Or maybe not; maybe she'd enjoy it herself. She wouldn't have thought of maple and amber as her colors, but they'd brought out something in her; she'd liked the way she looked in the mirror. She should experiment with colors more often. Perhaps she'd been in a rut with her usual blues and roses. She was thinking of lavender, imagining a cashmere sweater with perhaps a necklace of red beads. That might be kind of fun—wasn't there something about red and purple? Yes, but it was for old ladies, she now remembered. No, she wasn't ready to go there yet. She was in the parking garage, just about to unlock her car, when someone spoke her name.

Freezing, Sylvia felt a hot flush spread through her. How would they know her name? From the credit card, of course. They'd been following her throughout her ramblings. She imagined handcuffs, perhaps a frisking— and then, across the roof of her Lexus, was the smiling, vaguely familiar face of a young woman whom she couldn't quite place.

"Sylvia Ott, right?"

Syl nodded dumbly.

"It's Carla. I used to babysit Beth, when you lived down the street in La Jolla."

So great was Sylvia's relief that she dropped her bags and rushed around the car to smother the woman in a hug. She dimly remembered her—they'd been renting in La Jolla when Beth was little, before buying in Carlsbad.

"It's been forever," she gushed, taking in Carla's expensive if garish sweater, a claret-colored cowl-necked affair with something glittery woven through it. She wore it over bright-green leggings, giving her the appearance of an overfed elf. "How's your mother?" she asked, remembering the cranky old woman who used to peek out her window at passersby.

"Dead." Carla practically sang the word.

"I'm so sorry," Syl murmured, but Carla said, "Don't be—she's at rest now, hopefully."

"Are you still in the house?" Now that the danger had passed, Syl grew impatient with chitchat and wanted to get out of there. She retrieved her bags, busied herself with unlocking and loading the car.

"Absolutely," Carla replied. "I've redone it. And I'm in the process of turning it into a writers' retreat."

"That's nice," said Syl, sliding into the driver's seat. But Carla had followed her around the car, and stood holding on to the driver's door. "Have you ever thought of writing?" she asked. "I'm actively looking for local writers. I give stipends. And I have fabulous teachers."

"Me?" Syl laughed. "Oh no. I'm no writer."

"Oh come on," Carla pressed. "Everyone has a story to tell."

"Mine isn't very interesting."

"That can't be true. They're all interesting, in their own ways."

Sylvia looked up at the woman's face, animated and earnest. "Well," she said, "I'll certainly think about it."

"Great!" Carla fished in her bag and produced a business card, which she handed to Syl. "Right now I'm accepting open submissions, since we're just getting off the ground. Feel free to send me something; I'll give it special consideration."

Syl took the card, stuck it into the visor. "Lovely to see you, dear. You look wonderful, by the way."

Actually, she didn't. Syl glanced back at her in the rearview as she maneuvered out of the garage. She'd been a strange girl, but Beth had liked her. And it had been so convenient, with her just a few houses down. Memories of those years burst forth as if released from captivity: Beth, little and adorable, Carl so pumped up about their future, everything new and promising. She recalled an afternoon at the Cove, Beth delighting in the footprints she made in the wet sand, Carl, taking advantage of their daughter's distraction, lifting Syl's bathing suit strap, ostensibly to rub lotion in but really to tickle her breast.

A writer, she thought, as she swung onto the 5. She remembered how, when Martha Stewart hit it big, she'd felt a twinge of bitterness. "I could have done this," she'd said to Carl, tossing the magazine onto the table. "Yeah, but you didn't," he'd replied.

Hmmm, she thought now. A writer. This could be just the thing. Of course she had a story to tell! She just had to figure out what it was. What fairy godmother had plopped Carla down beside her, just when she most needed a little pickup? She reached inside her blouse and pulled out the necklace, fingered its smooth beads. It would be fun to take a class, she mused. It would get her out of the house; she would meet new people. Wasn't life funny, the way something always came along to lift your spirits when you were blue? It was as if a little window had opened, and right then and there she decided to go get a Starbucks and then get a mani-pedi, because, as that model on those TV commercials said, she deserved it.

Twenty-seven

News of Danny Gold's engagement spread like the Santa Ana wildfires, bursting into the preoccupied minds of the adults who had watched him grow up. He was the first of the children to marry (Beth's cohabitation with Franco didn't count) and the most unlikely. Sylvia insisted on throwing an engagement party. "Your condo's too small," she explained to Adele, "and I want to do it, really. Maybe I can get Beth to come home for it. Maybe she'll even bring her boyfriend. Maybe he'll take the hint."

Sylvia and Carl traditionally threw a holiday open house, and as the absence of a festive spirit this year threatened to cancel it, Syl was quick to jump at an excuse for a party. Plus, she was genuinely fond of Danny, who had always, discreetly and respectfully, flirted with her.

"I can't imagine why you would want to take this on," Adele protested. "You won't even know most of the guests." Privately, she didn't expect a marriage to emerge from this engagement. She was steeling herself for weepy phone calls from the girl after Danny extricated himself— it wouldn't be the first time. But Adele was engulfed in lethargy, and didn't have the energy to throw any flags of caution in the wind of Sylvia's enthusiasm.

After a triple bypass, Drew was home. Or, if not home, exactly, ensconced in the second bedroom of the condo, which had turned into the musty cave of the invalid. He had to follow a strict regimen of diet, meds, and exercise, and was adhering to it in his usual type-A way. Adele was a spectator; she was neither impelled nor asked to participate. They lived together like siblings, apologizing if they happened to bump against each other in passing, politely accommodating each other. After dinner they retired to their separate bedrooms, where each had their own TV. Mornings, they would meet in the kitchen and exchange pleasantries. Always, the great white elephant crouched in the corner, silently reminding them of their failure and loss.

But Adele stared it down. She was becoming aware of a new sense of acceptance, which had settled on her like a light dusting of snow. Which is not to say that she didn't still harbor feelings of rage. Sometimes Drew would make some offhand comment, and she'd be about to respond as if everything were still normal. But her response would be choked by the cold hand on her throat, reminding her of how irrevocably life had tilted. Then she'd ignore him, or make a cutting remark, and immediately feel remorse when she saw she'd hurt him. But these were passing things. Her overall state of mind was calm and focused, grateful for at least the semblance of normalcy. It occurred to her that this state of mind might be resignation, a word tainted with judgment, but that didn't alarm her. *Maybe resignation isn't such a bad thing,* she thought. *It beats throwing myself, or Drew, off the balcony.* So she wouldn't get her house. Cry me a river. She was alive, after such an ordeal! And her husband was alive, and their children. They had a roof over their heads. Not just any roof, she reminded herself, but a San Diego roof! Isn't that what everyone was supposed to want—a place in the sun?

She'd always been a good sleeper, and now sleep, the great healer, cocooned her nightly in velvety oblivion. She was grateful for that. The only thing she dreamed of, and she seemed to dream of it nightly, was her house. Kaleidoscopic, labyrinthine dreams of hidden doors leading to secret passageways, rooms appearing out of the mist, shapes floating and settling, the sigh of the pieces as they fit together. She'd wake with the fully rested optimism of a child, blinking on her pillow as she adjusted to the shapes her life had taken, feeling no weight of sorrow as she rose, but rather wonderment that she was whole, that the sun shone outside and her husband was under the same roof. The star house, so vivid in the aftermath of her ordeal, so insistent in its nightly recurrence, seemed now like something she had scribbled after a drug-induced dream—congealing, in the light of day, into something almost silly. She was a little embarrassed at having told her friends about it.

When she told Drew about Sylvia's offer he said, "Let them throw a party if they want. Carl should throw a party because I couldn't get him into the fund."

Adele smiled wryly. These kinds of comments were the only reference Drew made to their catastrophe. "But do you actually think he's going through with it?"

Drew looked at her, knowing exactly what she meant. "Better an engagement party that comes to nothing than a wedding that shouldn't be."

"Like ours," Adele said.

"No, not like ours. Don't say that."

She'd known her comment would annoy him. It was like sticking a little pin into him. In the past, she'd been so attuned to Drew's feelings that even the offhand rudeness of a cabdriver stung her for him. She watched him flinch now, and enjoyed it. "I'm going to the market this morning," she said. "Make a list. I used the last of the Jerusalem artichokes last night, if you want more."

To say that Drew was stepping carefully around his wife didn't begin to describe the minefield he negotiated.

Adele seemed, to him, alternately an angry mother, a brooding wife, a simmering teacher. Childish sparks of rebellion flared up in him at his mortification, followed quickly by crashing waves of remorse. He longed to find a formula to dispel this fog of tension; he felt, sometimes, that if Adele would make a wisecrack and cast him her familiar glance of collusion, all would be cured, instantly. His shame was deep and rueful, clashing with his sense of outrage and injustice. At night, lying in the guest bed listening to the muffled sound of the TV in Adele's room, he laid his hand on his miraculously still-beating heart and allowed himself to feel safe. Despite everything, the world had endured another day; his family was alive and intact. The worst had happened; the bogeyman that had fueled his anxiety over all these years had actually leapt out of the dark and ambushed him, and he had survived. Some of the victims of the Ponzi schmuck had killed themselves. Every day there was another tragic story on the news. Drew was pleased to have discovered, within himself, a kind of level, something that righted and anchored him and dispelled the despair that would cause such an act.

And he was impressed that Adele hadn't ripped him apart. She hadn't pointed out all the times she'd protested his decision to invest, she hadn't played the old record about the sacrifice she'd made, coming to California. She'd been, all things considered, a champ. A little bitchy at moments, but it was a rough time for a woman; the mid-fifties. And no question, he'd been a bit of a prick. Although really it had nothing to do with her, those girls, still, he'd hurt her. No question about that. Basically what he'd done was not think about her. He was guilty of the malice of thoughtlessness.

It soothed him to think about his wife, and how they'd both survived these physical tests, and how this would be one more bond between them. It was a comfortingly familiar challenge, facing down adversity with Adele. He just wished she wouldn't be so caustic, wouldn't act like they were practically divorced. All he'd said was he was unsure! He wasn't into building a house! Then she goes and turns it into a big mishegas. Truth be told, she'd been on his case in one way or another ever since they'd left New York. To the point where yes, he'd considered leaving her. Not seriously—he wouldn't have gone through with it. She was the one pushing. He'd been a good husband, a good father, a good provider. So he got restless, so he maybe went a little crazy, did that make him a bad person? Did that make him deserve this kind of punishment? Just when he'd felt so on top of his game? California. The golden ring, Adele called it, sarcastically. The glittering prize. And now look at him, frail and enfeebled, under the roof of a jerry-built condo that, let's face it, could crumble beneath him at the first rumbling of the inevitable quake. There was nothing solid left to stand on. And it was all his fault, his fault, no one's but his.

It was weird, how much it felt like 9/11. Bam, everything changed: one minute this; the next minute that. All that beautiful money, flourishing in the loamy soil of this guy's hands like the ranunculus in the Carlsbad Flower Fields, poof, gone. That money had been his backbone. He'd have denied it, before. He'd have said money isn't everything; he'd have shrugged philosophically, when it was hypothetical, and declared himself fundamentally indifferent. I've been blessed to keep my family clothed and sheltered, he'd have said, to have given my sons a good education.

He couldn't say that now. It would be a lie. The gaping hole that had appeared where the money used to be felt like a vivisection, even as he struggled to keep it in perspective. It felt as if his spine had been drained of fluid and he was being held up by the sheerest, most brittle thread. As if his heart kept beating like Chinese water torture, each tick reminding him of the flimsiness of his existence. It pissed him off that he'd managed the whole exodus out of New York so well, had created such a beautiful second act out here, had been all poised to leap into a whole new life, only to be flattened like this. Slammed.

And then his thoughts would shift to contemplation of his ventricle and his bypass valve. Feeling the steady thump beneath his skin, he visualized the left circumflex artery, the adipose tissue, the saphenous veins.

The mortal coil. No one knew better than he how abruptly it can shuffle off, and yet he'd given very little thought to his own turn. "Wake-up call," was the expression they'd used. He'd used it himself, usually meaning, This guy has to quit smoking, or lose fifty pounds, or cut down on his stress level.

None of which applied to him. It was the jolt, he knew, everything happening at once.

As for the girls, well, that was like a dream. Now that life had been restored, he was sure that whatever aura he'd exuded was gone. No longer a totally hot old guy; just an old guy. Sad. It would be interesting, he mused, to test it, just for the hell of it. Not that he'd do anything. He uneasily pushed thoughts of Adele out of his mind. At any rate, even if the magic wasn't all gone he'd have to cut back. Cut back; who was he kidding? It was over. In the long hours of his solitude he tried to relive the exhilaration of those encounters, but it was like trying to recall the details of a memorable meal, fast fading from the intensity of its pleasure. He couldn't remember any particular girl, only the lips of one, the ass of another, the scent of a different one. When he tried to concentrate, a flush of embarrassment would sweep through him. He began to imagine the girls as an army of Valkyries, swooping on him to feast, cackling over his puniness. For he was puny. He saw, in the mirror, how his trim body had, seemingly overnight, shrunken into the leathery folds of an old man. He felt no stirring of sexual desire, no surge of revivified sap. Just the weight of his bones, and the itch and ache of his sutures.

This morning Adele had tossed the mail on the table, one of those gestures of hers that seemed calculated to remind him how detached she was from their shared life. Unless *The New Yorker* was evident, she dumped the lot indifferently, for Drew to sort through. It was the usual junk, headed straight to recycling, except for a pink envelope that almost got tossed, stuck in the pages of the PennySaver. It was addressed to Adele.

"My God, it's an actual letter," Adele said. "From Cordelia."

They were silent, then, each of them immersed in their own discomfort at the mention of their old friend and all that she reminded them of. Adele fingered the envelope, tracing the writing. "Look at her. Personalized stationery. She doesn't even have an e-mail address."

Drew said nothing, shamed into silence by his own self-pity. Adele poured coffee and took the letter out to the balcony, shutting the sliders behind her. Drew reflected on Cordelia and John, once their best friends. It was shameful, how they had dropped that ball. One more thing for him to feel like shit about. Was this what it would be like, forever? Wave after wave of his own shit washing over him, burying him? He pushed himself to his feet, using the table as a brace. Today he'd think of something nice to do for Adele. Maybe suggest an outing. Balboa Park, or Hillcrest for dinner and a movie. No, he was too tired for the park. And a movie would be all right, but they could more easily manage the multiplex at La Costa. There was never anything playing there that Adele wanted to see. She'd get snide if he even suggested it. No, he'd have to think of something else.

⁓

Adele sank down in the fake wicker chair on the balcony that had become her command central.

On a table next to it was a stack of magazines and the game sections of weeks of the *Tribune*, folded over to the crossword and Sudoku puzzles. She cleared the makeshift footstool of the things from yesterday that she'd meant to bring in—completed puzzles, a plate, a book she'd tried to read and given up on—and settled back, holding Cordy's letter as if it were a fragile leaf that might crumble or be snatched by a breeze.

Ever since Canada, Adele had felt time as a bendable presence. She couldn't wrap her mind around the passing of the hours, but felt them warping and weaving, so that one moment it seemed she was young and her life was just beginning, and another moment she was watching it all unfold behind her. There was no sense of progression. When Adele saw the envelope from Cordy she'd had a funny response, like, Why's Cordy writing me a letter? In her mind she tucked Danny into his stroller and walked out the back way, through the deer path in the woods to Cordy's house, where she'd enter without knocking and yell out, "It's me!" But of course those days were over, and she and Cordy weren't even close anymore. How had that happened? "We're not close," she said aloud, and the word, *close*, seemed to materialize before her as if skywritten in puffs of white clouds. How could they be close, living thousands of miles apart? How could they be close, when Cordy's life had burst into flames and Adele's was still relatively intact in comparison?

Cordelia and she had been such unlikely friends. They'd met in a Tumblebears class, each with her first son. Adele remembered making snap judgments about Cordy, snickering inwardly at her pearls, her cashmere sweaters, her Gucci loafers. So typical, she'd thought. That was when she was still learning how to be suburban, having convinced Drew that the boys should grow up out of the city, with a lawn and their own basketball hoop. That had been before she'd fallen in love with her life in Bedford.

Cordy and John lived in a custom-built house at the end of a cul-de-sac that backed up onto Adele's property. Soon they were back and forth all day, wearing that little deer path into a lifeline. John was a banker and traveled frequently, and Drew was keeping horrendous hours at the hospital, so the two women clung to each other's company during the long winters. The boys adored each other. When she and Cordy each got pregnant again around the same time, they rejoiced. John and Drew forged a gruff if not spontaneous friendship. Years had passed in easy camaraderie.

Tripp and Henry. Adele spoke their names aloud. Their faces appeared before her, as when they were little. Her hands were fluttering, but she clutched Cordelia's letter and forced herself to look at the boys, to allow their faces to assume familiar expressions.

Tripp had been working for a hedge fund whose offices were at the World Trade Center. The morning of September 11 he had arranged an interview for Henry, who had recently gotten his MBA. The night before, they'd all had dinner together. Jake and Danny were both in California by then, but Noah, Drew, and she joined the Ruskins at Thierry's in Bedford Hills. They had had a wonderful time, toasting to the success of the interview. She had hugged Henry good night, she remembered. Henry, who had plucked Noah out of a riptide in Amagansett once, who had, as a cherub-cheeked boy, brought her a picture he'd drawn of them all, all nine of them, which she still had at the bottom of a box somewhere.

There were those who spoke of getting phone calls. Fathers and sons calling as they ran down the staircases, final words of love before the connections broke. Tripp and Henry, on one of the top floors of the north tower, hadn't had time for any calls. They vanished, mingled with the ash and smoke of that day.

Cordelia and John had continued to look and act like Cordelia and John, but they couldn't muster more than appearances. At the memorial service, Adele had been horrified at their graciousness, their veneer of stoicism. "I'm glad we're Jews," she had said to Drew. "I'm glad we wail and rend our garments. I can't stomach this zombieness."

She had helped Cordelia pack up the boys' things. She was the only friend Cordelia let in, which humbled her, as they came in droves, daily, leaving casseroles, flowers, cards. In Henry's room Adele had taken a T-shirt out of his drawer, one that she'd bought for him at the Bronx Zoo. It had undone her. She'd pressed her face into it and wailed. Cordelia had snatched the shirt from her. "Stop it," she'd said. "Or you'll have to leave."

~

When Drew and Adele sold the house and left for California, she and Cordy had made promises they meant to keep. They'd visit often; they'd call at least every week. Adele believed, deep down, that they'd never have left if 9/11 hadn't happened. But what was the point of going there?

Cordy had written "Mrs. Adele Gold" on the envelope. She'd gone to Miss Porter's, and then Bard. She had oil paintings of her ancestors and a little gold pinky ring with her family crest on it, but her father had had a nervous breakdown and lost all their money. Cordy had been a working girl when she met John. He was a ruddy WASP who drank too much. It had always concerned Adele. She held the delicate envelope up to the light, traced Cordy's writing with her fingertips. How was any of this possible, she wondered. How could she be sitting here in Carlsbad, California, holding a letter from her ex–best friend who had two dead sons, when five minutes ago they'd been sitting by her pool, yelling at the boys not to run on the wet slate?

And Adele had come out here and seen her third son grow strong and tan, learn to surf, go off to college. She had made new best friends who didn't stink of tragedy, friends for whom 9/11 was lumped in there with Pearl Harbor and the Lockerbie Pan Am crash, horrors they couldn't smell and taste on their skin.

Adele craned her neck and peered through the sliders to check on Drew. He was attempting to unload the dishwasher, reaching up to put the coffee mugs on the shelf. The doctors had been explicit about not reaching, not using his arms excessively, not straining the sutures. She whacked on the glass, glared at him. Made a "no-no" gesture with her finger, as if he were a naughty toddler. What was the matter with him? He knew better than that! He gave her a sheepish look, shrugged, left the mugs on the counter. A hard little voice in Adele whispered, What do you care? And she shushed it. It wasn't easy, seeing your husband shrivel up in front of you, no matter how much you wanted to hate him. Some nights, after she'd put out the light and lay in the dark listening to the muffled sound of the TV in his room, she experienced a tenderness toward him that felt purely maternal. How fast everything had changed, without any warning.

December was usually a nice month in San Diego. The sunsets could be spectacular. The days were cool and blue. The late morning sun peeked around the edge of the balcony, splashing over her legs; she threw off the polar fleece throw she'd been huddled under. What had Cordelia done, while she was starting over in Carlsbad? She'd thrown herself into charity work, Adele knew, from occasional Christmas cards and e-mails from mutual friends. She had told Adele, in one of their sporadic phone conversations that had finally petered out, that the new owners of Adele's house weren't very friendly. That the deer path had grown over. Adele closed her eyes and felt the wild myrtle brushing her bare ankles as she chased the boys, laughing and whooping, down the path. She inhaled the scent of Cordy's house as they burst into the back door: lemon oil, damp wool, the spicy potpourri she kept in antique china bowls in all the rooms. When she'd been in the woods that night in Canada, running from tree to tree while the panic rose up in her throat, she'd thought, for a brief moment, that she was on her way to Cordy's, playing hide-and-seek with the boys.

But here she was in Carlsbad, and here was a letter from Cordelia. She couldn't imagine what it would say. She dreaded opening the envelope. She didn't want to relinquish the innocence of anticipation she felt; she was afraid of what the words might actually contain. Perhaps Cordy had finally cracked, and this would be an outpouring of blame and accusations. "You never . . . You didn't . . . Why did you . . ."

"I didn't know what to do!" she said aloud, to the envelope, not to excuse herself but to agree. "Yes, I was inadequate. I failed you. I abandoned you. I took my three boys and left."

Or it could be something worse, something casual and almost impersonal, like a clipping from *Bedford Magazine* that she'd thought might interest Adele, with an exclamation point or a star jotted in the margin, and nothing else. The kind of thing Drew's mother used to do, sending them articles about things they couldn't have cared less about.

What if it was the first, a diatribe accusing Adele of all the things she feared she might be guilty of? She might welcome that. Just to have Cordy back, on some level. They'd never dreamt their friendship wouldn't last. There'd been an assumption—such as the one between her, Maggie, and Sylvia—that the children would hold them together, if nothing else. Just like a marriage. Syl had been so over the moon about Danny and the stupid party she insisted on throwing. It was lovable, it was Syl all over, but Adele couldn't help sensing a note of desperation in it. Apparently Syl had been a bit of a "butthead"—her word—during Adele's banishment to Gehenna, as she thought of that night in the Kootenays. "A total butthead," Maggie had agreed. Adele thought it was funny that Syl had behaved badly; she wished she could have been a fly on the wall to watch Maggie getting madder and madder. It didn't bother her that Syl hadn't worried. She was touched that Maggie had been so vigilant, but she was glad Syl had been so completely Syl-like. It reassured her. "What did you expect?" she had said, at Maggie's spluttering description of Syl's defection. "Some things don't change." Maggie had no idea, of course, that those words, "some things don't change," had been as fervent a prayer as Adele had ever uttered.

Carefully, so as not to rip the delicate paper, she unsealed the envelope. There were two sheets, crammed full of Cordelia's neat, assertive handwriting. Drew stuck his head out. "Want some more coffee?"

Instinctively, she held the letter up against her chest and shook her head. She could feel him waiting a moment, hoping for more. Then he faded back inside, pulling the sliders shut behind him.

Dear Adele,

It's been such a long, long time. I miss you. Remember how, when you moved out there, we promised each other we'd still talk at least once a week? So much for promises. Don't take that wrong; no criticism intended. Anyway, I hope the reason I don't hear from you is that you're wildly happy out there, and just too busy having fun in the sun to give much thought to those of us back here, still shoveling out our driveways and cranking up the oil burners. (Oh my God, the heating bills—the

snowplow. Let's hope this winter isn't like last year!) Bet you don't miss
those days.

I think of you so often. Wonder how the boys are, and Drew. Of
course, I see Jake and Danny on a daily basis—their picture is still on my
fridge, with Tripp and Henry. Remember that day, when we took them on
the hayride? So cute. (Here, Adele had to put the letter down and grip
the armrests of her chair.)

It's funny, but when I was a young career girl I used to dream of
having pots and pots of money. I thought it would be so great! I assumed
the other ingredients of happiness would fall into place, as long as there
were six big figures in the bank.

There are more than six figures in my account now. As if money could
pay us back. But that's not what I'm writing for. I'm writing to tell you
something, and to ask you something.

Last fall John was diagnosed with glioblastoma, a very aggressive brain
tumor. We've been concentrating on keeping him comfortable. He's home
now; we're just basically waiting. Please forgive me for not letting you
know sooner—I just more or less shut down. I'm sure you understand.
I mean, here I am in my dream house, rolling in money, and I have nothing,
Adele. Nothing.

The doctors seem to have turned their concern to me. They keep telling
me I have to think of the future, have to make a plan (other than suicide,
I guess is what they mean!). I can't think about the future. I can't even
imagine it. They just started me on Prozac again, though, so I'm thinking
in a few weeks, when it kicks in, I might be tempted to sign up on Match
.com or Outward Bound or the Peace Corps. Help!

Sorry if this sounds melodramatic or self-pitying, but frankly, my life
is over. That's what I feel like. But sometimes, after I've squeezed the last
drop out of my eyes and I'm as dry as an old wreath, some little thing
seems to stir inside me. Some dim, distant light flickers, and I know that
I still have miles to go before I sleep.

So then I wonder what I'll do. One thing I know, I want to get out of
here. I can't stay in this house. I haven't set foot in the city since 9/11, and

*everywhere I go, everything I do, is full of memories I need to get away
from. So where will I go? What will I do? You know everything is such a
mess now. So many of our friends lost their money, some in that Ponzi
scheme, some just overinvested in the market. Thank God John was always
conservative! I can go anywhere, do anything. So I started thinking, who
do I want around? If the phone or doorbell rings, who would I like it to be?
It's a very short list, Del. I know you're laughing now—you know I have
the fattest Rolodex; I was Miss Social Hubbub for so long. But in the end,
the list is short. And you're on it.*

*I'm writing this on the sunporch. It's weirdly Indian-summer-like
today, there's a light in the sky I think might be the sun, though it's been
so long since I've seen it I'm not sure, and it's warm enough to sit out
here, where we clocked so many hours drinking tea (or whatever) while
the boys played in the yard. Remember how we bitched? Oh, to have
those days back.*

*So I'm rambling, but here's what I want to ask you: Will you build me
a house? I remember how you always meant to build a house, someday.
You had so many ideas. You used to sketch things and show me, remember?
You are so talented. I want a little house, on a lake or something, and to
spend what's left of my life in peace. You know, reread the classics, that
sort of thing. Crochet booties for my friends' grandchildren.*

*You don't have to decide right away. For all I know you're in the midst
of building your own dream house, up on some lavender-covered hillside
overlooking the sea. I hope you are! But think about it. And please don't
feel like you have to jump on a plane because of John. He wouldn't know
you. He doesn't know me. I envy his oblivion.*

Love,

Cordy

Adele closed her eyes and pictured John as he'd been during their many
dinners together. Courtly, jovial, refilling wineglasses and deferring to his
wife on matters of the menu. Telling one of his drawn-out, oft-repeated
stories that always wound charmingly back to Cordy's laudable gumption,

or brains, or resourcefulness. Always ending with a toast to her, while she rolled her eyes in exasperation. "To Cordelia, the baleboste of Bedford," Drew would joke, and John would throw his head back and laugh, repeating the Yiddish: Ball-a-boost-eh! Cordy and John were the WASP version of her and Drew; two peas in a pod, to use Sylvia's expression. Now he was leaving her, too.

Adele reached for her pencil and began sketching on the back of Cordelia's envelope. She wasn't even thinking; just letting her hand move. Her heart was racing with a sort of coffee buzz, clamoring inside her. An odd kind of excitement clashed with the shock of another loss. She imagined Cordy standing on a porch, in cool sunlight, gazing at a sparkling lake. The porch would face the lake, but it would be the back of the house. The lake would be fringed with pine trees. She drew an octagon, and saw a widow's walk for stargazing. Her pencil flew.

"It's good to see you sketching again." Drew stood there, earnest as a teenager, freshly showered and with his hair slicked back. He'd put on a polo shirt and chinos. He looked as if he were about to ask her if he could borrow the car for a date.

"I didn't hear you come out," she said. "Going somewhere?" She laid her hand over the paper, a gesture he registered with an almost imperceptible wince.

"I was going to ask if you'd like to go out on a date. With me."

She clamped her lips against the flock of sarcastic responses that flew to her mouth. "What'd you have in mind?"

"Whatever you want. We could take a drive out to Temecula, have lunch at a winery. Or go downtown, stroll along the Embarcadero. Whatever you want." *I am at your service*, he started to add, but that was laying it on a bit thick so he left it at that.

Adele sighed, folded the envelope. "What brought this on?"

A muscle in Drew's jaw twitched. "Do you have to be confrontational?"

"No, Drew, I don't have to be confrontational. What is this, an olive branch you're holding out to me?"

"Okay," said Drew, nodding. "Okay, Adele. You want me to toddle off back to my room, you want me to continue my time-out? What do you want, you want me to write 'I'm a schmuck' a thousand times on the black-board? Is that what you want?"

Here was that question again: "What Do You Want?" The coffee, the sun, the letter from Cordelia had lulled her into a sense of well-being out there on the balcony. The sketching had given her a surge, a sense of purpose. The constrictions of her present circumstances had momentarily evaporated; for a few lovely moments she had dwelt in possibility. This is what I want, she wanted to say to Drew. I want to sit here and be left alone with my little ball of hope.

But that little ball of hope was fading as quickly as her rainbow had, and she had a skidding, thudding sense of herself as she was defined in the world: an aging, broke woman with a sick, unfaithful husband. "What do I want?" she echoed, thoughtfully. "That is the question."

Drew sank down in the other chair, pushing Adele's stack of papers and books out of the way. He sat with his hands on his knees, licked his lips, said, "I miss you, Adele."

"Mmm." Adele detached herself from his gaze, looked out at the hori-zon. Her grandparents had taken her, one summer, to the Jersey shore, where she had stood in the mucky wet sand and imagined the world that lay be-yond the Atlantic, a world she was sure contained the answers to all her adolescent yearning. "That's what Cordy said. That she misses me."

Drew grasped the straw eagerly. "How is she? What did she have to say?"

"You know," Adele replied, "I don't think she's forgiven me for leaving. She loved Noah."

Great, thought Drew. Next thing she'll blame me, personally, for 9/11. He clenched his fists and tried to swallow the lump of rage that surged in his throat, and was astonished by the jagged sob that escaped from him. It startled both of them; their eyes flew toward each other; scuffling creatures suddenly united against a larger predator. And at that contact, at the look of fear in Adele's eyes, Drew was unpinned. He covered his face with his hands, shuddering and swallowing his gasps. Tears ran through his fingers and splashed onto his freshly ironed chinos.

Adele sat still as a stone, watching her husband as though he were an actor on a stage. What is Hecuba to him? she wondered, perusing the way his shoulders shook and noting the real tears. And then she felt her own wet face, and heard a sob escape from her own frozen mouth, and without meaning to she clove to her husband, wrapping her arms around him, soothing, murmuring, mingling her tears with his. Cordelia's letter dropped to the floor and scuttled with the breeze up against the painted wrought iron of the balcony, where it leaned and gently fluttered, buffeted by the gathering wind off the Pacific.

Twenty-eight

SYLVIA HAD ALERTED the neighbors to the probability of a parking glut on the night of the engagement party. Sixty-five invitations had gone out to the list supplied by Danny and Kirstin. By the Saturday of the event, only fifty-two RSVPs had been received. Sylvia fumed, attributed the rudeness to "the young people" and instructed the caterer to be prepared for sixty. Carl glowered at the girl from the florist's who backed her pickup truck into the drive and unloaded four flats of arrangements. Sylvia hovered, smoothing pink tablecloths over the tables that had been set up on the patio, tweaking the flowers, issuing commands. "Don't even," she warned Carl, raising her finger in the air before he'd said a word.

The only reason he'd agreed to this was because he felt bad for Drew. Drew had been a fun friend, always ready to play a round of golf or buy a round of drinks, quick to reach for the check, slow to take offense if Carl blew up over a missed putt, which he was prone to do. Drew had a soothing influence on Carl, maybe because he was a doctor. Carl had been shaken by the difference in him since the heart attack, how quickly he'd aged, become fragile. Carl tried, really hard, not to gloat over the Ponzi thing, and the pang of guilt he felt over his impulse toward schadenfreude made him acquiesce to the party. But now, of course, Sylvia was sticking it to him every which way. "A caterer?" he'd asked. "Why can't we just grill burgers?"

"It's not the Fourth of July, Carl. It's a wedding engagement."

"What's with the flowers? It's overkill."

"What would you like for centerpieces, Carl? Ashtrays?"

She'd even hired musicians! He'd insisted on a written proposal with an itemization of expenses, and she tried to camouflage the five hundred dollars she was paying them as part of the catering fee. He had hit the roof about that, and she'd paid him back by serving him some kind of Russian pancake swimming in sour cream for dinner. He'd been up all night with heartburn, and all she said was, "Oh, I thought you'd like it. It's Russian cuisine."

So Carl stewed in silence as the minions Sylvia had hired descended upon his home, fussing and feathering for a party for someone else's kid. It particularly galled him that Beth had refused to come home. "It's not like I'm friends with him," she'd said, on her BlackBerry, the shrieks of the Manhattan streets making it impossible to converse. "They're your friends, not mine!" she'd added just before the connection was lost.

The guests began arriving at six. The first to arrive were Kirstin's parents, Kathy and Scott. At least Sylvia assumed they were Kirstin's parents, but much later in the evening it was revealed that Scott was just Kathy's boyfriend, at which point Sylvia was way too irritated to care who the actual father might be. Kathy looked to be in her thirties from a distance, but up close her face was weathered and stretched too tight across her bones. She was dressed similarly to her daughter, in yoga pants and an Indian peasant blouse, with ropes of silver and turquoise around her leathery neck. Scott, who was a lifeguard, looked like a lifeguard. They came with a vegetarian casserole in a covered dish and a six-pack of Fat Tire. "Oh, that's so sweet!" Sylvia said. "I'll just put it in the kitchen and we'll bring it out later." They were having grilled salmon and roasted new potatoes, haricots verts and a salad of mixed baby greens and papaya. *They can just eat this themselves if they won't eat fish,* Syl thought, shoving the casserole on a bottom shelf in the fridge.

Next came various relatives of the soon-to-be-bride, introduced as Uncle Nico or Nicky and Shandra something or other, dragging preteen twins who positioned themselves at the nut bowls and practically strapped on feed bags. They were followed by somebody's grandmother and an old man with a walker who winked at Sylvia and said he had his harmonica in his pocket for later. Sylvia had expected more oohing and aahing over her home and was put out by the seeming lack of appreciation. No one had any trouble making themselves at home, and soon there was a crowd milling around, most of whom Sylvia had never laid eyes on before.

Carl had put his foot down about a bartender and was manning the makeshift tiki bar, wearing a Hawaiian shirt and a Padres cap. The musicians shambled in, dragging their equipment. They staked out their territory and began unpacking and spreading out, which alarmed Sylvia. They were to play only for an hour, during cocktails; she couldn't understand why they needed so much stuff. "By the time you get all this unpacked and set up, your hour will be over," she muttered to the keyboard player, a pale young man in a rumpled thrift-shop suit with a face like a puzzled cherub. He looked up from his labors and smiled reassuringly at her. The bass player was an older, bigger man with too much cologne wafting off of him, and the singer was grotesquely overly made-up and wore a clingy, floor-length red dress.

Hordes of young people were now pouring into her house, bringing with them a rising din and an exuberant energy. Glancing out at the patio, Syl saw that Carl had recruited help bartending. They seemed to be having a jolly time fiddling with a keg. Sylvia had been opposed to the keg, but Carl had insisted, and since any display of enthusiasm for the party mollified her she gave in. The bottles of Pinot Grigio and Chardonnay glittered in the sunlight untouched, she noticed; nearly everyone out there had a beer in their hand. She ducked into the powder room to make sure there wasn't lipstick on her teeth and was horrified to discover the toilet seat up. Gingerly, with a piece of toilet paper between her fingers, she lowered it. "It's for Adele," she told herself in the mirror.

Adele and Drew arrived a little before six-thirty. Sylvia had wanted them to be early, to be there to greet the guests, but there was no rushing Drew, these days. In the car, Adele said, "I'm dreading this. Isn't there any way we can get out of it?"

"Not that I could come up with," Drew answered. "I can't really play the heart attack card, not when it's all for Danny."

"Harumph," replied Adele. She had tried to have a heart-to-heart with her son, and had been gently rebuffed. It had begun to occur to her that this time, this girl may have succeeded where so many others had failed. She felt eerily distanced from the whole affair. Every now and then it hit her with a dull thud, like something falling in the next room, that her son might actually be married soon. It didn't seem real, but then what did, anymore? The holidays had come and gone with hardly a ripple in their daily routine. The boys were busy with their own lives, and spent most of their time off with their girlfriends. That's how it went, wasn't it? The girlfriends kind of took over. "A son's a son till he takes a wife," wasn't that the expression? She stood and waited while Drew paused to catch his breath. He had exhausted himself getting out of the car, and stood sucking in air like an asthmatic.

"So, are we getting divorced or not?" she had asked him earlier. Casually, as if she were asking, "Are we eating in or out?"

"Not," he'd said. "Are you okay with that?"

She'd been in the bathroom putting on her makeup. He'd come in to ask her about what shirt to wear, and was sitting on the edge of the bed, putting on his socks. She'd looked at herself in the mirror and noted, dispassionately, that there was no flicker of joy or triumph in her eyes, no change in the grim set of her mouth. If it hadn't been for the heart attack. If it hadn't been for the loss of the money. *So that's it*, she thought. *I'm keeping my marriage after all.*

"You okay?" she called out to Drew now. He straightened up, patted himself on the chest. "Fine! Slow, but fine!" He gave her a brave little soldier's smile. His polo shirt hung loosely on him. A breeze rattled the tops of the palm trees. From where she stood she could glimpse the ocean between two houses, a glittering sliver. The breeze on her cheek, and a trick of the light, turned it into a mountain lake. A wheeling gull twirled like her snatched umbrella, rooting her on the pavement. Drew caught up with her, took her hand, brought it to his lips. "Danny, a husband," he said.

"I think he's going to go through with it," she replied. "I just had a feeling. I think this is it."

A few blocks away, Jake Gold and his girlfriend, Kristin, sat parked in his RAV4. They'd been arguing on the way to his brother's engagement party, and he'd pulled over to finish the fight. Jake was anxious to get to the Otts' house. He was protective of his brother and felt it was incumbent upon him to be there on time to meet and greet, run interference for Dan, not to mention their parents. He and Kristin were already late, and he was getting anxious. Kristin had started the argument over nothing; his pants. She didn't like the pants he was wearing. He tried to joke with her, but somehow her not liking his pants had turned into an MRI of their whole relationship, which actually was pretty good. He was happy with it. They got along great, for the most part; they had fantastic sex; she was funny and smart. He had to admit he probably loved her; they'd been together longer than he'd been with any of his other girlfriends. But she was on some kind of rag today, and now she was huddled into herself actually crying, and Jake had just seen his parents drive by on their way to the party and he was trying to figure out if he could somehow extricate himself, leave Kristin here to pull herself together and get himself to where he was expected.

"Baby," he said, "I don't know what's wrong."

"Yes you do."

"No, I really don't. If I did I'd do whatever I could to make it better."

"You would?"

"Of course I would! I mean if it's just the pants I'll go buy some, but now you're saying it's not the pants, and I just don't know."

"The pants are the tip of the iceberg."

"I mean . . . I just don't know what the fuck that means."

"How long have Danny and Kirstin been together?"

"I don't know." Another car drove by, party-bound. Jake tightened his grip on the gearshift.

"Longer than us or shorter than us?"

"I don't know."

"I know. Shorter than us."

Jake's jaw twitched, just like his father's did.

"How do you think that makes me feel?" Kristin's voice had risen an octave and taken on a petulant, girly tone.

"I don't know. Like you want me to change my pants?"

"Did you even notice what I'm wearing?"

"I told you you look nice!"

"What did I say to you last night? Do you remember? I said, 'Tomorrow I'm wearing what I wore when we met.' I said that to you last night, last thing before I said good night."

"Okay, Kristin, you look nice, and gee, you're wearing the same thing you were wearing the night we met. Okay?"

"You just don't understand anything."

Jake dug his fingernails into his flesh. "I need to get . . . I need to go. I can't do this right now. Baby, come on. Please?"

Suddenly Kristin unfurled herself and was on top of him, wedged in his lap with the steering wheel shoved against the small of her back. She wrapped herself around him like an octopus, pressing her hard breasts against him, breathing into his ear.

"Marry me," she whispered.

Music started up from somewhere. Had the Otts hired a band? In the rearview mirror, over Kristin's shoulder, Jake saw another line of cars wend into the cul-de-sac.

"Okay," he said.

"Really?"

"Sure."

"Ask me."

"Ask you what?"

"Ask me to marry you."

"Kristin, will you marry me?"

"Yes! Yes, Jake, I will marry you!"

As he aimed his keys behind him to beep his car locks, he thought how really bad that had been of her. He wouldn't have expected it. But look how happy she was now, skipping along, bouncing like the cute cheerleader she'd been. It was only words he'd said. Nothing was written in stone. She must know she'd coerced him. Of course he meant to get married someday, have a family. Maybe to her, why not? But he didn't like feeling bullied. He'd imagined a different scenario when the time came, one in which he might actually kneel down, or maybe hire a plane to skywrite the question like he'd seen someone do one day. He'd imagined—not that he'd given it a whole lot of thought, but certain vague things would occur to him, like how surprised and delighted she'd be, whoever *she* was, after he popped the question. Not like this, when he was preoccupied and late. Kristin was doing a little dance in front of him, a dance of . . . triumph? She had a killer ass. She really was cute, especially now that she was in a good mood again. Well, they could talk about it later.

⤫

Maggie and Paul sat in a corner of the patio together, sharing a chaise, listening to the music. The band had set up in the living room next to the open French doors, and they had their amps turned up high. The singer was taking a break and was at the bar, where Carl was pouring her a glass of wine and proclaiming loudly about her "mellifluous pipes." Danny and Kirstin were still entwined from their lingering kiss after dancing to "Our Love Is Here to Stay." The bass and keyboard had launched into a jazz tune that considerably raised the level of their previous offerings, which had pandered to the singer and her sugary renditions of love songs. "Now you're talking," Paul said, leaning in to concentrate on the keyboarder's solo. Maggie had never shared Paul's enthusiasm for jazz, but she was feeling lazy and contented, lolling in the chaise with a glass of wine and her husband's strong hands casually rubbing her foot. Paul had never been affectionate in public. Touching her in any way seemed to be foreplay, for him, so he saved it for the bedroom. Since their talk at the beach, however, things had shifted between them. They were being shy with each other, like newlyweds. He'd taken to impulsive bursts of affection; kissing the back of her neck in passing, holding her hand in public. Maggie was thrilled by it. There was something sweet and high-schoolish about their exchanges, as if they'd long harbored crushes on each other and finally discovered their feelings were shared. Each of them felt private relief and wonder at having emerged from the ragged, fraught weariness that had become their life together. Even

their lovemaking had changed; a new tenderness had sprouted where edgi-
ness had been. This morning they had lolled in bed together, talking. Maggie longed to tell him about Mitch, about her realization; she wanted to
share it with him, validate it by speaking it out loud to the one most affected.
But she held her tongue, suspecting that too many revelations at once
might tip their fragile new relationship. Unburdening herself would only
hand the burden to him, and he'd spent too many years feeling threatened
by Mitch. Once, Paul made a comment about the "man thrashing" he was
sure they'd indulged in on their trip, and she laughed. "Trust me, we didn't
spend enough time together to get into all that," she'd said. "Besides, Adele
and Sylvia adore you. Any thrashing wouldn't have targeted you, so you can
let that one go." For a brief moment he looked as if he wanted to pursue it,
wanted to press her about details, but then he dropped it.

Now here came their son, Josh, weaving through the crowd, plopping
next to them to say hello. He hadn't brought a date—Maggie'd been hoping to meet the girl he was seeing, but he'd shrugged and said not this time.
Paul squeezed her calf, warning her not to pursue it. Josh was secretive by
nature—often they'd found he'd kept things from them; never anything
serious, sometimes even things that would have pleased them. Maggie
chalked it up to his being a Cancer, the Crab, but Paul sensed it was trepi-
dation and eagerness to please that censored him. It was a characteristic
he understood all too well. As the three of them sat together, chatting
casually, Maggie felt a rush of well-being. She leaned into her husband,
listened to the sound of their voices and the background of the party's din.

They saw Adele and Drew come in, and then be swept away by Sylvia
to be introduced to Kirstin's relatives. At the sight of Adele, Maggie felt
what was becoming a familiar impulse, to throw herself on her knees in
grateful prayer. Drew looked awful—like a little old man. Sylvia had stopped
walking and instead was dancing to and fro, clutching her wineglass, pulling people around.

"Is she ever in her element," Maggie chuckled. "Look at her. Queen for
a day."

Paul had once made the mistake of agreeing with Maggie's disparaging
remarks about Sylvia and had been startled by Maggie's abrupt 180, in

which she starchily announced that her friends were not "fodder" for his "ridicule." So he kept his mouth shut now, as he had ever since. Personally he could take only so much of Sylvia, but fortunately that was all he ever had to take of her. Here she came now, swooping, Adele in tow.

"Mother of the groom," she announced. Adele looked disoriented.

"Come with me," Syl commanded. "I have to show you guys something." She rumpled Paul's hair and twitched her hips to the music. "Isn't the band fabulous?"

"They are," Paul agreed.

"Josh, where's your date? Look at you, you hunk. You hottie. When did you get so gorgeous?" Josh looked helplessly at his parents, blushing in his Irish-skinned way.

"Syl, you look so pretty," Maggie said. "I like that necklace. It's different, for you."

Syl's hand flew to her neck, touched the silver heart that hung from amber beads. "You like it? It's yours." She took it off and extended it to Maggie with a gesture of largesse.

"Get out of here. What are you, Japanese? Just because I like it doesn't mean you have to give it to me."

"No, I want you to have it, really." Sylvia draped it around Maggie's neck, stood back to admire it. "To be honest with you, Mags, I bought it with you in mind, but then I got selfish and decided to keep it. It's much more you than me, though, so please. I love it on you."

"Okay, then. Thanks." Maggie shrugged and looked to Paul, who smiled noncommittally. Adele wasn't paying attention; she was gazing off at the view.

"Come on!" Syl pulled Maggie up, herded them through the crowd. She put her hands on Maggie's waist and Maggie felt her knocking around, trying to get her to conga. Pulling herself away, she yelled in Syl's ear, "How many people are here? It looks like a lot more than sixty."

Sylvia waved her arms above her head in a gesture meant to convey complete abandon.

"Not a clue," she bellowed.

Upstairs, she positioned them in the hallway in front of Beth's room.

"Ready?" she said. "Ta Da!" She threw open the door, beamed expectantly at them.

"The Shrine," as Maggie and Adele referred to it between themselves, had been transformed. Gone were Beth's dolls and stuffed animals, her posters, all vestiges of the teenage girl's room. The bed had been stripped of its frilly linens, pushed against the wall, and converted into a sort of daybed, with bolsters. The white-painted dresser and skirted vanity were gone, in their place a no-nonsense desk, a computer, a bulletin board.

"It's my office," Sylvia announced. "What do you think?"

"Huh," said Adele.

"Nice," said Maggie. "What's it for?"

"Well," said Sylvia, "I have an announcement to make. Better sit down." Maggie and Adele sat, obediently, on the bed turned sofa.

"I'm writing a book," Sylvia announced.

Politely, Adele said, "About what?"

"It's self-help. Like a how-to. I have it all outlined, I have the title, I even have the names of the chapters. I'm taking a writing class with a professional writer. She's actually published novels! She's going to help me."

"Wow," said Maggie.

"Well, I'm not actually in the class yet, but I've applied, and I've gotten a lot of encouragement for my idea."

"So what's the idea?" Adele spoke in a measured, serious voice, causing Maggie to have to fake a cough to cover her mirth. Sylvia was flushed and expansive, her freshly permed hair a staticky nimbus around her glowing face. *She looks insane,* thought Maggie.

"It's called *Get Outta the Passenger Seat and Drive Your Man Home,*" Syl announced.

"Wow," said Maggie.

"What? Say it again?" Adele tipped her head as if she hadn't heard right.

"*Get Outta the Passenger Seat and Drive Your Man Home,*" Sylvia repeated slowly, enunciating as if speaking to a retarded first grader.

"'Outta'?" said Adele.

"It's colloquial. Don't you think it's a good title? It's about how to keep your husband. Or get him back. Do you have any idea how many women

need this book? Carla says I'll probably make the *New York Times* best-
seller list!"

"Who's Carla?" said Maggie.

Syl waved her hand impatiently. "A friend. But don't you like it? Don't
you think it's a great idea? I'm going to interview a bunch of women—you
included, Del, hope you don't mind—and get their stories about what they
went through, and then present them like hypothetical cases, with my sure-
fire recommendations for what they needed to do to turn the situation
around. Then I'll have a part, like an epilogue, where I do the payoff and
reveal what actually happened. Fabulous?"

"Fantastic," said Adele.

"Super," said Maggie. "Bloody fucking super, Syl."

Sylvia beamed. "I couldn't wait to tell you guys. Carla thinks it's brilliant. And you know, I always was a pretty good writer. I always thought I
could write something if I put my mind to it."

There were shrieks from outside. The band started to play the wedding
march. The women ran to the window and looked down. "My God, there's
a lot of people out there," Adele remarked. There was the sound of glass
breaking, and a roar from the crowd. The women ran downstairs, where
someone had shaken up a bottle of beer and was squirting it all over Jake.

"What's going on?" Adele said, to no one in particular, and a woman
she'd never seen before turned to her and said, "That's Danny's big brother.
He just got engaged, too!"

Adele looked through the crowd to find Drew but instead saw Noah,
who appeared to be trying to dance despite the girl who was wrapped
around him, sucking on his neck like a greedy piglet. Adele tried to catch
Jake's eye, but he had a dopey grin on his face and was wiping beer out of
his eyelashes. Maggie and Syl each put an arm around Adele. Where was
Drew? The girls with trays of sushi had stopped circulating and the waiters
were attempting to get through the throng to set up the buffet. People had
begun milling around the tables, claiming seats, a group was righting the
one that had been knocked over, salvaging flowers from the shards of broken glass. Oh, there was Drew, with Carl—he was laughing. His children
were leaping like lemmings and he was laughing, Carl no doubt goading

him with smut. Someone was tugging on Sylvia's arm—the caterer, red-faced and sweaty. "I have dinner for sixty," he was shouting. "Your party is out of control! I don't have food for all these people!"

"I only got fifty-two RSVPs," Syl murmured, looking baffled. "Who are all these people?"

"I told you it was a bad idea," Adele said, but no one heard her.

The band was packing up as fast as they could. Someone connected an iPod to the outdoor speakers and there was a blast of reggae, greeted with an ecstatic roar, and the patio turned into a zoo of writhing bodies. Carl had abandoned the bar and was dancing like an idiot. His Padres cap floated in the pool, along with champagne flutes and flowers and what looked like one of the new patio cushions Syl had bought for the party. A girl wiggled out of her dress to reveal what could have been a bathing suit and jumped into the pool; others followed. The door to the powder room banged open and a couple staggered out, the boy holding up the very drunk girl. Maggie intercepted them and said, brusquely, "Time to go," steering them through the house to the street. Someone was vomiting in Sylvia's rose garden.

Sylvia grabbed Adele. "What should I do?" she wailed.

But Adele was staring through the crowd at Drew, who was now lurking behind the tiki bar with a tall redhead. There was something furtive about the way they'd positioned themselves; they appeared to be conversing with an intimacy that belied party chat. The girl—for she was a girl; even from a distance Adele could see that she was young, not out of her thirties—reached up and stroked Drew's cheek with her fingers. Drew averted his face and glanced up nervously, with an expression exactly like Danny's when as a boy he got caught in the act of some misdeed.

"Adele!" Sylvia pleaded. "You have to talk to Danny, get these party crashers out of here!"

To Adele, the whole scene had begun to resemble a Hieronymus Bosch painting. Distorted images of leering, twisted bodies seemed to be winding themselves around the furniture. The cacophony sounded to her like hell itself. Something brushed against her, and she looked down to see a child trying to negotiate through the forest of legs. She touched the downy hair and the girl looked up, but instead of an innocent in need of comfort Adele saw the face of a demon, eyes glazed and burning, mouth stuffed and chewing, with crumbs of something dribbling out. She looked back to where she had just glimpsed Drew but could see nothing now except a wall of undulating people. Had she imagined that look on his face? Had it actually been Danny she'd seen? The *thut thut thut* of helicopters flying overhead sounded dimly through the din, and Adele looked up to see a formation, she counted fourteen, on some mission from Camp Pendleton. She wondered idly if they'd been dispatched to break up the party. Imagined an amplified voice coming from above: "You down there, stop it right now." They hovered clumsily, like huge bugs, and Adele gazed up at them, imagining the boys who were at their helms, boys just like her own, who were down here behaving like satyrs at a Bacchanalia. She turned to Sylvia, who had mascara smeared under her eyes and lipstick running into the thin lines above her upper lip, and had latched onto the arm of the ethereal keyboard player and was preventing his escape, demanding that he disarm the speakers.

Sunset was turning the sky into a pearly lavender, like the inside of an abalone shell. The silly palm trees stuck out against the opalescence like pinwheels. The scent of pot wafted across the patio. A girl screamed "FUCK!" followed by a loud splash and a swell of laughter. The music thumped. "White man something something we gonna fight . . ."

Everyone was behaving with abandon. Syl and Carl were dancing now, bumping their hips together. Syl was waving her arms in the air. Adele had a sense of nakedness, vulnerability, standing there under the sweep of sky, surrounded by the bare brown hills. *Human beings are affected by climate and topography*, she thought. *Formed by it, even.* She hadn't clarified this perception, before. The realization struck her as significant—she had to tell Drew. All his "why why why's" had made her defensive; she'd never been able to articulate her objections. But this was something he'd have to consider. This was palpable, almost scientific. Consider the landscape, Drew, she'd say—bleached, vast, stark. Home, it's lush and fecund, curled and coiled, with winding roads and coves and pockets of forests. Even the city is filled with hidden lanes and mews and secret places. People take their cue from the landscape. Here they're in your face and barely dressed and aggressively happy. Home, they're private and reserved. Respectful, polite.

It was true that she had tried to love California. But not with her whole heart. Of course Drew saw that. That's what he meant when he'd said those things to her, during that awful fight. "You're never there, you're always judging, criticizing." She had thought it unfair. But he was right. He saw her refusal to love their new home as a betrayal. So somehow he'd worked it out to betray her back. The thought brought a kind of clarification. She wanted to share it with him.

But if she had failed him by not embracing their new life, hadn't he failed her equally by turning his back on their old life? After 9/11, Drew couldn't wait to get out, whereas she had actually contemplated moving back into the city. Her city. She'd been so proud of her New Yorkers, felt such a swelling of loyalty and connection.

And if she had leapt off the cliff with him, if she'd been able to dive into their new life with equal glee, would that have kept him faithful? She had to ask him that. There were so many things they had to discuss. It had been too long since they'd talked. Since she'd wanted to talk. Now she felt an urgency, a need to understand.

Drew had accused her of being unhappy, negative. Now it occurred to her that the times when she'd been happiest were precisely the times when he hadn't been. The things she'd thought were the meat of their shared life were, for him, hors d'oeuvres on a passing plate, casually savored while anticipating the main course. A nasty thought leapt up: Had he planned this? To get his family out here, liquidate their assets, dole out her portion, and cut loose? A sinister contemplation; the very thought shocked her. Drew? Her husband, Drew? She would have squashed anyone who might have suggested such a thing. And yet here was the thought, rising of its own volition in her own mind. She'd never have believed herself capable of such a treacherous suspicion. The mere existence of the thought set off a quake in the very foundation of her life. Even the discovery of his grotesque infidelities hadn't rumbled as deeply as this. She and Drew had been together more than half their lives. Their relationship was as entwined around the core of her life as her own tendons.

She couldn't see him now. She could see nothing but a tangle of bodies. He might be in the bushes with the redhead, for all she knew. And this was her son's engagement party! She used to imagine the boys' weddings taking place at home, in Bedford. She'd entertained fantasies of how they'd set it up, with tables on the slate terrace and a dance floor erected on the lawn. Never, in her musings on the future, had anything like this occurred to her. It was wrong, all wrong. It had nothing to do with her. Everything about California shut her out, shoved her aside, negated her. When they'd first gotten here, she'd gone through a period in which she'd agonized over the history of all exiles. She'd lain awake at night thinking of the mothers in Auschwitz, unable to comfort their starving children. Her own grandmother had been one of those children. Adele had been severe with herself, passing judgment on her unhappiness as shallow and spoiled, reminding herself of her countless blessings in the face of things. Every time she heard an accent—South African or Middle Eastern or any of the unidentifiable hints of exile—she had been ashamed of her own petulant grief.

Yet the grief persisted. Thoughts rose, unbidden, demanding attention like a toddler. Thoughts like the one she entertained now, of cardinals outside at the feeder, the muffled sound of fresh snowfall. Not this. Not this scene; this was not for her. For her boys, perhaps. For Drew, apparently. They were all grown up now, all of them flown off. She'd never been meant to tag along. She was done now; she had finished what she had never realized was a job. And yet Drew wanted their life together to go on. He'd said there would be no divorce. "Are you okay with that?" he'd said.

No, she wasn't okay with that. If they were going to stay together they would have to reforge. She would not be one of those disappointed women, shrugging away her bitterness in order to hold on to a flimsy, straw-built life.

Maggie and Paul were dancing together now, too, smiling at each other. Maggie looked beatific. Paul put his arm around her waist and twirled her; she laughed up at him and he leaned down and kissed her lightly before she twirled away. Suddenly Adele wanted to dance with her husband. She

wanted to hold him and move to the music with him. Of course he'd have
to take it easy, but he could certainly just stand there and sway with her.
She'd let him know she was ready to talk. Maybe tonight they would begin
to attempt a way back to communication.

She had to bushwhack her way through what had become the dance floor.
Someone sloshed a drink on her, someone stepped on her foot, someone
backed into her while attempting a dance move. There they were. They had
ducked behind the pepper tree. Drew was leaning against it; he had a stupid
look on his face as he gazed at the girl. A fond, gluttonous look, as if he were
about to lick his lips. The girl was pressing a hand into his chest, talking ear-
nestly.

"Excuse me," Adele said. They both stared, startled. "Sorry to interrupt."
To the girl, she said, "I'm Mrs. Gold. Would you excuse us, please?"

Flashing an alarmed look at Drew, the girl backed away and was absorbed
by the throng of bodies. Like a released fish, disappearing into the seamless
water to dart back into its fishy depths. Drew gave Adele a goofy smile.

"Thanks," he said. "Adele to the rescue."

"Do you know her?"

"Adele."

"Did you sleep with her?"

"Stop it."

"Stop what? I wanted to talk to you. Actually, I wanted to dance with
you. I had some thoughts I wanted to share with you. I was missing you."

"Well, let's go dance, honey. Let's talk. Anything you want."

"Is she one of your girls?"

"Knock it off."

"No, Drew, this is what it is. This is what it will always be. I'll always
wonder. We could be on a plane and some stewardess could plump up your
pillow and I'll wonder, Did he sleep with her?"

"Not now. Can we do this later, at home? She works at Scripps, for
Christ's sake. She was asking about the heart attack."

"Uh-huh. I'll be hearing that one a lot."

"What's the matter with you? Come on, let's go get a glass of champagne and toast our son." He reached for her arm to propel her back to the party. Adele held her hand up to stop him.

"Drew. I can't do this."

"You can't do what?"

"This." Adele stood in front of her husband, shaking her head. "I can't do it. I can't live like this. I won't."

"Adele . . ."

"No. No, Drew, no. I don't trust you. I can't ever trust you again."

"You are completely overreacting. Nothing was—"

"It doesn't matter. I don't care." She looked into his face, and before she knew she was speaking she heard herself say, "I don't even know if I love you anymore. I don't even know who you are anymore."

They stared at each other. Drew reached for her. "Adele. Please."

She backed up. "I miss you! I don't know where you went."

He took a step toward her and she held up both her arms. "No. I'm done. I'm sorry. But . . . no more. I'm going home. You can get a ride with one of the boys."

"Adele, stop it, for Christ's sake—"

But Adele walked away from him, skirting the crowd as much as possible, back into the house, where she had stashed her purse. Then out to the car, to the silence of driving home, alone, back to the condo that was the only home she had, where she poured herself a glass of wine and sat on the balcony, pulling the quiet and solitude around her like a blanket, and read, and reread, and read again the letter from Cordelia.

Twenty-nine

THERE COMES A TIME *in the course of our hour upon the stage when the music stops. For most of us it doesn't stop abruptly, but fades and disperses and then, on some bleak morning when there are no eggs and the milk has gone off, a sense of persecution descends. The money's gone, love has soured, the sap has dried up, and simple joy is but a nostalgic haze. What then? Plow on? Push your lump of clay through the ticking tocking day? Cordelia is one of the few for whom it ended abruptly. For her, there are no expectations. She summons the past and fishes up memories of a friendship once dear, and because she doesn't know what else to do, she offers it some breath. Nothing like hope is involved. Just a whisper into the darkness.*

You've seen Adele around. At the market, in line in Starbucks, in the back of yogacize class. A short, crispy woman, wizened beyond her years, her face a mask of defensiveness. She's not quick to smile, but if you listen you can hear some interesting, funny things. She doesn't miss much.

Adele has spent the two-hour ferry ride in the bow on the sundeck, buffeted by the wind. Long after everyone else went to the lee side or the cafeteria, long after the interest of departure eased into the journey, she stayed in the bow like a figurehead, peering ahead and around as they cut through the sea. Except for the trip to Canada, she had not been in the Pacific Northwest before. She had not expected such beauty. The mountains rose and fell into the mist, some of them glistening at the top with blue-tinted snowcaps. Islands appeared, fringed to their rocky shorelines with pines, houses hugging the cliffs or peeking through the woods. What were the lives of these people like, Adele wondered. Reliant on boats to access the mainland, tucked away in the middle of this archipelago in this mall-less and multiplexless moist and verdant land? The greenery and the moisture were delicious to Adele; she breathed them in deeply. The ferry maneuvered through a pass and emerged again into open sea, and suddenly a huge black rock dislodged and slid, then another, and another, and then they disappeared and reappeared, and then a fluke split the water's surface, caught by a shaft of sunlight streaking out of the cloud bank. A commotion from somewhere on the ferry confirmed the whale sighting, and as Adele was cursing herself for not having her camera, a high-pitched, urgent sound reverberated, and she looked up to see an eagle soaring purposefully toward some unsuspecting prey. Despite herself, gladness began to seep into her. The wind whipped her; the sun warmed her.

This was an unanticipated adventure. She had simply followed Cordelia's instructions about where to fly, how to get to the ferry landing, which ticket to purchase. They had spoken on the phone briefly, in a businesslike way, each assuring the other how delighted she'd be to see her. When the plane had lifted off from Lindbergh this time, Adele had felt a rush of relief, lightness in her bones.

As the ferry approached its destination, the deck filled up again. Children pointed and exclaimed, were lifted up to better see. Tourists snapped pictures of each other standing at the rail. Adele watched as the land crew rushed about and the ship crew strapped on their life jackets; the ferry bellowed its arrival. Inside, the passengers for whom this was simply their commute nudged each other awake, folded newspapers, gathered children.

Cordelia was there, waiting for her. Adele spotted her instantly among the crowd of meeters: tall, slightly stooped, an unmistakably patrician air about her. She smiled and waved as Adele approached. They hugged. It was a jolt to see how Cordy had aged; Adele wondered if Cordy was think-ing the same of her.

They tossed her luggage into the rental car and headed to the B and B. Through the harbor, with its fish and chips shacks, past the long line of cars waiting to board the ferry for its next trip back to the mainland.

"How did you find this place?" Adele asked.

Cordy gave her a twisted smile, an expression Adele wasn't familiar with. "I pointed on a map."

"That's not like you. You didn't research, investigate? Send out surveys?"

"Of course I did, after I pointed. The main thing was, it had to be as far away as I could get and still be in the country. I'm not ready to leave the country—not yet. Mind you, this isn't definitive. We're just scoping."

"I'm surprised you don't want to go to England. You love it there."

Cordelia flinched, almost imperceptibly, and Adele realized her error. The point was, Cordelia needed to go somewhere she'd never been, some-where that held no memories. Adele was furious with herself for her insen-sitivity. She was trying to formulate something to say to smooth over the moment when Cordy said, "People seem to like it here."

"What's not to like?" Adele gazed out the window at rolling green hills, glimpses of the sea through the trees, mailboxes clustered at the base of a dirt road leading into a forest. "It looks like Hobbit Shire," she offered.

Cordy didn't respond, and the silence fell uneasily on Adele. It was unreasonable to expect things to fall instantly back into how they'd been, she told herself. It had been years since they'd seen each other. Ages since they'd even chatted on the phone. How could she begin to understand what Cordelia's life had been like; how could she expect to effortlessly re-sume a friendship whose context had been shattered? She wondered if this whole enterprise would be as uncomfortable as she felt now. It was possible that their friendship would never revive, that this would be a business ven-ture only. If that was the case, she decided, so be it. She would give Corde-lia what she could, and hopefully it would be well accepted. And Cordelia's gift to her was immeasurable. On her deathbed, she would bless Cordelia for making her dream come true, even if it was a slightly edited version of the dream.

Cordelia had booked them into the B and B that was a working farm. Adele's room overlooked the cutting garden, where flowers were grown to sell at a roadside stand. In the distance she could glimpse the mountains. She unpacked and went across the hall to Cordy's door and knocked. "Come on in," Cordy called.

Cordelia had chosen the smaller room for herself. Its windows overlooked the driveway. Embarrassed, Adele said, "We should switch rooms. Mine's bigger."

"I chose this one."

"Okay." Adele sat in a little Victorian stuffed chair next to the window. Cordelia was on the bed, propped up with a pile of pillows, looking at brochures of local attractions.

"Cord, we need to get a few things straight. I'm a little uncomfortable, I have to tell you. You're paying for everything—I'm not accustomed to this."

"I have nothing but money."

"Yes, but I just want to clear the air. Basically, what this is, is—you've hired me, right? Just so I'm clear."

Cordy laughed. Clapped her hand over her mouth, said, "Oh my God. You actually made me laugh. See, I knew I could count on you."

"Is that in my job description? Making you laugh?"

Cordelia glanced at her sharply, then went back to her brochures.

"I'm sorry," Adele said. "I don't mean to sound defensive. I'm just not sure—I mean, I'd like for us to . . . you know, have a dialogue."

"Adele, have you gone California on me?"

"If I have, shoot me."

Cordy frowned. "You still don't like it there?"

"Like it? My hatred of California has taken on depths of loathing even Woody Allen can't approach. I don't even find it funny anymore. It is an insidious, parched, cultural and moral wasteland. The beast is slouching across the desert toward L.A. I am a plucked cadaver; don't tell me you can't see it in my face."

"Wow." Cordelia stared at her. "Wow, Del. I had no idea. I've been picturing you lounging on your deck chair with a gin and tonic, watching the sunsets."

"Really? That's how you've been picturing me? Boy, were you watching the wrong movie."

"But, Drew—he still likes it there?"

"You couldn't get Drew out of California with a crowbar."

"And the boys?"

"All turncoats. Every one of them. They've even become Padres fans."

"Oh, but this is incredible news. No more Yankees?"

"They've actually turned on them. Broke my heart."

Cordelia stretched her long legs out, pulled another pillow behind her. "And your house? What's the status? Let me guess: Drew's trying to talk you into building it in California; you're holding out for . . . hmm . . . Vermont?"

Adele snorted. "I won't be building my house, in California or anywhere else. I'll be building your house, hopefully, and that will be fine. More than fine."

"But Adele, honestly, this is terrible news. What about your agreement? Didn't he promise you, when you left?"

"His promises haven't turned out to be worth much."

"I didn't know you'd been unhappy, Adele. All these years, I imagined you living this golden life—no pun intended!"

Adele smiled. "I don't want to get into this right now, but the marriage is over. In the course of destroying it, Drew also managed to lose all our money—my money. Maybe that's why I'm feeling a little raw, a little like hired help."

Cordelia stared at Adele for an uncomfortably long time, then nodded and turned away. "You lost all your money," she murmured.

"We still have the condo, free and clear. I'll probably stay there; he owes me that much."

"But you hate it there."

"Yup. Maybe in a few years, when—if—the market comes back, I'll sell it and go home. Wherever that is. Rent somebody's guesthouse, something like that."

Cordy said, in a dreamy voice, "Once upon a time there was a family of four, a husband and wife and two good strong boys, and a yellow Lab and a parakeet. They all lived together in a beautiful house on a beautiful street in a beautiful town in the most wonderful country on earth. Now there is one; the rest are all gone. All dust. Only the mother is left, alone in the big house, with nothing to do but wait until she too can crumble away."

Adele rose and sat next to Cordelia, took her hand.

"Why am I left? I ask the question daily, hourly, but God is stony. God and I are no longer on speaking terms. God can go to hell."

"Oh, Cordy." Adele made no move to stanch the tears that burned her eyes. Cordelia stared up at the ceiling, dry-eyed, and spoke in a sleepy voice.

"I went to an island full of children nobody wanted. Children thrown away at birth, because of their defects. An island of mutants, hopeless and imprisoned in their grotesque bodies. My priest sent me there. He thought it would heal me, to administer to the less fortunate. For years I went there. I learned their names, I read to them, I pushed their chairs into the garden so they could feel the sun on their skin. I brought them sweets and combed their hair, painted their fingernails—those girls who had fingers—and drove them to church, sometimes, on holy days."

Cordelia extricated her hand from Adele's, reached over to the bedside table and yanked some tissues out of the box, handed them to Adele. "The priest thought it would heal me," she continued, "but he was a poor judge of character. Those children made me mean, Adele. They dug up every nasty buried seed in me. All those years of Mother's careful guidance vanished in the weedy garden those children unearthed. I felt it sprouting and tried to ignore it, but one day I pinched a girl. I was braiding her hair; she was slumped in her chair, breathing that labored, raspy breath that set my nerves on edge. I pulled too tight, and she grunted. And I pinched her arm, hard. All I could think was, 'How dare you be alive?'"

"Cordelia, it's not your fault. Someone should have been caring for you. It's perfectly understandable that—"

"These are the thoughts that went through my head. How dare God waste life on them and take it from my boys," Cordelia interrupted, ignoring Adele. "I became a monster. I gave birth to two perfect boys. Smart, brave, beautiful, healthy boys. God took them away and kept churning out these mistakes. That's how I thought of them: mistakes. I hated myself; I knew I was losing my mind. I tried to talk to the priest about it, but he said to work through my feelings, and pray. Pray! Can you believe that? My heart was corrupt, and the less fortunate fed its corruption. I began to resent everyone, Adele, everyone who was taking up space my boys should have inhabited. Breathing the air they should have breathed. I was full of hate. I felt my heart shriveling up inside me. I kept waiting for it to just stop beating; I wanted that. For it to just stop. And then John got sick, and I stopped going to the island. And now he's dead, too."

Adele kept her eyes on Cordelia's impassive face; her own was wet and raw from rubbing it with tissues. She had no idea what to say. She knew that Cordelia's words had been a gift to her, an offering to the years of silence between them. She was so deeply moved that silence was all she could offer in return.

"It's funny how I ran to church." Cordy combed her fingers through her hair, gave Adele a wry smile. "All the staunch Episcopalians; you can always count on us to stay well-dressed and dignified. I sat through Father Andrew's elegant sermons, stayed for tea in the rectory."

"Where was this island? It sounds like a horror movie."

"Yeah. It was worse, actually. It's a hospital for the hopeless. Just a tram ride away from midtown. Roosevelt Island."

"Roosevelt Island? Wow. Who knew?"

"There's a group from church that goes there regularly. They do their good works and manage to stay sane. Not me."

"Sounds like the kind of thing my friend Maggie would do."

"Maybe," Cordy said, looking at Adele, "you'll come live with me. You'll build a house for both of us."

Adele smiled. "Life could be one big slumber party."

"I'm serious." Cordelia sat up straight. "Would you consider it?"

"You're very generous, but I bring nothing to the table."

"Adele, how many times do I have to say this to you: I have nothing but money."

Adele bit her lip and stared hard at the floor, where a gnarled knothole swirled like the eye of a tornado.

"Can I tell you something really odd?" Cordy was cross-legged now, hugging a pillow on her lap. "A few months ago I had a dream. I have lots of weird dreams; I don't even try to figure them out. But this one was different. It felt like I wasn't dreaming at all, but having some kind of visitation, an out-of-body experience or something. Remember that fish you swore you saw, in the pond? How everyone used to tease you about it? In my dream, Henry was calling me to wake up. He wanted to show me something. But it wasn't grown-up Henry, it was little Henry. Adorable little towheaded Henry, at his absolute cutest. Remember? So I got up and followed him, and he led me through the house, only he kept going through doors and down hallways that weren't actually in our house. I kept stopping because I thought some trick was being played on me, but then he'd turn around with that impish look on his face, so I kept following him. And then we were running down the deer path to your house, but it was scary. Dark. The path seemed to go on forever. I kept losing sight of Henry, and I was terrified. I kept yelling at him to stop, go back to the house. And then we were in your backyard, looking at the pond. There was a crowd there, all these people milling around, a sense of expectancy, like something important was going to happen. I lost Henry in the crowd, and I had that feeling you get, you know, when your child gets separated from you. I was pushing people out of the way, calling him, and then I heard him say, Look, Mom. I turned toward his voice and he was standing with Tripp, the grown-up Tripp, only he was still little Henry. I tried to yell at Tripp to watch his brother, but I couldn't make any sound. And then they both pointed at the water, and a big, silver fish leapt up, shooting out of the water and spiraling into the sky, where it burst apart like a fireworks display. All the shiny little pieces began to fall back toward the earth, and each of them assumed the shape of a star. Some of them fell back into the pond and sunk, and some of them fell on the ground. And then I was alone. The crowd was gone, and so were Tripp and Henry. I looked at the ground where the stars had fallen, and they had grown into the size of a house. I went inside to look for the boys because there was something important I had to tell them, and I was calling them. But the house was empty. I knew it was empty, but I kept calling them. There was something so important that I needed to tell them. I wandered all around inside that house, even though I knew they weren't there. And then

I realized I was inside a painting. The house was full of sunlight and rainbows—someone had hung crystals in the windows. I wanted to live in that house, but I didn't have the key. But you did."

Cordelia stopped talking, looked expectantly at Adele.

Adele had to lick her lips; her mouth had gone dry. "I had the key?" she said, weakly.

Cordy nodded. "I woke up and wrote the whole dream down, every-thing I could remember. For days I tried to figure it out. I still don't really understand it. But here's what I got from it, here's what's clear: Who's left that I care about? Adele. Where do I want to be? Anywhere but here. Who can build me a house like that? Adele. So I wrote to you."

"Cordy," Adele said, "I don't think, in all the years I've known you, that I've ever heard you talk so much."

Cordelia's mouth twisted. "Me either. I've never had that much to say."

"That's some dream you had."

"Don't you think it's odd? I never used to dream at all. Please consider it, Adele. Please. You can build a whole wing for yourself."

"Drew said we might be able to recoup some of the money."

"Great, whatever. Do you not understand? I have more money than the two of us together could figure out how to spend. I have nothing but money."

Nothing but money. Not the fruit of her father's or husband's labor, not her own scrupulous savings, not the hard-earned reward of a life well lived, but blood money, death money. Money paid in compensation for the loss of everything else. Adele understood, then, how little it meant. For so many years she had lived with Drew's measurings, his continual appraisals and valuations. She was proud of him as he rose in stature and accomplish-ments, but he marked it all by how much he got. Just like the ruler on Jake's bedroom door, where the boy's growth was marked in pencil. Drew might as well have had his own penciled ruler: this is how much they paid me for that, this is how much I got for the other, this is when I doubled my this or that. Adele had experienced the loss of her money as the theft of a dream, whereas Drew had been gutted. He'd lost his very self. That's why he'd aged so rapidly; it wasn't just the heart attack. Adele wanted to call him and share her epiphany with him, offer him some consolation. It was a lifelong habit; the urge to share her thoughts with him. A habit she would have to break. Just as she knew now that she would have to stop dreaming of home. She would never go home, never assume the familiar cloak of her life back east. A profound shift had occurred, something far more vast than anything specific she could identify, and she felt carried in the swell of it.

Outside the little window new guests were arriving, a young couple. They lifted their bags out of their car, uttering pleased exclamations at the charming place where they were to spend a night or two. He reached for the heavier of the bags; she turned her face up to him for a kiss. Adele watched them from above, tucking her wings about her, steady on her branch. Wise old bird.

"So let's go look at these properties," she said.

Thirty

THEY HAD A MAP, and instructions from the Realtor. There were three lots available. The first was in what was obviously on the cusp of becoming a development of overbuilt vacation homes. It was on a freshly bulldozed cul-de-sac in the woods, and the lots on either side were already buzzing with construction.

The second was a teardown on the island's main road. Behind the dilapidated house was what had once been a lovely yard, stretching into the woods. The remains of a vegetable garden lay strewn among broken toys. Cordy's face tightened, and Adele spoke for both of them when she said, "Let's get the hell out of here." In the car, she suggested they save the third one for the next day. "No," Cordy said. "I want to get that last one out of my head. Let's get it over with."

"It's pretty here," Adele said, "but I don't know. What do people do?"

"Do?" Cordy, at the wheel, smiled that twisted smile. "Do? Who cares?"

Adele's own research on the place had informed her of the temperate climate, the encroaching gentrification, the abundance of educated dropouts who ran organic farms and dairies. There were several art galleries to serve the resident artists and craftspeople. There was a bit of an old hippie flavor to the area, she sensed, like up in the Kootenays, but it was not as remote. It was civilized. Full of old hippies with laptops and lattes. As she was mulling over the idea of life in such a place, Cordelia turned sharply off the road onto what seemed like a deer path in the woods.

"What are you doing?" Adele pressed the imaginary brake on the passenger side.

"It said three quarters of a mile past the last stop sign to take a sharp left onto what looks like a footpath."

"Footpath? For who, elves? This can't be right, Cord."

But Cordelia bumped along, while Adele gripped the seat, envisioning a trek back to the road to flag down help. Soon, however, the path began to widen, and they passed a tree with signs nailed on it, names painted in cheery colors with arrows pointing in different directions. Cordelia thrust a sheet of instructions at her. "What does it say to do after the sign tree?"

"Continue until the road seems to end," Adele read, "then turn right into the clearing."

The rental car surged ahead, shuddering over a huge pothole, and Cordy whooped, yelled "Yee hah!" She swung hard, and sure enough they found themselves in a clearing, with a circular dirt drive. "No Mc-Mansions here," she said.

"Nope." Adele got out of the car and stood, transfixed. She was looking at a big, silent, glistening lake, fringed by towering firs. She and Cordy stood for a moment in silence—utter silence; the only sound was the breeze soughing through the tops of the pine trees. Then, without breaking the quiet, each walked off alone. Adele paced the lot, referring to the description in the sheaf of listings. It was level, facing southwest to the lake. She turned to say something, but stopped at the sight of Cordelia, who was standing in a shaft of sunlight on a floor of pine needles, staring out at the water. It was the look on her face that silenced Adele. It wasn't the excitement of a real estate score or the thrill of discovery, both of which Adele was experiencing. She just looked relaxed. Utterly peaceful and relaxed.

They had fish and chips for dinner at a place on the non-touristy side of the island that the innkeeper recommended. The fish, halibut, had been

caught hours before. The chips were made from potatoes grown at an organic farm up island. They drank beer from a local brewery. Adele brought
her sketchbook and showed Cordelia some preliminary drawings. Doodled
ideas in the margins. She told Cordy a little about her night in the Kootenays, a little about the house that had floated into her consciousness. Not
too much, because she didn't want to trivialize the awe she felt at their
shared vision. Cordelia noted the strangeness of their similar ideas; said
something about the collective unconscious.

Adele recounted a condensed version of Drew's infidelities. Cordelia
listened, absorbed, expressed sympathy. She offered no advice or opinions,
just shook her head sadly. Adele insisted on picking up the check. Cordelia
smiled that new, twisted smile.

"What is it about money?" she mused.

"Don't ask me. I'm the last one to ask."

"People get so strange about their money." Cordelia laid a twenty-dollar
bill on the table and studied it. "Look at it. It's all about trust and promise
and good faith. But I swear, I've never met one single person who wasn't
weird about their money. Most women don't even want to talk about it.
They'll give you a detailed description of their orgasms, but mention money
and they tighten up. Men think it's what their balls are made of. Ever look
into a man's eyes when he's threatened about his money? It's like you've
whetted the castration knife."

"Well, it's easy for you to say, Cord, because you've got a lot of it."

"Adele, one more time: money is all I've got."

"You've got me," Adele said.

Cordy was touched. She nodded, then said, "Maybe we should build
extra wings on the house. You never know. Remember Polly Hemple? We
were close for a while, after you left. She's getting divorced. And your friends
Margie and Sophie—we could be a Home for Crones."

"Maggie and Sylvia. Maggie drove me to the airport. She and Paul might
be moving. She said Paul's burning out on his job and they might want to
make a change. Sylvia . . . well, she's welcome to visit."

"I'd like to not be mean anymore. I'd like to think I can still be human."

"All I can do is help you build your house, Cord."

"I know. But don't you like the idea of making it a place where our friends can come, when they're at the end of their rope? How many arms can a starfish have, I wonder?"

"The thing about starfish is, they keep growing them back." Adele looked around the little restaurant. Who were these people? She hadn't realized how insulated she'd been, assuming that her life was the only kind of life on offer. Here were whole different ways of being, ways that had never occurred to her. Humbled, she bent her head and absorbed herself in studying the lovely whorls on the slab of wood their table was made of when the waitress plopped two more mugs of beer on the table.

"From the gentleman at the bar," she said.

The women looked at the man, who was sitting alone. Fifty-ish, wearing mud-caked boots and a worn flannel shirt. He approached their table, and Adele noticed a tattoo on his forearm, a shrewdness in his eyes.

"Ladies," he said, laying a business card between them. "Howard Burns. Can I be nosy and ask, were those house plans you were looking at? If you're looking for a builder, you could do worse. Check me out. I've built several homes here on the island. I'm not the cheapest, I'm not the most expensive, but I'm the best, and I'm honest."

Cordelia put his card in her purse. "Thank you, Howard. We'll certainly keep you in mind."

"Vacation home or permanent residence?"

"We're in the preliminary stage."

"I've lived here for twenty-two years. It's getting pretty built up. Not what it used to be. But it's still paradise."

Adele snorted rudely. To Cordelia's raised eyebrows, she said, "Oh, please—paradise! Can we lay that one to rest, for the love of God?"

"Thanks for the beers," Cordelia called to him as he retreated, having thought better of trying to engage them in conversation.

"No offense!" Adele added.

In the car on the way back to the B and B, Cordelia said, "What do you think? Could you do this?"

"I'm pretty confident." Adele swiveled around to watch the moon rising behind them, through the trees. "I can design your house, and I can work with the builder. It's up to you. If you're nervous, you can bring in a real architect. I'll do the preliminary sketches and they can correct my mistakes."

"You are a real architect."

"You know what I mean."

"I know what *you* mean. Do you know what *I* mean?"

"You mean, could I live here?"

"Exactly."

"Could you?"

"Absolutely. But then, I have no expectations."

"And I do, is what you're implying?"

"I don't know, Del. That's what I'm asking, I suppose."

Adele stared at her dim reflection in the window. "It would certainly finalize things."

"With Drew, you mean. Adele, you need to search your heart. Are you sure you want to leave him?"

Adele didn't reply. She felt crushed, suddenly, as if an immense weight were pressing in on all sides. She pressed the button to lower the window and leaned her head out. Above, more stars than she had ever seen glittered in the night sky.

"My God," she said, "it looks like the Hayden Planetarium out there."

"You don't have to stop loving someone because they've hurt you. You don't have to be ashamed for still loving him."

Adele caught her breath, choked the rush of emotions down. "Of course I still love him. He's Drew."

"Is he?"

"God, Cordelia, I don't know! I don't know anything anymore. I thought I knew everything. I thought I was safe. Of all the things I was worried about, this one never made it onto the list. The thing that happened was the one thing I forgot to worry about happening."

Cordelia made a little grunt of agreement. "But it did happen," she said. "And now what?"

"Now what?" Adele echoed.

"I'm going to put in an offer on that property, tomorrow," Cordy said. "I'm going to hire you to build my house. I want you to include, in the design, at least one extra wing, or whatever, of living space. And I want you to know that there's no pressure, but the wing is yours. Can we agree on that?"

She pulled into their parking space and turned off the engine. They shook hands, solemnly. Cordelia went up to bed, but Adele lingered on the porch. She knew that if she laid her head on the pillow, the thoughts tumbling around in there would push any hope of sleep away.

The moon had risen and cast a bluish light over the pasture across the street. The silence was deafening. No white highway noise, no trains, no passing cars blasting their stereos. Adele sat in a wicker rocker and remembered the silence of the forest in Canada, where she'd thought she was going to die.

Instead, here she was. With a clean, warm bed awaiting her, and her dear old friend across the hall. The stuff you worry about, she mused, is never the stuff that actually happens.

There was a rich, moist scent of earth and hay and lilies and animals, with a faint hint of the sea and a lingering aroma of cooking. Adele rocked, breathed in the air, listened to the silence.

Suddenly there was a movement on the lawn. A snuffling, labored breathing. Adele froze, her heart thumping. But it was the owners' old chocolate Lab, coming to keep her company. He heaved himself up the steps of the porch and collapsed next to her, leaning on her legs and laying his head on her feet. She reached down to pet him, and he uttered a grateful, contented sigh.

Once upon a time, Adele thought, *there was a big old farmhouse, and a husband and a wife and three sons and a black Lab, and they all lived happily, but not ever after.*

And now there's this.

A few days ago, while she'd been vacuuming, she knocked over her New York snow globe. It broke right open, the glittering flakes seeping all over the carpet, the tiny Statue of Liberty skittering under the couch. Oddly, it gasped out a last few dying notes—"those little town blues . . ."

Adele had wept as she swept it up and thrown out all the pieces. It had felt so cruel, so mocking. Into the trash went St. Patrick's, Rockefeller Center, Saks Fifth Avenue. Into the trash went her home, her marriage, her dream.

But now there was this.

Could she do it? Cordy had asked.

What, she wondered, was "it"? Could she build a house? Could she live on an island in the Pacific Northwest? Could she live without expectations? Without her family? Without her dream of home?

Could she let it all go and start anew, she and Cordy, two old crones in the woods, gardening and fishing and, in the evenings, reminiscing on the porch?

Or maybe she'd have a shop in the village. She could sell books, or gardening tchotchkes.

Or maybe she'd build such a good house that others would ask her to build one for them.

Or maybe she'd just sit on the porch and read, and swim in the lake, and the boys would visit with their children, and she'd cook meals for them from their garden.

And maybe, during the long, rainy winters, she and Cordy would fly off to sunny places; two old broads with guidebooks. Or not. Maybe they'd just stay home, by the fire.

Maybe something new would come from this. No expectations, Cordy had said. But expectations were irrepressible. They were like waves in the sea, ebbing and swelling; ceaseless.

She had expected to die in the forest, but she hadn't.

She had expected her marriage to be indestructible, but it wasn't.

She hadn't expected Cordelia to emerge from the past, with her redemptive offer, but she had.

"Yes," Adele said, aloud. The old Lab raised his head, startled by her voice. She scratched his fat, velvety ear, and he sighed and dropped back to sleep. His warmth and weight on her feet filled her with tenderness. "Remind me," she whispered to him, "to talk to Cordy tomorrow about getting a dog."

Epilogue

THESE ARE THE DAYS of reconfiguring. Of lack. It's a new millennium, and what we held to be true is lost or changing. The very planet we inhabit is shifting; all our laws and rules, our pacts and assumptions, have fissured, and we must wonder: Do we glue them back together? Do we patch and stitch and dam and fortify, or do we let it go and watch the rising tides, consign ourselves to the tsunami, and let ourselves grow fins?

Adele and Cordelia build their house in the woods. They have many visitors. Children come, and grandchildren, and old friends. They are always welcome; there is plenty of room, and, when needed, new rooms are added. Jake lives with them for a while after his divorce, and then returns regularly, and then brings his new wife and baby. Maggie and Paul come, and stay for a summer, and Paul builds a dock in the lake. Sylvia and Carl don't come, but they send gifts each Christmas. Sylvia sends a copy of her book, which she self-published. It makes a very nice trivet in the guest kitchen. Drew comes, too. At first Adele invites him only when the boys and their families visit, but eventually he shows up more frequently. They never bother to get a divorce, and their old friendship resumes. He continues to live in the condo in Carlsbad, and Adele worries about his lifestyle, but not too much. Cordelia buys chickens and gives each one of them a name. The dogs chase them at first but soon get used to them and learn to let them be.